The Untimely Undeath of
IMOGEN
MADRIGAL

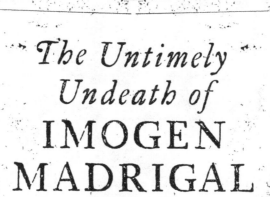

The Untimely Undeath of IMOGEN MADRIGAL

GRAYSON DALY

NOSETOUCH PRESS

Chicago • Pittsburgh • MMXXIII

To my own chosen sister, Jane.

The death of a poet ought to be a glorious affair.
Ideally, it should take place in a four-poster bed with velvet drapes, with mourners clustered tight about the dying, and roses of every hue perfuming the place. There should be tears, and black lace handkerchiefs, and it ought to take place deep into the night, such that the city falls into an appropriate hush as the last breath draws near. And at that last moment, a pen should be in every hand, prepared to catch the poet's final words as they fall from their lips. Poets' words have power, you see, and the words they utter within sight of the far side of the veil may as well be divine. Words have power, and if no one is around to receive a poet's last, they may not go gently into that good night.

Imogen Madrigal's last words were: "Oh, fuck—"

They did their best to make up for lost time; when her body was found, throat slit in the alley by the lobster docks, they wrapped a velvet ribbon around the wound, laid her in a mausoleum, and poured out enough absinthe to leave the ground muddy. The funeral was a bright, but short-lived affair; she had no family, and once her patrons and peers had dispersed, her grave was left alone. Winter came, burying the mausoleum in snow, and the wind howled. Spring and summer passed on, and the few roses still left on the steps of the crypt dried and desiccated to dust. Fall dropped leaves through the metal bars before the door, and no one came to sweep them away. Her grave was left alone, and for a year, Imogen Madrigal's only companion was the wind.

Sister Maeve poked through the bucket of flowers, glancing back over her shoulder at the marble obelisk she had just swept. It was an imposing monument, with hard square edges and an air of sternness. She selected a white lily, and headed back over, her boots crunching on the gravel path. There—she placed the lily down carefully, said a quick prayer, and then took her broom back up and headed onto the next. This headstone was much smaller, with curly carvings, and a glance at the name and dates revealed it to be the resting place of a twelve-year-old girl. A daisy, maybe? Maeve swept off the stone, considering, and then made her way back over to the bucket. Perfect. A pretty yellow daisy, sitting right on top.

"You know," Shivani said lightly, plucking up a flower beside her and heading back out along the gravel path, "you could get through your section quicker if you didn't spend so long trying to pick flowers out specially. I'm sure they don't mind."

"But I mind," Maeve returned, placing the daisy down and moving onto the next marker. "And their spirits might, too. I'm sure—" she squinted at the headstone, scrubbed at it a bit with her broom. "Eustace Cooper doesn't want a daisy. No, he strikes me as a poppy sort of person."

Shivani rolled her eyes and tucked a strand of wavy hair back up under her coif. "Well, when Mother Superior ditches you, I'll have tea waiting for when you finally get back."

"Such loyalty!" she teased and got to work on the mud caked to the bottom of Eustace Cooper's headstone. This was the time of year when tending to Lenorum's neglected dead was the most work; summer had left the stones encrusted in mud and pollen, and flowers were hard to come by this late in the fall. Of the chores and charities the Sisterhood of Good Death undertook, however, it was one of Maeve's favorites. A walk through the hustle and bustle of the city, followed by quiet work among the trees and little ponds? The contrast was delicious. Not to mention, now that she was one of the older Sisters, she could usually get Mother

Superior to leave her behind to finish up—a prospect in no way as disagreeable as Shivani made it sound.

The sun sank below the tops of the buildings surrounding the little cemetery, and as expected, Mother Superior looked up from her prayerbook, and let out a piercing whistle.

"All right—excellent work!" She rose to her formidable height and tucked the prayerbook away in her bag. "Everyone done?"

"Not quite!"

Mother Superior tutted and raised a knowing eyebrow at Maeve as she and the others made their way back from the corners of the graveyard.

"Yes, well. You feel comfortable finishing up on your own?"

"Of course," Maeve assured her, picking up the bucket of flowers and giving Mother Superior her most competent smile. "I've got it."

"Alright then." Mother Superior looked out over her head, counting under her breath. "We'll see you back at the convent, dear."

So, Maeve turned away with her blessing, and walked against the flow of the crowd, trying not to grin in the face of any of her sisters. The younger ones ignored her, chitchatting about things they saw on the walk over or plans for their evenings. Shivani rolled her eyes again and gave her a fond smile; Frances and Thalia offered dire warnings.

"You've got to watch out for the Wraith," Thalia said darkly. "I saw it in the papers—they mugged someone a block away from here."

"Are you sure you don't want me to stay?" Frances added anxiously, her eyes wide. "I hate the thought of you all alone out here in the dark. Not to mention, you know, if anywhere would be haunted—"

"It's okay, it's okay," Maeve promised quickly. "The Wraith has no reason to rob me—I don't have anything valuable!" She squeezed Frances's arm. "And I've never seen so much as a funny breeze around here. I'll knock on your door when I'm back, so you don't have to worry."

"Okay," she replied uncertainly, but went, along with the others, as Maeve took up her broom again and began working down the rows. Now that she had the bucket to herself and no reason to stall, things went quicker, and as the sun finally slipped below the horizon and the streetlights flickered on outside the fence, Maeve came to her final grave.

She cleaned it first, making sure to take in the little details. Intricate scrollwork, carvings—this mausoleum looked old, though the only nameplate she could find was much more recent. Maeve paused and looked at it for a moment as she scrubbed. Twenty-three—her own age. She looked the structure over with a new eye, wondering what someone her age had done to receive such unusual treatment. What sort of person had the deceased been, to be laid to rest in such a fancy grave and yet abandoned for at least a year? For abandoned the place had been, undoubtedly—ivy grew in tangled mats over the doorway, and dried leaves hung from cobwebs in the corners. Maeve knocked the latter down with her broom and did her best to peel the former away. She could see steps down into the dark inside, beyond wrought iron bars, but the whole place was locked up tight. Too bad—she was curious. How deep did it go? Who was the woman buried here? She detached a bit of ivy from the nameplate and amended that thought. No, maybe she had been curious, but she probably ought not to be. Because the woman buried here had a poet's laurel under her name.

She finished the cleaning rather quickly after that—the sisters and the poets disagreed on more than a few counts, and she didn't want to give the place any special attention beyond her duties. Not that there was anyone there to know, but—ugh. She'd know, and then she'd feel guilty. And anyway, the light was starting to fade in earnest, and she didn't want to lose it. She gave the steps one last sweep, propped her broom up against the door, and pulled her sketchbook and a pencil out of her bag, beginning to sketch even as she backed away down the steps, away from Imogen Madrigal's tomb.

Which was when she backed directly into someone coming up them.

Maeve spun sideways off the stranger's shoulder, tripped over the hem of her skirt, and fell gracelessly on her knees at the base of the stairs. She gasped, both from the pain of the gravel in her palms and from the utter faux pas she'd committed.

"I'm so sorry," she said, and spun to help the other person up. "I should have been looking where I was going—"

She stuck a hand out toward the stranger, and only then noticed that she seemed to be just as mortified as Maeve was. She seemed to be mostly legs, dressed in a white shirt much open at the neck, with a scarf thrown over short brown hair that she blew out of her eyes with a huff. She eschewed the hand Maeve extended in her direction, and when she did rise to her feet, Maeve could see two spots of color in her pallid cheeks.

"I—I'm with the Sisterhood of Good Death," she said quickly. "I was just cleaning this grave because—well—er, it seemed like it had been...abandoned." Rude—obviously this woman was here to visit. Maeve cursed herself. "But, um, you're here, and uh—sorry." She bent to pick up her things in a hurry, found that her sketchbook had wound up behind the other woman. "Um—if I could—"

The stranger glanced back, then picked up the sketchbook herself, and—to Maeve's distinct discomfort—paged through it, revealing a whole lot of drawings of other grave markers.

"Er...yeah, I, um—I wasn't—" She had been, though—drawing the mausoleum right in front of this person. Maeve felt her face get even warmer. "Uh—sorry."

The stranger still hadn't said anything, and Maeve was starting to feel worried that she would never give her sketchbook back. She chanced a glance up, and found the woman rolling her eyes in annoyance, her hand outstretched. Maeve frowned. "I, uh—"

The woman made a noise of frustration and pointed at the pencil in Maeve's hand.

"Oh!" Maeve passed it over, slightly nervous, and only grew more nervous when the stranger flipped to a clean page and... started to write? She held it back out, and Maeve took it a little more quickly than was strictly polite. Ornate cursive looked back at her:

Do not mistake my reticence for anger; I have recently lost my voice and am not yet in the habit of carrying means to communicate. If you want to draw the mausoleum, do not let me stop you. I myself am only here to sit for a small while.

Maeve blinked a little, looked up dumbly. "Oh, I'm...I'm very sorry to hear that." She stopped herself just before she asked what happened. "I...um, I will, then, if you really don't..." The woman waved permission, and so she sat on the grass, opened the sketchbook up and, after a moment's hesitation, pulled another pencil out of her bag. She still felt embarrassed, but that impression she'd had—of the stranger also being embarrassed, perhaps with no one who would take the time to converse with her—stuck in her mind. And though it wasn't the first thing people knew the Sisterhood of Good Death for, compassion toward the grieving was absolutely her duty. She held the pencil out and balanced the sketchbook on her legs such that she could sketch on the right page and the stranger could write on the left. "I'll be here a few more minutes, if you want the chance to…to talk to someone."

The stranger looked a bit startled, those spots of color rising back to her cheeks, and Maeve set the pencil down, taking up her own and continuing her sketch from where she'd left off. With company, the poet's mausoleum didn't seem quite so lonely—just a fine marble building, cleaner than it was before, tucked into a shady hollow of the cemetery. "I wonder what sort of person she was," she murmured, half for herself and half in case the stranger should want to talk about it.

The smell of jasmine perfume was the first clue to the stranger's proximity, but after a moment the dry grass crunched beside her, and Maeve felt the other side of her sketchbook dip as the pencil hit it. She glanced sideways—*She was naive. She didn't see it coming.*

Maeve frowned, her pencil stilling for a moment before she forced it on.

"See what?"

Her death.

"Oh. Was it…a long illness? Or something like that?"

Or something.

She snuck a glance at the stranger, her elegant profile silhouetted against the growing twilight, and found her expression surprisingly angry as she looked up at the mausoleum. Her instinct told her that maybe she shouldn't ask—that though the stranger seemed well-intentioned, she was still a stranger, and could be… unpredictable. So, Maeve let her alone, and kept sketching, trying not to feel too self-conscious. It was a lovely structure, and the lines came together easily on paper, but the stranger's claim to the place made her feel like an outsider.

She finished more quickly than she would have liked, and stood, brushing grass off her skirt. "Well—I'm sorry for your loss and…um, have a good evening. May you find peace." She felt more solid with familiar words in her mouth. The stranger stood as well, quite a bit taller than Maeve, and inclined her head with a rather sarcastic expression on her face. Or maybe Maeve was just reading too much into it.

Either way, she supposed if the stranger had a rejoinder she had no way of making it known, and so, awkwardly, Maeve took the last rose out of her bucket of flowers and handed it to the stranger. The stranger looked surprised. "For you—er, for her. For you to give her," Maeve explained, feeling her face get hot again. She quickly recovered her broom, ignoring the stranger's response, and turned back toward the bustle of the city for the short walk home. Only within the glow of the streetlight did it become apparent just how dark it had gotten, and Maeve chanced a glance back, not wanting to leave another woman alone at night. She watched the stranger mount the steps, unlatch the grate over the mausoleum's door, and descend inside, taking the rose with her. Curiosity burned in her stomach, but with no good reason to stay and enough recent embarrassment to dissuade her, Maeve was forced to continue on her way.

Chapter

II

The next morning arrived bright and chilly,
forcing Maeve deep under the covers to pretend she didn't hear the
bells. Her comforter certainly muffled the sound, but Maeve's room
was two doors down from the chapel—nothing on earth was going to drown them out completely. So, after a few futile moments,
Maeve sighed, and got out of bed.

The stone floors were frigid under her bare feet, and she
searched for her stockings in a rush. They were a gift from Frances,
like many things Maeve owned. Frances liked to knit when she felt
nervous, and she felt nervous a great deal of the time. These were
thick and woolly and just the ticket to keep the October chill out.
She pieced together the rest of her ensemble—fresh underclothes
and habit and boots—and pulled her silver hourglass necklace over
her head. Doing her hair was a necessity given its untamed volume:
she took it down out of her scarf, fixed the frizzy curls, and braided
it tight to fit it under her veil. She settled her glasses on her nose
and smiled at herself in the mirror—or what patches of herself she
could see under the layer of sketches taped to it. A flash of bright
white coif under a tall ship; a square of dark skin between two flowers; a slightly bleary brown eye next to a teapot. She took up her
bag, threw her prayerbook and sketchbook into it, and left her cold
room behind.

The others had left her usual spot open, and she settled between Shivani and Thalia just as Mother Superior and the elder
sisters entered the chapel.

"Want to—" Shivani said, then hushed as Mother Superior passed them by. She paused for a moment, then leaned in closer. "Want to go out tonight? Thalia said she saw a teahouse near the whaling district that had rose tea, and I want to try it!"

Maeve raised an eyebrow—now that was an odd coincidence. She'd sketched a poet's grave last night, and now here her friends were, wanting to go to a teahouse that would undoubtedly bring her into contact with more poets.

"Of course," she said thoughtfully. "Have you got a good excuse? You know Mother Superior doesn't like—"

"Frivolity!" came a thunderous voice from the podium, and Maeve snapped to attention. "It is something we allow—no, encourage—in this convent. We want you to lead happy, full lives outside of your duties, and to have a little fun once in a while." It would not, Maeve thought amusedly, be easy to tell—under Mother Superior's steely gaze, the whole chapel was sitting ramrod-straight. Even the little sisters had quit their giggling for once. "After all, we follow the teachings of the Blessed Sister Artemisia, whose words come from the Hallowed Mother herself—" Maeve nodded to the veiled statue on the altar. "—and she teaches that a life well-lived means a long and happy rest in the next world. However, frivolity can be dangerous. In the wrong circumstances, it can lead to materialism, hedonism, and worst of all, dissolution. Acting only on whims, seeking the easy route, desiring one's own comfort above all else— that leads to aimlessness, and aimlessness leads to regret. A regretful death is not a Good Death." Mother Superior raised her finger sternly. "The Blessed Sister Artemisia knew this. The Lenorum of her time was much given to such dissolution, and as a result, the spirits of the uneasy roamed constantly. That was what she founded this convent for—to lay them to rest. And though those spirits are less…personable these days—" Maeve pursed her lips. Less personable, indeed—the few hauntings they got each month were less of a laying-to-rest and more of a cleanup of amorphous ectoplasm "—we must remember the human being inside the ghost. It is our work that has helped this city to die a better death, and so must we help it in life. In your work, in your conversations, and yes, in your fun, strive for purpose, for diligence, and for empathy toward those around you. And when change comes and you do not get your way, do not rail against fate. After all, few wish for their current life to end, and that change must be taken, come what may. Be not like the scientists, meddling with forces they do not understand. Be not like the poets, wasting their days away in heedless hedonism. Take change in stride, live well, and think of those around you. Only by doing this in life, do we go to a good rest. So…" A minuscule smile made its way to Mother Superior's lips. "If you must sneak around the halls at night, so be it, but be compassionate, and think of the poor old ladies trying to sleep the next wing over. Now, Exorcisms 21:3, if you please—"

A nervous titter rolled through the crowd, followed by the rustling of pages, but Maeve hardly recognized the humor. The poets, again! She chanted along with the others, the words tripping off her tongue without conscious effort. She was lost in thought.

"Maevey-wavey, are you ignoring me? Helloooo?" Shivani shook her back to herself, and threaded an arm through hers, hauling her up and out of the chapel along with the others. "You look like you've seen a ghost. A properly scary one, I mean."

"No, I—" She blinked a bit in the morning sun as they entered the courtyard. "No, just a funny coincidence. Um. You never answered my question—about the excuse?"

Shivani shrugged. "Oh, Thalia's got something. Shopping for Frances's nameday, I think?"

"Won't that look suspicious when Frances comes with us?" Maeve pointed out.

Shivani started to speak, then pinched the bridge of her nose in exasperation. "Wait—yes. Okay. I'll make her come up with something smarter after I run choir." She patted Maeve on the cheek. "This is why we need you—we're all idiots." And with that, she whisked away in a twirl of skirt and veil, leaving Maeve blushing slightly. Shivani was always flirtatious, even with her friends.

She didn't have time to think on that or the odd coincidence of the poets too much for the rest of the morning, however—she had duties to get to, just as Shivani did, and if she wanted to get through them before they snuck out to the teahouse, then she'd have to get moving.

First it was teaching the younger sisters literature and scripture and a bit of art; then working in the gardens for a couple hours, winterizing the rose bushes and tending the oil grow-lamps in the greenhouse. She stole a moment for herself, sketching a late-season rose, and then kept on, making her way down the long marble hallways of the convent toward the kitchen. Her boots clicked and echoed as she went, and she shivered as she blew into her hands, trying to warm her fingers. Alright—maybe the season for outdoor sketching was drawing to an end.

"—cut their allowance for now; they won't notice anyway. But I would like to leave something for the older girls, just so they don't get too bored. Shivani always wants new sheet music, and Maeve's sketchbooks—" The sound of her name from a nearby closed door caught her attention, and she slowed her pace, coming to a stop without really thinking about it. Mother Superior's office lay behind the frosted glass—the place where the files and things were kept, where she usually only went to man the convent's phone.

"Perhaps the excursions, too." That was Sister Priscilla, Mother Superior's right-hand-woman. "The streetcar fares to West Cove could have been used for this month's food budget—"

"I know." Now Maeve identified the second voice as Mother Superior herself, sounding drained. "But I don't want them getting sheltered—they have to go out and see this world to know how to interact with the next. If we keep them completely cloistered here, they'll be afraid of life, to say nothing of death."

"And yet." Priscilla sighed. "And yet, and yet, and yet. We need to feed them, to keep them warm, even if we can't train them properly. They're our responsibility, Bethel. We have to balance spiritual and physical needs."

"We have to balance our finances." Maeve stayed quiet, stunned to have heard someone use Mother Superior's first name. Of course, she knew the number of sisters was smaller than it had been in the past—the empty rooms lining her hallway were a testament to that—and she knew from food-shopping that their budget was on the meager side. But she hadn't known it was particularly dire. She realized she was standing with her ear to the door, eavesdropping, and straightened quickly, her face getting hot. She should keep walking. The elders would tell her and the others when it was their time to know. "It's those damned poets—playing medium, all that seancecraft." Mother Superior sounded bitter. "Why do the hard work of grieving when you can just pay someone to call up your dead mother from her peace? Sure, she may not go back entirely, but echoes are easy to lay to rest, right? They make more work for us and make the people begrudge us for performing it." She should absolutely keep walking.

"Well," Priscilla said, sounding weary. "Perhaps people will figure that out and stop taking the easy way. Hallowed Mother knows we won't take it, right?"

Mother Superior sounded slightly cheered by this, and not a little amused. "No, we won't. Maybe if we shut down the elders' wing—less heating oil...."

With a tremendous effort, Maeve wrenched herself away from the door, and hurried down the hall, now undoubtedly late for her part in making lunch. She managed not to think about it too hard—think about the elders' wing being shut down, or the shrinking population of the convent, or the food budget dwindling or Lenorum's lack of faith in their beliefs. Lack of faith in *them*. She did a fairly good job of not worrying about her sisters, or about the little girls she had just taught their exorcisms, or about the beautiful old building and its gardens and echoing hallways. She very nearly didn't wonder what the easy way out would be; she didn't think at all about whether it might ever be worth it. And the fourth mention of the poets didn't even cross her mind.

"This feels bad," Frances complained as they stood in the alley near the teahouse, stuffing their veils and coifs into Shivani's open bag. She had cut her hair shorter since the last time Maeve had seen it; now it stuck up in little reddish tufts. "We shouldn't be doing things that we can't be properly in habit for. And what if Mother Superior finds out?"

"I have no doubt that Mother Superior already knows and has decided that she hasn't got the time to yell at us," Shivani said brightly, winding a normal scarf over her head. Maeve found herself immediately jealous—without her veil it was much colder, and she had spent most of the last five minutes fighting the wind to keep her hair out of her face. She grumbled in annoyance, raking the top part back into a bun, and jammed a pencil into it to keep it in place.

"We're not doing it to hide from Mother Superior," she said consolingly to Frances. "We're just trying not to stick out so much."

"Come on, it's late enough as it is," Thalia said impatiently. "The place will be full if we keep hemming and hawing."

So, with Frances still dragging her feet, the four of them left the alley and crossed the street toward the Lobster Pot, advertising its selection of rose teas as promised. The building was weather-beaten and rimed with salt, as were most buildings on the seaward side of the island, and Maeve could practically hear the beams creaking inside as they approached. Her fingers twitched for her pencils, but the others were disappearing through the door. She sighed, smiled, and made a mental note of the experience anyway—of the smell of old wood, of the clink of the lanterns hanging from the eaves, of the glow from the windows. It was worth sneaking out just to see what beautiful little things Lenorum was hiding in its nooks and crannies.

The interior was similarly aged, tables made from barrels and the smells of whale oil and tea mingling headily. The place was busy, but the four of them managed to find an unoccupied spot in the corner under a rusty harpoon. Shivani snatched up the menu.

"A pot for the table?"

The rest of them assented, and Shivani dove into the crowd to find the counter. Frances immediately pulled out her knitting, her hands working nervously as she glanced around. "Okay, this is… kind of nice."

"That's the spirit!" Thalia thumped the table, making Frances jump. Maeve snickered and gazed around. It seemed the clientele of this teahouse matched its decor—lobster hands in oilskins, whalers on shore leave. They swore and grinned gold-toothed and jostled their little table on occasion, squeezing by gruffly. Shivani looked quite small among them as she returned with a pot and a stack of stoneware cups. In fact, that stack was at elbow height, and the old sailor had thrown his arm out into a gesticulation before Shivani could dodge.

"Ah—watcher, there!" A young man in a knit sweater caught the stack just as it was about to clatter to the floor, and Maeve hastily got up to help the two of them. "You want to watch out for Ol' Bart—he's a bit of a gesticulator."

"I can see that," Shivani said, laughing. "Thank you, Mister—?"

"Mister nothing," the man scoffed, and gave Shivani a white-toothed grin. "Name's Nicky."

"Well, good catch, Nicky," she returned, and Maeve fought the impulse to roll her eyes at the tone of Shivani's voice. Another good reason to take the veil off—the opportunity to flirt with strangers unaccosted. She took the teapot from Shivani's absentminded hands and poured out drinks for the four of them.

Shivani was long in returning and looked rather dreamy once she did. "I like sneaking out, Thalia. We should do it more often."

Thalia tilted her hand good-naturedly—evidently, she hadn't noticed Shivani's state, or she didn't find it as ridiculous as Maeve did. "Only a night out every so often for me, I think. That way it's special."

Shivani opened her mouth to say more, but before she could, everyone fell into a seat, leaving the man in the sweater standing above them. His hands were laced behind his back, and the room went silent as he began to speak.

"I beg thy time," he said. The traditional poet's greeting. Shivani's face fell; Frances and Thalia shifted in their seats.

There were a few reasons the Sisterhood tended to be distrustful of poets. Of course, there was Mother Superior's argument from the morning's sermon—the infamous Court was known for its decadent taste, wild parties, and hedonism as a guiding principle. In a convent where helping others to lead good lives and die good deaths was the goal, the selfishness of the poets' quest for pleasure seemed plain. And there was the issue of seancecraft, which the Sisterhood seemed to be the only party on the island left willing to condemn.

There were other reasons, too, more rumors than anything—rumors that the Court clearly enjoyed. They had developed their process for raising the spirits of the dead relatively recently—had gotten even richer off it—but it had long been whispered that poets' words held power beyond their meanings. That a poem for prosperity could attract wealth, or a romantic verse, properly composed, could enchant a lover. To most, the subject was dismissed as superstition or, to the credulous, a strong reason to stay on the Court's good side. But among the sisters, it was a matter of deep suspicion. The Hallowed Mother kept the natural order of things for good reason, and the poets certainly couldn't be trusted to mess with it.

So, Maeve and the others tried not to get too familiar. Usually, poets came on to perform late enough that the four of them could head home and avoid, in Maeve's case at least, feeling too guilty. Sneaking out was one thing; rubbing elbows with unapologetic mediums was another. If it hadn't been for the coincidences of the morning, she'd have turned away.

The other patrons weren't nearly so hesitant.

"Given to thee!" thundered the sailor—Ol' Bart, according to the poet—and a chorus of ayes followed his declaration.

"My thanks times three," he replied with a wink, and took a step up and back onto the stage.

"Should we go?" Frances whispered under the murmur of the crowd.

"We just got here," Maeve pointed out, and sipped her tea, trying to seem nonchalant. She wasn't sure she believed in the significance of coincidence, but it couldn't hurt to be prepared for something to happen.

"Maeve's right," Shivani said reluctantly, spinning her cup back and forth with a bruised expression on her face. "It's not like Mother Superior's going to come down here and chew us out. Even if poets are stupid."

Maeve winced—Shivani was never the quietest of whisperers—but it seemed no one had noticed under the sound of the poet beginning his performance. It was not, to her surprise, the sound of words; no, he had begun to hum, a low pitch that seemed to swell and fill the room. The other patrons were humming along, she realized—it must be something that he did regularly. The poet stamped the front of his foot, then his heel, and Maeve caught sight of flashy gold disks tied around his ankle that clinked against each other when he moved just right. The rhythm continued—thump, clink, thump, clink—and the crowd hummed, and just as it seemed that that might be all that was going to happen, the poet opened his mouth and sang.

"*Oh, I've been away / from my love bright and gay / for a sounding and a sundering year / and the pale blue skies / in the hue of his eyes/ makes my heart take a turn quite queer....*"

A shanty, Maeve realized—the poet was singing a shanty like the fishmongers and whalers did on the docks did as they butchered their catches. It was rather more complex—the tap of his boot led them far from the even beats needed to work to, and his words chased each other playfully—but it was a far cry from the performances she'd half-heard slinking out the door of other teahouses. *Those* poets had been decked in low-cut blouses and diadems, clearly members of the Court. Maybe this man, Maeve thought, was new to the business. So maybe listening to him was fine.

He ended the song sharply and bowed to applause. "Thank you, thank you kindly. My laurels say Nickolai Shantier on 'em, but you all can call me Nicky."

Maeve had spoken too soon—he withdrew a crown of laurels from behind his back, finely wrought in bronze, and settled them on his brow. They glinted in the lantern light.

"Now, words have power, or so we say—we're blessed with calm winds outside this evening, so I'll ask the crowd. Anyone need the winds of fate beseeched on their behalf? I've got a fair number of love songs that need a debut."

He looked out over the crowd and winked in the direction of their table. Maeve heard Shivani make a strangled sort of noise and felt a hand close on hers with sharp nails.

"Next time," she gritted out through clenched teeth, "I try to open my idiot mouth, Maeve—"

Maeve pried Shivani's hand off with a wince. "I'll drag you back to your room and throw away the key, yeah."

"My wife's ship was drowned, ten years ago today." A quiet voice from near the stage hushed the murmurs in the room, and the poet—Nicky—narrowed in on the drawn-looking man who owned it. "A sign, to know she's alright wherever she is?"

"Oh, that's just—" Shivani began under her breath, but Maeve shushed her. Yeah, yeah, they were edging toward dangerous territory, but it wasn't like the man was being conned out of his money, or worse. A sea shanty wasn't going to drag a spirit unwilling from the grave. Why was Shivani so annoyed? Maeve didn't trust the poets either, but she wasn't about to strangle the man.

A lower hum took over the room, followed by the rhythm of the poet's foot, and in a croon, he sang a perfectly normal dirge for the man's dead wife. That was followed by a prayer for good catches, a warning against winter storms. It seemed innocuous enough, and Maeve found herself making justifications against the disapproving voice in her head. It was just music—Shivani played the organ all the time, and that wasn't bad. Any sign of seancecraft, they'd intervene.

In the meantime, it was warm, and the crowds around them were full of good cheer, and despite the guilt of sticking around to watch the performance, Maeve at least found it within herself to enjoy when he sang *The Whaler's Wife*. Anyone who had grown up in Lenorum was practically required to know it, and she had more reason than most. They were coming to the bottom of their third pot of tea, rose-mint that tingled on the tongue—miles more flavorful than the cheap Lenorum Public tea the convent bought.

Frances and Thalia were happily engaged in conversation on the merits of knit versus crochet with a sailor at a nearby table, and Maeve was lazily wondering whether they could get away with coming here weekly when Shivani stood abruptly.

"I'm going to get some air," she announced, and left before Maeve could ask if she wanted someone to go with her. She bit her lip as she watched Shivani thread her way up and out of the basement. Was that dangerous? Walking home from the cemetery alone was one thing, but she didn't know this neighborhood—or not after market hours, anyway. A tug in her gut told her that people didn't go for air for no reason, and so she stood. She ducked under the arms of a half-dozen lobster hands singing at the tops of their lungs and followed.

It was much colder outside, and Maeve found herself glad of the high collar of her dress. The door had spat her out in the alley they'd entered through, extending both ways out of the reach of the glow from the windows. She shivered and peered as far as she could in each direction. "Shivani?"

Well, they had come in from the left, so Maeve started walking that way. "Shivani, you okay?" The alley hadn't seemed particularly long on the way in, but now that Maeve was conscious of it, it seemed to stretch for miles and miles of brick and dark windows. "Shivani, come on, come back inside—it's kind of late. We'll head out soon anyway, okay?" The wind whistled disconcertingly as it rushed between the buildings, whipping at her skirt, and after peering into the dark and realizing that something could be peering back and she might not realize it, Maeve decided that Shivani had definitely gone the other way. She turned on her heel.

It took a great deal of her self-control not to scream when she found Shivani right behind her, and then the rest of it not to bolt when she realized the figure wasn't Shivani.

They had approached nearly silently, and now stood blocking Maeve's path from about five feet away. For a disarming second, she thought it might be a ghost—but no, the figure's feet were firmly on the ground under their full-length veil, and their outline was too clear despite it. From there, it took Maeve a moment to remember where she'd seen that long veil, the porcelain-and-silver carnival mask, but the sketches from Thalia's newspapers came back quickly, and with full impact.

"Um," she said quickly, taking a couple of steps away from the Wraith. "I hardly have any money—please, I'll give it to you, but I'm not worth it." Had Shivani gotten mugged? Maeve's stomach dropped. "Leave me and—leave me alone."

"Leave you and your friend," the Wraith said, so quiet and whispery that she could hardly hear it. "Your friend."

"Sh-Shivani," Maeve stammered. "You didn't hurt her, did you? Where did she go?" What had Thalia said about the Wraith? Did they hurt their victims? Could they be swayed by bargaining?

"How does your friend…" Here the Wraith paused for a long moment, till Maeve was nervous she was missing something they were saying. "…know the poet inside?"

"What?" Maeve blinked. "Er, she doesn't—she just bumped into him tonight."

"Lying to me…is a dangerous game to play…darling," the figure hissed out. Maeve caught a glint of metal from somewhere within the folds of the veil and felt her blood run cold. "And I'm… feeling much…too…serious. Shall we…try it…again?"

"I swear," Maeve insisted, and tried to back up further. The Wraith moved towards her, quicker than thought, and pressed her toward the alley wall, the brick cold against her back. "I p-promise, we've never met him before." The Wraith took another few steps forward, shaking their hand free of the veil. It was gloved in black lace, and held a twisted, wicked dagger. Maeve swallowed hard and gave up her only card. "We're nuns, we don't know hardly any men, and certainly not poets!"

The masked face cocked sideways, impassive, the knife hovering a few inches to the left of Maeve's face, and she rushed with fumbling fingers for proof.

"See? Sisters of Good Death." She pulled her hourglass pendant out of the neck of her dress. She swallowed hard as the Wraith snatched the pendant, holding it up to the veil for inspection. But the tug of the cord around Maeve's neck brought them closer, and now Maeve was within range to notice something that shocked the fear out of her system. The scent of jasmine perfume.

The Wraith dropped her pendant like she'd been burned just as Maeve started in recognition, and the two of them stumbled back from each other.

"You—at the cemetery—" Maeve said accusingly, and nearly took a step forward. "At Imo—"

"Do *not*," she hissed, her voice horribly strained, and spat a wracking cough before leveling the dagger at Maeve. They were barely louder than the sough of the wind, but somehow, the words gave Maeve pause. "Speak...that...name. It will get us...both killed."

"You were going to kill me!" Maeve shot back, indignant. "Where's Shivani? What did you do to her?"

"Headed...home...looked like." The Wraith took another long-legged step back and swung up a fire escape that Maeve hadn't even noticed before she could make the decision to move. "You... should, too. And *forget this*." And then she had made it to the roof, and then she was gone.

The wind rushed by, cold and whistling, but it couldn't extinguish the flame of stubbornness that sparked itself to life in Maeve's stomach. She glared at the roofline for a moment more, then turned, balled her fists in her pockets, and went back inside.

Chapter III

"*But you have to admit,*" Mother Superior said, with a zeal that Maeve could only imagine possessed lawyers arguing their cases, "that there is a potential for danger."

"Yes," the wispy-haired woman—Professor Nadia Chrystos, head of the parapsychology department at the Lenorum Academy of Sciences—said, removing her overlarge spectacles and polishing them agitatedly, "as there is with any research. With the development of electrical theory, or the vaccine, Reverend Mother. Surely you would not begrudge modern society these conveniences?"

"I would," Mother Superior said proudly, "if electricity or vaccination were my area of expertise. As it stands, Professor, my expertise is in spectral phenomena, and as such, I will offer it. What you are doing goes against the natural order of things."

It was an argument Maeve had heard half a dozen times now; Mother Superior liked to come here every so often and pick a fight with Professor Chrystos over her topic of research.

Privately, Maeve thought it might not be such a bad thing to know a little more about the science of the ghostly, but she didn't want to undercut Mother Superior, and so she kept her mouth shut. It seemed the professor's backup—a pale-faced girl with blonde curls standing in approximately the same attitude across from her—was similarly reticent, or maybe just bored. She glanced at her watch, then blew her bangs out of her face with a sigh.

Maeve tried not to feel intimidated by her nonchalance, and took to glancing around the room, taking in the skeletal specimens and strange glowing vials. Was that ectoplasm? She squinted harder. Ghostly detritus was typically short-lived, and the purple color was unusual. Maybe the professor or her students had collected it out in the field—which in itself would probably anger Mother Superior even more when she noticed it. Sisters of Good Death were trained to treat ghosts with the utmost respect and reverence; Professor Chrystos had probably been scraping this stuff off the walls during a manifestation. Well, perhaps it would help them all determine why the ghosts were coming through so fragmented these days. The closest thing she'd seen to a proper spirit in a month was the woman calling herself the Wraith.

The glowing purple vial in the cabinet blurred out of focus as her thoughts shifted. Shivani, as promised, had gone home— half-defensive and half-apologetic when Maeve had looked in to check on her, and had slept late this morning. She had been supposed to be standing on Maeve's other side here; instead, Thalia was filling in, looking extremely stern and quite intimidating at her full, big-boned height. She was secretly glad of Thalia's presence, though. Typically, Mother Superior and the professor would argue for fifteen minutes; then, the professor would invite her in for a cup of tea, which would lead to about forty-five minutes more of arguing over biscuits, during which Maeve and Shivani were typically free to roam the campus. In this case, Maeve was free to grill Thalia on the subject of the Wraith.

"Well, I first looked into them because, well, the *Wraith*—" She held her hands up, and Maeve nodded. "But it seems whoever it is, they've got the motivations of the living. People have been robbed and threatened—always at night, always by someone in a mask and a long veil. They move quickly, and no one's even gotten close to catching them—except once, a few weeks ago." Her eyes were shining; Maeve could tell she was hoping Maeve would ask more.

"What happened?"

Thalia's expression turned conspiratorial. "A noble walking near the cemetery—*our* cemetery, the one right by the convent. He was near enough to a constable's station when he got accosted that they were able to give chase. And they nearly had the Wraith cornered, too. But then—they disappeared. There was a constable at every exit. They searched everywhere, the groundskeeper's hut— everything, and never found them. They vanished. And that just follows everything else...."

Maeve said nothing; she had something of an idea of where the Wraith might have gone if she was, in fact, right about her identity. Was that the sort of thing she should report to someone? She was certainly annoyed by the Wraith's audacity in threatening her, but she was curious, too. Why had she asked about the poet in the bar? What kind of information was the woman trying to find?

"Anyway, I can give you some newspaper clippings if you're interested in it, too," Thalia offered, at the end of what Maeve blushingly realized had been a monologue she had not caught a single word of. She nodded.

"Definitely. I'll let you know if I come across anything." A thought occurred to her. "Another question—have you ever heard the name Imogen Madrigal?" She glanced around as the words left her lips, suddenly wary of the Wraith's warning.

That name will get us both killed.

Thalia shook her head, looking blank. "Who's that?"

Maeve pursed her lips. "Just...nothing," she said, after a moment. "Just something I was looking into."

"Come on—nothing to be afraid of!"

It was midday, though it was impossible to tell through the dust-occluded windows of the townhouse attic. Amal hesitated on the stairs, her arms wrapped tight around her prayerbook, and eventually Maeve was forced to go down and take her hand.

Not that Maeve begrudged her at all; exorcisms could be scary, especially for little ones, and this was Amal's first. The spirit in question today, however, seemed like an excellent one to start with; only a few knocks and bumps, the owner of the house had assured them nervously. She had been all in mourning for a grandmother who had recently passed, which gave them a clue as well. There had been a rush of cold air when they'd entered the attic, which had spooked Amal, but Maeve could tell from old familiarity that the spirit was just the lingering sort.

"W-what if I mess it up?" Amal whispered, her eyes darting around. "That poor lady—this is her grandma, isn't it?"

So, Amal had figured that out—good for her. Maeve shook her head. "You can't mess it up so badly that it can't be fixed, Amal. Just do your best! You remember what you do first, right?"

Amal gave a very small nod, smoothed out her skirt, and very hesitantly cracked open her prayerbook as she made her way up the last few stairs.

"Er—h-hi, Mrs. Gardener. My name is Amal, and I'm here to, to help you. Um, just to start—can you hear me? One knock for yes, two for no?"

There was a quiet moment, then two quiet taps echoed from somewhere in the vicinity of the far end of the attic. Amal looked up at Maeve, desperately confused, and Maeve suppressed a laugh.

"Sometimes," she said gently, "they like to tease. She wouldn't have known to knock if she didn't hear you, would she?"

Amal nodded quickly, flipping through pages of her prayerbook.

"V-very funny, Mrs. Gardener. Anyway, um, is there something that's keeping you from moving on?"

One rap in the rafters. Amal looked buoyed by this success. "Oh, okay! What is it?"

Silence, and Maeve patted her shoulder. "Yes or no questions, if that's how you want to do it," she reminded her. "I have a spirit board if you want."

The opportunity for choice seemed to paralyze Amal for a moment, but she nodded after a second. "Yeah, yeah, let's do spirit board."

Maeve reached into her bag, shifting aside sachets of salt and a few loose candles, and plucked out her little planchette and board. She took a glance through the planchette's window as she went, just to check—a few wisps of greenish mist hovered about the room in the fish-eye lens, but nothing suggested danger.

She passed it over to Amal as requested and Amal made a quick circuit of the room, finally settling on a particular area near the window. Maeve followed and found it colder than the rest of the room. Good instincts.

She watched as Amal took a deep breath and sat, and let her hands rest lightly on the planchette. It wasn't against the rules for her to give Amal aid, so she noted down the letters for her as they came out—R...O...S...E...S....

The cold faded, and Amal opened her eyes. "What did she say?"

"Roses."

"Roses." Amal bit her lip, glancing around the attic for inspiration. "I suppose she was Mrs. Gardener...."

Maeve, from a standing position, had a slight advantage—she could see the rose bushes in question out the window, clearly unprepared for winter. "Perhaps..." she began to suggest.

"Maybe she wants someone to take care of her garden!" Amal said, snapping her fingers, and looked up at the ceiling. "Is that it, Mrs. Gardener? Do you want your granddaughter to take care of your roses?"

One knock, an excited scramble down the stairs, and a conversation on horticulture later, and Amal was striding down the street confidently, prayerbook tucked back into her backpack and two silver ammonites in hand for the streetcar fare. Maeve smiled at Amal sitting very straight and tall in her seat, and pulled out her sketchbook, doodling and gazing out the window in equal measure. The townhouse had been on the edge of the sea, and even now in the streetcar the air smelled of brine, the sky grey and heavy with spray. It was beautiful, even if some might have called it bleak, and unbidden, a twist worked its way into Maeve's stomach. Mother Superior and Sister Priscilla had talked about the seaside, and how the streetcar fares might be better spent. But losing this—a little sister's first exorcism, and the chance to go out and see the city— that would...change things.

Mother Superior had just talked about the importance of accepting change, too. But this existential sort of change, that might end the Sisterhood as they knew it completely? Maeve was used to contemplating the end of things, but somehow the end of her order had never crossed her mind.

Mother Superior blamed the poets, and it wasn't hard to agree with her. The younger Miss Gardener was one of only a few calls they had gotten that month, and Maeve could see at least three seance parlors from where she sat as they rode back downtown. But she imagined that the poets would be even less likely to listen to them than the scientists at the university were; to them, she and the others probably seemed like relics of a Luddite time. She snickered—if only she could find the ghost of Imogen Madrigal haunting the cemetery; she could get her to talk to the poets in exchange for sweeping her grave. Though Mother Superior would undoubtedly disapprove of that, too.

Though…Mother Superior might not disapprove of her making a deal with the living.

Maeve's pencil paused. No, Mother Superior wouldn't like her trying to bargain with a spirit for her own gain, but a living person…a living person who had known a poet well enough to have a key to her mausoleum…Well, Maeve had already been curious enough, and the possibility that dealing with the Wraith might save her beloved convent only fanned the flames. Yes, yes—she'd find the Wraith, and drag out of her exactly who the dead poet was to her, and demand that she do something for the Sisterhood in exchange for Maeve's silence. Because unlike the rest of her victims, Maeve knew where her hideout was.

Isn't that blackmail? a small voice asked inside her head. Maeve scoffed to herself. It wasn't blackmail! It was getting aid from an unwilling party who really ought to be willing. It was simply setting right the moral order of things—after all, Maeve *had* done the hard work of looking after the Wraith's friend's tomb. She nodded to herself squarely, and let Amal drag her off the streetcar at their stop. Yes, this was something.

Only at night, Thalia had said—that was when the Wraith came out to do her work. Maeve had a few hours to wait, and a stack of newspaper clippings to go through. She would've preferred to know something about Imogen Madrigal too, but for obvious reasons she knew there wasn't going to be anything in the convent's little library. She took what Thalia had given her, pulled a cardigan on over her habit, and made her way up to the balcony of the chapel. She hadn't properly seen Shivani all day, and she still wanted to check on her.

Strains of soft organ music echoed down the hall as she made her way over, and as she opened the door, the sound swelled louder. Something slow and in a minor key—melancholy, and a fitting compliment to the growing shadows within the chapel. She made sure to let her boots click on the floor so Shivani would know she was there and stretched her legs out along the length of the pew. They often sat like this—Shivani practicing, Maeve sketching. The pipes of the organ usually made for an excellent study in perspective, but now she was opening her sketchbook to the page where she and the Wraith had had their conversation and writing EVIDENCE at the top. She pulled out Thalia's newspapers and got to reading.

There wasn't much there that the two of them hadn't already discussed, but she noted it all down anyway. Fourteen people since September—mostly alone, sometimes in pairs—had come into the constabulary reporting the same strange story. Some had found themselves missing some but not all of their money; others had lost nothing at all. Maeve tapped at her lower lip with the end of her pencil, reading it all over. A gravedigger, a teahouse waiter, a couple of rich young ladies, a poet. She read this one over especially carefully, but it wasn't a name she knew. Hopefully what she had would be enough.

The music petered out, and Maeve heard a sigh and the sound of sheet music being collated. She poked her head up over the side of the pew.

"Hey—feeling okay?"

"Mother's grave!" Shivani jumped as Maeve spoke, and spun around, clutching her sheet music tight. "Don't sneak up on me!"

"I didn't, promise!" Maeve sat up further and inspected Shivani. She looked a little tired, and a few wisps of hair had escaped her coif, but her hair was always doing that. "You good? We didn't really talk after last night."

"Oh." Shivani absently brushed those strands of hair back. "Yeah, no, sorry—just got a little annoyed at that guy, and then...I wasn't really having fun anymore, and I didn't want to put a damp-er on things. And then I didn't sleep well." She heaved another sigh and gave Maeve a small smile. "I'll be okay—just a little blue today."

"Okay," Maeve said, unconvinced, but she returned the smile and followed Shivani out along the balcony. "Dinner?"

"Dinner," she agreed, and linked her arm through Maeve's. "And maybe a sit in the garden after?"

Maeve winced. She hated saying no. "Er—sorry. I…actually have to do some shopping for Frances's nameday," she said, hoping her laugh didn't sound too fake. "But I'll take a rain check on that?"

Shivani pouted. "Fine. But before it snows."

She would have little time to fulfill Shivani's ultimatum, Maeve thought crossly, drawing her scarf tighter around her face as she made her way down the street toward the cemetery. The sun was long gone, and she was prepared to stake the mausoleum out for the whole night and the rest of the next day if necessary. That was if she didn't freeze to death while she waited. The Wraith had better be polite enough to keep her from waiting long.

The gates were shut, but not locked; whoever the keeper of the cemetery had been, it had passed into public hands some time ago, and Maeve made her way inside without issue. The place looked different by moonlight, though, and it took her a while to find the mausoleum she'd cleaned before. It seemed to brood at night, its gothic carvings taking on a sinister cast. Maeve wasn't scared of cemeteries; the dark, however, made her wary. She found a spot to hide with her back to a wall and began her watch.

The rustle of wind through ivy lulled her into complacency and drowsiness, and when a shadow did stretch along the grass, she hardly noticed it. But the screech of iron on iron she did notice, and as the figure slipped through the door and down the steps, she started to her feet, and rushed forward as quietly as she could. She just managed to catch the gate before it closed, and eased it open carefully to avoid letting it squeak again. She let it fall shut with a crash to avoid suspicion and took a deep breath. She had just locked herself in here with a person with a dagger. Perhaps that hadn't been her smartest idea.

No options but to keep going now. Maeve took a slow, careful step down, then another, squinting in the darkness. It was cold down here, even colder than it was outside; her breath fogged in front of her. She'd been into mausoleums like this before—the structure up top was an entrance, and the stairs would take her down into an underground vault. That was what would be behind the velvet curtains up ahead, and it would be tight quarters. When she pulled them back, she'd have to be ready to confront the stranger within. A chill breeze ruffled the fabric before her like an invitation.

She breathed deeply and took it.

What stood before her was surprising enough that the words she had planned died on her tongue. She had expected a sarcophagus, maybe the Wraith brooding in the corner pawing through stolen goods. She had not expected what seemed to be a pleasant, if cluttered parlor. Oh, it had surely been a tomb originally. A stained-glass window was set into the back wall, glowing faintly from the moonlight outside, and the ceiling arched like a chapel. But the marble floor had been disguised with a heavy rug, and upon that had been set a wingback armchair, a side table with a veil and porcelain mask resting upon it, a small bookshelf crammed with books. A taxidermied crow, a porcelain tea set, a full dozen candles scattered about the place—this wasn't a parlor; it was an apartment! The sarcophagus had even been shoved against the wall, and from what Maeve could see, stuffed with pillows. She bristled—whatever all this was was one thing; but disturbing the remains of the dead was within her purview and not something she would allow. Where had the woman gone, anyway?

She crept forward, and another thrill of anger and revulsion rolled through her. The pillows and blankets within the sarcophagus entombed the figure of the very-much-living Wraith herself, curled up and seemingly quite asleep. She must have been dead on her feet to have fallen asleep that quickly. Maeve pushed her compassion aside with annoyance; this meant she had the advantage, and she had ought to find the dagger before she woke the Wraith to demand answers. There, next to a stack of papers and an inkwell. She hid it inside the teapot and steeled herself. The tomb was silent but for her own breathing.

"Wake up." Her voice sounded reasonably stern, and she hoped she could follow it up. But the Wraith didn't stir; Maeve stepped back over and found her face just as slack and dreamless as it had been before. She scowled and raised her voice. "Wake up! I want answers!" Still nothing. Fine, then—Maeve was nothing if not stubborn, and her irritation was outweighing her nervousness. She pulled the covers back roughly and took the woman by the shoulders. Her skin was cold under Maeve's hands, colder than she had expected, colder than was actually…healthy. Maeve startled and dropped her. Which was a bit squeamish for her, really, but she had seen the woman alive and now she was dead—she shouldn't even be that cold, yet!

She shouldn't have opened her eyes, either.

There was a flurry of motion as the two of them scrambled back from each other, Maeve falling back against the wingback chair and the stranger pressing her back up against the wall of the sarcophagus. She didn't say anything, or maybe couldn't, but her eyes stared with shock and anger and fear. Maeve found her lips a little looser.

"You—you were dead! How are you not? What are you doing here? Who are you? Where's the body that's supposed to be here?" Her flailing mind caught at that. "You can't disturb the dead! That's a crime, and it's dangerous to do, besides!"

The stranger's chest heaved once, twice, and then she gave Maeve the angriest look she had ever been on the receiving end of. She stood and climbed out of the sarcophagus, and snatched up a dressing gown from its edge, shoving her arms into it and storming past Maeve to the tiny writing desk in the corner. She wrote with violence, and practically threw the blotted piece of paper at her.

How dare you break in here in the dead of night? What right have you to do that? And I told you to stay away—are you an idiot or do you have a death wish?

Maeve raised her chin indignantly. "When people threaten me, I want to know why. And you're avoiding my questions—two wrongs don't make a right!"

Curiosity killed the cat. See, we can all use clichés, but maybe you're not clever enough to come up with something on your own. Or to take a hint. Here's something more explicit—fuck off.

The woman's eyes bored into her, warning, dangerous.

Maeve curled her lip. "No. You're disturbing the person who was laid to rest here, and I cannot allow that." Not to mention the threats and the robbery, but Maeve was too shocked by the situation at hand to recall her plans. "I bet you didn't even know her, did you? You just lied to me to get me to go away the first time! You have no claim on this place!"

The woman's face took a turn toward a grimace, and she stood, still scribbling her responses but forcing Maeve to recall that she was taller than her, even barefoot.

Oh, I have every claim. Trust me. She glanced up, looked Maeve over with disdain in her expression, and wrote more. *I don't want to hurt anyone who's innocent, but I do* not *appreciate you breaking in here, and I do* not *want to see you again. I won't hurt you this time, but if you put yourself in my path again, I won't be so merciful. I'm in the midst of something dangerous—you get in my way, you put both of us in danger. And your little friend from the teahouse wouldn't like that, would she? If you were in danger?*

Maeve scoffed. "Are you threatening me?"

Not yet.

"Well," she said, curling her lip and glancing around the room for inspiration. "Well, I can tell the constables where to look for you!"

They won't find me.

The woman's expression was even, but Maeve sensed a tension in her shoulders that hadn't been there before.

"Maybe not—but they'd find all this," she pushed, gesturing sharply. "Got to be years of work down here, doesn't it?"

The woman shoved a note toward her in an irritated way.

What do you even want, anyway? Why did you come here, if telling the constabulary wasn't a given?

She phrased it like an interjection, but Maeve recognized it for what it was—the beginnings of a negotiation.

"More information," she said carefully. "Poets are powerful people, and you knew one...how?"

The stranger almost looked amused. *Well, well—curious indeed. You didn't come here for that alone, did you? You have to want something.*

Maeve looked back stonily—best to play her cards close to her chest. The woman seemed unconvinced.

Poets are powerful people, hmm? You want some of that power—for yourself. You want a poet's ear. You want a poem.

"Not for myself!" Maeve protested, then bit her tongue in frustration. The other woman looked smug. She growled under her breath. "For my sisters. Our convent—the poets, their seances, they've…made things tough."

The woman looked more interested at that. *I see. This is a devil's bargain. Crossing the divide to speak to the enemy.* She leaned in, looming over Maeve. *Does your abbess know you're here?*

Maeve stayed silent, unsure of how to reply. The Wraith didn't seem to mind the lapse in conversation, though; she strode away from the desk, paused with her back to Maeve, and then turned and perched on the edge of the sarcophagus. She picked up another scrap of paper from yet another table and began to write anew.

You come here, seeking a poet's aid to save your convent, and you tell no one. You told me you were a Sister of Good Death. Tell me—what, exactly, does that entail?

Maeve glanced up from the note; the woman's expression was all mock-innocence. Maeve narrowed her eyes.

"Well. We care for the dying. We help prepare those who want us to for burial. We maintain abandoned graves, we advocate for the deceased, and…we help uneasy ghosts onto their next lives."

And how do you do that?

"A…variety of methods," Maeve said warily. "We communicate with them to determine why they've returned, help lay to rest any unfinished business, and if needed, we have…stronger methods."

"Unfinished…business," she whispered aloud, sounding contemplative, then returned to her pen. *Well. I think a proposition presents itself quite nicely—if you're feeling brave, little Sister. And if you can keep a secret.* She fixed Maeve with a piercing stare. *Can you?*

"Depends on the secret."

Ooh, you'll like it. Right up your alley. She pulled out a fresh piece of paper and began writing even faster. *The two undersigned enter into an Agreement; the Sister will provide her services, and in return the Poet will provide hers. If the Sister should break this agreement and snitch to the Constabulary or any other soul at any time, the Poet shall tell her Abbess that she has been consorting with Unseemly Hedo-nistic Sorts, and the Sister shall be free to do the same in reverse should the Poet fail to hold up her end of the Agreement. The Sister shall aid the Poet in solving the murder of Imogen Madrigal, and in return the Poet shall aid the Sister in the resurrection and protection of her Sisterhood.*

She looked up at Maeve with an eyebrow raised.

"And you'll quit desecrating this place," Maeve put in. "And stop robbing people. And I won't commit any crimes." This felt bad—a devil's bargain, like the Wraith had said. Maeve hadn't known that the woman was a poet as well. Or that Imogen Madrigal had been murdered. But necessity drove her on.

Criminal activity will be kept to a minimum, the woman added to the end of the contract, and drew two lines, placing Xs before each of them. She held it and her fountain pen out to Maeve and looked at her calculatingly.

Maeve took the pen, her fingers brushing the other woman's. They were still cold as ice, and Maeve watched her out of the corner of her eye as she put pen to paper. Right up her alley, the woman had said. And unfinished business. But if the murdered spirit was restless and out haunting, where—?

She handed the contract back. The woman took the pen and signed with the flourish of someone well-used to doing a great deal of writing. Cold hands, but not stiff. No rigor mortis. A living, breathing—or…no…living, perhaps, but not….

Maeve took the contract back, already half-knowing what she'd see, and already shaking her head. "That's…not possible…."

Imogen Madrigal smiled at her in the dark and traced a finger absently over the velvet ribbon around her neck. "Get used…to… disappointment."

Chapter

IV

Maeve woke the next morning with a start.
She'd been in such shock last night that the poet had managed to
shove her out the door, and by the time she came to her senses,
she was already back at the convent. Now, she leapt out of bed,
yanked on her stockings, and sprinted down the hall to Thalia's
room. She rapped on the door, bounced on her toes for a moment,
then rapped again a little more insistently.

A disheveled Thalia came to the door, looking still half-asleep.
"Maeve, wh—?"

"Your newspapers—how far back do they go?"

She yawned. "The ones about the Wraith, or just in general?"

"Either."

"Wraith stuff started last month." She rubbed her eyes. "I only
got a subscription for my nameday. But the library's got a back-cat-
alog—that's where I used to get them. Why?"

"Just curiosity," Maeve said, shutting the door in Thalia's face
and running back to her own room. Okay, okay, information—
she needed to know more about unusual hauntings in general,
and Imogen Madrigal in particular. She sat at her desk and paged
through her prayerbook hopelessly. Why, oh why didn't the sisters
make studies of this sort of thing? She didn't want samples and
statistics and ethically reprehensible dissections like the scientists
at the Academy, but would a little bookkeeping be such a crime?
Would it be so bad to put a leaflet in the back with a bit more information on how ghosts actually *worked*?

It might not, but as far as Maeve knew, no one had ever put such a thing together. The prayerbook was only vague folklore and the Blessed Sister Artemisia's automatic trance writings, and beyond that Maeve only had what she knew from her own years in the field. Nothing she'd ever seen had come close to this. Ghosts didn't have bodies—at most, they were wispy, vaguely humanoid. They couldn't touch—they couldn't pick things up. And they certainly couldn't show the level of living consciousness that this woman did. Ghosts got stuck on things; they became broken phonographs. They didn't *scheme*.

So, she wasn't a ghost—but she was convinced she had been murdered. She must have been considered dead by someone, if she had a mausoleum. Unless it was an elaborate hoax—but Maeve had felt how cold she was. She had thought her a corpse before she had woken up. And Maeve knew what a corpse felt like. She huffed in frustration, slamming her prayerbook shut, and stood, then fished the contract out of her coat pocket and scanned it over, shaking it down for secrets. Nothing but the words they'd both agreed to and the meeting place she'd managed to demand. Eleven tonight, at the Northside Lobster Dockyard. It would be a torturous wait; already questions were buzzing around her head and doubts were creeping in. She shook her head sharply. Even if she had been mistaken—if she had been fooled—it would be in her interest to go. She'd at least find out who this woman really was, and if…if what they had discussed last night was really true, then…She shivered, and took up her sketchbook. Well, perhaps she should see before she thought too far out ahead.

"The library? Yes, of course—and bring the little ones with you," Mother Superior said thoughtfully, sipping at her morning cup of tea. "Lavender is starting to develop quite the interest in history, and we ought to encourage it."

Maeve was already headed for the door, wrapping a muffin in a napkin, but Mother Superior's words slowed her, and she sighed under her breath. She doubled back to the little ones' table and forced cheerfulness into her voice to disguise her impatience. "Alright—who wants to come to the library?"

A chorus of excited affirmatives came in reply, several of the little sisters nearly knocking their glasses over in their haste to stick their hands up. "Ten minutes," Maeve told them, tapping her watch, and then forced herself to walk slowly over to her own table. Frances was reading her prayerbook, Thalia a newspaper; Shivani sipped at her tea and raised an eyebrow at Maeve. She knew it was an inquiry after the state of Frances's supposed present, but somehow it felt accusatory. Maeve forced a wink and shoved the muffin in her mouth to keep from blurting anything inconvenient. *Should she snitch, the Poet will tell the Abbess...*Of course, Maeve didn't think that her cohort counted against that agreement, but... for now, it could be uncomfortable.

"I told you to go to the library—I didn't tell you to bring all the little ones, too," Thalia commented behind her paper. "Lobster is only two ammonite a pound this week."

"What's at the library?" Shivani asked, setting her tea down.

"She told me to take them," Maeve said carefully. "And—books are. You know, stacks of paper....?"

"Ha, ha," Shivani said dryly, and rolled her eyes. "You know what I meant, Maevey-wavey."

"Old newspapers, right?" Thalia folded hers down. "About the Wraith or something?"

"Oh, don't tell me you're getting into all that too." Frances set down her book, looking at Maeve pleadingly. "Don't do anything dangerous."

"Not about the Wraith," Maeve promised, and smiled reassuringly at Shivani. "Like Thalia said—just looking at some old news for a tricky haunting."

"Well, best of luck finding it and minding them at the same time." Shivani tilted her chin over at the little ones' table, where Sister Priscilla was sternly telling one of the girls to take her fork out of her nose. "I try not to do it before noon."

Maeve sighed and poured herself a cup of strong tea. "I do, too."

Imogen Madrigal had been found dead in an alley near the Northside Dockyard on November 12th one year earlier. The police determined that the murder had occurred on the spot, and that there hadn't been a struggle. A quick, clean betrayal. The obituary was plain but sprinkled liberally with quotes from an emotional

Orion Cantor—*the* Orion Cantor, whose name would be known even to young nuns in an order that despised the poets and their court. "A silver tongue taken from us too soon," he had said, and had sacrificed a forty-year-old pinot noir to her funerary offering.

Some whispered that that really wasn't that fancy of a wine, especially for the Laureate of the Poets' Court, but it wasn't so much out of indignation for the dead woman as it was spite against the living man. After all, following verse, the chief export of the Court was gossip, and silver tongues could still wag. Or at least they could with vocal cords intact.

When Imogen Madrigal awoke the first day of autumn the next year, she was appreciative that any wine was there at all. She was parched beyond belief, and the liquid soothed the searing pain in her throat by some small measure. It was night, and she was cold and uncertain of where she was; she had heaved a stone lid out of her way with difficulty, and her attention had seized upon the wine before she could come to her senses. Her body felt numb, and so it was a moment before she noticed the feeling of cold soaking down her chest. She raised a hand to her throat, which came away red; too thin to be blood. Detached horror led her to taste it and found it a very nice pinot noir like the one she had just drunk. She opened her mouth to scream; no sound came out. It was that, rather than the wound to her throat, that caused her to faint.

Maeve had been very lucky indeed and had found a great deal of information on her new associate. She had had a book of poems published, for one; Maeve couldn't spend long looking at it, not with the little sisters and their inability to keep secrets threatening her, but she paged through it quickly. She didn't know how to tell if poetry was good or not, but the few ones she saw about the ocean seemed nice. Perhaps, if she were to be working at this for a long time, she would actually check the thing out.

In addition to that, she'd found a number of newspaper articles detailing the poet's rise to fame, and whole front pages on her extremely public and scandalized death. So, she had definitely died, but whether the woman claiming to be her *was* her was another question. It was hard to explain how she might look so much like the person in the photographs if she wasn't, but Maeve strove to stay suspicious. If things were going to get dangerous, she couldn't go into this naively.

One final—and slightly sad—piece of information was a wax cylinder, stored along with a great number of others in a listening room with a phonograph. The label on the end declared it to be the *Performance of 'Rootbound' by the Poet - I. Madrigal.* The little sisters were occupied outside with the stacks of novels they had picked out, and so Maeve quickly slipped the cylinder out of its case, fitted it into the phonograph, and flicked the switch on. The recording spat and crackled but settled into the sound of a woman's voice—enunciated, rather low-pitched, and with a driving, hypnotic cadence.

"Iron drives away the fey, so they say
The trees, the leaves, those flushes of green
That seep between cobblestones and fight up to breathe
It drives them away, so they say, and the safe and the tame shall walk unafraid.

What is a chase, and what is a wait? I have seen trees, in infinite patience, devour fences in a matter of short decades, and time lies on their side..."

Maeve found herself thinking of the little patches of moss in the cracks on the sidewalk and that lost voice as she made her way to the dockyard. She looked up and drew her coat close as she neared the appointed spot. It had a great deal of significance, she now knew; this was the spot where they had found the corpse— where, according to the constabulary, the murder had occurred. Probably meant to scare her, but Maeve wasn't the type to be easily spooked by death. She found the alley in question, and after looking around carefully, entered it. Now, to wait.

A scrap of paper drifted down on the wind, seeming to linger near her, and she snatched it on a whim.

You came. I wondered if you'd thought better of it.

She looked up to find a figure seated on a fire escape far above, her legs dangling.

"Not yet." She winced internally—that wasn't exactly the wittiest of comebacks—but she heard an amused huff from above, followed by the rasp of creaking iron, and watched as the poet climbed down. She was wearing the flowing shirt tucked into tight trousers she'd worn when Maeve had first run into her in the graveyard, without the Wraith mask. "I've learned a lot about you."

The poet came to a stop before her and held a finger to her lips. She gestured with her chin for Maeve to follow, and after a moment, Maeve did, letting the poet lead her out of the alley and across the street to a teahouse. She paused on the threshold in confusion—wasn't the point of their meeting spot to maintain secrecy? Or was it all just for the theatrics?

The entrance led up a set of extremely steep and twisting stairs, and once at the top the poet slipped another note into Maeve's hand, which she struggled to read in the dark.

Ask the host for the private room under the name Seek. And order a pot of the belladonna.

She held the door open, and Maeve passed through. A woman in a long black dress with a great deal of kohl about her eyes met the pair of them and looked them over with an unimpressed expression.

"Room for Seek," Maeve said carefully. "And, er, can we get a pot of...belladonna?"

"As you wish," the woman—who Maeve now realized was more of a teenage girl under the makeup—intoned and beckoned them deeper into the black-lacquered interior. It was nearly empty inside, and what patrons Maeve saw were universally dressed in black, with their noses in well-worn books. Maeve glanced down at her own sweater and skirt—lavender and charcoal grey, respectively—and wished the poet had warned her where they were going. She stuck out.

Presently they came to a pair of rice-paper doors, through which a diffused light could be seen, and with an air of utmost disinterest, the hostess slid one open.

"We'll have that right up for you," she sighed, and glided away.

Within, a small table with a lantern in the center sat, a pouf on either end. "I've...never been to a place like this," Maeve said carefully as she sat and unwound her scarf from over her head. Her companion sat opposite and scratched something quickly in a notebook.

It was wise of you to come out of uniform. This place is a haven for sad teenagers to discuss macabre literature. If they knew they had a Sister of Good Death in their midst they'd be beating down the doors to ask you about all the corpses and ghosts you've seen.

Maeve folded her hands and pursed her lips—she was well-aware of the morbid interest their order drew. "I...suppose I can understand their interest. Though all the black is a bit gloomy."

The poet smirked. *Oh, unquestionably. Lavender's a bit cuter. Suits you.*

"Er—"

She shook herself. *Of course. To business. I have four main suspects—the Court, the Academy, the Warwicks, and of course, your convent. So, to start—*

"Wait, wait, wait," Maeve interrupted, reading upside down. "Ignoring *that*—" She pointed an indignant finger at the mention of the Sisterhood— "I have some questions first. And some ideas that might speed this up. Okay?"

The poet looked up in slight annoyance, then started a new line.

Ideas?

"Yes," Maeve said crossly. "I've been working with ghosts for ten years and you've been one for, what, a few months?"

A number of unpleasant expressions crossed the poet's face. A quiet rap came at the door, followed by the hostess with a pot of something strong and floral smelling, who placed it between them. Maeve murmured a thank-you, not taking her eyes from her companion's, and the door was shut again. At length, the poet gave a tight nod.

"Thank you," Maeve said, and poured a cup for each of them. Her companion didn't touch it. "If we're safe to speak plainly, let's do so, and lay out the facts. Your name is...."

"Imogen Madrigal," she whispered. Her eyes burned with purpose as she said it, like it was important to her to use her voice to do it.

"Who was widely written up to be murdered one year and a few months ago. A story which you yourself corroborate." Maeve pulled her own sketchbook from her bag and began taking notes. "I believe that to have been the case, but for the purposes of our investigation, I would like to prove that you're her." She reached back into her bag, and laid out her spirit board, her planchette, her prayerbook. "When did you...find yourself in this state?"

September 21st. Imogen eyed the items. *The first day of autumn, this year. I can produce proof quite easily, Miss…what was your surname?*

"It was Whaler. But you can call me Sister Maeve, or Maeve." She noted the information down and looked up. "Proof? Have you experienced…anything unusual, then?"

She smirked. *Something like that, Sister Maeve.*

Maeve watched as she tucked a napkin into her collar and untied the ribbon around her throat with the other hand. Below, Maeve could see evidence of the gash that had been the killing blow—a wound that, to her knowledge, was unsurvivable. It curved wickedly from one extreme on the left to the other on the right, and if it went as deep as it seemed to, must nearly have beheaded the woman. She frowned, bent in closer, then pulled back as Imogen took up the cup of tea, and took a sip.

It took precious few seconds for the napkin to grow stained and brown, and Maeve watched in fascinated horror as Imogen stuck her finger into the wound—not a scar, as Maeve had thought, but a still-gaping wound—and ran it around the edge. Her finger came away bloodless, and she wiped it off on the napkin before writing once more.

So there's that, obviously. There's also more.

"M-more?" The fascination was quickly superseding the horror, and the words that came from her mouth sounded painfully eager. "Tell me."

What first?

"Do you eat? Does your heart beat? What temperature is your body? Do you bleed?"

Imogen numbered out a list, looking slightly amused. *1. I don't seem to have to, but I can if I want. 2. No. 3. Cold. Very cold.* Her pen hovered above the paper, and she looked up at Maeve, a perplexed expression on her face. *4. I haven't gotten cut since I woke up. I don't know.*

The two of them stared at each other for a long moment, and very slowly, Maeve poked about in her bag, till she came to the small knife she used to sharpen her pencils. She held it out apologetically, and Imogen looked at her disbelievingly for a moment, before snatching it up with a huff and quickly pricking her thumb. She, it seemed, was almost as curious as Maeve was. The two of them watched the cut tensely, and in the dark room, Maeve almost thought her eyes were playing tricks on her. But no, there was a definite glow around the cut, and before her eyes, a trickle of pale purple ectoplasm welled up, and dripped onto the table. The two of them looked back at each other, and Imogen swallowed painfully, before wrapping her thumb in the napkin and folding her arms.

Maeve was itching to ask more questions, but she was also well-aware of the bedside manner necessary for an undertaking of this sort. Usually, it was a distraught loved one, who had to be carefully comforted and shepherded away while another sister could do the requisite dirty work. In this case, the distraught and the deceased were one, and so she was at something of a loss.

"Well," she said, and then said it again. "So yes, there's ghostly activity going on." She paged through her prayerbook, looking at the few sections she had bookmarked as even possibly helpful. "If I had to guess—have you ever heard of possession?" Imogen shook her head. "Well. It's...an ability that some particularly strong spirits have. Not so common nowadays, but back in..." she coughed; the poet probably didn't want to hear history. "Anyway. A spirit can inhabit a physical object and use it as a vessel to interact with the physical world. Usually that's something the ghost owned in life—books or jewelry or canes or things like that. In your case...it would appear that the object was your own dead body." She didn't mention the logical inconsistencies—that possessions were hardly a permanent, month-long occurrence, that possessed objects were invariably small and inorganic, that the complex system of the human body would be far beyond the mental faculties of the typical ghost....

Imogen seemed to accept it, however. She nodded and went back to her notes. *So, that's the what. The who and the why is what I want to know. Which is why I didn't want you getting involved with this—whoever killed me probably wouldn't be pleased to find out it didn't stick, and any associates of mine will probably be in similar danger. I intend to stay alive this time, and I'm sure you do, too.*

Maeve blinked. She had been approaching this from the angle of helping a ghost— albeit an unusual one—find peace and go to the grave. She hadn't considered that she might want to stay. Her goal was to help ghosts out of this world and into their own, but Imogen wasn't quite...she frowned and realized she had been scanning the page Imogen had written without reading it. She pushed the conundrum from her mind; there would be time to consider that later.

Again, my four suspects: the Court, the Academy, the Warwicks, and the Sisterhood. I can imagine motives for each of them, and while I suppose I may have just been mugged, I doubt it. Her face was grim when Maeve glanced up to look at it. *I am not the sort of person to be killed in such an undignified manner.*

Maeve raised an eyebrow; she didn't think many people would consider themselves the type to get killed at all. "So…what exactly happened, then? Did you not see the person who killed you? Where were you?"

Imogen canted her head in a frustrated manner, and gestured to the top of the page. *I cannot remember anything of the day I was killed beyond waking up; it was raining, and I was hungover.*

"Right," Maeve said, feeling her face get hot. "Sorry."

Have you got a pocket telegraph?

"No." They didn't exactly come cheap.

Neither do I. I'll rectify that. It'll be quicker. Maeve opened her mouth to ask just exactly how the poet planned to do so, but she kept writing. *I've been forced to gather information piecemeal to this point—I can't show my face to any of these people, or I'll lose the only safety I have. Which is where you come in.* Imogen topped up Maeve's tea, the smile on her face just failing to hide the calculating look in her eyes. *You're going to be my eyes, ears, and most importantly, my voice.*

"Why do you suspect the Sisterhood?" Maeve asked warily, taking a sip of her tea. It took a bit to get past the overwhelming floral taste.

Imogen shrugged noncommittally. *It's a tenuous motivation, to be sure—just that nuns hate poets. I don't know any Nuns of Good Death, so it wouldn't be a personal thing. I doubt any of you having the stomach to slit my throat, but I figured I'd be thorough.*

"Sisters," Maeve corrected, not sure whether to be offended or not by the logic. She pursed her lips and set down her tea. "What are the motivations for the others?"

The Court—general backstabbery. I was rather well-known by the end, and some idiot might've been worried I was coming for their laurels. Which I was, of course. She angled her chin in a proud sort of gesture that rubbed Maeve the wrong way. The poet was beginning to reveal herself as rather self-absorbed. *The Academy—lover's quarrel, I won't bore you with the sordid details. The Warwicks—political disagreements, and you just know how Lady Marlene gets when she doesn't have her way.*

Maeve most certainly did not know that; Marlene Warwick was of such astronomically high social status that Maeve had never spared a thought for what she might be like personally. This list of Imogen's enemies was a veritable catalog of Lenorum's powerful elites—people who moved and machinated in ways that hardly touched Maeve's little life except to elevate the price of lobster every so often. She swallowed hard; she was making enemies of them now, if Imogen was to be believed.

"So, you want me to help you investigate them?"

Imogen nodded. *I'll work behind the scenes, and you'll take the stage.* Another smirk brushed across her lips. *Not the split I typically prefer, but the circumstances necessitate it, I suppose.*

"As in, I go talk to…to people in the Court, and to people who know the Warwicks, and…?"

Indeed. Darling, you look a touch pale—must I find another actor?

"No," Maeve said quickly. It was intimidating, but the thought of losing her chance at helping the convent was worse. In fact, if she was talking to the Warwicks she could throw in her own endorsement. "No, no, I can handle it. I'll just…need some coaching, I suppose."

Oh, indeed. That was already on my to-do. Along with clothes. Like I said, it's a cute outfit, but certainly not the sort of thing one meets Orion in.

"O-Orion Cantor?" The indignant reply died on Maeve's lips, undermined by the horror of this prospect. The rich and educated were one thing; the Laureate of the Court was another. Imogen watched her fumble for a moment, then wrote with great deliberateness and not a little sarcasm and pushed the notebook across the table.

Perhaps we won't start with him, then.

Chapter

V

"I'll just be a moment—I want to go back and look
at those oranges," Maeve said, feeling a twinge of guilt as Frances
nodded cheerfully. They'd been food-shopping for the convent for
most of the morning, but it was only now that Frances was waiting
in line for the fishmongers to come in that Maeve saw her opening.
She headed back into the indoor portion of the market, weaving
her way among stalls selling fresh-baked breads and preserves and
all possible manner of teas. Aside from the cemetery, the market
was one of Maeve's favorite spots to gather inspiration: the bustling
patrons and busy shops held all sorts of lovely little details, from
beautiful raincoats and scarves to meticulously arranged displays.
It was a challenge to avoid being distracted by gilded tea sets and
violently green absinthe bottles, but eventually she made her way
back to the eastern entrance and outside into the rain.

The barrel Imogen had told her to look for her message in was
there all right, though it took Maeve a bit of awkward maneuvering to open it with one hand and hold her umbrella with the other.
Inside, sporting a few water stains but no worse for wear, she found
a small package of brown paper and twine. A tag tucked under the
string told her to *open when alone*. She slipped it into her bag and
went back to look at the oranges.

Frances met her with a package of her own, though hers gave
off the overwhelming aroma of fish. "Let's get this in the icebox,"
she said with a wince, and wedged it into the wagon alongside
the rest of their purchases. The wind threatened to yank the tarp

they'd secured over the top of the wagon from its place, but they made it back with the food dry, if not themselves. Maeve tried to wring out her skirt as Frances rang the doorbell, hopefully to summon a few little sisters to help them put the groceries away. That helped with the worst of the water, but she was still damp when they finally got everything put away in its place. Blech—Maeve always hated being cold and wet. She'd spent too much time that way as a small child to ever want to experience it again.

She cut up the orange she'd gotten to reward the little sisters— Eleanor, Una, and Lavender this time around—and split half a wedge with Frances. Juicy and bright with acid, this was a good orange, maybe one of the last good ones of the season. Certainly, one of the last ones they could afford before the price of citrus rose to its winter height. She winced, did her best to savor the taste as she headed up to her room, and shut the door, shucking off her wet clothes. And now, for the package. The anticipation was almost exciting, though the reason for its delivery still made her nervous.

Stripped of paper and twine, the box within was of white cardboard, sturdy enough to seem expensive. The stamp on the top of the box proclaimed it to be a product of Clothier and Daughters, the ink shimmering silvery in the light from her window. Maeve swallowed hard. Mother Superior's last sermon on hedonism was by no means the first, and where exactly the line between enjoyment and hedonism fell was a matter of some anxiety for her. Maeve had a few nice things—her drawing pencils, and the hourglass pendant that all sisters wore—but clothes seemed to be an impractical thing to spend much money on.

She lifted the lid off carefully and found a folded sheet of paper on top.

My contact code is in the telegraph; send me a message if the dress is the wrong size. I'll have it re-tailored. This should be good for daytime appointments, I think—your own clothes will work for more casual assignations. Enjoy as much as your austerity permits. —yours, I.

The same sentiment she had felt but framed much more rudely; if even the poet thought the gift might be too much for her, then now she felt certain it was. She inspected the pocket telegraph sourly, trying to determine whether it was stolen. She'd never seen one up close. It was about the size of her palm, with a few toggle switches and a button underneath a tiny glass screen. She flipped one of the switches experimentally, then set it aside.

Onto the dress. She shut her eyes and pulled it over her head blind, nervous of what she would see. Hopefully it wouldn't fit, and that would be that. She peeked in the mirror with trepidation.

She was surprised to find something far less objectionable than she had been expecting. The dress was long and black, with tight sleeves that flared into lace cuffs and a cinched waist. The neckline swept a little lower than she was used to, but a collar in that same lace buttoned up to her throat, so she wasn't too uncomfortable. It rather reminded her of her habit, in fact, though quite a bit more stylish.

Maeve fell in love with it, and then felt a rush of guilt for doing so.

She rolled one of the silver buttons between her fingers nervously. It couldn't have cost that much. It wasn't so bad to have nice things or enjoy them. It wasn't a crime to dress up; it wasn't a sin to fawn over a bit of lace. It wasn't hedonism to twirl a bit in front of the mirror, or to appreciate the match between the buttons and the frames of one's glasses. The dress was a business expense, a necessity, a tool for navigating society. It just happened to be a nice coincidence that it was very pretty....

A rapid knock came at her door, and she jumped.

"One second!" she shouted, struggling out of the dress and feeling her way over to her dresser for a dry habit. "Just changing!"

"Well, pick it up!" Shivani's voice, sounding eager and impatient. "We've got a call!"

"Oh!" She stuffed the dress back into the box, shoved it under her bed, and yanked her coif over her head. "I'm coming, I'm coming!"

Shivani was looking at her watch when Maeve stumbled a little breathlessly into the hall. "Twenty two seconds?" she complained, a smirk twitching at the corner of her mouth. "What, are you trying to make us late?"

"Shut up," she returned, and finished shoving her spirit board into her bag. "What kind of a call? Where?"

"Edgewood Heights." Shivani raised her eyebrows and put on a haughty accent. "And just the most *awful* ruckus the poor Lord Robert has ever experienced. A really terrible shock to his system, and all sorts of horrible goo on the tapestries...."

Maeve laughed and started down the hall in high spirits. A normal ghost—that was a nice change of pace. "Great. Seance party gone awry?"

"Undoubtedly." Shivani grinned. "But some fun for us, at least."

"And your sacred and solemn duty?" A stern voice caught them both in their tracks, and Maeve felt her face go hot as she turned back to find Mother Superior tapping her foot.

"Er—we're just excited to be helpful?"

"Indeed." Mother Superior's voice was dripping with sarcasm, but the barest hint of a smile belied her true feelings. "Clean up that bedside manner before you get there, ladies. Lord Robert called the Academy, too, and I don't want us looking bad in front of Professor Chrystos."

Maeve and Shivani glanced at each other, and Maeve stood up a little straighter. "Will do," she promised, and quickened her pace as Mother Superior watched them leave.

"Idiot," Shivani muttered under her breath. "The Academy? What does he think he's going to get from them?"

"Don't know," Maeve said, flagging down a cab outside the gate with a nervous feeling in her stomach. She'd never been part of an exorcism with a third party involved, and the odds that it went smoothly were low. A motorcar pulled over for them, and Shivani gave the address. "We'll just have to work fast and get it right the first time, before they can get involved."

"Maybe we can leave them to clean up the old tapestries."

Normally the two of them would have walked or ridden the streetcar to an exorcism, but Edgewood Heights was on the mainland, linked to the island exclusively by a narrow cribstone bridge too long to walk in a timely manner. This was where the city's nobility lived, families who had carried titles down from the annals of history and retained a great deal of political sway despite the fact that the tea companies and whaling armadas that had made them their money had largely been replaced in public hands. Maeve's family's whaling ship had been part of that redistribution, and she retained a hereditary disdain for their old bosses. She had been out here once or twice and had found it singularly lonely—the houses were acres apart from each other, and one would need to take a motorcar just to have tea with a neighbor. She preferred the crush of townhouses in the city proper, or better yet, her friends under the same roof.

The cab brought them out onto an oak-lined lane, and Maeve watched as the estates in question rolled by, each surmounted by a sprawling and slightly-decayed mansion. It made sense, she supposed—the nobles were so concerned with names and blood ties that they would have to keep adding wings and floors to their houses to keep the whole family line sheltered. Newport, Sinclair, Warwick....

Maeve remembered what Imogen had said, that she and Lady Marlene Warwick had political differences. She wrinkled her nose; she didn't like nobles, but she didn't think she would be brave enough to stand up to whoever lived in that brooding green house, with its wrought iron fence and twisted topiaries. She was just Maeve—once Maeve Whaler, now Sister Maeve, and never Maeve with a surname that meant anything more than an occupation. She preferred it that way, but still.

Finally, to the estate of the Heathcliffe family, of whom Lord Robert was the patriarch. The cab dropped them at the end of a long driveway, and the driver refused to stick around. Shivani tried to argue with him as Maeve put up an umbrella over the pair of them, but he left them in a cloud of exhaust.

"We'll have to borrow the phone, I suppose," Shivani grumbled, and turned toward the house. "No wonder it's haunted."

Maeve agreed. The mansion looked far more labyrinthine than its neighbors, even from the outside, and the hedges out front were unkempt. She glanced at Shivani, then started forward, the gravel crunching under her boots. The pair of them said nothing as they passed the cream-colored coupe with chrome details parked out front. It appeared they had been beaten to the scene.

Shivani pressed the buzzer by the door, and a stooped man with a mustache opened the door with a suspicious look in his eye.

"Pardon my bluntness, young ladies, but the Heathcliffes are spoken-for in terms of—er—religion."

"Oh, Lord Robert called us," Maeve explained, and Shivani nodded. "We're from the Sisterhood of Good Death, here about the...strange events?" Sometimes it was best to come at these things obliquely; ghosts scared other people.

"Ah." The man's face took on a nervous cast, and he eased the door open a fraction more. "Yes, well, the representative of the Academy has already gone through with Lord Robert, but I shall bring you along as well, I suppose."

"Thank you," Maeve said, trying not to feel slighted, and followed what she assumed was the butler deeper into the decrepit old house. Cobwebs, peeling wallpaper, grim family portraits—yes, this was the sort of atmosphere in which things could get left behind. Or called up.

"Was there a seance here lately?" Shivani asked, voicing her thoughts as they crossed through a marble-floored great hall and up a wide staircase. "Or a party of that sort?"

"It is not my place to snoop into what Lord Robert and his guests do at their social gatherings," he said reproachfully, then darted a glance upward as a heavy thump echoed down from above. He brushed some plaster dust off his uniform, then added as a nervous afterthought—"The poet Estelle Chanteuse is a friend of the family."

Shivani glanced at Maeve, and the two of them followed silently until they reached the top of the stairs and the source of the knocking—a closed door with a gaunt old man and a round young woman outside it, both listening intently. The butler cleared his throat; the man jumped, and the woman turned, looking impatient.

"The Sisterhood of Good Death, m'lord."

"Excellent, excellent, yes." Lord Robert mopped his brow and gestured to the young woman. "Ms. Camille Sinclair of the Academy, ladies. Ms. Sinclair, er—"

"Sisters Maeve and Shivani," Shivani said coolly. The pair of them both recognized the young woman—she was the curly-haired student of Professor Chrystos's that stood opposite them every time Mother Superior went over to argue. Sinclair—Maeve hadn't known she was of noble descent. She decided she liked her a little less even than before.

"Charmed," Camille said shortly, and pulled a pair of goggles down over her eyes, looking as uncharmed as one possibly could. "Anyway, as I was saying, m'lord, the readings in this room are particularly high, and of course the sounds are suggestive. I would love to set up a few instruments, take some readings, perhaps collect some samples if you'll allow."

"Excuse us, m'lord," Maeve broke in. The formal address was unfamiliar and unpleasant on her tongue, but she wasn't about to be boxed out. "But we thought you wanted the spirit removed from your—er, parlor? Not researched."

"Er—" Lord Robert glanced between them uncomfortably, perhaps only now realizing that he shouldn't have called them both. "Well, yes—er, but is it safe? Perhaps Ms. Sinclair should be allowed to take her readings, if they will give us a better idea of what we're dealing with."

"Oh, we can figure that out without issue," Shivani said sweetly, gently prying Lord Robert from the door and strolling him down the hall. "Now, I was wondering—have you hosted any sort of seances recently? Or tried to contact any relatives who have passed on?"

That was Maeve's cue, typically—Shivani took the social aspect. She turned back to the door, which was blocked by the scientist.

"I'd like to go into that room."

"I'm sure you would," Camille said coolly. It seemed she recognized them, too. "Unfortunately, I have a number of delicate instruments set up already, and whatever you plan to do might pollute my results." She looked down her nose at Maeve like her being there was already pushing it. "Of course, you can have your turn at it once I've collected my data. I shouldn't expect there to be much left, though."

"You'd be surprised," Maeve said, sizing the woman up and determining if she could slip past her if she was quick. "I've seen your lot's handiwork, and it usually entrenches the spirit even more. Don't suppose Lord Robert would like that. Not to mention, of course, it's inhumane to the spirit."

Camille gave her a pitying look that said very clearly that she didn't care about Lord Robert. "Inhumane is irrelevant to the inhuman," she replied, and turned away. "Now, if you'd let me get back to my work—"

"Lady Aurelia!" Shivani proclaimed cheerfully, returning to their end of the hall. "A beloved grandmother, spent her time in the parlor, quite enjoyed cards. No worries, m'lord, we'll have no trouble—"

"Excuse me, m'lord, but I thought we agreed that the nuns should get their turn second?" Camille pulled her goggles off, looking displeased. "For your sake, of course, since we have no idea how long their...er, rituals might take? Since science is founded on *reliability?*"

The embattled nobleman glanced between the three of them, beginning to sweat once more, and began to murmur something that sounded nearly like an assent.

Shivani swooped in neatly. "Now, now, no need to argue— it might agitate dear Lady Aurelia, and we wouldn't want that, would we?" Maeve shook her head warningly. "No, no, Lord Robert—what you want is tried and true methods to take care of your grandmother, lay her to rest, back at peace. After all, she may not understand all of this newfangled machinery, but people are people, and most spirits recognize that. You wouldn't want her to get uneasy, entrench herself further, would you?"

"No, certainly—er—not," the lord agreed, and Shivani nodded kindly, backing toward the door before Camille could protest. "Won't be half an hour, sir." Maeve turned the knob surreptitiously, and the two of them slipped through, shutting out Camille's noise of indignation and locking it behind them.

"Smooth," Maeve said dryly, and Shivani smirked.

"We're in, aren't we? Now, let's be hypocrites—grab me the camera, would you?"

Maeve fished the device in question out of her bag and passed it over, then took out the planchette and peered through its aperture at the shadowy room. Oof—Lord Robert hadn't been exaggerating. A riot of spectral energy kaleidoscoped around the room, lurching sickly green into corners in time with the knocks. She lowered the planchette, and noted the ectoplasm leaking from the walls, the levitating poker chips strewn through the air. This was a strong spirit, and one that had come back corrupted.

A click came from beside her, and Shivani shook the photo as it came out of the camera, peering at it appraisingly. "Bad," she said shortly, and looked up at Maeve. "Another fractured one. Botched seance, do you think?"

"Or the machines she's got running out there." Maeve jerked her chin at the door and looked at Shivani's photo. There was an apparition visible if one squinted, though it was broken into several fragments across the room. An arm and part of a skirt near the bookshelves, a hand grasping at the curtains opposite. Shivani cleared her throat and stepped forward.

"Lady Aurelia? Is that you? Please knock once for yes, twice for no."

They didn't get a knock; rather, an unpleasant clinking sound, as though long nails were tapping on the glass windowpane. Maeve shivered as a chill leeched into the room.

Shivani soldiered on. "I will take that as a yes. Lady Aurelia, we're very sorry that you've been called up from your rest, and we'd like to send you back as painlessly as possible. Can you help us do that?"

The clinking continued, though it increased in tempo.

Maeve jumped in. "Lady Aurelia, I have a device here that you may be able to use to speak with us. If you can, please tell us what holds you here."

She pulled the spirit board out of her bag, but before she could set it on the floor, it and the planchette were torn from her hands and flew to the back wall with a clatter. She followed it across the room, her breath visible, and tried to decipher the jerky movements of the planchette.

W-H-E-R-E-W-H-Y-D-O-N-T-K-N-O-W—

"You're in your home, m'lady, and we don't know exactly why. Are you in pain?"

P-A-I-N-P-A-I-N-P-A-I-N-P-A—

"Yes, yes, okay, we'll be quick. Is it something to do with Robert, m'lady? Or the poet Estelle Chanteuse? They were the ones who called you up, so far as we—"

F-O-O-L-S-F-O-O-L-S-B-O-T-H-H-A-T-E-D-W-A-S-T-E-F-U-L-W-O-M-A-N—

"S-she's not here now!" Shivani interjected, shivering as the room dropped another few degrees. Maeve could see frost forming on the edges of her glasses. "Lady Aurelia, you should g-g-go back to your rest! We'll relay your message—"

R-U-N-I-T-I-N-T-O-T-H-E-GR-O-U-N-D-C-A-N-T-L-E-A-V-E-I-T-T-O-H-I-M—

The poker chips that had been floating gently up to this point began to vibrate, and then flew deadly fast to the door, burying themselves in the wood just as Shivani ducked out of the way. The planchette's movements had devolved into gibberish, and Maeve looked back at Shivani, urgently drawing her finger across her throat. Negotiations had failed; time for exorcisms. Shivani nodded and knelt to extract her prayerbook from her bag as Maeve turned back to recover her spirit board. A good thing she turned—now books were beginning to rattle from the shelves, and as she spun, she narrowly dodged one that had thrown itself at her head.

"Oh, fuck!"

Maeve spun back to see Shivani's prayerbook slip from her fingers and fly across the room to join the other books. Typically, she'd tease Shivani for the language—she'd picked it up in her youth outside the convent—but she rather agreed at this moment. Her own bag was trying to tug itself out of her hand, but she held fast, and dodged a small card table as it was caught up in the maelstrom.

"What's she trying to do?" Shivani complained.

"Probably trying to—wait, move, move!" Maeve realized the books were headed like a battering ram for the door an instant before they hit her and dove over to the windows along with Shivani. The door groaned but held against the onslaught.

"I'll hold it!" Shivani shouted. "You do the exorcism!" She rushed back to the door, and Maeve fumbled in her bag as the books flew back to the other side of the room. Her prayerbook twitched, but she held fast and began flipping, ignoring the frost on her glasses and the horrible cold in the air. It felt like it was digging into her very bones—

The sudden grasp of a spectral hand at her throat startled a scream out of her mouth, but it was immediately choked off as the hand began to squeeze. Shivani nearly ran forward, then was forced back to the door as the fusillade of books gave it another hit. The hinges squealed, and from outside Maeve could hear commotion.

"What are you two doing? Let me in, let me take over!"

"Do not open this door!" Shivani shouted back. "Get the lord out of the house and hold it shut!"

"How dare you give me orders!"

Maeve only heard this exchange in snatches; she was preoccupied with her ongoing strangulation and was beginning to run low on breath. She tried to choke in some air, and blindly groped in her bag for salvation. Salt, not properly encircling her, but it might help a bit—she tucked the sachet under her chin where she felt the hand, and managed to suck in a single breath. The exorcisms in her prayerbook were blurred by frost, but she knew near all of them by heart—hopefully, needfully enough.

"Hallowed Mother preserve this lost soul—" she choked.

Immediately the grip loosened, and an unseen force yanked at the prayerbook. She held fast and shifted into the old language in which the exorcisms were half-written, ducking debris and joining Shivani by the door. Under control, under control—Shivani batted away the shards of a tea pot with her spirit board as Maeve chanted, and though the scent of ectoplasm was acidic and sharp in the air, she could feel it starting to take hold. Yes, yes—back to the grave, back to rest, and hopefully out of pain. The books paused in their flight and shivered; Shivani snatched up her camera and took a picture.

"Yes, keep going, she's coming back together!"

Maeve couldn't look, focused as she was on the text, but the room was certainly coming back up to its normal temperature. There were a few more half-hearted knocks, the planchette slid to GOODBYE on the spirit board, and then it and everything else that had been floating in the room tumbled to the floor. It was loud, to say the least. They winced in parallel.

Three seconds elapsed in peace, and then the door swung open to admit the irate scientist, arms full of instruments.

"Great," she snarled. "Thanks to you—"

Lord Robert peered in the door, arresting the burgeoning confrontation.

"Is...is she gone?"

"Yes," Shivani told him, beginning to recover books from the floor. "Apologies for the state of things; she got a little...belligerent."

Maeve opted not to mention the old woman's fears that Lord Robert was letting the estate fall into ruin; it may have been a symptom of the corruption, and in any case picking a fight with the man might undo the gratitude plain on his face. She joined Shivani in tidying up while Camille scraped ectoplasm off the walls into test tubes, glaring daggers at them. The lord's presence kept her quiet, though, and the pair of them managed to finish their work and escape unaccosted. The lord gratefully passed them off to the butler, who saw them out the door with a word of thanks, and they started down the gravel path once more.

"Shit—we should've asked to use the phone," Shivani said, smacking herself in the forehead.

"I'm not going back," Maeve said frankly. "Do not want to put myself face-to-face with Little Miss Academy."

"Suppose you're right." Shivani blew a strand of hair out of her face, then tucked it back into her coif thoughtfully. "Another fractured ghost. We never found out if it was a botched seance, either."

"I wanted to make sure we got paid—didn't want to insult him." Maeve pulled her umbrella out and held it over both of their heads as they passed under the still-dripping oaks. "We should ask Mother Superior to ask him when she checks in."

Shivani nodded. "Good call. And nice work—I should memorize the—" She suddenly looked closer at Maeve and pulled her collar down with a frown. Maeve shivered; Shivani's hands were still cold, and her neck was sore from Lady Aurelia's grasp. "Oh, Mother, I completely forgot. Are you okay?"

"Yeah," Maeve assured her. "Just bruised, I think. She didn't have me for too long."

"The hand by the window." Shivani cursed, and took the umbrella from Maeve, holding it for her instead. "I'm so sorry, Maevey-wavey. Shouldn't have let her get you."

"It's okay! That's why we're partners." Shivani looked over at her, her gaze regretful but her mouth quirked in a smile. Maeve smiled back. "You schmooze the old men, I get strangled, and we both walk three miles back to the convent in the rain."

Shivani groaned, her sincerity departing as quickly as it had appeared.

"We walk one mile to a phone booth and then we call a cab, or I'll freeze to death and strangle you for good."

The rain continued into the night, and by the time Maeve changed into her pajamas and made to get into bed, she had forgotten about the pocket telegraph she'd left lying on the pillow. She picked it up as she burrowed under the covers and flicked the toggles methodically until the screen glowed green. She blew out her lamp and inspected the device under the covers. A few rows of options—MESSAGES (1), ADD NEW CONTACT, SETTINGS. She hesitated for a moment, then selected the first.

The screen displayed dots and dashes for a moment, then resolved into alphabetical text. Maeve was a little relieved—her Morse education was from back before she joined the convent and was consequently rusty. She squinted at the letters in the dark.

Did you like the dress?

Her finger hovered over the key as she chewed her lip, trying to decide how she felt about that message. There was something almost familiar about the tone; she could imagine Shivani saying it teasingly. But this wasn't Shivani, and the poet's intentions might range anywhere from sincere to mocking. She frowned at it for a moment longer—should she be sincere herself, or bury the lede? Was it dangerous to be friendly? She growled to herself; Lady Aurelia's ghost hadn't forced her to doubt herself like this. Poets just had to complicate everything. She stared at the message for a few more moments, then began to send a reply. Dit-dit-dah, dit-dit-dah. She tapped it out, and the device translated her words into text. She'd treat it like she would any other client—after all, this was a professional relationship.

Yes. Thank you.

A reply came almost immediately; she raised an eyebrow and opened it.

Most welcome, darling.

She glared at that for a moment, then shoved the damned thing into her sock drawer and rolled over. Poets just complicating everything....

Chapter

VI

The next morning was both warmer and drier,
and so when Maeve received a message from Imogen asking
whether she'd like to meet for brunch at a cafe near the seaside, she
nearly found herself looking forward to it. Her chores for the day
were minimal—a bit more work in the garden, then an art class for
the little ones, spent touring them around the chapel and explaining all the symbolism in the stained-glass windows.

"The hourglass represents the two worlds, or so we think—the
one of the living above, and the one of the dead below," she told
them as they gazed up at the image of the Blessed Sister Artemisia. "As above, so below—that's what the Blessed Sister seemed to
think the symbol meant, and it trickled down into our culture. But
it's not just the actual image of the hourglass—artists will often
lay out their figures in an hourglass shape too, to emphasize the
message." She pointed up and traced out the hourglass formed by
the Blessed Sister's outstretched hands and the corners of her habit.
"Someday we'll go to the Museum of Fine Arts, and you can see
it there too, especially in paintings of her first meeting with the
Hallowed Mother, and of her death."

Amal raised a hand, and Maeve nodded. "If Sister Artemisia
learned what the world of the dead is like, why didn't she tell anyone any more about it?"

Maeve pursed her lips—not really an art class question, that
one.

"Well," she said carefully. "She did a great deal of her writing under a trance—automatic writing, you know. Frances is particularly good at that if you want to see someone do it. Except instead of talking to a spirit like Frances does, the Blessed Sister was chosen to speak with the Hallowed Mother, and She only revealed a little. We learn today that it's a divine mystery—not meant for anyone to understand. As Sisters of Good Death, we try to have faith in Her about the whole thing."

"Yes, but why?" Amal pushed. "Wouldn't it be better if we didn't have to wonder?"

Maeve paused for a moment, trying to determine how to phrase her understanding of the issue. "Well, think of it this way. If you were going to receive a gift—for your nameday, say—would you want to know what it is before you get it?"

"Yes!" Amal looked exasperated.

"Not so fast." Maeve tapped her nose. "You know what it is, but you have to wait. If it's something good, then all you're going to want to do is get to your nameday, right? You're so excited about the future, you forget to pay attention to the days you're trying to skip over. You might even go looking for your present early! And if it's bad, then you're going to dread it the entire time leading up to getting it. Now—" she said placatingly, "we don't believe death is a bad thing. The hints we have from Sister Artemisia are good ones, we think. But wouldn't you rather get a nice surprise on your nameday, and enjoy the days leading up to it too?"

"Maybe." Amal still looked slightly unsure, but she didn't seem to have any more questions right now. It was a natural part of finding one's faith, and Maeve wasn't worried—she'd had those questions herself a long time ago. She moved onto the next window, smiled at the bright colors and kind-faced prophet therein, and kept on with her lesson.

Ten thirty arrived quicker than expected, and Maeve made her way out to the street, careful to avoid getting caught in any conversations with other sisters. She hopped on the nearest streetcar headed west, and folded her veil and coif into her bag, pinning her hair up with a pencil. The ride would take a while, so she used the time to make a list of questions in her sketchbook. Had Imogen stolen the dress or the pocket telegraph? How had she gotten them, if not, and what was Maeve to make of her past robberies?

It seemed strange to be thinking so darkly on such a pleasant day—a few clouds scudded fast through the sky, and the cry of seagulls could be heard more and more as they drew closer to the strait between the island and the mainland. This was the kind of weather that her family had always tried to convince her to go in for.

"Imagine this with a sea-breeze in your hair and the salt on your tongue, love," her mother had said, shaking back her own braids and waving at all the whaling ships down at the pier. "Oh, nothing better."

Nothing better, perhaps, but nothing worse than the rest of the time at sea. Maeve's few excursions with her family—storm-lashed, with the nauseating scent of whale-oil and gore thick on the air—had done plenty to dissuade her from the sailing life, and she had preferred to spend time on land with her grandmother before she passed. They were family by blood; the convent was a family by choice, and she was lucky to love them both, if one from a safe, land-based distance. They were probably sailing far away to the south now, chasing the migrating herds.

She hopped off the streetcar within hearing distance of the clink of the rigging—nobles' yachts in the western harbor—and made her way down to the cafe near the Academy that Imogen had specified. Time to focus. The Bookshop Teashop, entertainingly named, was not difficult to pick out—its pink siding and windows stacked high with books stood out from across the street, and the door was propped open invitingly. Maeve glanced around in an attempt at caution, and after seeing no one she knew or suspected of bad intentions, stepped inside. It was busy within, waiters bustling to and fro with pots of tea and neat little sandwiches. A small chime issued from her pocket, and she pulled out the telegraph to find a message waiting.

Booth in the back on the left.

She glanced up, and spotted a hand gloved in lace wiggling its fingers. Another chime came as she sat down.

You ought to try the elderflower iced tea here. They put sugar on the rim. Imogen mimed a kiss from within the scarf enshrouding her face.

"Good morning to you, too," Maeve said, only half-sarcastic. "I have a few more questions."

Imogen had set her telegraph on the table, and set to tapping fluently. *Ask away. Shall I get you that tea? I ordered one for myself already. Hope you don't mind.*

"No—I don't have quite have the money to—" Maeve said absently, digging in her bag. She heard herself say it and cut herself off. Be professional, not antagonistic.

To throw around? It's my treat. No need to get snippy.

"Er...."

Imogen raised her eyebrows. *Only trying to be hospitable, darling. No fun to drink alone.*

Maeve frowned at the message. "Can't you not drink without—?" She gestured to her own neck.

I can, it's just difficult! And anyway, I'm a poet—a sensualist, if you like. A hedonist if you're feeling rude, which I think you are. My murderer didn't take my taste buds and so I shall continue to use them and enjoy whatever pleasures I can in this sorry state.

Maeve almost laughed, incredulous. Mother Superior hadn't exaggerated in the slightest. "Alright, well, answer me this, hedonist—where'd you get this dress?"

She hadn't taken her coat off yet; Imogen leaned over, trying to peer down its collar. She buttoned it up a little higher.

Clothier and Daughters—it's a fashion house out by the Court. They do divine things with lace, like these gloves. She made an elegant gesture. *No more than I would spend on myself, dear Sister, so worry not.*

Maeve imagined that what Imogen would spend on herself would be well outside her own comfort zone. "I mean, how did you pay for it?" she pressed. "And the telegraphs?"

When I died, they impounded the contents of my apartment to auction. But there were legal complications due to the murder, and so it all apparently sat in a warehouse for the year. I tracked all that down two months ago, stole what I could back, and have been liquidating it into more prescient assets. I was loath to part with my portrait of the Blessed Sister, I can tell you that, but it fetched enough for your dress, these telegraphs, and about a thousand elderflower teas besides.

Maeve swallowed.

"Alright," she said, trying not to think about how much money that was. "Er, then, if you have all that money, then why were you robbing people?"

A smirk rose to Imogen's face within the folds of her scarf. *Oh, I wasn't—those were my victims' shoddy attempts at revenge. People with secrets don't like being threatened with being revealed, but you can hardly call the constabulary on someone for uncomfortable conversation.*

Maeve wrinkled her nose. "So they lied? That seems unlikely."

To you, I'm sure. I shouldn't have shaken you down for information—I didn't know any of your secrets. Didn't have enough leverage.

"I don't have any secrets."

Then what am I? A waitress arrived with a glass of sweet tea garnished with some sort of herb, and Imogen nodded in thanks, taking a sip with her head tilted carefully back. *Everyone has secrets, darling. It just depends on who they're keeping them from.*

Maeve decided to let that pass without comment. She was still suspicious, but she supposed she had no choice if she wanted Imogen to hold up her end of the bargain. "Alright. So why am I here today?"

I want to start interviewing suspects. Imogen tapped this out, then withdrew a notebook from the satchel on the seat beside her. Maeve looked at the pages she indicated; the evidence, it seemed, she had collected so far. *Mr. Orion Cantor, Laureate of the Poets' Court, and/or assoc. underlings. Lady Marlene Warwick, Socialite. Reverend Mother Bethel, Abbess of the Sisterhood of Good Death, and/ or assoc. underlings, save Sister Maeve. Ms. Camille Sinclair, Scientist.*

"You've got to be kidding me," Maeve muttered under her breath, remembering what the poet had said last time, and looked up at Imogen in disbelief. "A lover's quarrel? You dated that odious woman?"

Imogen looked surprised. *You know her?*

"More than I'd like." She wrinkled her nose. "Surprised she has time to date with all the time she spends committing heresies and things."

Imogen rolled her eyes. *Sex isn't a heresy, darling—*

"I meant her area of study." Maeve swallowed back a laugh as Imogen's expression flicked briefly into mortification. She recovered her neutral expression, though two spots of purple arose in her cheeks like a blush. "Anyway. I'm not investigating Mother Superior for you. So, what's your plan for the other three?"

Imogen looked mutinous for a moment, but blew out a sigh of frustration and tapped a new message. *Well, I had thought Camille since she'd intimidate you the least, but now I don't trust you not to embarrass me entirely.*

"You're dead—you can't be worried about your reputation!"

Shh! Undead! And someday I plan to have a reputation again. She looked over her dossiers again, frowning. *Can't have you go to Orion first, or you'll die on the spot. Marlene might not even let you in. Ugh. You know Camille, though?*

Maeve nodded grumpily. "She got called to the same haunting as I did yesterday. Did not end particularly civilly."

No way around it, I don't think. Imogen pinched the bridge of her nose. *At least this won't require acting. Just…I don't know, tell her I'm haunting my old apartment or something. Without a body, I mean. Proper dead. See what she thinks of that.*

"Any particular information you're looking for? Do we have any leads so far?"

I want to nail down my movements that day. The constabulary got that I went to a teahouse near my apartment that morning, but I seem to have avoided witnesses after that point. But if I went to visit any of my suspects, then, well….

"They're going to lie if I come straight at it," Maeve pointed out, taking an annoyed sip from the tea that had just arrived at her elbow. "I need to know a bit of prior information too, so I can try to guess if they're lying. Like a detective would have."

Imogen sighed. *Sensible, I suppose. Camille and I dated for approximately six months before our separation. We met at some ball out in Edgewood Heights; one of my auditions for my laurels. It went well— the audition, I mean.*

"Was it an amicable separation?"

Imogen looked down her nose at Maeve. *Have you ever broken up with someone?*

"The Sisters of Good Death eschew worldly attachments in order to better fulfill their duties without the distraction of their own grief," Maeve said primly. "Anyway. I'm going to take that as a no."

No. Imogen paused, looking down at her hands. *Well, I didn't quite break up with her either. It was only a week or so—a little time away—ignoring her calls and such. Which got rather angry by the end.*

"And did you see her again after that break?"

No. I was going to have to do so, but I hadn't made plans to do it, yet.

Maeve sipped her tea again, processing the information. "Why did you have to see her again? And what's the motive, if you hadn't broken up with her?"

Imogen hesitated for a moment, looking torn. *Well, actually she…she proposed to me. And I didn't respond affirmatively right away, and I wanted some time to think about it. She was…insulted.*

"Hmm." Maeve wasn't sure that could lead all the way to murder, but she supposed Imogen would know better. She drummed her nails on the table, then finished off her tea and stood. "Well, that's enough to get started with. When do I talk to her?"

Imogen glanced out the window. *Well, I was planning to set you up on some sort of Academy tour, but now I suppose it would be more sensible to just have you meet with her directly. Are you free sometime soon?*

"I am now—let's get it over with," Maeve said, standing and putting her telegraph back in her pocket. "No need to dance around and try to be polite if she already dislikes me. You coming too? In disguise or something?"

Imogen swept all her papers up quickly, getting to her feet. She shook her head, and pointed to Maeve's pocket, tapping out one more message.

I'll lurk. Her office has a balcony outside.

Maeve nodded in reply, secretly relieved to at least have that much backup.

"The tea was your treat, right?" She suppressed a smile as Imogen rolled her eyes. "Give me twenty minutes."

Ten minutes found her at the reception desk of the parapsychology department. "Not Professor Chrystos this time," she assured the stressed-looking secretary. "Ms. Sinclair and I were at the same haunting yesterday, and we planned to compare notes."

"*You* were comparing notes?" He looked incredulous.

"Of course." Maeve tried to make it sound natural. "Not every member of the Sisterhood of Good Death is so reluctant to embrace progress." She muttered an apology to Mother Superior in her head, but her guilt evaporated as the secretary shrugged and took up the telephone receiver.

"Ms. Sinclair? You have—er—a collaborator here to compare notes?"

Five more minutes after that saw her led back through a dark hallway and to a door with a brass nameplate declaring it the office of C. Sinclair. She nodded to the secretary, then knocked and let herself in.

"Oh, good, Theo—" The scientist's voice sounded much less shrill when she wasn't shouting, but the reprieve didn't last long. She glanced up from a desk covered in neatly-piled papers, and made a noise of disgust. "Oh, what do *you* want?"

Maeve paused a moment, making sure to take in the office and its possible clues. The room had one glass-paned door that opened out onto a balcony and was otherwise occupied by an overlarge mahogany desk and bookshelves. It was impeccably organized, or at least appeared that way to her—not a personal effect in sight, not a pen out of place. "I...am working on a new haunting," she said, trying not to look like she was trying to read the papers on the desk. Camille began stuffing them away anyway.

"And you wanted my help? Your window for collaboration already closed, Miss—"

"Sister Maeve," she said, trying not to rise to the argumentative tone. "And I don't want your help, per se—or not in terms of exorcism, at least." She pronounced the next part carefully and watched for a reaction. "You see, I believe the spirit I'm dealing with to be a woman called Imogen Madrigal. I heard the two of you...knew each other."

Camille's expression betrayed nothing that Maeve could see; she raised one eyebrow, and stood, crossing to the window.

"I see."

Maeve sincerely hoped Imogen wasn't out there right now. "Or at least that was the last deceased resident of the apartment in question. Have you ever been there?"

"Several times, yes." She looked back with a frown. "What exactly do I have to do with this?"

Maeve raised her hands apologetically. "I need more information on her to lay her to rest, and your name was mentioned in a newspaper article in conjunction with hers. I...rather hoped you might want to help, seeing as the two of you had a relationship."

That was a good excuse—with any luck, Camille would assume she was trying to sway her to the sisters' view of ghosts as people to be reasoned with.

The disdainful scoff levied her way seemed to confirm her hopes. "Sorry to disappoint, but the relationship wasn't much of anything."

"Oh?"

Camille shrugged coolly. "I ended it; she was...insulted. She was always given to theatrics." She gave Maeve a hard look. "What does she seem to be stuck on?"

The soft scuff of boots landing on metal caught Maeve's ear, and she tried her hardest not to let her recognition of it show. She cleared her throat and made a small show of taking her sketchbook out of her bag and flipping to something that looked like notes. Camille looked impatient but didn't turn around as the door eased open a crack and Imogen hid herself somewhere outside once more.

"Er—" Well, the truth of Imogen wanting to solve her murder would absolutely put Camille on guard. "She's upset about her possessions, I think. She had a portrait that she's talked about on the spirit board—of the Blessed Sister Artemisia?"

Camille rolled her eyes. "Figures—all her stupid stuff. I know the painting you're talking about, but I haven't the faintest idea where it is. Is that all?"

Maeve raced to come up with another excuse to keep asking questions. "Well—er—I mean, I think that might be what it is. Hard to tell. These ghosts who die violent deaths, you know. Did they ever find her killer, anyway?"

Camille wrinkled her nose. "How should I know?"

"Well, the newspaper that mentioned you came from a few weeks before her death," Maeve lied, hoping she sounded convincing. "And, er, so I wondered if maybe you had heard anything? Or if you had been in touch with her?"

She opened her mouth, looking annoyed, but was interrupted by the glass door—creaking open in the wind with an unmistakable squeal of its hinges. Camille turned slowly, and took a few steps toward the door, looking suspicious. Maeve's heart caught in her throat; she had nothing to call Camille's attention back, nothing to distract her from Imogen's hiding place.

A breeze tugged one of the papers off Camille's desk, and Maeve caught it, stuffing it into her sketchbook on instinct as the wind turned suddenly violent and slammed the door open. It sent the rest of the papers flying, and Camille spun, slamming the door shut and snatching them up with a muttered curse. She looked up, as if realizing Maeve was still there, and glowered.

"Look," she said irritably. "If you want to know what she was up to so badly, go bother some poets. I didn't have anything to do with her that week—I was busy writing exams, and I didn't have time to think about soppy, overemotional, alcoholic—" her voice was icy as she delivered the last damnation— "*artists*. So, if you please, I have a lot of work to do."

Maeve decided not to push her luck. She retreated with a bow and walked very carefully back down to the reception desk and out of the parapsychology building, conscious of the feeling of eyes on her back. She hoped they were Imogen's.

She paused a few blocks away, ducking into an alley and out of the way of traffic, and after a few minutes, Imogen joined her, her scarf pulled tight over her head such that only the fringe of her bangs sticking out could be seen in profile. She turned, and Maeve could see her eyes shining bright out of the shadows. A chime came from her pocket.

I'm impressed—nearly got sticky there.

Maeve winced. "Sorry I couldn't think of a way to distract her that wasn't suspicious. But," she set down the device and pulled her sketchbook out, extracting the stolen paper. "I managed to grab this."

Imogen pulled her scarf down a fraction, and in her eagerness and distraction, actually smiled at Maeve. Maeve found herself struck by the expression—struck like she'd find herself before a cathedral or a monument or the expanse of the sea. A moment of loveliness in what was otherwise sharp and inhospitable. It turned to more of a smirk as Imogen took the paper and read it over. "What is it?"

Not a clue, she typed, and passed the paper back. Maeve had no better idea; it was a technical drawing of some kind, a sketch of straight lines issuing from a central point, along with a list of what seemed to be waveforms annotated in a spidery and illegible hand. She frowned at it, then secreted it away for further study.

"Did you hear everything she said? I noticed she—well, had a different story as to how the breakup went."

Imogen waved a dismissive hand. *Lies, all of it. She always was proud—probably unwilling to admit how it really happened.*

Maeve pursed her lips; Imogen herself was proud, too, and she was rather unsure of how much she could trust either of the women.

"Did she lie about anything else? Did you hear it all?"

Not the first part. That's why I had to open the door. But the rest of it sounded right—she called me soppy or overemotional or alcoholic on a pretty regular basis. Sorry about the artist comment, by the way—she doesn't think much of the finer things in life. Imogen winked, and Maeve blinked back uncertainly. She was a nun, not an artist.

"Can ghosts—or, er, half-ghosts—or, um, undead people even get drunk?" she asked to mask the awkwardness. The smile dropped from Imogen's face, and she tapped at her telegraph furiously.

It takes a hell of a lot more to do it. And I'm allergic to salt and iron now—the iron's not so bad, obviously, but have you ever tried to eat an entirely unseasoned meal? Mother's grave, I've been taking the burning over the tedium of it. She raised her chin. *Truly a cursed existence I'm leading.*

Maeve was inclined to roll her eyes, but there was a note of sincerity in the line of Imogen's mouth that stopped her. She, it seemed, had a way of telling the truth that made it seem like a lie—too much bravado, or too much pride. Or maybe Maeve was just imagining that.

She put her sketchbook and the paper inside it away and considered the poet. "Well, er—successful first attempt?"

Imogen looked up from her sulking, and nodded. *Yes, I think so. We should follow up on that alibi—if she was here at the Academy that night like she says she was, then I don't know if she'd have had the time to get over to the alley where I died. And the motive doesn't quite fit her, either—like she said, overemotional.* She pondered the tips of her boots for a moment, then glanced back up at Maeve. *I'll do some snooping. You go to the library—*

"For what? More newspapers?"

For poetry. Quit interrupting me, I can only tap so fast. Maeve gave an apologetic look, and Imogen sniffed. *But yes. I'm in talks to get an appointment with Orion—you're pretending to be a critic with the* Lenorum Herald, *and I'm your photographer. So, study up.*

Maeve winced—maybe Imogen hadn't forced her to break the law, but she was stretching her comfort zone pretty aggressively.

But if she had to go against the convent to save the convent, it seemed like a fair trade. She sighed.

"Any recommendations?"

Imogen seemed surprised to have encountered so little resistance, but a grin quickly rose to her face. *Yes. To start, me—*

Chapter
VII

Maeve sat on her bed, a cup of tea on her bedside table and a halo of open books arranged around her. Every creak of the old building caused her to jump—how would she explain if someone walked in to find her surrounded by all this poetry, all the names of the people who threatened their way of life? Imogen had changed her mind and dragged her back to her mausoleum to give her the books herself and seemed to have selected her recommendations largely on the basis of whether they would irritate Maeve. There was an anthology from Estelle Chanteuse, who expounded in rhyme about what spirits had told her in seances of the afterlife—heresy, plainly, and wildly self-contradictory at that. There was an autographed volume of Orion Cantor's own work, which bore an enormous wine stain that had seeped throughout the book and made deciphering the salacious verse even harder than it had to be. There were long songs from what Imogen called the Shanty School, and scattered collections of loose characters that formed art pieces more than they did poetry. And there was a folio, unbound, of the stuff Imogen told her she had written in the weeks leading up to her death.

Don't lose it, she had messaged her sternly, and had produced a ribbon from somewhere and tied the folio and other books into an attractive little package. *There's good stuff in there when I get around to editing it.*

If I can fashion a ship in a bottle,
If I can put my own heart in this bottle,

The saltwater thrashings of love in this bottle,
She'll need not the water;
She'll have her own ship;
She'll stay as the kiss of sweet salt on my lips—

"Maeve!" A knock came at the door, and she had just enough time to shunt everything under her pillow and pull out her sketch-book before Shivani opened the door anyway. "You're late!"

"Can't a woman get a little privacy?" she complained, before noticing the bottle of wine in Shivani's hand. "And girls' night never starts this early!"

"It does when we've all been assigned to dinner duties," Shivani pointed out archly. "Which you're also late for."

Maeve grumbled under her breath—she had forgotten that—and got up off the bed, taking the corkscrew out of her sock drawer while trying to make sure Shivani didn't see the telegraph secreted in there. The tiny light bulb at the top of the screen blinked. That meant there was a message pending. She bit her lip and shut the drawer, then handed Shivani the corkscrew.

"Happy?"

"Quite," Shivani said, and grinned at Maeve, then took her by the wrist and pulled her down the hall. "What are you even doing up here all alone, anyway? I feel like I haven't seen you in days."

"Research," Maeve said with a wince. Technically it was the truth, but she still hated having to hide anything from Shivani. "And, um, doing some drawing. For Frances—a little portrait of all of us."

"I thought you were shopping for her this year?" Shivani glanced back crossly as she slid down the banister of the spiral staircase down to the kitchen. "Don't tell me you're going to make me look all cold and materialistic when I buy her yarn."

"I didn't have any luck shopping," Maeve said apologetically, mentally making a note to keep better track of her excuses. Shivani was sharp as a tack—if she wanted to protect her from the danger Maeve and Imogen were in, then she had to keep her from digging too deep. "But don't worry, she loves yar—ah!"

This last comment was precipitated by her falling off the last few feet of the railing, too busy thinking about her lies and not busy enough thinking about her balance. She managed to land on her feet, staggered a few steps, and was finally caught by Shivani, who burst out laughing. "Mother's grave! Be careful!"

"That was your fault!" Maeve laughed, swatting Shivani's arm and ducking as she tried to pat Maeve haughtily on the head. "You distracted me!"

"You almost made me drop the wine," Shivani shot back, and cradled the bottle in her arms. "I had to hide this in my rain boots for a week so Mother Superior wouldn't find it. A week!"

"Well, let's put it somewhere even safer," Maeve teased, and allowed herself to be pulled the last few feet down the hall and into the warm, brick-walled space of the basement kitchen. It was a cavernous room, built for more sisters than currently lived here, but the long trestle tables were worn with the cooking and baking of hundreds of years, and the scent of spices burnished into the wood and walls made it feel like those sisters were still there with the four of them. Frances was tending soup by the fireplace; Thalia was giving a ball of dough a stern kneading; Shivani pulled four glasses out of the cabinet and poured the wine with an almost-professional air. Maeve felt herself relaxing as she took a sip and started chopping vegetables at Frances' behest. Maybe for a little while she could forget about the secrets.

(!) 1 New Message(s): Orion's set for Monday. I look forward to seeing you.

Maeve took a deep breath, gazing out the window of the streetcar, then stood, hopped off, and crossed the street. There was little question as to where she was headed; this was called the Arts District for good reason, and though she would have liked nothing better than to take a detour and walk the quarter mile up the road to the Museum of Fine Arts, she was forced to wait here. White-washed gates, each side bearing an ironwork sprig of laurel. They were open; it felt intimidating anyway.

A beep came from the pocket of her nice dress, and she turned to survey the cobblestoned square behind her. Imogen was no-where in sight, unless her disguise was quite good. Maeve was a little worried about that; she didn't want to go in alone, but she didn't want Imogen getting recognized by her murderer, either. That would be bad for both of them. She checked the message.

Guess who?

She looked around again, growing more surprised by the second, and finally tapped a message in reply. *The woman with the stroller?*

Close.

Something tapped her shoulder, and Maeve jumped, turning to find who on first inspection seemed to be an older man with a beard and an unfashionable overcoat. Imogen grinned, held up her camera, and then went back to her telegraph.

Good, no? My guardian Oleander used to be in theater when they were young—taught me a few tricks of the Northern style.

"Very good," Maeve said curiously, trying to detect the seams of whatever appliances were giving her crows' feet. "Your guardian? Where—?"

Predeceased me. Imogen's mouth twitched slightly as she typed, whether in a laugh or some other emotion Maeve couldn't tell. *Currently in the same cemetery as me, in fact—or at least their earthly portion. Anyway, let's get going.*

Maeve acquiesced but made a mental note to look into that further. Imogen had lost someone, and Camille had been quite plain about her drinking; she supposed it wouldn't hurt her bodily now, but she was a little worried for what might happen to Imogen emotionally once her quest was complete. Which she supposed she wasn't responsible for—well, maybe she was, since her duty was to help ghosts find peace—ugh. She couldn't travel too far down this road right now. Her goal in all of this was to get some help for the convent. That would be Imogen's new purpose once this whole investigation was complete, and that would keep her going long enough that Maeve wouldn't be obligated to care anymore. She ignored the question of whether she would anyway and stepped through the gate.

It was a cool, clear day, and within the fence, the pair of them walked through an impeccably maintained garden, still blooming with mums and asters. Maeve couldn't tear her eyes away as they passed it by; it put the convent's garden to shame. A path of stones that sparkled in the sun led to the building itself—a palace of white marble at least twice the size of the convent. Ornate trim topped each arched window, and a crest of laurels sat above the door. Scrollwork in the same ancient language as the exorcisms trailed from the crest, and Maeve translated it before she heard Imogen whisper it under her breath.

Verba Potestatem Habent—"Words have power."

Imogen's subsequent coughing fit was interrupted by the creaking of the door, and before Maeve even had a chance to knock, she found it opening to reveal a young man in a low-cut shirt and a semi-transparent skirt. Alright. No easing into it, then. Maeve took a deep breath and bowed.

"Hello, there. My name is Maeve Pagewright, and I'm a reporter for the *Lenorum Herald*. I have an appointment with Mr. Cantor?"

The man stared at her dully for a moment, which gave her a chance to notice how dilated his pupils were, and then smiled. "Sure—follow me." He stepped aside, allowing them in, and Maeve had to force herself not to stare as they did so. She was a reporter, she reminded herself sternly. She probably saw places this breathtaking every day.

But guilt hit her hard as she followed the young man down a sunlit corridor, Imogen following behind and snapping pictures haphazardly. It was too much, certainly—too opulent, too decadent, too…oh, too beautiful. She couldn't deny that. Absolutely beautiful. The windows in this hall were slightly rose-tinted, casting a balmy glow over the whole scene. An elegant waltz echoed in from some other wing of the building, whether on phonograph or from some musician's practice she wasn't sure. The white marble walls were adorned here with gold trim as well, and with art—tapestries with metallic thread, paintings of nymphs and faeries and mythological figures, sculptures tucked into alcoves. The barrel vault of the ceiling was the most tempting to look at—frescoed in blue and pink and purple with scenes of the Hallowed Mother, the Blessed Sister at her side, the spirits of the departed scattered around them. She could have stared at it for hours—hell, she could have sketched it for days and not gotten tired of looking at it. She was surprised, though, to see religious art in a place like this, given the tension between the poets and the actual stewards of that same religion. She wasn't going to say anything—Maeve Pagewright, reporter, wouldn't have much of an opinion either way. But it was curious.

"This is the painting room—he's usually here in the morning," said the young man, who Maeve was beginning to realize was less of a doorman and more of someone who had happened to be in the area. He made a vague sort of curtsy and wandered off. Imogen snorted, then rearranged her face into a mask of neutrality.

Sorry, she mouthed, and waved Maeve ahead.

She knocked—she wasn't sure if just walking in would be rude.

"Come in!" came a voice, and so she pushed the door open. She blinked a few times, tried not to show on her face any of the many emotions she was feeling, and folded her hands behind her back as neutrally as she could.

The painting room was lovely—a round space with huge windows that looked onto the grounds beyond, with sheer white curtains that blew in a slight draft. The floors were glossy wood, upon which a ring of easels and stools had been set up, each with a canvas, paints, and a painter staring over their shoulder at her; about a dozen of them in total. Their subject sat in the center—a basket of fruit and a bottle of wine and some other random objects that were less noteworthy than the man draped languidly among them. Despite Mother Superior's best efforts, Maeve recognized his face—olive skin a few shades darker than Imogen's, high cheekbones, heavy eyebrows. His long hair—a streak of grey in the black the only clue to his thirty-odd years—was held in place by a silver circlet made to look like laurel branches; the circlet was, in fact, the only thing he was wearing. "Ah, excellent," Orion Cantor said, flashing a bright white smile, and sat up, waving a dismissive hand to the painters. "My eleven o'clock."

Maeve pursed her lips, and forced a smile to her face, exercising every ounce of self-control in her body to keep from showing a reaction.

"Ms. Maeve Pagewright, and photographer," she said sweetly, and gestured around the room. "I must confess, I've never been to the Poets' Court before. It's very beautiful."

He clicked his tongue, looking touched and raised a hand to his chest. Maeve tried not to track the motion or stare. She really,

really, did not spend much time around men. Especially not men with what she really hoped weren't nipple piercings.

"Thank you," he said sincerely. "We've done a lot of work over my tenure." He stood, crossed to the side of the room, and began to thread his arms through a green silk bathrobe. Maeve breathed an internal sigh of relief. Orion returned to the central pedestal, pulled over one of the stools from the easels, and gestured for her to take another. "Sit, sit! Love your dress, by the way—Clothier? Lovely. Can I get you anything to drink? Tea, or something else—?"

Maeve snuck a glance sideways at Imogen, who nodded subtly as she raised her eye to the viewfinder of her camera and nodded back to Orion.

"Tea would be nice for both of us, yes." Damn—now she'd stuck Imogen with having to try and drink in front of the man, but she hadn't been able to think of another way to excuse her glance.

Orion didn't seem to notice anything amiss; he stood and strode energetically to the door. A bell sounded from somewhere deep within the walls, and he returned, twisting the cork out of the bottle of wine beside him and gesturing to them. "You don't mind if I...."

"Of course," Maeve assured him, watching as Imogen wandered over to the windows, aiming her camera out over the grounds. "So—to business, I suppose."

"Yes, yes." He crossed his legs, pouring a splash of wine out into a glass and taking a sip. "I was told you wanted to do a sort of career piece—how one might go about becoming a poet and my recommendations for aspiring hopefuls, that sort of thing?" His voice was smooth and resonant, his accent just shy of posh.

"Indeed." Maeve took a small notebook and pen out of her pocket—she had decided that taking notes in her sketchbook in this setting might look suspicious—and looked over the list of questions she and Imogen had come up with. They'd agreed it might be best to come at it from a circuitous route. "So, how does the structure of the Court work? How does one join, how are the members organized, that sort of thing?"

Orion smiled. "Of course, darling!" He traced with his finger in the air as he spoke. "So, to start, we have one hundred laurels—ninety-nine bronze, and one silver." He flicked his diadem as he spoke, making a ringing sound. "They're very old, and have a lot of ceremonial worth, of course, but really, we keep our numbers there because it just gets hard to *know* everyone beyond a hundred!" He had a very theatrical way of speaking, Maeve noticed, and a similarly theatrical vocabulary of gestures. She could see exactly where Imogen had gotten her body language from. "Too big, and we couldn't collaborate, too small and we'd get dreadfully boring. I say this out front just so you don't think us cruel or exclusive later on." He pouted, like he was worried Maeve might think that anyway.

"I understand," she said consolingly, and pretended to take notes. "So how do laurels pass from person to person, then?"

"Depends on the laurels."

A knock came at the door, followed by a young woman bearing a platter with tea and cookies, who set it on a stool between Maeve and Orion. She leaned in to take her cup—mmm, something sweet with honey. Definitely not Lenorum Public. The woman retreated, and Orion resumed his speech.

"The silver laurels, which denote the Laureate—me," he gave a winning smile—"are passed on in terms of five years. The hundred of us vote, and the winner leads the Court for their term. The rest of them are a lifetime deal, if desired—older poets usually retire, though, so we have plenty of turnover. Or we can vote people out, but—" he clicked his tongue, "that's nasty, unless they're really not writing anything." He swirled his wine around, then leaned forward and snagged a cookie off the tray. "You should try these, sweetheart—lemon and lavender. Really divine."

Maeve reached for one as well, balancing it on her saucer as she wrote. There were an awkward number of things in her lap now. "Makes sense. But I see that young woman—and the man who met me at the door—they weren't wearing laurels. Do you have any sort of organization for those who there aren't spots in the one hundred for?"

He gestured vaguely. "Typically that's left up to individuals—many of us run a sort of school. Adolai Anchorman, for one, has a really impressive following down on that boat of his; they do shanties. I've been working lately on trying to pull in more of the arts, for my part—musicians, painters, the like." He held up a hand. "They all get a stipend for their services, of course, and we frequently vote new poets in from the schools. I really dislike the rumors I hear flying around about us, so forgive my defense."

"Not at all," Maeve said, not entirely sure which those rumors might be and whether they might have to do with the dilation of the young man's pupils. "A stipend, you say, but not enough for them to live on, I imagine. What else do these young people do for work, would you say? Are they working at their poetry full time, or is it possible for people who have to, say, send money back to their families to make their way?"

Orion tilted his head, looking interested. "I see—sort of an inquisition into elitism, hmm?" He steepled his fingers. "I...will say this. We have had, in the past, problems like what you are describing. I would like to say now, though, that we are doing our best to make things fairer. How are we supposed to canvas the whole of the human experience, after all, without people from every walk of life?" He took another sip of his wine. "I have, right now, one student from the Greene house, three who run a seance parlor, eight teahouse waiters, and at least four who moonlight as absinthe girls."

"Will they be voted in, do you think?" Maeve asked, trying not to let any of the rumors she did know make her judgmental. Not even on a night out did she or her friends dare to go to absinthe houses; the combination of extreme intoxication, risqué costume, and harder drugs had never seemed like a draw.

He shrugged. "Too early to say, dear. I've only had them for a year." A spark came into his eyes, and he leaned in. "But I can tell you the story of the top student in my last class—a story you've maybe heard of. Maybe it'll even fit into your piece. Heard of Imogen Madrigal?"

Maeve saw Imogen's shoulders raise for just a moment, then lower. She was behind Orion, so it didn't matter, but Maeve had no such luxury. Either their questions had, in fact, led to the story they wanted, or it was a strange coincidence. Or...she shook herself internally, trying not to let fear of the lurking third option influence her.

"I have," she said carefully, "though I'm not sure I recall all the details."

"Well, if you want a success story, there it is. She grew up Imogen Grave—her guardian was a cemetery keeper. A foundling, and poor as the dirt she grew up digging. You could always tell it, too—once she really got going, she put on the most tremendous of airs. Absolute taste for luxury; she reminded me of myself, though I can't claim such humble beginnings to justify mine." He smiled again. "But anyway, she told me she worked on a lobster boat during the day, served at a teahouse at night, and was allowed to do fifteen minutes of poetry—unpaid—at the end of her shift. Which is what got her noticed, and ultimately got her out of that situation." He sighed. "She had three very good years—meteoric, really. And the horrible thing is that we had made the vote the night she died. It was incredible—the Laureate's not allowed to vote on these to avoid ties, but I absolutely put in my two cents. I wanted her here. And ninety-nine to naught, she was going to be."

A sudden draft caught Maeve by surprise, causing her to shiver. Orion seemed to notice it, too, drawing his robe a little tighter over his chest and looking back over his shoulder.

"My dear friend, would you be so kind as to shut the window?" Imogen had her back to the two of them, but acquiesced, and Orion turned back around. "They found her not so far from here, actually—out by the docks. We hadn't told her we were voting, but I always wondered if she'd guessed and gone down to do something sentimental near her old haunts. It was…terribly sad." He did look genuinely upset. "Anyway. Success story, the dear Ms. Madrigal—and a curious one, too. Maybe that should be your next piece—trying to solve a year-old mystery."

"I'm an arts and culture writer," she demurred, keeping an eye on Imogen over Orion's shoulder. She seemed to be in some sort of distress, retying the scarf around her neck with a worried expression and ignoring Maeve. Maeve took a deep breath. "Er—speaking of which, I would love to include a few details on the Court building itself, and some of those artistic efforts you mentioned over your tenure. Could we—"

"A tour?" Orion leapt to his feet, grinning hugely, and rubbed his hands together. "Darling, I thought you'd never ask."

Maeve had just enough time to set her tea aside and jam the lemon-lavender cookie into her pocket for later before Orion took her arm and practically dragged her into the hall. He was nearly as liberally perfumed as Imogen. She didn't glance back to check if Imogen was with them; right now, she needed a distraction for whatever was going on, and Maeve needed to provide it.

"You already came in through the east wing—let's go through the topiary garden…."

The tour was a bit of a whirlwind, but Maeve's main emotional experience was one of first, extreme jealousy, and second, deep self-doubt. They passed through a garden past a deep, clear pool with gorgeous swirling mosaics of whales and serpents and more mysterious leviathans at its bottom, their forms almost seeming to wriggle through the shadows of the ripples on the surface. She barely had time to admire the effect before they passed in quick succession through an airy room full of marble statues, a cavernous library with thirty-foot frescoed ceilings—the painters' scaffolding still up in some areas—and a hall of personal rooms whose windows looked over the cliff and out to sea. It was all just as gorgeous as the rooms she'd seen on the way in, and just as diverse in style and subject—some of the statues were the solemn sort that Maeve was used to watching over her at the convent and the cemetery, while others danced and battled and took on more…suggestive positions. Orion was walking much too fast for her to have time to really take it all in, but the few bits of information he threw over his shoulder served as explanation enough.

"From its founding, the Court has been on the cutting edge of culture, and we try to keep it that way. Nothing is off limits—today's taboo might be tomorrow's trend, after all." He waved a hand up at the ceiling. "Here we've got the Court's history—Portia Mate's first seminars, the convocation of the Beacon Society, the forging of the laurels, all that. You'll notice it's not finished, and that's by design. Leave it to museums to record the past—the artist must always be looking forward. Stagnancy is a fate worse than death, in my mind."

They passed various personages as they went—knots of young people gathered in the gardens, a few solitary figures pacing the halls. Some had laurels, and some did not; the Court seemed to have a whole ecosystem of art and writing thriving within its walls. Maeve winced at the talk of stagnancy. She was beginning to wonder whether the Sisterhood had an interest in demonizing the poets, given that their entire foundation rested on tradition. To be fair, it wasn't the complete opposite of what she had grown up hearing—Orion was still carrying his bottle of wine though it was eleven thirty in the morning, and some of the others they encountered on their way seemed shy of sobriety. Taboos, indeed.

"Orion, baby," slurred one woman in what looked to be a sheet carefully pinned into a dress. "I've just had the best idea for a bit of performance art—the next party—"

"Best behavior, Beena," he admonished, gesturing to Maeve. "Ms. Pagewright here is writing a story about us."

"Ooh—get my good side." Beena assumed an artistic pose, undercut by her swaying. Maeve glanced back, and found Imogen gone. *Uh-oh.*

"Ah, we seem to have…lost her photographer for now," Orion said easily, putting a hand on Maeve's shoulder and steering away from the inebriated woman. "We'll come back for your closeup!" They started back down the hall.

"Er—maybe I should go look for him," Maeve said after a moment. She wasn't fully sure of which way was out, and not having backup was starting to make her nervous. She glanced back again.

"I can send someone to look for him," Orion assured her, and positioned himself in front of a closed door. "Or we can go look in a minute—but I've got one more room I think you might like to see—a little surprise. Game, Ms. Pagewright?"

Maeve swallowed—she wasn't sure she liked the idea of what might constitute a surprise in this place, but he seemed harmless enough so far.

"Of course," she said, injecting a false sense of cheer into her voice, and was rewarded with a beaming smile from Orion.

"Excellent," he said, and pushed open the door. "After you!"

The room in question was dark, and it took Maeve's eyes a moment to adjust—moments during which the door shut behind her, and she found it even darker. She made out curtains of heavy black velvet over the windows and rich green wallpaper instead of the airy scheme that dominated the rest of the place; a few more moments let her pick out several old portraits in gilded frames. Poufs littered the floor, and the faint perfume of what Maeve dimly remembered Shivani telling her was the smell of opium graced the air. There was a definite cold in the room, and as she stepped in further her senses, honed by years in the business, began to pick up other details. The sour smell of ectoplasm under the opium. The hairs on her arms pricking up. Her foot nudged something as she stepped forward and found a spirit board and planchette below her. She picked up the planchette almost instinctively and peered through it. The whole room was green—practically dripping with ghostly energy.

"This is our seance room," she heard Orion say, his proud tone a gross contrast to the disgust she felt congealing in her stomach. "Sort of a corollary pursuit of ours nowadays, which I'm sure someone would be much interested in writing about at the *Herald*. Someone who did work there, of course." She blinked, and set down the planchette carefully, a thrill of dread running down her spine. Had she misheard him? "Now, I'll talk to anyone who will listen—no grudges there—but I hope you won't begrudge me a question of my own, seeing as you're not even going to do anything with everything I told you." Maeve felt a disturbance in the air behind her, and turned slowly to see Orion, his light tone and easy expression a sharp contrast to the wary line of his arm. His knife looked familiar—Maeve had been threatened with an identical one before. He smiled, and it looked like a threat.

"How is it, darling, that Imogen is alive?"

Chapter

VIII

"She," Maeve said, on instinct, "isn't."

Orion's smile grew wider. "Please, don't lie to me. I'm cleverer than I look."

Maeve narrowed her eyes. "Where did you get that knife?"

"Don't be lewd, darling—I have pockets."

She just barely managed not to wrinkle her nose. "I meant where you got it, originally."

"Ah." He cocked his head. "You're cleverer than you look, too. It's one of a pair—I see you know the other. I gave it to her, in fact—you need that sort of insurance when dealing with my... mother." He raised his eyebrows in an exaggerated wince.

"I've been on the end of that knife, too." Maeve crossed her arms to hide the shake developing in her hands. Who was his mother? For once she wished she paid attention to the tabloids a little better. "I'd appreciate it if you quit pointing it at me."

She was feigning the confidence, but to her surprise, he listened to her. "As long as you don't try anything," he said lightly, dropping the knife back into the pocket of his robe and holding his hands up. "Would be a shame if you had to leave without your... colleague. Now, as I'm sure you know, the story I told you before wasn't quite all of it. Would you care to fill me in on the rest?"

She hesitated for a moment, sizing up the door behind him and wondering if Imogen would be able to find her. Unless Imogen had been taken prisoner, somehow...She took a deep breath and looked back up at Orion. She would try to stall.

"How do I know you don't already know it?"

He sighed, and reached for a chair, dropping into it and kicking up on the back two legs.

"Sweetheart, you're not in a position to bargain. I've told you what I know, in very good faith. Now—you've been on the end of dear Imogen's knife. That means she mugged you in her persona as the Wraith. So far as I can tell, she's been doing that to people with things to hide." Orion studied her for a moment from under his eyelashes, the languor that had originally characterized him wholly absent. His gaze was steely, now. "I'm going to say…fisher putting on airs. Private detective, perhaps. That's enough for me to start with, tracking you down, and though I would like for us to be friends, I will warn you that I have a great many resources."

Maeve swallowed. She didn't doubt his threat, but his guess was wrong enough that maybe, maybe she could get out of this. "I only know," she said carefully, "what I've been told—which is that you are a suspect. Convince me otherwise, and I'll spill."

"Ugh—how tiresome." He drummed his fingers on his knee. "I have an alibi for the evening, but he's married. And I'm sure you think I just bought some assassin, anyway. I don't suppose you'd believe me if I said I cared for Imogen and didn't want her dead?" Maeve shook her head. "Does she not remember who assaulted her? You could introduce me to them, and watch me very carefully for a reaction…and of course, if you told me exactly what happened, maybe I would be exonerated…."

His eyes cut back to hers.

She was about to tell him that he was out of luck when the door slammed open. For a moment the brightness dazzled her eyes, but she managed to duck as the figure in the doorway dashed towards her. Imogen, undaunted, doubled back, and put herself in front of Maeve, pushing her towards the far wall of the room and drawing her own knife from somewhere within the folds of her overcoat. This was escalating concerningly quickly, but Maeve couldn't pretend she wasn't a little relieved. Orion glanced at the door, back at Imogen, and then sighed.

"Must I do everything around here?" He stood, shut the door, and looked over his shoulder at the two of them petulantly. "No manners. Now, Imogen and our mystery guest, would either of you care to actually explain to me what's going on?"

Imogen glanced back, looking betrayed.

"Don't blame her," Orion interrupted. "There's police sketches of the Wraith's knife in the papers. And contrary to what seems to be popular belief, I do read them." He smirked a little. "The mustache suits you, by the way."

Imogen glared back at Orion, and Maeve heard a ping from her pocket.

Read these out loud to him for me, she tapped one-handed, keeping the knife up with the other.

"'You low-down vicious, vile snake,'" Maeve read, and glanced up with a wince. "This is her, not me," she clarified, and Imogen nodded vehemently.

The front two legs of Orion's chair hit the floor, and he leaned forward, looking surprised for the first time.

"Why...are you reading for her?"

"'You know very well why,'" Maeve read out, and Imogen curled her lip. "'I knew you were a venomous double-crossing son of a...bitch but I didn't think you'd sully your pretty little hands with murder. I still don't think you did. Who'd you send to do your dirty work? Naomi? Horatio?'" She decided to keep her own thoughts quiet—Imogen should probably be in charge of what information she wanted to reveal.

Orion's eyes flicked back and forth across the floor, seemingly uninterested in what Maeve was saying, until suddenly he gasped and lurched to his feet.

"Your...your voice," he said, his own voice barely a whisper. "They cut your throat...."

Imogen swallowed hard; Maeve knew that was a painful effort for her. "Spare me your false pity."

Maeve didn't think the pity was false; there was something in his expression that seemed far too sincere.

"You can't think I would do this," he insisted, taking a step forward. "To take away another artist's gift—that's a crime worse than murder. Imogen, you must—"

But that was a step too close, and Imogen lunged, kicking the Laureate of the Poets' Court in the shin and throwing him to the floor. He went down with a yelp, and Maeve didn't know whether to laugh or take off running—what was she thinking? Her telegraph chimed again, and she read to herself—*obviously you were trying to kill me, you snake, but it didn't stick. I agree it's a crime worse than murder, and so I think you'll pay for it like I have. That work for you? That what you wanted out of all this, you lying, traitorous*—the words were still coming in, but Maeve realized belatedly that Imogen was using one arm to choke the man out and the other to point her knife at his throat. How was she—? She then realized that Orion was trying to speak, staring at her frantically, and she dove forward, prying Imogen's arm back and pulling him away.

"You don't know he did it!" she shouted, while Orion coughed and gasped for air and did a bit of unimpressive clinging to her. Imogen's eyes were glowing with rage, but she brushed her hair back from her forehead, dusting off her coat, and Maeve saw a new message flick across her fallen telegraph.

With Orion, sometimes you have to cut through the niceties.

Maeve didn't believe that excuse for a second—there was no way Imogen had been bluffing—but Orion was trying to speak, and she had to let it go.

"I," he said to Imogen raggedly, making no move to get up out of Maeve's lap, "never took you for such a *businesswoman*, Imogen." His mouth curled up in a grin, but his tone dripped with acid. "Whatever. So be it. You want me to be a snake, I'll do it. You have something I want, and I have something you want." He sat up and held out his hand. "Tell me what you know—let me help you solve this—and I'll make sure you get your laurels."

That, Maeve could tell, hit Imogen square between the eyes, though she tried to hide it. She stood very still for a moment, then reached into her pocket, and looked at Maeve. Maeve nodded; Imogen took a deep breath and shook her head.

Tell him to get used to disappointment.

They left quickly after that; Imogen took Maeve's hand instead of Orion's, and he made no move to stop them as Imogen pulled her out the door. Back through the labyrinthine palace, their only accompaniment that faraway waltz and the click of their shoes. They made it to the door, and a ringing sound startled them both within sight of it. They turned to see another languid-looking youth, this time holding out a telephone trailing long cords behind them. Imogen picked up the earpiece.

"This has been fun! I'll see you again soon, darling," Maeve heard tinnily. "Make sure you bring that cute little friend of yours next time—I'm so looking forward to learning more about her."

Imogen slammed it back onto the receiver, threw her shoulder into the enormous front door, and stormed out.

Maeve caught up to her a few blocks down the street, breathing heavily from trying to keep up with Imogen's long strides.

"Okay," she said nervously. "I know you're angry, but we need to talk about what just happened."

She glanced down at her telegraph as a new message appeared and Imogen snorted. *Which part? A lot just happened.*

Orion's foreknowledge of their coming, Imogen's homicidal rage, the messages appearing on their own? Now that they were out of danger, at least temporarily, Maeve was a little frustrated.

"All of it." Imogen strode heedless toward the streetcar station, and Maeve hurried after her. "I don't know, call it a debrief, but—"

Imogen paused and huffed a sigh through her teeth, dragging her hands through her hair as she stomped back.

Are you sure you still want to be here? she typed, looking down at Maeve.

Maeve blinked. "Why...wouldn't I be?" Was this Imogen kicking her off the investigation? They had a contract!

Imogen stared at her a moment longer, seemingly reading her mind. Then she sighed, pulled off the false beard and the other parts of her disguise, and tucked them into her pockets.

Look, this...it's...you seem like a nice person, and I don't like what they're doing in that seance room much more than you do. And you've helped me this far. I can...I'll write something up for you, and you'll be free to go.

Maeve looked up from her telegraph; Imogen's face was unreadable.

"Am I hindering you in some way?" she asked, still unsure of her motives. "I'm sorry I intervened, but...even if he did kill you, you can't...."

Imogen sighed again, leaning back against the pole of a streetlamp, and looked up at the sky. It was growing dark out now; the sun never stuck around for long in Lenorum, and the sound of raindrops slapping into the sidewalk grew to a crescendo within seconds. Maeve crossed her arms in the downpour and waited for Imogen to speak her mind.

Look, she tapped after a solid minute, then dragged Maeve under the streetcar shelter by the wrist, her eyes closed. *I...you've had two knives pointed at you, now. I thought I would be able to see through Orion, but I underestimated him, and you almost got hurt because of it. I'm starting to think that this might be even more dangerous than I previously did. And I...I'm on my second chance already. If I get killed again, that's...fine, I suppose. I'm already on time that's not mine. But you...this isn't your danger to face. And even if I can help you, even if I manage to find the words to help your convent...* The flow of messages paused, Imogen's hand hovering over the telegraph's key. *I don't want to bait you off the edge of a cliff.*

Maeve read this all quietly, the rain walling their little alcove off from the rest of the city. Imogen had offered her an out—a return to her normal life. Everything she had said was undoubtedly true; the danger was beginning to show itself, and the reward she had been promised had no guarantee of working. It was a bad deal that was beginning to get worse.

She looked up; Imogen was gazing out into the rain, her brow ever-so-slightly furrowed. Maeve remembered the first time they had run into each other, how she had immediately been struck by the thought that Imogen had no one to talk to, and how that had been truer than she had expected. How Imogen was, by the very circumstance of her existence, forced to be alone. How she could trust very few people, and how that might wear on a person. Maeve was exhausted just by keeping the few secrets she had; Imogen had to keep her entire existence a secret. She had to live in a tomb, and while her bodily needs were reduced by her condition, Maeve couldn't imagine it being easy. She bit her lip; things were getting dangerous, yes, and the reward was uncertain. But what was the point of being a Sister of Good Death if she left the living by the wayside? Or the semi-living, at least.

She looked at Imogen harder, noted the dark circles under her eyes. Her hair was rumpled, likely by her running her hands through it, but Maeve wondered when the last time she had had a bath was. When the last time she had been warm was. When the last time she had had a meal, however unnecessary to her survival that might be. The frustration and fear ebbed away, replaced by stirrings of protectiveness.

"I...would love if you could help me," Maeve said with a sigh. "But...you need my help, either way. I can't turn away from that. I don't want to. I want to help you through this, whether or not I get anything out of it."

Imogen looked at her sharply, her eyes roving over Maeve's face. There was a note of disbelief in her eyebrows, but Maeve stood her ground. Maybe in Imogen's world, people didn't do things out of kindness. But if she was getting dragged into Imogen's world, then maybe she could drag Imogen back into hers a bit.

"Here," she said after a minute, and peered out through the rain, trying to judge whether it was going anywhere. "I won't push you. And if you don't want my help, then that's okay. But...can you feel the cold?"

Imogen blinked a little, then nodded.

"Then, let's go somewhere, and get warm, at least." The street-car pulled up, and Maeve stepped on. "Follow me."

She had expected some argument, especially once it became clear that they were headed back to the convent, but Imogen kept quiet—or quieter than usual, at least. By now the pair of them had been drenched in the rush from the downtown station to the west side of the convent's block.

The main entrance was on the south side, but Maeve knew better than to march Imogen in openly. She'd run into six little sisters, Shivani, and Mother Superior herself that way. She took Imogen down to the side entrance and let them in with one of her lesser-used keys. She hadn't really thought out the consequences of doing this; all she knew was that Imogen needed a friend in addition to an investigative partner. Imogen hung back at the door, and Maeve heard a chime.

Is this safe?

"Safest place I know," she said, and managed a smile. "Come on. I'll get you something dry to wear."

They crept up one of the back staircases, and Maeve peeked ahead before waving Imogen on towards the bathroom.

"How have you been keeping clean?" she asked. "You can't have water in that mausoleum."

Imogen rubbed the back of her neck; she suddenly seemed to have lost her bravado. *I've been dunking my head in the fountain by the market.*

Maeve winced. "Okay. Here. Let's fix that first." She held the bathroom door open for Imogen, who went through, looking around nervously. Maeve had always thought the place rather lovely; it had a big brass bathtub, and a high, leaded window that let the light in. Imogen glanced back at her, then turned the hot tap, and let her fingers trail in it for a few seconds.

No one is going to come in and find me here, right? This message came in without Imogen seeming to type it; Maeve was going to ask about that, but for now she would focus on other matters first.

"It's only the four in my cohort who use this bathroom," she explained. "And I'll come back in a minute when you're in. Get you something warm to wear." Imogen nodded, and unwound her scarf, setting it carefully on the floor before shucking off her coat and beginning to undress. Maeve was about to leave her to her privacy when she noticed the strands of ectoplasm smeared across the scarf, and across Imogen's throat as well. She stared, then noticed Imogen watching her out of the corner of her eye.

"Is...that what happened in the painting room? Did you re-open the wound?"

Imogen swallowed, then winced.

It...weeps, when I get upset. Sometimes.

"Ah," Maeve said, and couldn't come up with anything else to follow it with. "I'll...be back in a little while."

She shut the door and hurried down the hall, but there was no one around. She wasn't missing something she was supposed to be at, was she? A thrill of nervousness hit her for a moment but left quickly. No. Today she was free, because today had been the audience with Orion Cantor, and she had rescheduled everything around it. God, had that just been an hour ago?

She reached her room without issue and cast about for something that wasn't a habit for Imogen to wear. A pullover sweater, a soft pair of pants she slept in sometimes—it was all going to be too short and too big at the waist, but at least it would be dry. She bundled up those, a pair of Frances' signature socks, as well as a towel and snuck back down the hall. She knocked, and then locked the door behind them.

It was much warmer and much more humid in here now, and Maeve's telegraph chimed as she entered.

Baths are so much better when you don't have to breathe!

That was the first exclamation point Maeve could remember seeing from Imogen; she glanced over at the tub with a snicker and found only the poet's feet sticking out of the water. Kind of an excellent image, really—the composition, the stark white of her skin, the sheen of light on the water. They submerged, and Imogen's head resurfaced, her bangs dripping and her chin hanging over the edge of the bathtub as Maeve sat down on the green tile floor nearby.

"I'd like to ask about how you're doing that, but I don't want to bother you."

Imogen cast about for her telegraph on the windowsill and tapped at it with a shiver. *Doing what?*

"Sending messages without typing. Is it like, a modern spirit board kind of thing?" She clicked her tongue and smiled. "I ought to try it next time I go to a haunting." She looked over to find Imogen frozen, her expression shocked. "Oh! Did you—?"

Not know I was doing that? Yes! Yes I did not know! Imogen typed furiously, then set it down and stared at it hard. Nothing came through, and Imogen picked it back up. *When did I do that?*

"When you had Orion at knifepoint, you were…yelling some stuff," Maeve told her, scrolling through the backlog of their messages curiously. She had figured, been annoyed that Imogen was keeping secrets from her, but…"And just now, when you told me that not breathing makes baths more enjoyable."

I didn't—I just thought that! Imogen's face split into a smirk, then shot to horror. *Oh no, that's less good than I thought. I don't want my thoughts being read.* She looked at the telegraph angrily, as though she blamed it for the situation.

"I wonder if that's an emotional thing, too," Maeve said, re-reading the stream of invective Imogen had thought in Orion's direction. "Only seems like it happened when you were really angry or really happy."

Imogen received that news with ambivalence. *I still don't like it. I'm angry rather frequently these days.* She frowned and resubmerged for a minute. Too long to be comfortable for living lungs. She came back up, then hooked her chin over the edge of the tub once more, looking at Maeve for a second and picking the telegraph back up. *I shouldn't have told you about all that. Or at least I feel like I shouldn't have. You nuns, you're not going to experiment on me and try to figure out what's wrong with me, are you?* Her eyes narrowed. *You're not just being nice to try to put me off my guard, are you?*

"No!" Maeve said, taken off guard herself by Imogen's sudden suspicion. "Our only goal is to help spirits—or, or whatever you are. We don't even really take notes on our hauntings. Which has not been helpful in me helping you, but...."

A knock came at the door, and they both froze.

"Hello?" Thalia's voice.

"Taking a bath, Thalia!" Maeve yelled as Imogen ducked back underwater. "Give me twenty?"

"Ha—midday bath, what are you, a poet? Kidding. See you at dinner!" A few seconds passed without further interruption. Imogen poked the top of her head back out and narrowed her eyes over the rim of the tub. She glanced over at Maeve after a moment.

Maeve took a deep breath. "You're fine. We're not scientists. Is that what you're afraid of?"

No, I— Another message was long in coming, and Imogen frowned, blinking down at the floor. *I don't know why I thought that. Or why it alarmed me so much.* She shivered, and a water droplet fell from the tip of her long nose. *I'm warm now. And I stole some of someone's shampoo. Can I get dressed?*

"Of course," Maeve said quickly, and turned her back, until Imogen cleared her throat. The height gap was more of a problem than expected; the pullover's hem sat slightly north of Imogen's belly button. Oh, well—Imogen routinely walked around with about four buttons undone at the top of her shirts; modesty didn't seem to be a going concern for her. Maeve pulled the bathtub plug and led a hasty retreat to her room.

It was only once they had made it back safely that Maeve realized she had never had any outsider in her room before, much less a poet. Self-consciousness crept up her spine, and she shoved her hands into her pockets as Imogen looked around. It was deathly austere compared to Imogen's mausoleum, and she was certain she was confirming all of Imogen's ideas about what nuns were like.

Cozy, came the only response. Imogen took a few steps over towards the dressing table mirror, and then looked back over her shoulder. *I'm sorry for making you risk sneaking me in here.*

"It's nothing," Maeve said, hoping Imogen wasn't looking too closely at the sketches taped to it or judging her based on their quality. She shook herself and refocused on trying to comfort Imogen into opening up a little. "I'm the one who made you come here. You just seemed…shaken."

Imogen looked back, pursed her lips, and nodded, sinking to a crouch. *I didn't know they had voted. Especially not ninety-nine to…* She rubbed her eyes. *He gets bored with people. I thought he was getting bored with me.*

Maeve hesitated, then sat down across from her. "But it seems like the rest of the Court liked you—they all voted for you. Does his opinion matter that much?"

Imogen shook her head. *I wouldn't take that at face value. If they all voted for me, it's as much fear of Orion as it is liking me. The Court is ruthless, so you can imagine what it takes to get to the top.* She worried her lower lip with her teeth. *But I guess that is evidence in favor of him, that vote—proof he still wanted me around. He had been weird that last week. We'd argued a bit. He'd been keeping his distance.*

"What did you argue about?"

Camille, actually. I told him about the proposal and how I wasn't sure about it. He said some nasty things—he hates nobles, though he is one by birth. She smiled. *And of course, he hates the idea of being tied down.*

A noble by birth. "Oh—who's his mother?"

Marlene Warwick. Maeve raised her eyebrows, and Imogen nodded. *So you can see how terribly tangled it all is. Having you as an outside perspective will be…important.*

"So, the argument and the connection to Lady Marlene—that's why you thought he killed you?" Maeve asked. She surveyed Imogen, curled up, and turned back towards her bed for a blanket.

That, and the way he is with everyone else. Merciless. Imogen rolled her eyes, then glanced up at her as Maeve put the blanket around her shoulders. She looked away just as quickly, and her cheeks glowed purple. *Getting into the Court is a cutthroat business—* she snorted as she tapped it—*and Orion took me under his wing. Keep your friends close and your competition closer, right? So, if anyone was going to hate me, it'd be him.* She tugged the blanket tighter around herself and made an attempt at her usual scheming expression, but it quickly faltered. *If anyone was going to care, it'd be him, too.*

"Will you go back?" Maeve asked, sitting across from her. "I mean, it seems like he's interested in what happened."

Imogen blew her bangs out of her eyes with a huff, and eyed Maeve.

What do you think I should do?

"I...think we should," she said after a moment. "Even if he isn't interested in it out of the goodness of his heart, I think he wants to hear the story. And he said he had resources."

Resources he threatened you with. Imogen gave her a wry smile. *I don't know if you want him getting closer to your identity, darling. Like I said, merciless—if he figures it out, he might go blabbing to your abbess just to stir up trouble.*

Maeve winced. "Well," she said, casting about for a solution. "I could just tell Mother Superior the truth at that point. Leave you out—" she said quickly, watching Imogen's eyebrows raise— "but say it was for a haunting. She would understand."

Would she really?

"Yes," Maeve said firmly. "So don't let me hold you back. We'll go back, if you...well, if you can do it without threatening him again, too."

Imogen sighed, and buried her face in her blanketed knees. *Maybe I can't tell smugness and sincerity apart anymore. Ooh, a crime worse than murder. I'm so sorry, Imogen, darling, he says—*she sniffed roughly, and wiped a trickle of ectoplasm from the corner of her eye with her thumb. She glanced at Maeve, seemingly only then remembering she was there, and bristled. *You didn't see that.*

"I...was looking out the window," Maeve said carefully, and then did look out the window to sell it. Now the scuffle at the Court made a bit more sense—that Imogen was too proud to take mocking and too hot-headed to consider other explanations. Maeve had gotten used to Imogen's chilliness, but maybe that, too, had been pride. "Anyway. I think it's lobster stew for lunch. I can... go down, and get you some—"

No, Imogen tapped, and stood, shrugging off the blanket. *No, I'm alright. I'll...I'll go work on getting you an audience with Lady Marlene. And I'll prep you something in advance—so you know exactly* *what you're getting into. And...*She ran a hand through her hair, and picked up the blanket, folding it without looking at Maeve. *I'll wait outside when you see her. So...nobody makes anymore hasty mistakes.* She set the blanket down, crossed quickly to Maeve's window, and unlatched the panes. She swung a leg over the edge and looked back. *Even if you are sticking around, it'll be over soon. So don't worry.* Maeve watched her go, that protective something pacing restlessly around her stomach again. She had thought she had made progress, but....

She waited a moment or two, then got up to close the window. As she turned away, her telegraph chimed, and she looked at it, surprised.

I like the sketch of those tall ships, by the way.

She glanced up at her mirror, looked at the drawing in question. A view of the harbor in black and white, with the waves beyond. It was an old one and she saw all its imperfections, but she still glanced down and found her reflection smiling.

Chapter

IX

And now," said Mother Superior, to the sisters assembled in the chapel, "on to another matter." She drummed her nails on the edge of the pulpit, and Maeve pricked up her ears, feeling a nervous twinge in her gut. "Not a cause for worry, I assure you, but a slight adjustment. As you may have noticed, there are… fewer of us than this convent has room for. And so, to make things a little cozier this winter and to conserve our resources, we're going to close up the elders' wing." She paused for a moment, during which the murmuring that had started up abruptly cut off as it found itself exposed. Maeve glanced around; she counted twelve little sisters, the four of her cohort, and ten older than her—full elders, and all with their mouths set somewhat grimly. Just twenty-six in total. She wondered if the other elders knew what Mother Superior and Priscilla had been talking about.

"Did you know anything about this?" Shivani hissed in her ear. "Is something wrong?"

Maeve swallowed. "I…heard they were a little tight on cash…."

Shivani's eyes widened, and she stared down at her laced-together fingers for a moment. Maeve looked down the line—Frances' toe was tapping, and even Thalia looked uncharacteristically sober.

"I also ask that we all try to conserve things like lamp oil and paper. We'll let you know if there's anything you have to worry about, but for right now, we're just going to be a bit more frugal. Thank you, everyone—any questions?"

One of the little sisters raised her hand. "Are Maeve and Shivani and Frances and Thalia in charge since you're leaving?" She sounded close to tears; Shivani looked similarly horrified by that idea.

"Oh, no, no." The smallest hint of a smile came to Mother Superior's face. "We're not going anywhere, Cissie. The other elders and I will be moving into their wing, in fact. So, we'll be right down the hall from all of you."

The expression of horror didn't budge from Shivani's face. Maeve didn't like that either; the stunt she'd pulled with Imogen the other day would be impossible now. And she had wanted to do it again, if she could—she'd gotten a few more messages from Imogen that led her to believe that the poet was beginning to open up a little bit.

Sent a few letters yesterday to try and get an audience with Lady Marlene. I'll tell you if anything looks promising.

Are your ghosts allergic to seawater? I keep sneezing whenever I go down to the harbor, now.

Where'd you get this rose, anyway?

"Hallowed Mother, Maeve, you're even spacier than usual, hmm?" Maeve shook herself, and Shivani rolled her eyes as the two of them found themselves alone in the chapel once again. "I said, we should talk about this with the others."

"Oh—what about it?" Maeve got to her feet, feeling her face get hot. She needed to be careful not to get too distracted with her outside obligations.

"Well—" Shivani waved her arms uncertainly. "I don't know, is there anything we can do, is there anything we need to do to get ready for the elders, that kind of thing? We can't have girls' night in my room anymore—they'll come through to yell at us! And what if they see us sneaking out? I've gotten used to having a little freedom!" She half-shouted that, then glanced around the echoing chapel, and lowered her voice.

"I'm...sure it will be fine," Maeve said, glancing up at the altar and at the veiled statue of the Hallowed Mother. "We just have to have faith, and...."

"Faith." Shivani sounded a little frustrated. "Faith means just waiting, more often than not. And things don't always work out by waiting."

Shivani had entered the convent when she was nineteen and though they had been friends for all that time, Maeve was never more aware that Shivani had fully grown up outside than when she said that sort of thing. She pursed her lips, reminding herself that she'd had a lot more time to adapt to the shock than Shivani had, and put an arm around her shoulders.

"Well, I'm game if you want to. Just let me know when, and I'll be there."

Shivani's body was tense, but she loosened up a little at the physical reassurance. "Alright. I will." She sighed. "Thanks. Let's get out of here."

"Of course," Maeve said, following her down the aisle towards the courtyard. She glanced back a little uneasily, but the statue of the Hallowed Mother stood as quietly as ever. Was Shivani right— was faith a fancy word for complacency? She didn't think so; she thought it was more about trust. But then again, she'd acted when she'd heard about the convent's trouble, and in a far more drastic manner than Shivani. What did that say about her? Imogen never waited; she had been so displeased about fate that, somehow, she had defied death itself. Maeve tasted iron, and realized she was worrying her lower lip with her teeth. Whatever. She'd stay her course; it hadn't contradicted her vows yet. Or at least the parts that didn't involve a nude Orion Cantor hadn't.

She was on-call for pauper's mourning today and had to fit in lesson planning for the little sisters, besides. The former meant going down to Mother Superior's office and sitting by the telephone, in case any funeral needed an officiant and couldn't afford one. Just another practice of theirs which, while lovely, didn't bring in any money. She swallowed, thinking of the Court's seance room kitted out to the teeth. Her hand was shaking when she went to knock on the office door, so she forced a deep breath before she went through with it.

"Come in!" Mother Superior's voice. Maeve complied and made her way to the old floral armchair that was set up beside the telephone for the on-call officiant. "Ah, Maeve." Mother Superior glanced up from her desk and gave her a small smile as she sat. "On-call?"

"Yes, ma'am." Maeve managed a smile in return, though it must not have been quick enough. Mother Superior's eyebrows twitched, and she looked harder at Maeve.

"Are you worried about the announcement?"

Maeve pursed her lips. "To…to be honest, a little." It felt refreshing to be able to tell the truth. "Of course, I don't know the whole state of our finances, but…" She looked around, laced her fingers together. "I just…I don't know, are we in a sustainable place?"

Mother Superior sighed. "I would like to tell you not to worry, Maeve, but…" She gazed down at her desk for a few long seconds. "You've been here for a long time now, dear. Ten years, right?"

"Mmm." Maeve found herself painfully conscious of the chair she was sitting in—probably the same chair Mother Superior had been sitting in when she had gotten a call from the constabulary about a scared little girl whose grandmother had passed in the night. That was when the two of them had met—Mother Superior the newly-elected abbess and twelve-year-old Maeve Whaler, who had felt a cold hand caress her cheek in the night and seen a spectral woman with tight grey braids take up a sentinel post on the stoop of their shoreside townhouse. Twelve, some might say, was old enough to mind the financials of a whaling business, but Tia Whaler seemed to disagree, counting her granddaughter as her unfinished business. When the sisters arrived for the ghost and found the girl, her grandmother's spirit had vanished, leaving only the consumption-wracked body. Mother Superior agreed with Tia; in the months it took for Maeve's mother and father and brother to return from the southerly whaling grounds, she or another sister came by on a daily basis with a meal and a kind ear to listen to Maeve's grief. And Maeve would never stop trying to repay that.

"Mmm," Mother Superior echoed, considering Maeve and maybe thinking the same thing. "Well, Maeve, I believe it to be a problem of awareness. There are fewer of us than there used to be, and so people don't know what we do. Not to mention, well, our competition…" Her expression grew dark for a moment, then cleared. "We'll keep on, as we always have, as long as we can, but…."

"What if we tried to reach out?" Maeve blurted, before she could catch herself. She couldn't sit here and see Mother Superior unhappy.

Mother Superior looked at her with a frown. "How so?"

"Well," she said, nervous that she was about to get herself caught. "I just...I've met Professor Chrystos, and I know she doesn't want to negotiate. But maybe the poets would—they don't all do seances, and...people listen to them." She laced her fingers together and looked down at them. "I don't know. I just...don't want this place to have to close. I think what we do is important."

"I agree, dear." Mother Superior's voice was soft. "And I'm not so stuck in my ways as I seem. I go back to Professor Chrystos because I think she can be swayed, not because I'm bashing my head against a wall. But the poets..." She sighed. "I have tried sending letters to the Poets' Court to get a meeting with the Laureate. I have been rebuffed several times by form letters—signed by him, I believe, but form letters all the same. I don't think they are willing to listen."

For a moment, Maeve was tempted to spill her secrets—to tell Mother Superior that it was okay, that she had a standing invitation back to the Court, that she could tell Orion what she wanted to tell him in-person! But the phrase *back* to the Court sat acrid and shameful on her tongue, and she swallowed it back. Her throat ached.

"Okay," she said, forcing herself to sound disappointed. "Sorry. I just...."

"I know." Mother Superior gave her a weary smile. "But remember your scriptures, dear. Sometimes, it is time for something to die. And we must not compromise our beliefs to keep it from going."

The convent's sprawl had its downsides, but there were definite benefits to living in one of the most ancient structures on the island. When Maeve had moved in, she and Frances had spent many late nights in their shared room discussing what mystery rooms and hidden corridors might lay within the convent's walls, and when Thalia had arrived, they had grown bold enough to go looking for them. The place didn't seem as huge or mysterious to Maeve anymore, but the secrets they'd discovered padding in slippers around the halls at night remained.

One had to count floor tiles to find the right spot to stand under, and then reach up on her toes to press the knot in the wooden ceiling that released the widow's walk stairs. Maeve did so, catching the rickety structure as it tumbled down from its compartment, and settled its feet firmly on the ground before climbing up and out to the roof. It was freezing, raining slightly, but Maeve had expected that. She pulled on her gloves, tucked her scarf tighter into the neck of her coat, and curled up beside the little gas stove Shivani had snuck up here for them to tell stories and boil a kettle over. It was a wonder they hadn't burned half the place down, Maeve thought wryly, lighting the stove and shutting its windows against any stray sparks. She looked out to the north while she waited for things to warm up a little—there was the fisher's harbor, with its lobster boats bobbing, and to the east, the cliffside and the Court, to the west the Academy and the bridge to the mainland, and to the south the whaling harbor. She nearly fancied she could smell the oilworks from here. Yes, she'd draw the whaling ships today, she decided. To replace that old drawing Imogen had liked. She pulled the stool and small table she kept up here over to the south, and settled in.

Framing first—catch the curve of the horizon, the rough edges of the coast. Piers jutted out into the water, and the boats stuck spindly straight towards the sky, though their individual masts were little more than toothpicks at this distance. Rooftops, crates and barrels, figures milling about. She wished for a moment that she knew how to use pastels or paints—the colorful flags that flapped from the rigging lent the whole scene cheeriness, but were hard to pick out in graphite. She chewed at the end of her pencil, frowning at the dreariness of the scene she'd roughed out, and looked back up at the harbor. Well, it *was* a bit dreary. Her mind went unbidden to the Court's pink windows, and to the painters who made art there. Not that she needed all that, but...it might be nice to draw *with* someone. To learn and share and collaborate. It was hard to make progress on one's own.

A thump on the trapdoor surprised her—who else even knew where that secret button was? It opened to reveal Shivani, blowing a loose strand of hair out of her face and hoisting herself up to sit on the floor.

"Good, found you. Come on down—I need someone to bounce ideas off."

"Um…" Maeve hesitated—she had snuck this time out of her schedule for herself. "Could…could you talk to Thalia?"

"She won't listen," Shivani complained, sticking out her lower lip. "Not like you will—she'll just say 'sounds good!' and stick her nose back in her books. Come on, Maevey-wavey—it's cold up here anyway. You're just freezing your ass off."

"Yeah, but…" Maeve muttered to herself, looking at her drawing. It was dreary, maybe, but it just needed a little time. A little care and attention.

"C'mon," Shivani whined. "Just ten minutes. Then you can go back to doodling yourself towards hypothermia."

Maeve closed her eyes for a minute, feeling something twist in her stomach, and then opened them.

"Okay," she said, and closed her sketchbook. Shivani's face lit up, and it nearly assuaged the disappointment. Nearly.

"Excellent," she said as she slid back down the ladder. "This'll make up for having to live with the ol' ladies. A good night out for Frances' nameday."

Oh. It wasn't thoughts on how to save the convent or anything. Maeve paused for a fraction of a second on the ladder, then sighed and kept going. Well, she'd help with this, too.

Maeve only got back to the drawing a few days later, as she sat on a bench in bustling downtown. She was keeping a wary eye on the sky—clouds sat low overhead, and she didn't want to get another sketchbook soaked—but for now, the weather seemed to be holding off. She put down lines over her sketched curves, firmed up the shapes, erased the smudges. Not so bad after all.

She was focused enough that it took her a few moments to recognize the woman in mourning who had sat down next to her. Well, it actually took her until Imogen reached a familiar lace-gloved hand out from under her veil, and tugged Maeve's sleeve.

Am I interrupting something? came the message she tapped out with her other hand, and under the black tulle Maeve saw the flash of one of those rare smiles.

"Sorry," she said, blushing, and turned to face her as she stuffed her sketchbook away. Somehow, this seemed an even stranger disguise than the man with the beard; under the veil, she'd dressed up in a black dress with petticoats and all, and buttons up to the throat. It certainly did a good job of obscuring her identity, Maeve supposed; between the veil and the uncharacteristically modest silhouette, she'd never have picked her out of a crowd.

Don't be. Imogen reached out and held Maeve's hand back from stowing the book. Maeve shivered—her skin was cold as ice despite the gloves. *May I look?*

"Oh—er, sure." Maeve drew the sketchbook back out and passed it over. "It's not quite done yet, but…."

Imogen looked at it for a moment, then huffed an annoyed sigh and hiked up her veil, pulling the sketchbook up underneath and scrutinizing it.

Oh, lovely composition. I like this even better than the last one.

Maeve laughed a little nervously. "Just drawing what's in front of me."

Not so, not so! There's art in choosing what you're drawing, darling, just as much as there is putting pencil to paper. She passed it back and smoothed her veil back down. *Anyway. Ready?*

Maeve sighed and nodded. "How long will this take, anyway? It's my friend's nameday, and I have to be back to the convent by seven."

Oh, won't be an hour, Imogen assured her. *You'll have plenty of time to spare.* She hesitated for a moment. *I thought nuns—Sisters, rather—wouldn't have namedays? Your name is just Maeve, isn't it?*

"We celebrate the day we joined the convent—gave our surnames up to serve," Maeve explained, glancing at the clock tower atop City Hall—it was four-fifty now. "But this is Frances' given nameday, anyway."

Imogen nodded in understanding. *My guardian had one of those too.* She cocked her head. *She didn't have to change her name to get into your convent, did she? I don't think I've ever seen a Sister who wasn't a woman.*

"Oh, no," Maeve said quickly. "She changed it long before she came to join us, she's told us. Preferred it that way. And we've had a few Sisters who weren't women, but it sort of follows traditional lines. I've read a lot of automatic writings by a Sister Matthew, so...."

Ah. She stood and tapped out a final message. *I'll be in deep mourning, so you can speak for me if we need to. But hopefully no one will bother a sad sad widow....*

She stuck a hand out from under her veil to help Maeve to her feet, and the two of them turned toward the library. Maeve hadn't exactly been looking forward to this trip; among other research, Imogen had deemed it crucial for her to have a better founding in the intricacies of the nobility before she went before Lady Marlene. Already she was bored. She didn't like nobles—few whalers did, given the nobles' theft of the fortune gained by their sweat and blood. Whale oil and tea held Lenorum together, and plenty of Maeve's forebears had drowned for the former. Drowning wasn't a good death; the elder sisters led a mass exorcism for the sea's dead each year, but spirits still staggered out of the waves. People would always die whaling, obviously, but when the masters of the whaling companies never risked themselves alongside their crew, well... Maeve didn't like nobles. Tia had spoken of Maeve's drowned grandfather at least three times a day and shook her fist across the narrow strait to Edgewood Heights every time they were on the landward side of the island.

So as Imogen led the way up the steps and began a long-strided circuit of the shelves, plucking down books without looking, Maeve made her way to a desk in an empty study room. She comforted herself with the promise of Frances' nameday party later and daydreamed about the hot meal that awaited her until a thump snapped her out of her reverie. *Courtly Manners and Practices* was the top book in the stack. She looked up at Imogen and snorted.

Imogen crossed her arms. *Don't give me that. Literally all of our suspects are nobles—we have to get inside their heads. Orion once told me that he paid two hundred ammonite for a bottle of champagne because it had edible glitter in it.*

"Mother have mercy," Maeve grumbled, and pored over the rest of the titles. "Fine, you start with the manners, and I'll do the newspapers—" She tried to pull the binder of *Lenorum Heralds* towards her, but Imogen smacked her hand and pushed the manners book toward her instead.

I already know what I'm doing. I'm going to search for stuff about myself. You read this, and I'll bring you back a cup of tea too if you can tell me three facts about nobles. Imogen slipped back out the door, and Maeve stuck her tongue out at her retreating back. She cracked open the book.

Nobles' parents will request other nobles to act as a sort of secondary parent, or godparent, for their newborn child—providing a built-in mentor to the ways of the social scene and also forging non-familial bonds. It is quite common for godchildren to marry their godparent's actual children, to provide a trustworthy partner and the strengthening of the line....

The sky went from its evening deep blue to night's full black outside, and by the time Imogen came back Maeve felt thoroughly vindicated in disliking the nepotistic, xenophobic, exploitative nature of the noble class. It seemed bad for the island, and bad for the people themselves. She could see why anyone would distance themself from the concept. Didn't mean she understood Orion buying a two-hundred ammonite bottle of anything, but she could see why he would leave.

Okay, this is everything. Imogen deposited another stack of library materials on the desk and slid a library-issue teacup over to Maeve's elbow. *It's Lenorum Public, but hopefully you can choke it down.*

Maeve took it gratefully. "I like Lenorum Public."

Imogen blinked uncomprehendingly. *Come again?*

"I like Lenorum—"

Never mind, don't say it again. Words have power. Mother's grave. Imogen wrinkled her nose at the cup like Maeve's assertion might have given it preternatural powers. *I took you to try the belladonna at Corvus's. And you had to have had something good at the Lobster Pot. Are you sure you like Lenorum Public?*

"It's nice! It's simple and tasty and—"

That's it! No depth, no complexity. The mouthfeel of dishwater! Maeve raised an eyebrow and raised the cup to her lips as Imogen's expression turned pained. She grinned behind its rim. *Look, I made tea at the Silver Pearl for three years. I know people in the business. I can source you some good tea.*

"All I need in tea is warmth and caffeine," Maeve told her sweetly, though her interest was secretly piqued. Orion had mentioned that Imogen had worked as a lobster hand and at a teahouse, but she hadn't really been able to picture the poet rolling up her sleeves and working. But something as fiddly as fine tea—mixing herbs, monitoring water temperatures, arranging flowers and leaves together to bloom in crystal pots—now that she could see. Her narrow hands seemed suited to detail work.

Hands that Imogen's face was currently buried in right now. Her telegraph key toggled of its own accord. *At least tell me you did the reading I told you to. Did you learn anything?*

"Yeah, I think the Sinclairs killed my grandfather." Maeve slid the first stack away distastefully. "I didn't know Arrow Whaling was owned by them before it broke up."

Imogen looked up, dropping her assumed drama. *Sorry.*

"Don't worry—never met him." Maeve pulled the new stuff towards her and took another sip of tea. "Explains why every time I see Camille I want to kick her, though. Tell me more about Lady Marlene."

Imogen dug in among the books and pulled out a green-covered tome with gold leaf. She cracked it open and folded a page out to reveal an extensive family tree, complete with portraits. She switched to writing in her notebook.

Well. Speaking of tea, the Warwick family were the tea magnates before the city publicized their holdings, and they've never forgotten it. They've been here for eons, and they lead the social scene. Marlene is holding the old ways together with spite and bits of string, and she's not releasing a penny of ancestral wealth.

She pointed a finger to a portrait a single generation up from the bottom—a sharp-faced pale woman of perhaps forty years with a single streak of grey in her hair. She looked like she was made of ice—even the drawing of her captured something ruthless and cold about her. She was linked by a line to a man who looked quite the opposite of her, with unruly curly hair and a smile. Orion, below, looked like both of them—Marlene's hard gaze and keen cheekbones and his father's good looks. He was still a child in this portrait, but the likeness was unmistakable.

He left at sixteen, Imogen informed her. *He renounced his name to do it, which—as I'm sure you know—means you lose it all. Camille, on the other hand, is still a noble—just a second daughter. So, she doesn't get the title, but she has a little more freedom.*

"And how did you get wrapped up in all of this?" Maeve asked.

I met Orion applying to his school. Met Camille at an audition, like I mentioned before. And Marlene is an old family enemy. Imogen laced her fingers together. *She's obsessed with the cemetery—the one I'm buried in, the one my guardian and I looked after. The land is fantastically valuable, obviously, because of the location, and she's been trying to buy it for years. Develop it, you know?*

"But disinterring bodies practically guarantees hauntings," Maeve protested. "It'd be inhumane!"

Which is why the law requires a grace period. Imogen nodded. *I agree with you, of course, but legally she only has to wait for a year after the last burial to be allowed to disinter. I didn't think she should be able to do that—so I did a bit of a campaign to extend the grace period.*

"Did it work?" Maeve couldn't remember hearing anything about this, but she wasn't exactly diligent about following the news. Imogen held up a newspaper clipping and shook her head.

She won the argument before city council, and the grace period remained the same. So, she only had to wait the year—the year for my guardian to rest. She blinked a little under the mourning veil, then kept writing. *It was the last thing they could do to protect the old place— to haunt it for a little while longer. They insisted on their death bed to be buried there. I didn't understand until months later.* She paused and shut her eyes for a minute. *I made room—one more grave. That was all I could do before it went into public trust.*

Maeve read it, then reread it a few times, pieces slotting into place.

"She grew up Imogen Grave—her guardian was a cemetery keeper," Orion had said. And Imogen had mentioned her guardian had passed. And that...oh. That she was a foundling.

"Because when your guardian died, you weren't able to inherit it?"

Imogen nodded. *Oleander never went and put it in writing that they had adopted me—they found me on one of the grave markers out there, on some cold December night. Someone trying to kill me. Not for the first time, I suppose.* She smiled a bit. *I had always gone publicly by Madrigal, so I didn't have a case legally. And I wasn't really in a state to fight for it—too sad. Oleander was—*she had written a few words, then scratched them out, finally opting for—*my person*. She began a new line. *I thought Oleander had just been paranoid about nobles, that it would be safe in public hands, but Marlene started making moves. Jolted me out of being sad. I started my campaign and ran up against her.* She smirked. *And now it's me holding that grace period. Whoever buried me managed to do me one favor, at least.*

"Do you know who that was?"

Imogen shook her head. *But maybe it's in here.* She patted the top of the stack, then caught it as it threatened to topple over. *So, if you want to do me the favor of helping me read, I would be most grateful.*

Now Maeve was more interested—she, too, would hate to see the little cemetery torn up for some noble's profit, and it was her duty to advocate for the dead. She took a binder of old newspapers, and let Imogen direct her to the dates of the City Council vote. She made notes in her sketchbook as she went. The arguments had taken place on May 23rd. The grace period had been set to expire six months and a bit later—November 30th. Maeve frowned and glanced back at the other articles—the ones about Imogen's murder. "You died just before the grace period ended, huh?"

Imogen nodded. *Only outlived Oleander by a year.*

"Is that…is that a motive?" Maeve tapped her pencil against the table, deep in thought. "You're an activist. You're willing to fight for the cemetery—could someone have made the decision that you should die for it, too?"

Imogen's eyebrows rose slightly, and she was long in hesitating before she wrote something down.

In that case, there's only one party I can think of who cares about the dead more than cemetery keepers.

There was absolute silence in the library as they stared at each other uncomfortably. The collapse of their pile of books was a relief; they both lunged for papers as they avalanched towards the floor, and Maeve firmly put her convent's disdain for the poet's lifestyle from her mind. Oh, Mother—she recovered a wax cylinder from the floor and pulled it from its case, praying they hadn't broken it. It seemed fine—*Performance of 'Magnetic North' by the poet - I. Madrigal*, said the label. Imogen glanced up from redistributing the papers into a hill with gentler slopes, and her expression went very strange for a moment, like she'd found something she'd never expected to see again. She pulled off her veil and tossed it over her shoulder, taking the cylinder from Maeve's hands. Maeve's telegraph chimed on the table. *That's what these are? They're recordings?* Her hands trembled, ever so slightly.

"Oh—there's a phonograph over there," Maeve said softly, placing down the cylinder's case and moving to the door to shut it if Imogen did, indeed, want to listen. Imogen looked at it for a long time. Then she moved dreamlike towards the phonograph, placed the cylinder in, and switched it on with a click. There was static for a moment, and then—

"I worked on a lobster boat by day
In an earlier life of mine
I had never set foot off the island before but
T'was all that was open to find—"

Maeve moved away from the door and sat, watching Imogen carefully. She wasn't sure of what she was worried about—if she might have some ghostly reaction, or breakdown, or what—but she remembered how she herself had felt, a few weeks ago, listening to another of these cylinders. Imogen turned slightly to lean against the wall, her head bowed, and Maeve could see now. She was mouthing the words to herself, eyes closed.

"The captain—a woman, Grismelda, which was
A fam-i-ly name she said,
Worked dawn till dusk; if I know her I trust
She'll do so until she is dead
"The sun beats down on a lobstering boat
Till you're redbacked and baking and raw
And the sea roils around you, boils and churns
And sears the salt into the cracks of your palms
"The catch of the day goes on ice belowdecks
And you wish it were you, you do, you do,
But Grismelda she sang ho-hey, ho-hey,
And heave in the lines, girl, we'll make a payday!
Oh ain't it the life, the salt-spray and strife?
Haul in the lines, girl, let's make that payday!"

There was a shantyish rhythm to the old performance, and Imogen replicated it now perfectly—ducking her chin with the beats, her toe nearly tapping. If it weren't for the crackle of the phonograph, Maeve would nearly believe it. She found herself really, truly wanting to believe it.

> *"I lose a fine buoy of red and turquoise*
> *The flag o'er the cabin displays its same shades*
> *I sulk to the bow and look to the waves*
> *Which have eaten our buoy, trap, and catch of the day*
> *Ho-hey, girl, you think you're the first lobster hand*
> *To lose to the pounding of wave, rock, and sand?*
> *The ocean's immeasurable, ancient, and vast*
> *We're closer to fish than to gods."*

And Imogen opened her eyes, a silent laugh on her lips as she noticed Maeve watching her, and crossed over towards Maeve, hiking up her skirts and stepping up on a chair. Then up onto the table, and she leaned down and wrinkled her nose in a grin—seized Maeve's hand, and spoke on:

> *"She takes my cracked hand in her hand and she says*
> *Lobsters head south for the winter*
> *The old ones—they go first in the line*
> *The young follow after—they learn the long routes*
> *Through canyon and valley, along the sea floor*
> *And they all go claw in claw as they walk*
> *The long miles down to Paradise*
> *They go claw in claw, the old and the young*
> *And they learn the way to Paradise."*

Maeve blushed—embarrassment at being caught watching, being brought into the performance herself, or some other harder-to-define reason. If this was how Imogen typically conducted a poetry reading, then she had no doubt of why she had risen so quickly to the top. She was…compelling. Her mind offered her the word "captivating" and she pushed it away with a deeper blush. Perhaps that was a little much. Nuns didn't like poets, after all.

Though in other lives, like she mentioned—Maeve had been a whaler and Imogen a lobster hand. Imogen let her go, and turned to some imaginary audience, but that remained. She knew what it was like to have salt-cracked hands. To watch the sea turn to gold in the sunset, and to tell stories belowdecks on stormy days. The poem told of the captain of Imogen's lobster boat, and a compass that pointed home instead of north, and she nearly laughed—it was a story she'd heard a thousand times from all manner of relatives.

No, it wasn't who she'd chosen to spend her life with, but the familiarity touched her all the same.

"I opened the note at a tavern that night
Drinking ale and watching the sun set
It's a map she's left me
Islands down south and a small epigraph
The old lobsters show the way, ho-hey
The old lobsters show the way."

The phonograph crackled into silence, and Imogen's shoulders lowered. She turned, smoothed her hair out of her face, her eyes cast down.

Ha. Sorry, read Maeve's telegraph.

"No, no," Maeve said quickly, startled out of a reverie she was surprised to find herself in. "Uh, snaps, right?" She gave a few hurried snaps, and Imogen gave a small silent chuckle, carefully stowing away the cylinder and placing it back in the stack before taking up her notebook again.

I've tormented you enough—I can make copies of these clippings later. Let's head out.

They stepped outside into a drizzling rain. It was quiet despite the bustle of the city—quiet, perhaps, because Imogen had to be quiet. Because there was so much left unsaid.

"When did you do those performances?" she tried, hoping to fill the space somehow.

Oh, I don't know. Every night a party in those days—and everyone would get up to say their piece. I did that one a few times at Adolai's. Went over well with his crew. A smile twitched at the corner of her lips as they turned into an alley, more protected from the rain. *But my best one was about a girl raised by wolves—these fancy wolves in suits, who find a baby left on the doorstep of their forest manor. It was something about people being feral and animals being elegant, and the line blurring, or what have you. There's a murder; it's told in three-four. I had a fun little prowl routine, and then I'd waltz with some girl in the audience. A bit sexier than Magnetic North—it's called—*

The clicking of the telegraph paused, and Maeve came to a stop a few feet after Imogen. She looked like she'd just been struck; a chill draft swept through the alley. "What...was it called?" Maeve asked, concerned.

Lupine. That's not important. But I gave it—at that party...at the Academy. The night I—

Maeve didn't catch the rest of the message, because before she could read it there was a gasp, and something hit her hard. Imogen's shoulder, catching her sternum in a way that knocked the breath right out of her and sent her spinning to the ground. She heard the breaking of glass, and a sound that sounded like nothing so much as a ship's butcher lopping meat off a whale, and then felt something ice-cold and liquid hit her face. She scrabbled at it, still gasping, and found that the broken glass had been the left lens of her spectacles. Her vision was still good enough to see that the substance that had hit her was ectoplasm. She settled her glasses back onto the bridge of her nose with shaking hands and found her nose an inch from a wicked black harpoon, which had impaled the wall just beside her. A hand seized hers—cold, and covered in ectoplasm, and as Maeve fought to get her feet running, she noted two things with absolute horror.

First, the thing that had produced the horrible sound and had diverted the harpoon, which was the gaping hole in Imogen's torso; second, the figure on the rooftop far above them, who had shot it. Whoever they were, they were reloading.

Chapter

X

They hooked around the corner, Maeve staggering
as another harpoon tore through her skirt and pinned it to the
ground. It ripped as she kept running, but there was no way she
was stopping now. Imogen yanked her on, looking left and right
for cover. There was none in this alley. She skidded to a stop and
Maeve bumped into her.

"Don't stop," Maeve panted. "Come on, we'll lose them in the
crowd—" Imogen pointed frantically to her chest, still soaked in
ectoplasm. "Doesn't matter!" Maeve snapped back, shrugging her
shoulders out of her coat and throwing it at Imogen. "Come on,
wear this, whatever, just come on!"

She started running again, now yanking Imogen along instead, and after a few lopsided moments the two of them got back
into step, Imogen holding Maeve's coat tight around her shoulders
and over her wound. They skidded out onto the busy street the
library was on, Maeve scanning the rooftops with what vision she
had available.

"We need to find cover," she muttered to Imogen, who nodded, looking back. She went, if possible, even paler than usual,
and dug her nails into Maeve's hand. Maeve looked back, too—a
tall man in an oilskin stood at the other end of the block, carrying a harpoon gun slung over his shoulder. He wouldn't be out
of place, except that they were nowhere near the whaling harbor,
and he'd taken the cable off his gun. Maeve's mother had always
been pedantic on the point that a harpoon was to tether, not to

kill. But that was for hunting whales—this man clearly had more vulnerable prey in mind. He scanned the crowd, and Maeve tried to make herself small, pulling the two of them in front of a gaggle of schoolchildren and quickening her pace. "Did he see us?"

Imogen glanced back, then mouthed a curse and nodded.

"Cemetery," she whispered, nearly too quiet to hear over the noise of the street, and pulled Maeve across it, narrowly dodging a couple of motorcars. Fewer and fewer people surrounded them—they were heading away from the crush of the crowd, and still the man with the harpoon came on, taking long strides that ate up the distance between them. Soon he would be on them, and in an area with very few witnesses. But there was the iron gate of the cemetery, and as they approached it Imogen broke into a run, pointing across the little hills toward a squat structure—the groundskeeper's hut. "You go there," she hissed with a wince, and let go of Maeve's hand. She cut left away from her, Maeve's protests dying on her lips as the silhouette of their pursuer arrived at the gate. She hesitated for a moment more, then turned unhappily and sprinted through weeping willows and mazes of headstones into the dark. She heard a piercing whistle, and saw, over her shoulder, the man breaking towards Imogen.

The groundskeeper's hut was dark—safe? She tried the door, and found it locked, but the window beside the door was loose in its setting and opened after a persuasive shove. She wedged herself through it and shut the window behind her. What was Imogen thinking? Just because that first harpoon hadn't killed her....

She glanced around in the dark, feeling horribly powerless, and then moved towards the door, unlocking it slowly and turning the knob. She had to see, at least, what was going on—otherwise she couldn't help. The door creaked as it opened, causing her stomach to drop, and the sound of a boot turning on gravel reached her ears. *Oh, no. Oh, no, no, no.* Maeve eased the door shut again, but the sound of footsteps approaching was unmistakable. She locked the door, and pressed her back to it, terribly conscious of the moonlight pouring in the windows. A shadow passed across the one she had entered by, and she pressed her hand over her mouth to keep from making any sound. The handle rattled a bit, followed by the tap of a boot testing the door's sturdiness. It wasn't very sturdy. Maeve closed her eyes, her heartbeat loud in her ears, and offered up what meager prayer she could scrounge. *Hallowed Mother, please protect us—I'm only trying to do the right thing, and Imogen has already suffered enough. Deliver us from evil....*

It was a good thing that she was already covering her mouth, because when Imogen's hand seized hers, she nearly screamed. She had slipped in through the other window, and as the man outside gave the door a kick in earnest, she dragged Maeve to the floor and pulled up a trap door, hidden under dust and clever carpentry. Maeve didn't stop to wonder how Imogen had known it was there; she simply jumped in, and let Imogen pull the door shut above them. Another heavy thump sounded, followed by a splintering and the fall of heavy footsteps, and Maeve held her breath.

After what might have been minutes or hours in the dark, the footsteps moved toward the door, and the hinges squealed again. Maeve didn't dare move; he could be faking them out. Her eyes began to adjust, aided by the weak lavender glow of the ectoplasm splattered over both of them, and with difficulty she made out a small cellar with a brick floor and walls, maybe eight feet across. Imogen was seated on the floor, her eyes shut, seemingly listening. If she hadn't had a hand pressed to her stomach wound, she might have been praying. Her eyes opened after a moment, and she pointed to Maeve's bag. Maeve pulled out the sketchbook and a pencil for her, and Imogen wrote in it shakily. Maeve had to squint to read in the dark.

Let's stay here for a little while, to make sure he's gone.

Maeve nodded agreement and wrote back.

Are you okay? Are you in pain?

Imogen nodded, then bent double, stifling violent coughs. She managed to get a handkerchief over her mouth, but its black silk only served to highlight the ectoplasm she coughed up. The sight put a horrible twist in Maeve's stomach—she couldn't help but remember seeing her grandmother's white handkerchiefs dotted with similar spots of blood. It was a long moment before she tuned back in enough to look at the notebook and register that Imogen was looking at her, now, with concern.

Sorry. Are you *okay?*

Yes, Maeve wrote, slightly shaken, and watched as Imogen hiked her veil up to peer at her. In the pale light of the ectoplasm, she looked ghastly—pale and corpselike, even more than usual. *You look...deader than usual.*

The slightest wince crossed Imogen's face, and Maeve knew when the *Oh, I'm fine!* arrived on her screen it was a lie. She hesitated for a moment, her first instinct to play nice, and then pushed that aside.

"No, you're not," she insisted, and peered right back at her. "What's wrong?"

Imogen glanced away and tenderly began unbuttoning the bodice of her dress. *Just a little discomfort*—She undid her collar, and Maeve noticed her throat wound weeping ectoplasm again. *It hurt like this when I woke up too—it'll go away once I've healed, I'm sure.* She smiled, but it looked like more of a grimace. *I'll tell you if it doesn't.*

Maeve wanted to protest further, but Imogen had started undoing her corset and Maeve's face was feeling rather hot. It was unlucky the harpoon had gotten through a corset at all. She averted her eyes and busied herself with pouring water onto one of her handkerchiefs until Imogen tapped her shoulder and held out the sketchbook.

Can you look at the wound and make sure there's no fabric left in it?

Maeve nodded awkwardly, and pulled out her telegraph, using the light from its screen to inspect the entry point on Imogen's back. To her surprise, it wasn't gaping like it had been previously—the puncture only went in a few inches, and though it was still bleeding ectoplasm, what was there seemed to be congealing. She picked out a few stray threads, watching Imogen carefully to make sure she wasn't hurting her, and then came around to the front. Things looked even less horrible here—she wiped away a bit of the ectoplasm and found beneath it was healthy-looking muscle tissue. She looked up at Imogen in confusion, then remembered that Imogen was shirtless and probably freezing and definitely wouldn't want to answer questions. She finished her inspection rather hurriedly, then used her pencil knife to cut a few strips from Imogen's trashed chemise and helped her wrap them around the wound. That seemed like all it was going to need—to be covered and left alone. She recovered her own coat from the floor and placed it over Imogen's shoulders.

Imogen had written a message for her when she sat back down. *I'm so sorry I put you in this danger.*

We decided we're in this together, Maeve wrote back. *You took a harpoon for me, so it all works out evenly, I think.*

Imogen read that, and her face crumpled into an unsteady smile. *Sans a dress and a pair of glasses. I'll pay for them, promise.*

A slight relief, that—Maeve's backup pair of glasses were exceedingly unfashionable. She took the broken ones off, plucked the remaining slivers of glass in the left frame out, and put them back on, her head starting to ache from the mismatch in her vision. At least there wasn't much to see down here.

How did you know this place was here? she wrote after a few minutes of silence.

Imogen picked up the pencil, a bittersweet expression on her face. *Well, it used to be my cellar. So I hope I'd remember where the trap door was.*

Right. She didn't push the topic—after all, she never went back to her old house. After her grandmother was gone from it, it hadn't felt the same. She chewed the corner of her lip, straining her ears for further sounds from above. *Who do you think he is?*

Imogen shut her eyes. *This says Marlene to me. If she's involved.*

Maeve stared at her. *How do you know?*

Imogen shrugged weakly. *Can't imagine he's Camille's—too bold for someone with too little influence. And Orion likes you, at the very least—he wouldn't hire someone to shoot at you.* Her eyebrows knit together. *Word must have gotten around. Probably his fault—the Court leaks secrets like a sieve.*

Maeve swallowed; she sincerely hoped her address wasn't one of those secrets that had gotten around. *So, what next? Do we just… have to live with this?*

Imogen's eyes popped open. *No. No, we…we're not powerful, but we do know how they work. I told you—getting inside their heads is key. I have an idea.*

What?

She bit her lip. *Like Orion said—he has resources. And he hates Marlene. If I'm clever I can…*She shook her head. *I'll handle it. But whenever you do things for me it should be in disguise. For your safety.*

Maeve glanced down at her shredded dress. *I'm going to need a new disguise.*

It had been several minutes since they had heard sounds from the hut above, but Maeve was exhausted enough by adrenaline and fear that she was in no great hurry to leave. She shifted toward the wall, leaning back against it, and watched the ectoplasm on her clothes slowly evaporate. The whole dress was a lost cause, of course, and her coat might be in the same sad boat. She glanced at Imogen, curled up inside it, and their eyes caught for a moment. Imogen glanced away, and picked up the sketchbook, weighing the pencil in her hand.

So, I made you learn a bunch of stuff about me. I don't know anything about you. Your grandfather died whaling, you said. And you were a Whaler. Can you shoot like that?

It was a non-sequitur and Maeve wasn't sure why Imogen was asking, but she'd take it. Any excuse to hide in safety a little while longer. She took the pencil back.

I know how to shoot a harpoon gun. But I was never any good at it. Mostly because I never wanted to hit anything. She smiled. *Not much to tell, really. My family owns a ship called the* Fletcher. *Bought it off Arrow Whaling Co. when they got broken up, like I mentioned. They're gone most of the year on it.*

So how did you go from not wanting to kill whales to being in a death nunnery?

That makes it sound like we're the ones causing the deaths, Maeve protested, elbowing Imogen lightly. She hesitated, and then began to explain—her preference for shore life, her time with her grandmother, the illness and her death. She tried to keep it short and informative—Imogen didn't want to know about Tia Whaler's prowess at knot-tying, or the times they'd skived off bookkeeping for an afternoon to go to the art museum, or the long nights Maeve had sat outside her sickroom, banished by Tia for her own safety but unable to leave her alone. Terrified that each wheezing breath would be her last, until one of them was. She had to go a bit more in-depth at that point, to tell Imogen why seeing Tia—her apparition no longer emaciated but strong and tall, the pale negative of her sun-browned face giving her a final, gentle smile, and her stride to the door steady and confident—for that last time had ignited a faith she'd never known was within her. Why it had convinced her that helping every spirit, every person find the divine peace that she had finally felt that night was a real, worthy mission.

Imogen read silently for a minute or two; she had, perhaps, written more than she had intended to. She looked up eventually, her eyes searching Maeve's face, until her lips curled into a smile.

You know, if anyone else had written that, I'd have thought it was sanctimonious bullshit. No one's that nice in real life. She paused for a moment more, tapping her nose with the end of the pencil while Maeve chewed the inside of her cheek in embarrassment. She'd been noticing that Imogen dropped her formal wording when she meant something sincerely, and this was practically Shivani-levels of familiarity. *Now I want to hear about your drawing—have you got a great life-changing story there too?*

Oh, no. Maeve shook her head as she wrote. *That's just...frivolous. Mother Superior says the key to a Good Death is a happy life, and so, when I'm not busy with Sister stuff, I do that for fun.*

She could feel Imogen's eyes on her; she didn't meet them, sure that her expression would reveal the transparent lie. That it was a bit more than fun, that she had to steal moments for it, that those trips to the art museum with Tia had been just as formative as her death. It was a lie she didn't feel too bad about telling; she only had so much time, after all, as the hourglasses all over the convent were constantly reminding her, and she had a better chance of helping people with her main occupation than her hobby.

The nudge of the sketchbook at her knee pulled her out of that slight reverie, and Imogen's spidery cursive informed her that she was more of an open book than she thought.

You help people a lot. Do you treat yourself with the same priority?

Maeve allowed herself a slight chuckle, and then a very slight confession. *I do wish I knew...*she paused for a moment. *How to make art-art. Like what...the poets do. How Orion said you all...collaborate? Not that I want to be a poet or anything—and if art requires me to wear my shirt unbuttoned and talk in riddles and be wildly ostentatious then forget I asked*—another hand stilled hers, and she glanced up, to see Imogen looking amused.

It doesn't, she wrote. *The Court has an image it likes to uphold, but at the end of the day, we're there to work together. To learn and grow.* Imogen thumbed at the edge of the sketchbook, flipping the pages a little. *Which, if you like....*

Maeve froze, then shrugged self-consciously. She relaxed a bit as Imogen paged through, making exaggerated facial expressions and fanning herself and miming gasps. It felt silly, but at the same time…nice. Almost a critique. She flipped back to the pages they were writing on a few times—*Oh, this one's screaming for a bit of color. Ooh, I like this one; where's this garden? Oh*— She flipped through a few portraits Maeve had done and landed on one of Shivani playing the organ. *Oh, you draw her like you love her.*

For a moment Maeve was speechless; she had no idea at all how to respond to that statement. Of—of course she loved Shivani; they were best friends, they were sisters. But the word meant something heavy and dangerous in Imogen's writing; something with greater meaning behind it. Words had power; she supposed that was what all poetry was, and she was beginning to recall why she didn't care for it.

"What makes you say that?" she whispered, forgetting their need to be silent.

Imogen pointed to the paper, running a fingertip over the part with Shivani's face drawn on it. *You've nearly gone through the paper erasing. Trying to get it just right.* She looked at Maeve, and though she had on her characteristic smirk, Maeve thought for a moment she thought she saw something else in her eyes. Hmph—undoubtedly, Imogen projecting some old dalliance of hers onto Maeve. But Maeve was a Sister of Good Death, and Sisters of Good Death didn't do that sort of thing.

She pulled the sketchbook back, aiming to tell Imogen just that, when her flipping of the pages led her to the portrait she had done of Frances and the others, for Frances' nameday. Frances' nameday—oh no. She checked her watch; she was an hour late already.

Do you think he's gone? Maeve scribbled hastily. *The others are going to miss me*—

Imogen's expression shot to incredulity. *It's been ten minutes at most. He's probably still casing my mausoleum or something. No way is it safe.*

Well, then, come with me, Maeve wrote impatiently. *You can stay in my room for the night and leave in the morning. But I have to get back—I've already missed half of it. Frances is probably worrying herself mad.*

She stood, heedless of whatever protest Imogen was going to make, and began to pack her things. Imogen watched from the floor sullenly, then finally stood and crossed her arms. She pushed up the trap door a tiny crack, peering out, and then glared at Maeve. Safe, Maeve imagined, but Imogen wasn't happy about it. She didn't need to read her words to know that.

The keeper's hut was, at least, close to an exit, and so after a few minutes of scouting, Imogen and Maeve broke for the street, and made it without issue. The weather had grown unpleasant—cold heavy rain that slapped into the pavement and made walking without slipping difficult. Without her coat, Maeve found herself shivering, sleet soaking through her ruined dress and her fingertips turning numb. Guilt twisted her stomach—they had been planning this night for a month. She would need an excuse, and an excuse meant a lie. If she could even get in without anyone seeing her, without anyone questioning her broken glasses and ripped dress. A dress she shouldn't even have had, from a friend who was also irritated with her. A friend with whom she was also growing irritated, to be fair. She spent half the time longing for the simplicity of her life before she had started dealing with Imogen, and now she had skipped a night that was meant to be just that.

By the time they arrived at the convent's side door, the fear and frustration of the night had brought her to the brink of exhaustion, and she turned, soaking, to Imogen.

"I'll let you in at my window," she said shortly. "Do whatever you did last time when you left." She turned away without waiting for confirmation, and let herself in. The kitchen fire was warm, and the whole of the room was empty, and for a moment she was tempted to just stay there and avoid whatever was coming next. But she took the spiral stairs up, turned the corner onto their hall, and walked head-down to her door. When she looked up and found Shivani standing outside, her arms crossed, she didn't quite have the energy to fake a smile.

"Where have you been, then?" Shivani said. Her tone was chilly.

"Would you believe I got mugged again?" Maeve tried. Shit—she had never told Shivani about the first time, either.

Shivani blinked slowly, then shook her head. She opened her mouth to say something, but before she could, the door two down from hers slammed open, and Frances and Thalia rushed out.

"Oh, Hallowed Mother, I was so worried!" Frances said, seizing Maeve by the shoulders, and looked her over with a horrified expression. "What happened to your dress? And your glasses?" She crushed Maeve into a hug, and over her shoulder Maeve could see Thalia, also looking worried, and Shivani, looking unconvinced. "Come on," Frances said, pulling back, and turned towards Maeve's door. "Come get into dry clothes. And then you can go to sleep if you need, or if you need to talk—"

Maeve hurried forward and put herself in front of the door. "Of course, of course, just give me a second—I'm so sorry I'm late, Frances—just let me get cleaned up and—" She turned the doorknob and had pushed open the door a crack when she was arrested by Shivani's voice.

"No, I want to hear her explanation now." Maeve didn't have a response ready; she was busy noticing that Imogen had not, in fact, waited for her to let her in, and had one leg in through the window. She glared at her as much as she could without tipping off the others. "Come on, Maeve—what was that about getting mugged?"

"You got mugged?" Thalia echoed, her voice much louder than Maeve would have liked. "Who by? Were you in the cemetery alone again?"

"No, no, I—" Maeve forced a laugh, but it came out sounding nervous. "I, um, went for a walk, and then I got held up—took the trolley back and it got delayed—"

"And you fell under the wheels, that it?" Shivani said dryly. Maeve didn't answer—she didn't have a lie and she didn't want to lie, but what else could she do? Shivani didn't even know what she'd done and she was angry already! Imogen pulled her other leg the rest of the way in, evidently having missed Maeve's glare. Maeve cursed internally, looked back, and found Shivani looking at her suspiciously. Then, before Maeve could react, she darted forward, wrenched the doorknob out of Maeve's hand, and slammed it open.

"Mm. Yeah. Okay." Shivani didn't sound surprised at all—a sharp contrast to the exclamations Frances and Thalia made and the cornered expression on Imogen's face.

"Who's…this, Maeve?" Thalia said measuredly, stepping forward and placing her arms in front of the other three of them. "Do you want me to remove her from your room?"

Imogen caught Maeve's eye, uncertain for a fraction of a second, and then immediately recovered herself. She stood to her full height, the effect marred by her ectoplasm-stained clothing and soaked hair and bowed. "I am," she whispered, "someone…who Maeve…is helping."

"Pardon?" Thalia asked, and Imogen sighed. She took a step forward, and Thalia pushed the rest of them back a step. The jostling finally shook Maeve out of her paralysis, and she ducked under Thalia's arm, standing between the two parties.

"Okay," she said, her voice catching in her throat. "I…have some things to explain."

A short bark of laughter issued from Shivani. "Yes you do. And no bullshit—" she reached into the top of her dress and pulled out a note, gesturing with it. "Everything you say better line right up with this, Maeve, or I'm—"

"Hey!" Frances piped up, ducking under Thalia's arm and leveling an uncharacteristically stern look back at Shivani. "No fighting on my nameday!" A little smile twitched at her lips, then subsided as she looked at Imogen. "I want to hear what's going on, too, but are you okay? Not injured or anything?" Imogen paused, then nodded very slightly. "Maeve, are you?" Maeve searched Frances' face, found only concern. She nodded too. "Okay," Frances decreed, then walked back towards Thalia and pushed her arms down carefully. "I'm going to go get some towels for you two; no one fight while I'm gone. Maeve and our…guest…" She looked Imogen up and down for a moment, then glanced over to Thalia. "Thalia, do you have anything dry she can borrow?"

Five minutes saw them back in Maeve's room, Imogen ensconced in a more size-appropriate sweater and Maeve wrapped in a quilt despite her protests. They sat in a circle on the floor, an uncomfortable parallel to girl's night, though with one more body. It was Shivani, not Imogen, who sat on the outs, glowering at her note and not speaking. Maeve had no idea what the note said or where it had come from, but she was certain Shivani wasn't going to tell her until she said her piece. She sighed, glanced between Frances and Thalia, and then told them.

She told them about meeting the Wraith in the alley; Thalia's eyes lit up and Imogen blushed a blotchy purple. She went through the particulars of Imogen's condition and skimmed over the investigations they'd conducted.

"She had...angered some people before getting killed," she explained, glossing over who those people were, exactly. "And it seems like maybe we're getting close, because, um, someone came after us." By the time she had explained what exactly had happened to her glasses and her dress, Thalia was openly cracking her knuckles.

"Oh, that won't stand," she muttered. "No one hurts my sisters."

"It's okay," Maeve assured her, "for now." She looked at Frances and bit her lip. "Any questions?"

"You mentioned," Frances said, almost to herself, "that Imogen had almost remembered something today. Do you know what triggered that? Or why she has amnesia?"

"And where, exactly, were you today?" Shivani piped up, still not making eye contact. "Because there are a few details that I have, Maeve, that you seem to have conveniently left out."

Maeve winced; she had hoped maybe Shivani would stop being angry once she told the truth. Or most of it, anyway. "Where did you get that note? What does it say?"

"Someone mailed it to Mother Superior," Shivani said, finally turning to look at Maeve. "And I was handling the sorting. For which you are Mother-damned lucky, Maeve." She clicked her tongue. "See, is honesty so hard? Now, Imogen—" and Imogen looked up from plucking at her sleeve— "what's your surname? What did you do before you died?"

Imogen looked at Maeve, and Maeve sighed. She could lie, say Grave, but this wasn't Shivani asking. She was fact-checking. "Madrigal," she admitted on Imogen's behalf. "Imogen was...a poet."

Thalia raised an eyebrow, and Frances looked at Shivani.

"Where were you tonight?" Shivani repeated.

"We...have been following a few leads," Maeve explained, staring at the floor. "The first was someone at the Academy—you know that scientist with the curly hair, Shivani?"

"Yes."

"She and Imogen...had bad blood. Um, and then we went to investigate other poets—mainly Orion Cantor, who was Imogen's teacher." She swallowed. "We went to the library to study up on him and on Marlene Warwick, who she also suspects, but we also...listened to one of her old poems. And she remembered one of her performances, on the night she died."

She looked up at Shivani, but she was studying the note, ignoring her. She looked back down to Thalia and Frances. "So, you're a poet—do you do seances and all that?" Thalia asked, sounding more curious than malicious. Imogen shook her head, then looked at Maeve and pulled her telegraph out of the mound of discarded clothes.

Maeve pulled out hers, explaining as she handed it to Thalia. "She can't speak, really. Without coughing or having to whisper."

But I'm getting pretty quick at this. No, I don't do seances—ghosts should be left to rest, and certainly not hauled up as a party trick. Imogen winced theatrically as Maeve and Thalia read the message. *I was a cemetery keeper when I was young. I'm...well, I'd like to think I'm on your side.*

"Where'd you get those little toys?" Shivani put in, looking at the telegraph with antipathy.

Imogen raised her chin and tapped a message. *What I do with my money is none of your business, darling. Made it easier for me to talk to Maeve.*

Thalia read it aloud as it arrived, looking rather interested. Maeve found a small spark of relief at that—Thalia, same as always, interested in the news and the new.

Shivani bristled. "My name is Shivani," she snapped, "and you'll call me that or nothing at all, thank you very much."

As you wish! Imogen tapped and turned pointedly away. Maeve glanced back and forth between the two of them, unsure of what this dynamic between them was or what she should do to defuse it, but before she could Frances spoke up.

"So, reliving old experiences helped you remember...do you think automatic writing could help?" She drummed her fingers on her knee. "I'm certain it isn't harmful to spirits, and I've used it to help them remember what it's like to be alive—to articulate things they can't communicate on their own."

Imogen cocked her head. *I don't know what that is, but I'm willing to try it.* She ran a hand over her face and through her bangs. *Willing to try most things.*

"Well, let's give that a shot," Frances said thoughtfully, "in the morning, maybe." She glanced at Maeve. "You two need some rest first."

"I'm fine," Maeve promised, pushing her spare glasses up the bridge of her nose. Ugh—she'd forgotten they slipped down at the slightest provocation. "Let's do what you want to do. This was supposed to be your day. And it's still early."

"Well, I want you to take care of yourself," Frances said dryly, then cracked a small smile. "But I have some knitting to get to—courtesy of Shivani—so I *suppose* if you refuse to go to bed, you can all come keep me company."

"I'll get some tea," Thalia put forward, getting to her feet eagerly. "Do you like chamomile, Imogen?"

Oh! Imogen blinked a bit and glanced sideways at Maeve. Maeve prayed she wasn't about to complain about Lenorum Public again, but she seemed to be playing it polite. *I don't want to intrude.* She glanced around for a few seconds before busying herself with the telegraph. *I'll just rest here for a little while. If that's okay. Stay out of the way.*

"You wouldn't be intruding," Frances said gently, and Thalia nodded agreement. Shivani, Maeve noticed, rolled her eyes. "But if you want to rest, absolutely." She got to her feet as well and headed for the door. "You wanted to come, Maeve?"

"Yes," Maeve said hastily, and after giving Imogen an awkward thumbs-up, followed Frances out into the hall.

Shivani followed a moment later. "I have a headache," she announced, and squeezed Frances' arm. "I'll come through later if you're all still there. Happy nameday." She turned on her heel and disappeared into her room without a glance back.

The three of them stood in silence for a moment, until Frances folded her hands and turned to Maeve.

"Well," she said. "I'm sure she'll...get over whatever's bothering her. Your friend seems perfectly nice." She bit her lip, wavering. "Tea? Were we getting tea?"

"Yes!" Thalia said, hastily taking up the mantle of maintaining their spirits. She pointed at Frances. "You relax, nameday girl.

We'll be right back!" And so saying, she dragged Maeve down the hall and down the stairs toward the kitchen.

"Thalia, I...I appreciate you being so okay with all this," Maeve managed as she stumbled along in the taller woman's wake.

"Oh, of course!" Thalia said, then thought better of full volume speech, and leaned in conspiratorially. "I don't mind poets, necessarily. I don't believe in that whole 'words have power' thing, and if there's one thing that history teaches us, it's that nuance is critical. Or we'll wind up like Lord Benjamin Darcy."

"Oh, right—Lord Benjamin Darcy," Maeve said, trying to sound like she knew who that was.

Thalia scoffed. "Mother, you people need to read the news. He was this old conservative noble who got a seat on the City Council and tried to abolish name-choosing. Said that blood lines were the *only* way to determine family. Whose disowned son came forward and reclaimed his name and took half his estate away? That Benjamin Darcy?"

"Oh," Maeve said, dimly recalling the event. "Funny mustache?"

Thalia grumbled, then assented. "It's really the case law that's important, but sure. Funny mustache." She pushed open the door to the kitchen, then paused in the doorway. "So, you actually met Orion Cantor?"

"Yeah," Maeve said, surprised. "Why do you ask?"

"Oh, no reason, just curious." Thalia took a few more steps forward, then paused again, and looked over her shoulder. "What was he like?"

Maeve looked for words, couldn't find anything besides rude ones. "Unusual," she said at last, very carefully. "He called me 'darling' a lot and pulled a knife on me."

"Wow." Thalia took the kettle down from the cupboard, started filling it. "He seems very glamorous in the papers," she said in a measured tone.

Maeve's mouth fell open behind Thalia's back, and she fought back an insane grin. She closed her mouth with effort, considered for a moment, and then hopped up on the counter beside the sink.

"Did I mention," she said, studying her nails, "that he introduced himself to us entirely naked?"

Thalia dropped the kettle into the sink. "He did not," she said, in a strangled tone.

A hysterical laugh burst out of Maeve, followed by tears, and soon she was holding Thalia tight in a hug.

"I don't know why *you're* crying," Thalia said indignantly. "You got to— oh, you can't say a word about this to Frances; she'll laugh at me! You're laughing at me! Quit crying on me, you—you— you—ugh!"

But she held Maeve back, her arms wrapped tight around her as she swore Maeve to secrecy, and that was the statement that really mattered.

Chapter XI

"*Okay,*" *Frances said, her eyes shut.* "*Just try* to relax."

Imogen looked the very opposite of relaxed, sitting on Maeve's floor once more. She had been curled up in the corner without a blanket when Maeve had reentered that night and had lain unmoving until about eleven in the morning, at which stage she had thrashed violently to her feet and startled Maeve out of her skin. She seemed to remember where she was after a few seconds, however, and folded her arms behind her back in slight embarrassment.

Morning.

"Nearly afternoon, more like."

Shivani had not yet made a reappearance, and no one felt quite brave enough to enter the chapel while the organ was thundering so furiously. Maeve could hear intricate passages issuing down the hall even now, played with precision. She was distracting herself.

Alright, Imogen typed, and took Frances' offered hand. She looked at Maeve warily, then shut her eyes as well, and lowered her shoulders by a fraction of an inch.

For a moment, the room was silent except for the muffled music. Thalia, keeping watch by the door, turned to look at the object of interest—Frances' hand, holding a pen and hovering over the page of a notebook. Would it take? Frances had told Maeve before that it was a difficult thing to coax a spirit to write, and harder still to get them to make sense. And Imogen was an unusual case— Frances' methods might not work.

She nearly missed it when Frances' hand twitched, the pen brushing over the paper unevenly. Maeve propped it up hurriedly and turned the page as her wrist began to move.

Solitary stalks the shadow hiding from the moon's bright eye / Lies 'neath sleepers, shrouds itself from pitiless open voids of sky.

Maeve dimly recognized that—it was a snippet of one of the poems Imogen had given her to read. "Imogen?" she asked carefully. "That you?"

No clear response in the writing or from the woman herself. Frances and Imogen's hands were clasped together loosely now, the smooth sweep of Frances' hand the only motion between the two of them.

"Ask them the questions you want to know anyway," Thalia advised from her position. "It filters through most of the time."

"What…happened, Imogen, the day you died?" Maeve asked firmly, glancing back at Thalia who gave a thumbs-up. "You woke up hungover, and it was raining…."

Rain represents a baptism they say / Which sins are mine to keep / When I run from my door to yours?

Maeve frowned. "Is it all usually as inscrutable as this?"

Thalia came over to look, and Maeve moved to the door to keep them covered. "This isn't too bad, really." She looked up. "Frances told it to me like this—when you speak, you choose which words you're going to use and you communicate in a way that makes sense to everyone listening. It's filtered. But automatic writing is supposed to just be the way that the person's mind processes their thoughts, no filter. Sometimes we get people who think in short little snippets, or even in pictures. Looks like Imogen thinks… well, in poetry."

"Huh," Maeve murmured, glancing back. It seemed awfully torturous to her, but she supposed, to Imogen, command of language was like her own command of a pencil. Muscle memory.

"You said you remembered a party, the night you died," Thalia said. "Where was that?"

Brick and book. Champagne in hand. A dalliance for the peacock's flock, a place to pretend to be something one is not.

Brick and book….

"The Academy," Maeve said. "She mentioned that before."

Thalia snapped her fingers. "The Academy Masquerade Ball!" She looked back at Maeve. "To be something someone is not, right?"

"I'll take your word for it—what's the Masquerade?"

"Big annual party at the end of the fall term—used to be a thing the students did, but it started picking up politicians and poets and now everyone who's anyone goes. The Academy's grand library is the only place big enough to fit all the guests."

"Anyone who's anyone." Maeve looked at Imogen thoughtfully. "Was Lady Marlene there?"

The ice queen. Yes.

"How about Orion?"

Green with absinthe, green with envy. No.

Maeve considered for a moment. "That squares with what Orion said." She crossed to her desk and flipped back in her sketchbook. "He said they were voting on her induction that night, and then he was with someone else."

"Any of them could have sent someone else," Thalia pointed out. "Everyone she's mentioned is rich."

No, Frances scrawled, and underlined it. *By their own hand. By their own hand. By their own hand.*

"Whose hand?" Maeve demanded. But they couldn't get anything clearer than that—the pen pressed into the page so hard it tore, and with a gasp Imogen lurched back.

Frances blinked her eyes open, grimacing, and looked around vaguely for a moment before Thalia took up a glass of water and gave it to her. She sipped at it, swallowed painfully, and then nodded a bit.

"I'm...very sorry, Imogen."

Imogen looked unsure of how to respond; she was pressed back against the side of the bed, her fists clenched tight. She reached into her pocket and withdrew a handkerchief, blotting at her throat carefully, then reached for her telegraph. Maeve glanced at it, then passed it over to Frances.

For what?

Frances rubbed her forehead for a moment and took another sip of her water. "For what happened to you. I can't quite see what it was—neither of us can—but I think your mind is blocking it from your spirit, for your own sake. The shape of it is...painful."

Imogen frowned at that, then glanced at Maeve. *I've still got to figure out what happened, don't I? Got to know who's trying to kill me so they won't manage it next time.*

Frances and Thalia glanced at each other; Maeve could tell they were having the same worries that she had had about where Imogen's spirit ought to be.

"Well, whatever you do, be careful," Frances said gently. "A lot of spirits have a lot of energy built up around their unfinished business, but yours has trauma, too. Which I suppose makes sense, but…anyway." She sipped at the water again and trailed off.

Imogen looked frustrated, and snatched up the notebook, reading it over. A few times she raised her eyebrows and opened her own notebook to copy something over. At length, she dropped it, looked around, and settled on Maeve.

By their own hand, huh?

"Camille or Lady Marlene or Orion," Maeve agreed, grimly.

But not some minion. It was personal.

"Mmm."

Imogen flexed her fingers a few times, glanced down at the notebook again, and sighed. *I've intruded long enough. We need to regroup and figure out what to do next. Or I do, anyway, and you need some time to…*She looked up at Thalia and Frances. *Attend to your own things. Your duties and your life and all that.* She stood and clasped her hands behind her back. *Read this to them. Thank you very much for your hospitality, and I'm sorry for making Maeve miss her obligations. Your kindness will not go unrewarded; I plan to help the Sisterhood as much as I can once I resolve this business. I hope I haven't offended your other friend irreparably—apologize to her on my behalf.*

Maeve read it aloud incredulously—she thought they'd progressed a little beyond the businesslike formality—and was surprised when Imogen turned and headed for the window.

"Hey!"

Imogen turned back. *What?*

"You can't leave!" Maeve got to her feet and squared herself in front of the window. "You don't know whether that man's gone—if you go back alone who knows what he could do?"

I'll be fine—I survived that harpoon. She pulled up her sweater to reveal her stomach, smooth and unblemished. A smirk twitched at the corner of her mouth. *Not the worst side effect of being half-dead.*

Maeve crossed her arms. "You don't know if that's reliable! What if it only works as often as the telegraph thing does?"

Well, if it's an instinct, then won't my body just kick in and do it?

"Not necessarily!"

Really, Maeve, I'll be fine—

"No. You need a better plan." Maeve glanced back, then raised her chin. "Or else."

Or else what?

"Or else I'll convince you that you need a better one." Imogen still looked stubborn, so Maeve folded her hands innocently. "Frances?"

Frances looked uncomfortable to have been called on. "What?"

"Worry her."

Frances blinked a bit, and Imogen stifled a laugh.

"Well, maybe you should listen to her," Frances said after a moment. "Because the harpoon man might still be there, and even if he can't kill you with harpoons, he could trap you, and bring you somewhere you couldn't contact us from—or, or, ghosts are hurt by iron and salt, so he could throw you in the harbor, or—" her eyes went wide— "he could cut you up into little pieces and salt those, and keep you from healing, or he might try to exorcise you and that might kill you!" She drummed her fingers on the floor. "Really, Imogen, if you lose your body, we can't help you and we don't know how this works and you should be being more careful all the time and the next harpoon might hit you in the head and make you lose more memories or—or—or—"

Maeve watched with a private grin as the smirk slipped from Imogen's face and she slowly began to fidget with the hem of her sweater. *Okay, okay, okay,* she messaged, wheeling to face Maeve. *Fine. I have another plan.* She tapped her foot for a few seconds, her face working as though she was having an argument with herself, and then finally sighed and nodded. *Can I use your phone?*

Maeve nodded primly and helped Thalia and Frances to their feet. "Thanks," she whispered to Frances.

Frances gave her a grim smile. "That's the first time that's ever been good for anything."

The four of them snuck down to the kitchen phone in tight formation and took the receiver into the pantry. The shelves were rather empty, Maeve noted as she took a seat on a barrel. Hopefully that just meant it was shopping day. That wasn't her responsibility this week, was it? Imogen spun the dial with some violence, and her gaze flicked back and forth as it rang. It was quiet enough in here that all of them could hear the dial tone. Finally, there was a click, and a posh voice issued from the speaker.

"Hello-o?" Imogen opened her mouth, then blinked, and mouthed a curse. "Hello? Anyone there?"

Maeve hastily took the receiver from her and put it to her own ear. "Hi, this is Imogen Madrigal—I'm speaking for her. To whom do I owe the pleasure?"

"Oh, is that our lovely mystery Maeve?" The voice sounded like its owner had just heard a juicy secret. "Orion Cantor speaking. What does Imogen need?"

Imogen, leaning over to listen, shook her hands in frustration and fished her telegraph out of her pocket.

I need a place to stay. Tell him I trust him. Provisionally.

Maeve raised her eyebrows and relayed the message.

"We, er, came under some fire last night, Mr. Cantor. I don't think it's safe for her to go back to her...current residence."

"Well, Mother's grave, of course not. And Mr. Cantor ought to be a preacher's name—Orion, please, darling." She could practically hear the blindingly white grin over the phone. "I can be anywhere on the island to pick the two of you up in about ten minutes. Yes, yes, you as well, Ms. Mystery. Where shall I direct my driver?"

Maeve winced, and hurriedly tried to ask the others where they should meet him.

"Just here," Frances whispered. "We'll make sure no one sees you go, and anyway it's safer than you going somewhere else. He can't hurt you because we know where you're going."

"I'm not going!" Maeve protested. She wasn't—she still had to patch things up with Shivani.

As if in response to that thought, Frances and Thalia glanced at each other. "We think," Frances said carefully, "that we can get Shivani to come around on her own, and then put the two of you back together. At least we can try to figure out what has her so upset."

"So, you're banishing me?" Maeve asked, incredulous. She could hear Orion saying something. She ignored it.

148

"Not banishing you!" Thalia said quickly. "Just…encouraging you to get some air, for the afternoon! And some allies!" She gave a smile and shrugged. "Maybe they can offer you some protection that we can't!"

Maeve glanced at Imogen with a frown, who bit her lip and tilted her hand back and forth. Maeve groaned and picked the phone back up. Only for Shivani's sake.

"Convent of the Sisterhood of Good Death. And don't try anything—our friends know where we're going."

"*Really.*" That overlapped her last sentence, like he had only listened to the first. "Of course, darling—safety first. See you two soon!"

The line went dead before Maeve could tell him to exercise discretion; she had a bad feeling that it was a necessary thing for her to mention.

The next ten minutes were rushed—Frances ran back upstairs as Thalia scouted a safe path for Imogen to exit by, and Maeve followed along, listening as the sound of the organ covered their footsteps. She'd be back, and she'd patch it up. She'd just go for the afternoon to see Imogen settled, and then she'd come back to her duties.

"Come back when it's safe," Frances said in a rush, catching them just before they went through the front door, and holding a mass of knitted fabric out to Imogen. Imogen looked at it hard, and Frances straightened her coif. "For you. Any friend of Maeve's is a friend of ours. Even if you are a…" She glanced around, then winked, and pressed the object into Imogen's hands. She and Thalia waved them on, and after mouthing a heartfelt "thank you", Maeve pushed the door open.

Under the arch of the convent's main entrance, they found that they were just a hair too late. Two figures waited for them there— one, the short figure of a little sister; the other, Orion Cantor in what appeared to be an atrocious attempt at being incognito. A bottle-green wool coat with a full skirt that went down to the tips of snakeskin boots; Maeve made a quiet prayer that no one was looking out the window. He was crouched with his fingers laced under his chin.

"Interesting. So would you say you see the Hallowed Mother as a supplementary parent? The Mother, if you will, that you never had?"

"Why are you wearing sunglasses if it's cloudy outside?"

Orion took off his glasses—gold framed, with tiny gold snakes curling over the top of green lenses—and tilted them back and forth. "They went with the scarf. I only had a few minutes to throw together this outfit, sweetheart. Ah!" He straightened, tugged his scarf a little closer over his hair—over his damned laurels, which he was still wearing for some reason, Maeve noticed with a stab of frustration—and gave a winning smile. "Our Ladies of Good Death!"

Maeve pursed her lips, and looked up at Imogen, who looked similarly full of regret. "Sisters," the little sister—it was Amal—corrected. "Who's this, Maeve?"

"A friend," Maeve explained, urging Imogen forward and trying to box Orion Cantor out of Amal's line of sight. She made a point to tread on his toe; he sucked a breath in through his teeth. "She came to visit and now she's going back to her house."

Amal frowned. "Why's she wearing Thalia's sweater?"

Maeve looked at Imogen in consternation, then back to Amal. "Her clothes got soaked in the rain."

She nodded. "Is she a poet, too, like this guy?"

Orion's face fell; Imogen smacked her forehead, and Maeve fought to maintain a neutral expression.

"No, she's a cemetery keeper. This is just—"

"I'll give you the sunglasses if you swear to tell no one we were here," Orion interrupted, and held the glasses down surreptitiously.

Amal frowned at him for a moment, glanced at Maeve, then shrugged and took them. "Sure. See you later—or for the first time, I guess..." She put the glasses on and slipped back through the door. Maeve wasn't entirely sure, but she thought she may have heard her mutter, "weirdo," as she disappeared back inside.

Well, having that particular pair of glasses kicking around the convent was a problem for her to solve later; for now, Orion was speaking entirely too loudly as he ushered Imogen toward a long black coupe. The back door was open, and Maeve could see plush red velvet within, like the lining of a coffin. Great.

"I'll have something else for you to wear when you get back—Maeve, sweetheart, you may wish to change as well for the sake of blending in, not that those habits aren't a lovely look, of course, perfectly macabre with all the black—Hargreaves, back to the Court, thank you—" Maeve had hardly sat in the back of the car before it had pulled away from the curb, and Orion shut the door as they pulled into the street. The front seat faced the back, and Maeve and Imogen found themselves shoulder to shoulder, avoiding Orion's legs as he stretched them out. "And Mother, wouldn't you know it, but we're having a bacchanal tonight! I don't know if you can go, Imogen, but *Maeve!* Darling!" He said her name in a way that made her feel like she was about to get in trouble. "You simply must—we've got Feyfolk Absinthe sponsoring, and dear Estelle will be there—I'm sure the two of you will hit it off! You know, I never would have known you were a nun, but I'm sure you'll find our seances—"

Imogen kicked him in the shin.

He looked like his feelings were hurt. "Imogen, I go to all the trouble of rescuing you from the crypt myself, and this is how you repay me? More bodily injury?" He looked down his nose as Imogen shoved her telegraph under it. "'*Maeve is not going to a bacchanal?*' I should think Maeve gets to decide that! Might be good for her to spend some time with the living...."

"I'm only staying to get Imogen settled," Maeve said firmly. She didn't quite know what a bacchanal was, but Imogen's reaction and the linguistic roots did nothing to attract her to the concept.

"Suit yourself, Sister," Orion said smoothly, and produced a small notebook and fountain pen from his pocket. Maeve snuck a glance at Imogen while he was occupied with scribbling notes of some sort; she was looking out the window, her knee bouncing. It stilled as Maeve watched, and Imogen looked back at her. Her expression was hard to read—some combination of relief and anxiety. Maeve didn't dare ask her what was wrong with Orion there, and anyway she didn't quite have time. It seemed like no sooner had they gotten into the car than they had pulled up to a side door of the Court, and a moment after that, the door was opened. The three of them stepped out of their velvet compartment, and Maeve made sure to mouth a "thank you" to the uniformed chauffeur. He nodded near imperceptibly.

The door opened before Orion even had to reach for the door-knob, and as Maeve followed him and Imogen inside, she found another uniformed servant just inside the door, shutting it carefully and moving to catch Orion's coat as he passed it off.

"Clothilde, darling. Have I got anything this morning?"

"No sir," the servant—Clothilde—said. Her eyes skimmed with studied disinterest over Maeve and Imogen. "Your next appointment is at three, followed by the party."

"Perfect." He rubbed his hands together and turned back to Imogen. "Give me a list of what you need, and we'll get you moved out of whatever place you've holed up in. Hargreaves and Clothilde can go collect your things." Imogen hesitated, then withdrew her notebook and began writing, and Orion turned back to Clothilde. "After that, take the afternoon off, my treat."

Clothilde nodded—a slight wince in her expression led Maeve to believe that getting the afternoon off implied something messy happening while she was gone—and after placing Orion's coat in a closet by the door and giving Maeve one more surreptitious once-over, slipped out the door.

Maeve's telegraph beeped.

"She's new," she read.

"Oh, yes, Imogen—that was Imogen?" Orion smiled over his shoulder. "Clothilde's the picture of discretion. The last man was far too...shall we say, judgmental?"

"Plenty to judge about you." Orion frowned, glancing between them. "That was her," Maeve clarified.

"Well," he said, apparently choosing to ignore her. "Maeve—should I call you Sister Maeve?—welcome to my apartment. Imogen, welcome back. Which bedroom would you like?"

Whichever one has had the fewest orgies in it. WAIT, DON'T SAY THAT OUT LOUD. Tell him the Sky Room, if it's free. Maeve managed to catch her tongue before she read the first message aloud and read the third fighting a horrified laugh. Orion didn't seem to notice anything wrong.

"Oh, of course. Excellent choice. Maeve, dear, would you like to pick? I've got—hmm—the Mosaic Room, the Flower Room—"

"I'm not staying," Maeve said, trying not to sound exasperated. "I'm leaving as soon as—" As soon as what? Thalia called her to tell her that things were all patched up? As soon as she knew the man with the harpoon wasn't going to find her?

"Well, you can at least take a tour," Orion said, waving a hand, and straightened his peacock-blue cravat. He winked. "To get your good friend settled and make sure she's in good hands?"

Maeve sighed, but she supposed that was what she was here for. She followed Imogen and Orion out of the entryway and into an airy apartment. There was a parlor with two very tall bookshelves and some plush-looking lounges, a kitchen with a bowl of oranges on the counter, and a staircase leading up to further reaches. The walls were papered in mint green and hung with hazy, near-luminous oil paintings, and as she stepped into the space, she nearly tripped over a bedraggled-looking grey cat that meowed unevenly at her. Oh—that was unexpected. She'd known a number of ship's cats in her day, and this looked like one, or at the very least a stray. A little out of place, like her.

"I'll make tea," Orion announced, sweeping a brown paper bag off the counter, and handing it to Imogen, "once we've got you unpacked. Maeve, you'll stay for tea, at least?" He led them up the stairs and onto the next floor, which contained another parlor stuffed with books and a few closed doors. They weren't stopping there, though; they crossed the landing to a spiral staircase, and took that up to the very last landing, with only two doors. "Sky Room as promised; orange peel tea sound good? Excellent. Ta!" He wiggled his fingers, and disappeared down the stairs, leaving a cloud of patchouli-heavy cologne behind that shouted more than hinted its wearer had been there. Maeve sneezed.

Imogen peeked into the brown paper bag, sighed, and beckoned Maeve in through one of the doors. It was bright in here, much brighter than Maeve would have expected, and she had to blink a bit to bring her eyes to equilibrium. But oh, it was clear why it was called the Sky Room. The walls and ceiling were painted in a blushing pink in one corner, a deep blue in the other, and between them the colors commingled and brightened into clouds, stars, whirls of night wind. A round skylight glowed white with daylight, and the rest of the windows were curtained in gauzy periwinkle. Maeve stood for a bit to look at it all and take it in; Imogen hardly hesitated before kicking off her shoes and standing on the bed, wrenching at what seemed to be a mirror attached to the ceiling. She got it down with some effort, made a face of disgust, and shoved it under the bed. Maeve, for her part, sat, and ran her hand over the bedspread—a soft flannel lilac. Imogen sat down too after a moment and pulled out her telegraph.

I'll give you three guesses as to what he's put in this bag.

"A bottle of wine," Maeve put forward, her stress beginning to lessen. Imogen would be comfortable here, for certain. Having this beautiful room all to herself...oh, yes, she would be okay. "Hmm...a book of his own poetry, and a lingerie set."

Imogen faked gagging. *Mother bless the man, at least he has boundaries when it comes to his students. It's worse.* She opened the bag and laid out in short order a loose white shirt, a tailored waistcoat, a pair of damask trousers, and a silk cravat—essentially, the exact same outfit Orion was already wearing. *Here at the Poet's Court, we value each artist's individuality! Unless you're Orion's understudy.*

Maeve laughed. "Better than him wanting to murder you! Which he still may have done!"

True. Imogen blew her bangs out of her eyes, and sat back down beside Maeve, unfolding the knitted object that Frances had given her. It turned out to be a cowl, grey and knobbly and deep enough to hide one's face within. Imogen pulled it over her head, tested the hood out a few times, and then pulled it down to look at Maeve. *No, I...I almost feel like...well, no proof. But I feel like maybe...maybe he's telling the truth, with that bit about my voice. I've never seen him make a face like that. And it would be nice to...*She stroked the cowl absently. *You have good friends.*

"I do," Maeve said simply.

I should probably change so you can bring Thalia her sweater back. And I'll ask Clothilde to get your stuff from the mausoleum. She surveyed the outfit laid out on the bed beside her with resignation. *Let me squeeze myself into these pants.*

Maeve headed out to the landing to give Imogen her privacy and peeked into the other door—a bathroom tiled in dark blue, with fluffy towels and a gilt-framed mirror. She sat down on the top step, gazing down at her old beat-up boots. How much of this was Orion's, and how much of it was attached to his office? The sum of Maeve's personal possessions could fit in a suitcase; the rest of it was interchangeable with any other sister's things. Spirit board, prayerbook, linens and habits and dishes. She'd be buried with her hourglass pendant, but the rest would be given to a new sister. She heard a ragged meow, and the cat poked its head up the stairs. Her mind floated back to her bunk on the *Fletcher* as she clicked her tongue to lure it closer. She'd had a single small trunk there, too, stuffed under a hammock. Always ready to turn over her space—never permanently entrenched except when she was at home with Tia. Home—it was a word she now only prefaced with "haunted," since the only time she spent in real homes was to cleanse them. She was as transient as the ghosts themselves, in a way.

Something nudged her shoulder, and she jumped—the toe of Imogen's boot.

Well, teatime?

Truth be told, her outfit didn't look too far off her usual sartorial choices, but she was standing with such annoyance in her body language that Maeve gave her a sympathetic wince. "You look… nice?"

Imogen rolled her shoulders awkwardly, causing her cut throat to gape, and at Maeve's actual wince she held a hand to it.

Oh. Right. Didn't wear the ribbon yesterday. She turned back, then sighed. *Don't want to bleed on that nice cowl. I'll try not to move too much.*

"Don't worry," Maeve said, and stood, giving the cat a final scratch. "Maybe it'll actually sober Orion up."

Imogen canted her head. *That's true. He doesn't know I'm dead.*

A mischievous grin found its way to Maeve's lips despite her bad mood. This could be entertaining.

"Well, let's go break the bad news."

Chapter

XII

"What," Orion said pleasantly, *setting his teacup* down with some violence, "the fuck did you just say?"

He stood abruptly when Imogen made a demonstration of her slit throat, and looked at Maeve, fear plain in his face.

"That's not my fault. She came to those seances of her own volition, and anyway we were all too far gone to get anything to show—"

"We never said it was your fault," Maeve said dryly. Just thought it. "But now you know what the stakes of this are. So, you've got to cover for her. She's got strengths this way, but she's got weaknesses, too."

Orion looked back at Imogen, who just barely managed to cover her smirk. Curiosity stole into his eyes.

"Like what?"

Imogen rolled her eyes, then stretched her hand out over her telegraph. Orion dodged back behind his chair, a move he tried to pass off as pushing it back in. Maeve's telegraph chimed on the other side of the table, and she read the message out.

"This, for one."

Orion snatched the telegraph out of Maeve's hand, then swept over to the hall closet and returned with another telegraph. "Message mine," he demanded. "Oh-oh-four-six."

Imogen shut her eyes, her eyebrows twitching together, and after a pregnant pause a ping came from his. Orion's eyes roved over it, then narrowed. "Bold words to the person holding your laurels, Imogen. You've gotten disrespectful since you…died." He handed Maeve back her telegraph, looking troubled for just a moment. Imogen put on an expression of mock-penitence.

"Got nothing to lose," Maeve read from her screen. "And dying's scarier than you are."

Orion glowered at Imogen from under his eyebrows, and Maeve privately disagreed with Imogen's sentiment. Dying was predictable; the Laureate was not.

"Are you sure about that?" he said, honey and venom in his voice.

"Deepest apologies, Young Lord Warwick." Imogen cocked her head insolently and bared her teeth in a smile.

Orion's lip curled, and his eyebrows rose back to their usual position. "I fold—you're playing dirty." He shook himself, as if shrugging off some unpleasant thought. "Anything else?" He looked at Maeve as though he had just recalled she was there. "Rather lucky you found a death nun, hmm?"

She found me. Imogen flipped a toggle to send the messages to both of them. *And she's a Sister of Good Death. They need more name recognition, Orion, so say it properly.*

"Invested?"

In line with my politics. They spoke back and forth so snappily that Maeve was having a tricky time parsing everything, but she caught that with a bit of a wince. Very cold of Imogen. *Anyway, I heal quickly. The room gets colder around me. Allergic to salt. Iron. Takes a lot more to get drunk.*

"We'll test that," he said, almost to himself, and turned to Maeve. "But that's not all ghosts can do. I've seen it. They can make things float and possess mediums and make ectoplasm. Could she do that with training?"

"Training?" Maeve echoed. The idea had never crossed her mind. "Ideally, we…I don't know, heal her somehow."

"Not necessarily!" Orion argued, and snatched the butter knife up from the plate of scones in the center of the table. "Stab, stab, I'm the Wraith, don't mess with me, but—" he wound up, and whipped the knife across the apartment, where it hit a wall and fell with a clatter, startling the grey cat off the sofa— "if she can float knives at her enemies, it'll *really* scare them. Fear's half the battle.

And not to brag—" he coughed, "but I'm rather good at it, myself. Which is why I've only had two assassination attempts this term."

"Only?" Maeve said disbelievingly.

"Down from six my last term." Orion smiled easily and rocked back on the back legs of his chair. "Granted, it's early still, but they're getting more half-hearted, too. Imogen—can't tell you all my secrets, but I will tell you to invest in this poison-detecting nail lacquer I found, if people are going to be trying to kill you."

Good to know. Imogen drummed her fingers on the table. *You might have something here—I'd been considering it a bit of curse.* She went silent.

Orion glanced at Maeve, a bit of a smirk on his face.

"Now watch her go," he mouthed.

Maeve wasn't sure how to respond, so she looked back at Imogen, who shook herself out of a reverie and picked her telegraph back up.

Anyway. You ever know anyone to hire a harpooneer as an assassin?

"No. Downright folksy." Orion stroked his chin. "I can put out feelers, though, if you'll let me."

Imogen glanced at Maeve, then nodded. *May as well. We're drawing too much attention doing all the investigating ourselves.*

"Ugh. Legwork. I hear you." He sipped at his tea, and glanced around the kitchen, before settling his gaze back on Maeve. "I've never had the pleasure of meeting a Sister of Good Death before."

For obvious reasons.

Orion ignored Imogen's message. "I've received a lot of strong letters from your people on the subject of seances—do those views go all the way down the chain?"

"Yes," Maeve said coolly. "Summoning is traumatic to the spirit. Imogen agrees."

"Imogen hasn't been summoned, though. I wonder if we could—"

"We will not be summoning Imogen—I'm the spiritual expert here and I say it would be bad for her health—"

Imogen is right here and would prefer not to be talked about in the third person. She raised an eyebrow at Orion. *I was against it when I was alive, and I really wouldn't like to go through it now. And Maeve's an expert, like she said—you ought to at least hear both sides of the story and not just Estelle's.*

"I'm listening," Orion admonished. "And anyway, I'm getting a bit bored with Estelle. Her poetry's just a vehicle for her ego." He inspected his reflection in the back of his teaspoon, and Maeve swallowed her arguments. She got the feeling that any impassioned defense might make him contrary.

After a moment he set the teaspoon down, and looked at Maeve again. "You have a good eye for art. I didn't expect that." She frowned, and he waved airily. "You've been looking around. I keep an eye on new people, and you keep looking at all the best things in here. And my cat."

"We…study a lot, at the convent," Maeve said slowly. "Lots of history, including art history." She managed a small smile. "Ghosts like to haunt paintings, actually. Ectoplasm's a nightmare for restorers—I've met a few."

"Hmm." Orion sipped his tea again. "Ever done anything yourself?"

"Pardon?"

"Any painting? Any art?" He ran his finger around the top of his teacup. "I imagine after all those stern letters to us you're not encouraged to take up poetry in your spare time." He glanced up, and fixed her with a pale blue stare, striking against his darker coloration. "But I've said before it takes all perspectives, and I cannot imagine what very interesting verse a Sister of Good Death could come up with."

Maeve kept her expression even. "Unfortunately," she said, "I am a bit too busy for that."

Orion shrugged. "Well, things ebb and flow. Maybe you won't be so busy in a little while. I imagine an ascetic's life is hard on someone who clearly has a taste for nice things." He held his teacup up to the light, where it cast a weak green shadow on his face—a fine translucence Maeve hadn't noticed before—and then downed its contents. "Imogen, I think I've figured out a way you can go to this party."

Imogen looked up from regarding her tea leaves sourly. Her expression shifted into guarded interest. *Oh?*

"Yes. We curl your hair, mess around a bit with some makeup, and call you my cousin from the next province. You don't speak the language, of course—but your translator or friend or girlfriend does." He looked back at Maeve, a hint of slyness in his manner.

"I retract my urging on the whole seance-with-Estelle thing—I can tell you're not arguing as much as you'd like to—but poets and nuns aren't inherently incompatible. You've got some maxim about a good life leading to a good death, don't you?" He held up a hand as if weighing the words. "And we believe in enjoying life to the fullest." He held up the other. "Sounds like maybe you even *ought* to come to this party."

"I appreciate the invitation," Maeve said firmly, "but I will have to go back once a few things are sorted out." She didn't want to keep Shivani waiting once she came around and was willing to talk, and anyway Orion's pitch sounded even more like a devil's bargain than her contract with Imogen. "I'll finish tea and then I would appreciate the use of your phone."

"Of course," Orion said with studied unconcern. "Imogen, are you in? I can play interpreter for you."

Imogen glanced at Maeve for a fraction of a second, then looked away. Yes. *I'd like a distraction, if you think it's safe.*

Orion grinned. "It's a *bacchanal*—if it was safe, I'd have to hand in my laurels and resign!"

You know what I mean. Imogen waved a dismissive hand. *You do what you want to do—I'll just lurk and write an explanatory note. I don't want to be the center of attention.*

"That's a change," Orion muttered coyly in Maeve's direction, and divided a scone in half. "Excellent. I'm going to take a nap, then. The phone's in the office, Maeve—through there." He pointed to a door beyond the staircase. "Dial two for Hargreaves when you want him to drive you back." He stood, wrapped the scone in a napkin, and clicked his tongue. "Pre-party naptime, Eliot." The grey cat emerged from wherever it had been hiding, and it followed Orion up the stairs and out of sight.

Maeve finished her tea—it was growing rather cold at this stage—and looked at Imogen. "I'm sure Thalia and Frances have gotten through to Shivani by now. She's got a little bit of a temper, but...."

Imogen said nothing, and after an awkward moment Maeve got to her feet and made her way to the closed door on the far side of the apartment. The office looked much like the rest of the rooms she'd seen—ornate, ringed by bookshelves, dominated by a writing desk in front of the window. Maeve allowed herself a peek at the papers on the desk. Orion's handwriting was surprisingly love-ly, and the brush pens arranged at the top of the writing surface showed signs of careful maintenance. She picked up the phone, and dialed the convent's number, mindful not to lean against any-thing.

"Hello, you've reached the Sisterhood of Good Death. This is Sister Priscilla—how may I help you?"

"Hi, Priscilla—it's Maeve," she said, hoping Priscilla wouldn't ask where she was calling from. "Could you get Thalia or Frances? I need to check in with them on something."

"Oh, give me a moment—Eleanor? Could you go find Frances and Thalia? I think they went into the chapel." Maeve winced—Priscilla was not familiar with the practice of covering the receiver while she shouted. "Eleanor's going, Maeve, dear. What's the sto-ry?"

"Shivani and I…" Maeve sighed, sick enough of lying for her whole life. "We, um, fought a little. I went for a walk. Frances and Thalia said they'd tell me when to come back so we could talk."

"Ah." Priscilla's voice sounded sage even over the phone. "That explains the toccatas."

"Yeah," Maeve said, closing her eyes.

"Here we go—best of luck, Maeve."

There was a bit of shuffling, and Thalia's voice came over the phone. "Maeve?"

"Hey, Thalia."

"Hey!" She spoke carefully; Priscilla must still be in the room. "How's…things on your end?"

Maeve glanced around. "Do you like old books?"

"Write down the titles," Thalia hissed, then raised her voice back to normal. "That's good, that's good. Good to get some air."

"Look," Maeve said, pinching the bridge of her nose. "Can I come back yet? Shivani's not still mad, is she? You get why I did it, right?"

"Of course," Thalia assured her, then hesitated. "Um, Priscilla, sorry, but can I talk to Maeve…thank you, yes, just a little sensi-tive, of course, sorry—" There was a pause, and Thalia got back on the line. "Make sure you write down the historical ones. I want to read what he's reading."

Maeve tapped her foot in frustration. "Are you deflecting?"

"No!" Thalia might be even worse at lying than Maeve was. "No, no, but I certainly get it, like I said—Imogen needs help. And you wanted to help us. You should've told the rest of us that the convent was in trouble…" Her voice went slightly reproachful.

"I panicked," Maeve said, swallowing back guilt. "But you're not answering my question. Is Shivani mad?"

She could hear Thalia swallow. "…yes. Just a little…well, kind of a lot, but, um…"

Maeve's stomach dropped and she clenched the fist that wasn't on the receiver. She was starting to get annoyed—it wasn't like she'd thrown out her vows or something. And who was Shivani, to be judging her?

"What, exactly, is she taking exception to?"

Thalia made an uneasy noise. "She won't really tell us—just keeps saying 'it's fine' and that—" She went silent.

"What?" Maeve pressed. "Tell me."

"She's…not in her right mind," Thalia demurred. "She wouldn't actually say it to you."

"But she sure is thinking it, huh." Maeve's eyes roved the bookshelves and lit on the stuffed shelf of anthologies bearing Orion's name. "Is it her grudge against poets?" Thalia's silence was telling. "Is it about Imogen? Because she's got no good reason to be mad at her for what happened to her, or about what she did in her life. She didn't like seances—she grew up like we did. She's a good person, Thalia, even if she isn't what we're used—"

"She said 'Maeve's going to throw her life away on that slut and ditch the rest of us to go paint worthless pictures, and won't we be sorry for caring about her then,'" Thalia said in a quiet rush. "I, um. I disagree."

Maeve sat in stunned silence, and Thalia spoke into it. "You're the most dedicated of all of us, and even if you did want to go paint pictures—they wouldn't be worthless." Her voice cracked. "And I would still care about you."

Maeve finally found her voice. "Then I," she said carefully, her throat suddenly sore from the effort of holding back tears, holding back rage, "think I will stay the night here. If Shivani truly thinks that she's better off without me, then I might as well give her a little time to get used to the idea."

Thalia was quiet for a moment.

"I wish you didn't have to," she said, finally. "And I'm sure we can, um, patch this up. Eventually. But I support you."

"Love you, Thalia."

"I love you, too, Maeve."

Maeve dropped the receiver, and it was only when the dial tone began to beep that she realized she had dropped it on the floor instead of back into the cradle. She picked it up and was about to replace it when a knock at the door startled her.

"Yeah?" she called out, a bit roughly.

Imogen opened the door, holding out her notebook.

Everything okay?

"Yes," Maeve said, and drew herself up to her full height. "Yes, Shivani's still mad, but I'm starting to think it's her problem and not mine."

Imogen blinked a little and added another line. *It's my fault. I'm sorry.*

"Don't be," Maeve said, and she meant it. She gazed at the paperweight on the corner of Orion's desk—a tiny brass whale. It was polished bright on top like someone had rubbed it for luck, over and over. "I'm my own person. Shivani's not my mother. I don't have to fit into the little box she's got in her head for me."

Imogen raised an eyebrow. *Dust that off and add a line break and it could be poetic.*

Maeve managed a smile, and picked up the little brass whale, inspecting it. "I've no quarrel with that," she told it, looking at its tiny wise eye. "Art is more important than some people give it credit for." She turned the whale over, weighed it in her hand, and finally looked up at Imogen. "Hang it. Let's go to this party of yours."

Imogen's other eyebrow rose to meet its partner. *It may be a bit of a shock to the system.*

"I'm not made of glass." Maeve put down the whale and raised her chin. "Let me take a look at the other side of the story."

Orion seemed very displeased to have been forced to his door in curlers, but once Maeve explained he perked up immediately, and dove for the phone.

"Let me think, let me think," he mused, pacing energetically around Maeve. "You're probably…Naomi's size. She's got some lovely clothes, too. Lives in one of the apartments—I'll call her."

Maeve forced herself not to wonder whether this was a good idea and waited by the door as Orion paced around inside.

"Naomi? Darling, it's been too long, too long! Yes, I'm excited for tonight, too—can't wait to see what you come up with! But listen, darling, I have a friend here—new to the scene, new to the scene—and wouldn't you know it, she hasn't got a thing to wear!" There was a moment's pause, and Orion struggled to interject. "Yes—well, the thing is—see, I was wondering—she's about your size. Did you have anything from last season?" He nodded a few times, held a finger up to beg Maeve's patience. "Very dark complexion, and…" He squinted at Maeve. "Long hair, I believe, and those tight-tight curls. She might need help with makeup, too, if you—yes, I know it's an ask, but she's new and I want—aren't these things supposed to be fun? Come on, a favor…" There was a bit of grumbling on the other end of the line, and Orion beamed. "Excellent. I'll send her over in a few. Owe you one, darling!"

From there, Maeve was urged by Orion through a back door and instructed to count eight doors down on the right past the circular reading nook. She quickly stuffed her veil in her pocket and her hourglass necklace down the front of her dress, but there wasn't much more than that she could do. She carefully counted her way down the pink-wallpapered hallway and knocked on what she hoped was the door in question.

"Are you Orion's new friend?" The woman who opened the door had high cheekbones and long, wavy hair, and already looked slightly exasperated. "He might have given me more than four hours' notice."

"I'm sorry," Maeve said earnestly. "I didn't know I would be here." Usually, posing someone an inconvenience like this would be enough to ward her off an idea completely.

Naomi's irritation faded with a roll of her eyes. "Not your problem—what was your name? Fool didn't even tell me—"

"Maeve."

"Maeve. Nice name. Alright, Maeve—" Naomi pulled back, and gestured for her to enter. "I don't know how to do hair like yours, and we've got four hours to develop you a whole costume!"

She threw up her hands in frustration, then settled into a wry smile. "But we'll do our best."

The theme, Naomi informed her as she led Maeve back to a dressing room with a gilt mirror and about a hundred dresses, was mythology.

"The Stars, the Muses, the Fairy Queen, that sort of thing," she explained absently as she pawed through the rack. "I'm doing the Huntress, so we'll do something opposite that for you. So, no one can accuse me of being a lazy stylist."

Her manner was very sharp, but she gave Maeve another smile as she held a slip of black silk up against her. "Oh, no, too much." She pulled it back, eyed Maeve's dress for a moment, and looked up. There was a glimmer of recognition in her eyes. "How do you know Orion, then?"

"Kind of a long story."

Naomi held her gaze for a moment, then shrugged. "Suppose we don't have time to hear it. Be careful, is all I'll say." She turned back to the rack, and Maeve forced down the pinpricks of doubt in her mind.

They went through a few more options, Naomi asking her about her clothing preferences and Maeve coming up with very few insights. Her education in the kind of mythology referenced in the theme was a little spotty, and her experience in formal wear was even weaker.

"I'm assuming you want something a little on the modest side, which cuts this down by a lot..." Naomi's hand brushed over the dresses as she considered, then darted out to seize a handful of candy-blue chiffon. "How about this?"

Several more people stopped by throughout the afternoon, offering hairdressing, accessories, and advice. Maeve found her acting ability sorely tested as their attentions turned her way.

"Oh, yes, I'm a translator—I work down by the shipping docks," she told the woman settling pearl-shaped hairpins into her hair. "One of the party guests needs my services, so here I am."

"How quaint! Love the ocean theme!"

"Do you get to travel much?"

"Who's this mystery guest?"

She got the impression that anyone new to the scene was a curiosity—Naomi shooed most of the visitors out by name, and

166

nearly all of them wore bronze laurels. Eventually, the two of them were alone once more, and Naomi pronounced her costume complete.

"Now I've got almost no time to do my own ornamentation," she complained. "Give me a little while and we'll go down together."

She disappeared back into the closet, and Maeve hopped down off the stool she had been perched on, getting used to the heels on her borrowed boots. The sun was going down, and a draft blew in from the far side of the room. She shivered a bit; hers and Naomi's definitions of modest differed slightly, and the open back of the dress was an adjustment as well. She looked out the window, drawing the white silk shawl she had been lent closer against the cold, and found a vertigo-inducing drop. She hadn't quite realized how close the Court backed up to the ocean; a cliff fell away to the sea below, and foam lashed the black backs of rocks in the dark. She backed up and paced back across the room, her stomach full of anticipation. She couldn't tell whether it was excitement or dread.

At last Naomi emerged, resplendent in a headdress of antlers and a long flowing jumpsuit. She disappeared into the bathroom, returning with her lips alarmingly green, and gave Maeve a smile.

"You look splendid, dear."

"You do, too!" She meant it, even if she was a little nervous that they were going to be out of place. Surely this was all a little decadent already?

The sun finally sank below the waves as the two of them departed from Naomi's apartment, and the moon peeked over the horizon.

"I'll stay with you till Orion comes down," Naomi told her, waiting patiently as Maeve picked her way down the stairs in her heeled boots. "Or whoever you're…translating for."

"Are we early?" Maeve asked, hiking the hem of her skirt up so she could actually see her feet.

"No, no. Orion likes to—well, you'll see." Naomi rolled her eyes, but Maeve thought it might be with a hint of fondness. "Make an entrance."

The first floor was already full of people milling around and chatting, but Naomi led them surely to what Maeve imagined would be called a ballroom. Its tall doors were propped open, and blue light poured from within. The crowd was denser here—costumed figures in dresses and robes and tight pants and tall heels. Laurels shone upon brows, and jewelry gleamed on fingers and at throats. She took a deep breath and looked up to the ceiling—frescoed cherubs dancing in and out of the shadows.

Naomi came to a stop, squinted through the crowd, and then positioned Maeve by her shoulders at a particular spot. "They'll come through there," she said, pointing a varnished fingernail at the door on the far side of the room. The corner of her mouth twitched up.

And a few moments later, as predicted, the door swung open, flying with a crack into the wall and startling the crowd to attention. Somewhere, someone lit a lamplight, and into its rays stepped Orion, grinning for all he was worth. Maeve's worries about being overdressed evaporated on the spot as she catalogued his costume incredulously. Silver laurels, his hair loose, gold eyeshadow, enormous shoulder pads and sheer flared legs on an open-chested orange jumpsuit. The Sun, unquestionably. He held his hands out and dipped his chin graciously. "Dear, dear friends—I beg thy time."

"Given to thee," came the refrain from every mouth. Maeve glanced around and found the people around her watching him closely—some with awe, some with admiration, some with resentment or outright loathing. Orion cleared his throat and began to speak.

"Fondly love I
the sea and the sky
as my moods flit on by
and they changeably lie
by my doorstep in shades of grey and of gold
and of wine-dark red, and in stories of old
the moon and the sea
are lovers, you see
and reach for each other as I reach to thee…"

He kept on, the words flowing into each other like the soughing of the ocean waves, and the blue lights rose and fell in rhythm with the crescendos of his voice. He spoke of the night sky, and the heroes painted across it in constellation, the Huntress and the Wanderer and the Magician. He told of the spray of the sea and how the first tide of a full moon brought a love potion in on the waves, and he told of how the Fairy Queen used it to tempt changeling children away. He spoke of ghosts and ghost stories, and the sailors drowned at sea and the Moon's great dragnet that brought them back from their icy graves. At last, he threw his arms out wide, and spoke of the poets of old who had told these stories, and how the catalogue of the present became the mythology of the future.

It was a bit self-congratulatory, but it was beautiful, too—vivid, vibrant images swirled through Maeve's head and left her wishing for that world of legend, where things worked out cleanly. She pushed down the bitter in her bittersweet. The point of tonight was, as Orion had said, to shrug on that legendary mantle and, for a few hours, pretend.

Orion came to the end of his performance and allowed a lingering moment of applause before cutting the crowd off like a conductor halting a symphony.

"And speaking of stars, our rising ones—please give my students a hand for their work in planning tonight's diversions!" The door behind him opened once again, and a dozen figures filed out in identical costumes, all black and diamond and tall silver boots. There was another cascade of applause, and the students bowed, sparkling alongside Orion. "But I've prattled for long enough." Orion hunched his shoulders in a self-deprecating manner that was undercut by the shoulder pads, then squared them again and clapped twice. "Let's make this bacchanal one for the history books, hmm?"

Chapter XIII

On cue, the shades were raised from the lamps,
bringing the room to life, and amid the cheers and surging of the
crowd, the third and final opening of that door was hardly noticeable. But Maeve had been scanning the room anyway, and so
was poised to see another figure slip out in a black-and-blush-and-
white costume, an opal brooch at her throat and a pair of beat-up
elastic-sided boots on her feet. They'd curled her hair and done
something to her cheekbones to make them cut glass like Orion's, but Maeve knew to be looking for Imogen. This was just an
Imogen she had never seen before—Imogen as she had been before she'd been slain. Imogen with her gaze roving the ballroom,
Imogen in black lipstick, Imogen sidling up to Orion as he waded
into the crowd and whispering something with a smirk into his ear.
Imogen the Moon to his Sun.

Peripherally, she saw Orion mouth "my cousin" to someone,
and watched Imogen raise her head, looking out over the room
once more. Her gaze passed over Maeve, then backtracked and
fixed on her, and Maeve managed a little smile. Now she was feeling a little intimidated again; she'd hoped she would recognize at
least one person here.

Imogen gave a little smirk back, and when Maeve looked up
from blushing at her shoes, she found Imogen slipping through the
crowd towards her. She wedged herself between a couple of particularly large costumes, then crooked a finger at Maeve and led her

over to an emptier space behind a marble column. She pulled out her telegraph, and Maeve did the same.

You look gorgeous, darling.

"You sound more like Orion the closer you get to him," Maeve demurred, making sure her hairpins were all still secure. "You look really nice, too."

Imogen rolled her eyes. *He's added me to his little night sky.* She touched the opal, pinned to a cream silk cravat, then loosened her collar slightly. *Anyhow. Drinks are in the bar room. Want to go get something?*

Maeve blinked a little. "Oh, you want to—wouldn't you rather spend time with, with Orion or something? Talk to people you know?"

Well, I'm making a pretense of incognito. Right—of course Imogen's only option for socialization was Maeve. Not to mention, Orion might have murdered her. *I'm sure some sort of rumor is going to get started, but I confess I don't much care. Maybe it'll flush someone out of the woodwork, knowing I'm alive.* She fiddled with the buttons on her waistcoat, which Maeve now saw were mother-of-pearl cut in shape of the phases of the moon. *But I'm not going to abandon you to the jaws of the Court, either. That's downright irresponsible.*

Maeve went to roll her eyes but found enough sincerity in Imogen's that she arrested the gesture. "I," she said, after a moment, "would like to try rosé. Do you think they would have that?"

Absolutely. Imogen proffered her arm, and with a snicker, Maeve took it. It was starting to be fun, putting on airs.

They made it about two-thirds of the way down the hallway before a voice hailed them, and they found themselves overtaken by Orion and his entourage.

"My cousin Isobel and her translator," he said as an aside, and kissed Imogen on the cheek, leaving a smudge of gold. "Dear, you must try some of the Feyfolk libations—Auntie Elena tells me you've got a great taste for such things." He winked at the two of them and swept on in the same direction they had been going. "By the way, Hermia, did you hear that Estelle isn't coming? I'm so sorry—I know how the two of you like to chat. But Melville—has Kiki made an appearance, or is that cough…?"

Maeve glanced around, trying to figure out exactly who Hermia or Melville were, but it seemed everyone was whispering. That reminded her of her false duty as a translator, and she leaned towards Imogen to keep up appearances.

"Doesn't stay on one topic for long, huh?"

Imogen glanced at her, then tapped wryly at her telegraph. *Oh, just wait. You didn't think they were scared of him because of his name or his scary eyebrows, did you? He's got a bucket full of bait, and he's putting it over the side of the boat, chumming the waters. They'll all go into a feeding frenzy, and by the end of the night they won't even know they're all trapped in his net.*

Maeve eyed the group with a new lens. "They fall for it?"

She shrugged. *They've all got secrets. If they learn everyone else's, then that makes them feel safer.*

"What's Orion's secret?"

Imogen smiled. *That's the question, isn't it?*

They made it to the bar in one piece, and Orion held the door as the group filed in. "I want to see her first absinthe," Orion stage-whispered to Imogen, who rolled her eyes and raised an eyebrow to Maeve. Whatever Orion had done, he had generated an uncanny resemblance between the two of them as they looked questioningly at her now.

"I'll try one," she said gamely, and Orion beamed.

What she hadn't realized when Orion had mentioned that the party was sponsored by some absinthe house was that the place would send its workforce with it. The bar smelled sharply of alcohol and a tangle of perfumes, and was already packed with bodies, some partygoers and some in electric green lingerie, all crushed together and blinking flirtatiously at one another. A scantily clad girl who couldn't have been quite Maeve's age smiled at her and offered her a cocktail off the silver platter in her hand, and Maeve was a little too surprised to say no without stammering. It was one thing to consider flirtations from the outside; it was quite another to be an active participant. She and Frances and Thalia and…well, they had giggled over silly youthful attractions and hypothetical romances none of them ever really thought they were going to experience. Not that she was doing anything now, of course, but… she was being dragged dangerously close.

That dragging brought her to the bar, where a young man wearing a corset took their order. "Absinthe for the ladies and a kiss for me," Orion said with a wink, then waved his hand. "No, no, make it three, I'm old enough to be your father, ugh!"

The man seemed unfazed, and indeed served them their drinks with a wink in return. "Anything else I can get our host?" he said in what Maeve decided she had to call a purr.

"All set, darling." Orion smirked and carried the glasses to a nearby table with a green-shaded lamp in the center. "So this, dear Maeve, is how you drink an absinthe." He took up a few tiny, slotted spoons from a jar on the table and placed a sugar cube in each. "Bit of chilled water over the sugar, get it all mixed in—" He poured the sugar water into the glass as he went, deft and clearly practiced. "And you can sip, or—"

Imogen took up her glass as soon as Orion was finished and knocked it back in one go. "Or you can shoot. Im—Isobel! Terrible manners!"

Imogen reached out, flagged down another boy in green, and got her glass refilled. She tipped it back and forth innocently, and Orion narrowed his eyes. "I'm not going shot-for-shot with you, darling. I remember what you said this morning." He picked up his glass and recovered his composure. "To new friends, anyway."

Maeve tried a sip, then decided to shoot it. No way was she having that in her mouth any longer than was strictly necessary. It burned her throat on the way down and nearly came back up her nose, but she choked it down with difficulty. It even had a horrid licorice-fennel aftertaste. She mustered a smile for Orion, and then gagged at Imogen when he turned away. She grinned, and got up, returning after a brief moment with a bottle of rosé.

Orion, meanwhile, had pulled out a whalebone pipe, and was busy stuffing it with something that absolutely was not tobacco.

"My father has a pipe like that," Maeve said conversationally, accepting the glass of wine that Imogen poured her. "He carved it himself off his first whale."

"Whaler—I guessed Fisher. I was close." Orion sipped his drink and lit his pipe with a gilded lighter. "Do you miss your family much? Wish my mother would develop an interest in the sea—preferably, the bottom of it." He took a long, sour drag.

"I left home pretty young." Maeve winced—maybe she shouldn't have mentioned that to him—but took a sip of her wine and found it much tastier than the absinthe. She smiled at Imogen.

"I like seeing them, of course, but I spend more of my time with my friends."

"Found family—classic." He blew a smoke ring off to the left. "I left at sixteen. Didn't want to ride Mother's coattails and didn't want to live by her rules. There's some Heathcliffe daughter back in Edgewood I left at the altar who probably dislikes me quite a bit. But I make it a point to never go to the mainland. Witches can't cross running water." He grinned.

"Is the daughter or your mother the witch?"

"Oh, the latter. Sometimes my tongue moves faster than my brain." He polished off the absinthe, and Maeve thought maybe she knew why. "Oh—Vienna! Vienna, darling, wait up—I want to hear about how things went with that sculptor—!" He lurched to his feet a few inches higher up than usual, and the crowd parted to allow his passage, then tangled itself back together.

The pace of socialization seemed to be a lot faster than Maeve was used to, so she sipped at her wine again and looked to Imogen for direction. Imogen had refilled her absinthe glass again and drained it before tapping something out to Maeve.

Absolutely don't do what I'm doing.

"Wasn't planning on it." She caught a whiff and winced. "That stuff is disgusting."

Grows on you. She smiled and looked around. *Is it the shock I expected?*

"I'm handling it. I've seen people...uh..." Maeve glanced around, searching for some landmark of similarity she could attach this to her usual life with. The only bare limbs she was used to were those of corpses, and what their owners were doing with them, well—wholly unfamiliar. "Orion did all the shocking when I met him so I think I'm okay."

Imogen laughed silently and spun her glass between her fingers. *You're very resilient, dear Sister Maeve. If I had to go do your life all of a sudden I think I might not take to it so well.*

"You've got relevant experience," Maeve pointed out. "You could teach literature to the little ones."

True. Imogen smiled. *I like old buildings and homemade meals. But I refuse to wear a habit. I can fight ghosts in tight trousers, promise.*

"I believe it." Maeve surveyed Imogen's current attire—cigarette pants with a sheer stripe all the way up the thigh. Those might be a little too impractical for an exorcism. She felt the jolt of what was probably the shot hitting her and steadied herself with the edge of the table. "Speaking of meals, I am now realizing I had nothing for dinner."

Well, we can fix that. Imogen snatched an unattended shrimp cocktail off a nearby table and looked around warily. *Can you go order me a bottle for the road?*

Maeve giggled and headed off to do so, trying not to blush when the bartender made a point of brushing her fingers with his as he handed it off, and returned to find Imogen. She was gazing around, looking pleased and exceedingly elegant, and again Maeve felt nervous, out of place. But their eyes met, and Imogen smiled and proffered the bottle of rosé and the shrimp cocktail. Maeve swapped the bottle of absinthe to her and ate a few shrimp to fill the hollow feeling in her stomach.

"Where are we going?"

Wherever you like. Imogen winked. *But Orion was nattering about a show in the library—do you like theater?*

Her eyes were twinkling; Maeve recalled Imogen mentioning her guardian's ties to the theater. Maeve herself knew nothing, but she trusted Imogen's taste.

"I've never been. But I'd like to."

The library was thinly attended; Maeve wondered if Imogen was trying to steer her away from whatever unsavory attractions might be drawing the bulk of the partygoers. She had been here before briefly, but it was transformed—plush rows of seats decorated the ground, and a dais had been set in their center, lights casting the divide between stage and house in sharp relief. A young woman in thick spectacles approached them as they entered, looking pleased to have more guests. "We'll be starting the show in five minutes if you care to stick around."

"Yes, we do!" Maeve said with as encouraging of a smile as she could muster as Imogen pulled her by the wrist to a pair of seats with a good view. "Between the wine and these cushions, I might fall asleep," she giggled.

Don't you dare! I'll pinch you!

"Then I'll pour all this cocktail sauce on you!" Maeve brandished the shrimp.

Imogen raised her hands with a gasp. *I surrender, I surrender!* She seemed more lighthearted than usual.

"Ugh, finally. Isobel!" It took both of them a few moments to realize that Orion was yelling for Imogen, but it became clear when he crouched down on his enormous platform boots and flicked Imogen's nose. "Hey. Are you drunk?"

Imogen shut her eyes and frowned as she typed. *Slightly.*

"Good. Come win a bet for me—Adolai thinks no one related to me could drink better than him."

No one could, Imogen shot back. *Warwick means "lightweight" in the ancient tongue.*

"Ease up on the 'W' word or I'll kick you out, Madrigal. I'll give you half the money."

Give Maeve half the money. I don't need it.

"Fine. I'll give a hundred ammonite to the winner's charity of choice."

Ugh. That's a lot. Imogen cracked an eye open and looked with displeasure at Maeve. *Isn't he a snake?*

"Hiss hiss," Orion said with a roll of his eyes. He pulled Imogen to her feet and began to drag her away. "Enjoy the show, Maeve!"

Maeve blinked a few times, but they were gone by the time she had processed what they'd said. A hundred ammonite was solid to her, but undoubtedly a drop in the bucket for them. She rolled onto her back and looked up at the dome. That was...very nice of Imogen to do.

A small knot of people came in smelling strongly of opium and sat down beside her. Maeve watched them for a moment, then took another swig of wine. She was glad that Imogen had done it, but she also rather wished she still had a friend to whisper to in the dark. She looked wistfully at the empty seat beside her, then settled into her own seat a little farther, and gazed up at the stage.

The show began, and for a moment it startled Maeve—was the play about the Wraith? But as more actors came out onto the stage, she realized that she had gotten it the wrong way 'round—they were all wearing the sort of masquerade mask that Imogen wore for a disguise, only matched with ornate costumes instead of long veils. That must be where she got the mask, she thought, as the actors played out a pantomime to the score of a small musical ensemble secreted somewhere she couldn't see. An inheritance from her guardian, or an interest in acting herself. The show had begun without preamble or explanation, and she didn't quite understand what was going on beyond broad strokes, until one of the opium smokers spoke up to another, their whisper louder than they intended.

"I've forgotten everything I knew about Southern theater, Christine. Who's that?"

"That's the *Donna*," their companion explained. "In the flowery mask. She's the lady of the house."

"And that fellow?" A character bedecked in bells with a hat of many points emerged to much pomp and was quickly and cringingly shuttled out of the way for other characters to emerge.

"The jester. Or the fool. The others coming in are the *Don* and his servants."

"And there's supposed to be a lover, right?"

"Oh yes. They'll be in black and silver. Or is that the assassin? Oh, I can never remember...."

With that primer helpfully gleaned, Maeve settled back, and watched as the actors cavorted across the stage, motion exaggerated into a manic dance as misunderstandings were had and lies were told and tensions escalated. The costumes gleamed and swished and shone under the spotlights—the masks seemed to fall away and the exaggerated features seemed to rave along to their music. It was all very stylish, very exotic, and Maeve thought that if she knew what exactly Southern theater was that she would appreciate it even more. Or if Imogen was there to explain it to her. It was warm and hazy with smoke in here, and by the time the show came to an end and the patrons filtered out, she felt like she might very much like to curl up and take a nap. Imogen—she was still missing Imogen, though.

She sat up and headed for the door, her vision lagging slightly behind the movement of her body. Imogen would probably be at the bar again. Did she remember where it was? She glanced left and right as she came out of the library, squinting against the relatively bright lights, and then turned as someone called her name.

"Guess who won her bet, Maeve, darling?" Orion called down the hall, supporting a stumbling Imogen, who picked her head up slightly and pointed at herself with a grin.

"How much did she have?" Maeve asked, vague disapproval filtering through her intoxication.

"She's fine, she's fine," Orion assured her, and shrugged off Imogen's arm, deftly transferring it to Maeve's shoulder and dusting his hands together. "She's all yours again, darling. Have fun with her!" He winked, and before Maeve could protest, he had disappeared once more.

"Are you good?" Maeve said, looking at Imogen with concern.

Abso-tively, came the message on her telegraph. Imogen's wasn't in her hand. *Sorry I left. I missed you while I was gone.* She pouted, then grinned, her eyes drifting closed. *Have you been smoking? You smell like dope.*

"I have not!" Maeve said with indignation, shrugging Imogen off and suppressing a giggle at her swaying.

You're high, though! Imogen's nose wrinkled opened in a silent laugh.

"Am not!"

Are, too!

"You missed the show." Maeve mustered what dignity she could. "So now we have to go find something else to do."

Okay, okay. Imogen giggled to herself, straightened up, and leaned over unsteadily. *How about a private viewing of the statuary room?*

"How do you know it'll be private?" Maeve asked primly.

Because they lock that room to keep people from kissing the statues, and I can pick locks. Imogen offered her arm once more with a smirk, and Maeve pretended to consider, then took it.

Imogen led the way down the mazelike hallways with surety, and at length they came to a quieter section of the building. Imogen stopped at a closed door and knelt in front of the handle.

Hairpin, please, assistant.

Maeve passed one of hers over, and within a few minutes the door clicked open. The pair of them slipped through, and Imogen shut the door.

Inside, moonlight streamed through the windows, the shadows of the trees in the courtyard falling on the statues and making them seem to move. It was eerie, but beautiful. The sound of the party was muffled here, and as Maeve took the few steps down into the room, her footsteps echoed loudly. She grimaced and pulled her boots off, stuffing them behind a potted plant. The marble felt cool on her feet, and she settled onto flat soles with relief. She looked back at Imogen, who gestured for her to go forward, and then did so, studying the figures in the dark. Marble fingers pressed into marble skin, carved curls of hair and tiny lines wrought into lips. It had depth to it, like skin—the light played under the surface and made it glow in the dark. Practically ghostly. Oh, how would she capture that on paper?

She took a sip of wine to quell the itch for her pencils in her fingers. "This is…beautiful," she whispered, feeling like anything too loud might shatter the magic. "Thank you."

Imogen looked up, trying not to stagger as she pulled her boots off too, and smiled. *Sometimes I think they—we?—forget how lucky we are to have all this. We see too much, we have too much, and we lose our wonder.*

"I understand that." Maeve slid to the ground in a pool of taffeta. "It's a tough line to walk in my line of work between mundane and…holy. There's a ghost in someone's house and it's a nuisance, but it's also a divine mystery. I forget to remember that, sometimes."

Divine mystery. Imogen slid over on bright purple socks and moved to sit beside Maeve with a kiddish smile. *I never learned much about religion—just enough to know what I was looking at in all those paintings.* She looked sideways at her, then over to where Maeve could see a robed figure holding an hourglass on a chain. She'd missed it before—the Visitation of the Blessed Sister. It was famous; she taught lessons about it. She hadn't known it was here. *Does it make it better, to understand more?*

Maeve stumbled to her feet and made her way over, peering unsteadily under the veil. Marble made practically sheer brushed over her face like cloth. Her expression was calm and wise, her eyes closed. A mysterious smile quirked her lips.

"I think it makes you take pause," Maeve said softly, "and seek out the little details. That's all wonder is, isn't it? Taking pause to notice your blessings."

That's why you draw. She felt a slight chill at her back as Imogen came to stand near her. *It's something like praying.*

She turned and nodded mutely, her stomach curling with emotion. Those were words she'd never been able to find for herself, and now that she had them, it was agony to have lived without them. Imogen gave her a small smile, then hiccupped slightly. Her cheeks were flushed pinkish-purple, and between that and the black lipstick she might have looked alarmingly close to hypothermia if Maeve hadn't known that the room was feeling quite warm all of a sudden.

Forget the statues—how would she capture *that* on paper? *You draw her like you love her.* Maybe Maeve would draw Imogen writing, the end of that fountain pen of hers balanced on her lower lip, her eyebrows gently knit in thought. The sharp lines of her jaw and nose would make a lovely compositional counterpoint to the flow of her shirt, and she'd blacken in the background, let the marble pale of her skin glow in the dark. She would miss the color, though. The flush in her cheeks and the periwinkle of her eyes....

The sound of the door opening startled them both, and quickly Imogen dragged Maeve behind the statue to hide.

"Everyone's in rare form. They're taking cues off him."

"What's his problem?"

Two voices, slurring slightly—a higher and a lower one.

"Word is the Warwick house is making a move on that little cemetery again. The year burials have to lie before being moved is almost up, or something like that. And he hates it when she gets her way."

"Oh, spicy. What do they want to do with it?"

"Shops, I heard. Luxury apartments. Something along those lines."

"I'd buy an apartment there. Chance of haunting, but boy, the view...."

"You won't if you want to stay in favor here." The voices came nearer, and Maeve pressed closer to Imogen. Their hands were still clasped, and noticing it made her stomach twist harder. Imogen's nose wrinkled as her face broke into a silent grin. Maeve shook her head in disbelief, fighting a smile of her own. They *really* shouldn't have been eavesdropping, and yet— "Because he'll block it with everything he's got, and when she gets it through anyway, he'll sulk."

"I heard a rumor that there's a death nun here tonight. D'you think he's trying to get them involved, then? To block Marlene?"

"Love, I heard a rumor that Imogen Madrigal was here to-night. You can't listen to everything you hear within these walls."

"But I should listen to you?"

"Well, of course." The higher voice had settled into a flirtatious register. "I'm always right."

"Ooh, I...bet you think...you are..." The conversation was beginning to trail off into something else, and Imogen nudged Maeve with her shoulder, pointing with her chin towards the window. Maeve gave a silent grin of assent and tripped over on her tiptoes while Imogen unlatched it. She boosted herself out and into the courtyard, the wind whipping her skirt around her legs. Imogen followed, her hand finding Maeve's again, and together the two of them ran as well as they could, drunk and barefoot and seized by paroxysms of laughter.

"That was bad information!" Maeve complained. "Why are we laughing?"

Because they stole our idea! Imogen wheezed a bit. *And because I forgot to lock the door behind us like an idiot, and, also, because we're drunk, and everything is funny when you're drunk. My socks are wet! This was a bad idea!*

"That's true," Maeve said begrudgingly, and took a swig of her wine. The bottle was starting to get light. "It's cold."

Oh, my fault. Imogen let her hand go, paced a few steps away. *Better?*

"No," Maeve said quickly, blinking as she tried to make her brain catch up with her mouth. The twist in her stomach returned without a distraction to hold it at bay. Was it nerves? "Um—wait, yeah, no—you—" She took another few steps closer, jammed her telegraph in her pocket, and took Imogen's hand in both of hers. It was, to her surprise, warm.

Imogen looked up slowly and gave Maeve a quizzical look.

"You're warm," she said lamely. Was the ground tilting, or was she just drunker than she had thought? Because it felt an awful lot like she was leaning towards Imogen, or maybe Imogen was leaning towards her, or maybe they were leaning towards each other—

A frantic series of chimes issued from her pocket, and Imogen jerked back. *You're a nun I'm so sorry I'm way too drunk let's go back inside—*

Maeve dropped the telegraph and kissed her anyway.

Imogen tensed up for a moment, then took Maeve's face in her hands and kissed her back—urgently. The knot in Maeve's stomach tightened, but it was with something like amazement—Imogen's lips were so much *softer* than she had expected. Mother, what had she expected? All she had thought was that she didn't want Imogen to pull away again. It was a long moment before she did, but only by a fraction of an inch—space to let Maeve breathe, which she did in a gasp.

"Was that...your first...kiss?" Imogen whispered, her lips still brushing Maeve's.

Maeve felt her face flush under Imogen's hands. "The answer to every first question is yes, so, um..." She breathed out a shaky laugh. "Don't expect too much."

Imogen just shook her head with a smile, bumping their foreheads slightly. "Is...there more...to expect?"

Maeve sucked in another breath. Frivolous, frivolous, frivolous—was she really ignoring her vows for the sake of a sudden, foolish, frivolous crush?

Drawing is something like praying. She had been wrong about what was frivolous and what wasn't before. She had been wrong about what she wanted before.

Maeve opened her eyes to see Imogen's, off-blue and warm, watching her, and nodded.

"If you like."

Imogen's grin spread wider, and she carefully bent down to recover Maeve's telegraph.

Let's get the fuck out of here.

"You want to leave?"

Imogen rolled her eyes. *It's a euphemism. Let's go back to my room.*

"Oh." She shook herself, embarrassed, and then took Imogen's hand herself. "Yes."

The party was starting to reach a crescendo inside; glancing to the sides was becoming perilous, and a haze of smoke hung around the ceiling. Shrieks of laughter echoed through the halls, and music drifted out of key. They ran across Orion once, who had shrugged himself out of the top half of his jumpsuit and was drinking a glass of water with feverish urgency. His face, neck, and chest were smeared with a rainbow of different colors, roughly matching the lips of the acolytes arranged in devotional disarray around him.

"Oh, Maeve, darling," he gasped, and set the glass down hard. He extended a hand in benediction to her. "I'm taking a breather. Want to go listen to the chamber musicians in the other room with me? I owe you after stealing dear Imogen—I can get us good seats."

"Imogen needs to go to bed," Maeve said carefully, and gathered her skirt out of the way of stepping on it, dragging Imogen behind her. Imogen coughed up a wheezy giggle, and Maeve elbowed her in the stomach.

"Oh, I'll bet she does," Orion said, narrowing his eyes irritably. The blue had been pushed back into thin rings around his pupils. "I'll just go alone!" His mutterings followed them down the hall, but Maeve drank some more wine and successfully tuned him out.

And then they were stumbling into the apartment, struggling up the stairs, and slamming the bedroom door. Maeve hiked her skirt up and collapsed onto the bed, and Imogen followed, adding a fresh, messy streak of lipstick to the one Maeve realized must have already been on her face. Well, Orion had no grounds to judge her on. She pressed herself in closer to Imogen, a thrill overtaking her body as Imogen wrapped an arm around her waist once more. There was a tangle of emotions in her stomach that she couldn't sort out individually, but the touch gave her grounding. Imogen lifted her chin with her free hand, surveying her down the length of her nose. Maeve had never noticed that Imogen had very long, pretty eyelashes. She felt a telegraph nudge at her elbow.

Let's take this slowly. I don't want you to regret anything in the morning.

"I'm drunk; I'm not out of my mind," she grumbled, but Imogen began to pluck the pearl hairpins out of Maeve's hair, and she found that she liked Imogen touching her hair, too. She also liked it when Imogen picked her up under the knees and swung her into her lap. She decided that taking it slowly might be okay when Imogen kissed her again, open-mouthed, and slid a hand into the back of her dress. In fact, Imogen's "slow" was very, very fast to her.

She tested her own hand at Imogen's hip, that feeling in her stomach warming approvingly, and twisted her other hand into Imogen's shirt to steady herself. She had been untethered all day, unsettled—like Imogen had felt, too. Was her skin being warm a sign that she felt more settled, now? There was a thump beneath her fingertips, and she pulled away from Imogen's lips reluctantly, looking down at her chest. Imogen didn't seem to notice, applying her mouth to Maeve's collarbone so indecently that Maeve nearly forgot what she was going to say.

"Imogen?"

Imogen looked up questioningly, her lips slightly parted.

"Is your heart beating?"

Imogen frowned and pulled her hand back from Maeve's waist to place it on her own chest. Her eyebrows rose, and she managed a few words. "That's untenably sappy."

Maeve giggled, whether from Imogen's upset or from surprise or something like wonder, she didn't know. But she didn't need to—she was comfortable in the dark, in the mystery. She spread her fingers out over Imogen's chest and closed her eyes and felt her heart beat every few seconds. Imogen's arms felt warm and safe around her, and her cheekbone nuzzled in close against Maeve's, a little sharp but with infinite gentleness. Touch blurred into warmth, and kisses into slow breathing, and in the dark and the divine, they fell asleep together.

Chapter

XIV

The hangover wrenched her out of sleep, and by the time she had staggered to an unfamiliar bathroom and emptied the contents of her stomach into the toilet, Maeve was coming to the conclusion that she had not, in fact, gone home last night. She pulled herself upright by the windowsill and peered out; no, the convent wasn't next door to open ocean. It figured that it would be bright and sunny out the one day she wasn't in a state to enjoy it. She scooped some water into her mouth from the sink, rubbed a bit more on her face, and ruefully surveyed the smeared makeup and frizzy hair that comprised most of the woman in the mirror. Ouch.

The memory of exactly how last night had ended was beginning to dredge itself up in her mind as she returned to the bedroom and began the search for her clothes. The headache was holding the emotions at bay, but she could feel them knocking at her mental doors. She studiously avoided looking at the bed, where furtive glances showed a body still ensconced in the covers. Wait—had she left her clothes at Naomi's? She swore, her head starting to throb, and slipped back out the door.

At least no one was likely to be up yet—the sun's position over the water put the time at about eight in the morning. Maeve crept down the spiral staircase, then down the next toward the kitchen. She would just go to Naomi's door, get her stuff back, get a cab home, and message Imogen after a long nap and a bit of thinking. Nap first, thinking after, she told herself sternly, as a nail of headache drove itself in behind her eye.

"Morning, sunshine."

Maeve swallowed back a noise of frustration and hovered on the stairs in front of Orion. She could go back up to bed—or maybe she couldn't. Who would she prefer to face? A possible murderer or...well...Orion poured a second cup of tea at the kitchen table and smiled her way. She cursed herself once more, and finished descending.

Up close, he looked about as worse for wear as she did—his hair was wet from a shower, but the scent of strong spirits hung in the air around him. A retch fought its way up Maeve's throat at the smell, but she managed to swallow it back and take a tiny sip of tea. "I'm surprised you're awake."

"Best to rip the bandage off, I find," he said, and rubbed at the bags under his eyes. "Plus, I think I may be avoiding the same thing you are."

Maeve gave him a glare, but she couldn't summon much ire. "I didn't think you were capable of shame."

"Ouch." He took a sip of tea, and for a few moments they were silent. The grey cat wound its way around Maeve's ankles, tickling her bare feet. "You're right though," Orion said after a few moments, sounding thoughtful. "Are you ashamed?"

"Don't let me keep you from your morning," Maeve said wryly.

"Oh, I don't mind." He took a bite of a cracker from the carton tucked under his arm, then set it on his saucer, looking nauseated. "In fact, I was hoping to catch you before you snuck out."

"I wasn't—"

"I just don't want you to hurt her feelings," he continued, as though she hadn't spoken. Maeve bit her tongue with slight annoyance, and with trepidation as well. She hadn't thought that she might hurt anyone's feelings.

"Which you might think is overstepping my role as a teacher, but I'd also like to think I'm her friend. And I've known her for a long time." His voice went faraway for a moment. Maeve looked up from her tea. "A long time," he repeated eventually. "So, I know what she wants, and I know what she's been through, to some extent."

She swallowed. "Come now," she tried to tease. "She's your student; I'm probably just the latest in a long list of...hookups..."

The idea hadn't actually occurred to her before she said it, and now that she had, she found it hurt.

Orion shook his head carefully. "She never was like that. Disappointingly. Of course, she'd flirt—practically a requirement to be here—but I've only ever heard her talk about a couple girls that way." He leaned in across the table. "I like to study people. It drives my friends crazy. But I've had a few good years to look at Imogen, and her death hasn't changed her a bit. She was abandoned as a child, nearly killed, and she's never forgotten that. She's slow to bestow her trust—I still haven't got it, and she's known me three years. But you..." He eyed Maeve, and Maeve wasn't sure if he was jealous or not. "Once she does decide to trust, she's loyal—violently. She loved her guardian first, and then that macabre girl from that tea shop. Then the Sinclair brat." His lip curled disdainfully, then relaxed. "She's too wary to let more than one person in at once."

Maeve sipped more of her tea; her mouth felt rather dry. "That's a lot of pressure for one person to live up to."

"Indeed." Orion scratched his cat behind the ears. "But habits can be broken with a little discipline. I imagine you know something about that. You and your friends at the convent." He winked. "I'm sure they're absolute sweethearts. Kind, honest, good with, ah...difficult cases...?"

"Hmm." Maeve didn't know what else to say—what could she? She could tell where Orion was going, but she couldn't...her head began to throb again, and she forced herself to stop thinking.

"Anyway. You, darling—you're a sort of person who is rare around here. You like to take care of people. To help them."

"I—yes, I suppose." Maeve sipped nervously—she could see why people didn't like Orion studying them. "Nothing wrong with that."

"Not at all. But I imagine if I were that sort of person, I should like to be the center of attention, every once in a while. To have someone take care of me." He took another stab at the cracker and managed a larger bite. "Not to sound vain or anything, but it's nice being worshipped. And I know just the woman upstairs."

"I'm a nun!" Maeve couldn't hold it at bay any longer. "I swore an oath that I would never take up any earthly attachments—I've been given trust by my sisters, and I can't abuse that!"

"Whyever not?" Orion looked mildly surprised. "Aren't you supposed to live a good life or something?"

"It's a check on the power we've been given," Maeve said, massaging her temples. "If someone I loved died, I might be tempted to misuse the tools I have for dealing with the spirit world to keep them around. I wouldn't be able to act objectively."

"Well, perhaps, but you've already shown a pretty strong antipathy to seancecraft," he said, his nose faintly wrinkled. "I have a hard time believing you'd toss your morals out the window even if your lover bit it."

"You don't know what grief can do to people," Maeve said sullenly.

"Yes, I do." Orion sipped his tea and looked at her frankly. "I watched them put my dear friend Imogen in the ground a year ago."

There was silence in the kitchen for a few moments.

"And yet," he said at length, "I didn't try to bring her back. Oh, I thought about it—talked to Estelle about it till she kicked me out—but I didn't. Because I knew she wouldn't have wanted that. Now, are you afraid that you have less of a backbone than me, or are you just a rule-follower?"

"I'm—you—I follow the rules I think are important!"

His eyebrows quirked together, and he grinned. "Well, if I were you, I'd hold that one up to my moral compass again. Decide if I cared more about stuffy absolutist codes than my own feelings."

"Did you follow your feelings into bed with whomever you're avoiding up there?" Maeve snapped before she could think better of it.

Orion blinked a few times, then smirked and drank more of his tea. "Touchy, aren't we?"

Maeve wrestled her face into something neutral, refusing to do him the dignity of looking his way. "Alright. Going home. See you next time I'm forced to do so."

"You stayed of your own accord, darling," he reminded her, and withdrew a paper bag from under the table. It turned out to contain her clothes. "Would you like to give me a message for Imogen? Or do you just want to disappear and leave her to wake up alone?"

Maeve stood without acknowledging him and took her clothes up to the bathroom to change. She didn't look in the bedroom—she definitely didn't notice Imogen's silhouette under the blanket, her shoulders rising and falling—she simply put on her habit and rinsed the makeup off her face. She hurried back down the stairs, and folded the dress into the bag, refusing to look at Orion.

"Will you take this back to Naomi?"

"Yes. Will you leave me a message for Imogen?"

Maeve gritted her teeth. It wasn't that she didn't want to leave Imogen a message. It wasn't that she wanted to leave Imogen, a voice whispered somewhere in her mind, but she quashed it down. She just...what did she say, when she didn't even know what she wanted to say? She would tell the truth, but she didn't know what it was!

"Tell her," she said to the table, her voice embarrassingly emotional in her ears, "that Thalia called, and there was a haunting I had to rush off to. That I will message her later...later today." That would be enough of a cushion to get her head on straight—it would have to be.

She chanced a glance up at Orion, who looked unimpressed.

"Not the best I've ever heard," he said, "but I don't know that you're good enough with words to come up with a more convincing one."

Maeve didn't consider herself the kind of person to have a quick temper, but the headache was leaving her less charitable than she would normally be.

"And I don't know that you're a good swimmer," she snapped back. "But I invite you to try the harbor regardless." Without a look back, she departed.

The convent looked no different by the time Maeve made it back, but she still felt as though something was painfully changed. She entered through the side door and found the halls abuzz with activity—little sisters carrying linens up the stairs, and Mother Superior directing some effort at the old freight dumbwaiter.

"Oh, excellent, Maeve," she said as she saw her. "Glad you're feeling better. Can you help pull?"

It was an effort, it seemed, to move furniture up to the second floor—the elders' move out of their wing, already underway. Maeve dutifully took up a share of rope behind Sister Cory and helped them hoist the dumbwaiter higher and higher.

"Got it!" came Thalia's voice from above, and Mother Superior pulled the brake lever down.

"Excellent," she said, and dusted her hands. "That should be the last of it, and then it's just draining all the pipes." Her expression was even—no sadness, just practicality. Maeve envied her certainty. "I gave your tasks to the rest of your cohort, Maeve. Why don't you head up and see what's left, if you're up to it?"

Maeve nodded, and took the nearest staircase to the second floor, trying hard not to feel nervous. It was Shivani's fault they were fighting—whatever transgressions Maeve had committed on the back of her spiteful feelings were separate, and she could take the hit for them later.

Hypocrite, her mind whispered. She ignored it.

Thalia was attempting to shove an overstuffed armchair across the floor on her own when Maeve found her, and she picked up the end of it to help.

"Moving day, huh?"

"You look terrible," Thalia said bluntly. "We told them you were sick, but I didn't know that was actually the case."

"Yeah." Maeve didn't trust herself to say anything about the night she'd had. "How's it going here?"

They made their way to an open door and maneuvered the chair through with difficulty. This room overlooked the courtyard and faced south—probably Mother Superior's new living space. It wasn't much larger than Maeve's room. She was sure Orion would find that offensive, having to stay in a room the same size as one of his underlings.

"Well," Thalia said, "there's...um...news. Which there is every day, but this is relevant news—which is that there was a fire at the cemetery last night. Someone burned down the keeper's hut, and a couple of mausoleums got vandalized besides."

Maeve looked at her sharply, and nearly dropped the chair. "Anyone who we...know?"

Thalia nodded shortly. "They are saying," she pronounced, "that it's a reaction to the purchase of the cemetery's land, which has been contracted as of yesterday to go through the day the last burial has lain there for a year."

"Who?"

"The buyer or the burial?" Thalia clicked her tongue. "The former is Marlene Warwick. The latter is Imogen."

"Ugh." Maeve set down the chair and rubbed at her eyes. "Okay, that's important. I'll tell—" she hesitated, remembering that she'd have to deal with the previous night's events before she could talk to Imogen. The thought made her feel lonely. "Well. I'll note it down at the very least." She bit her lip as they headed back into the hall and glanced around nervously. "So, what happened with—?"

"Maeve!" No chance to prepare herself, it seemed—here was Shivani, hurrying down the hall. Maeve didn't even have a chance to determine if she was mad or not before Shivani caught her in a hug. Maeve blinked, raising her eyebrows at Thalia over her shoulder. Thalia avoided her eyes. "Glad you're feeling better." She pulled back, and smiled at Maeve, no trace of ire or embarrassment in her face. "Best not to feel too sorry for yourself when you've been sick."

Maeve stared at her; had Shivani gone mad? Things had happened—she had said horrible things! She was just going to—to—to not think about it?! Or was she calling Maeve the sick one, saying that her decision to stay away was some kind of self-pity? But Shivani patted her cheek and turned on her heel, whisking away back down the hall, and Maeve was left open-mouthed in her wake. She looked at Thalia, who fidgeted uncomfortably.

"Maybe just forget what I told you she said?" she whispered hopefully.

"Fat chance," Maeve hissed. "What did she mean by that?"

Thalia made a noncommittal noise and began to retreat. "C'mon, let's finish this up, anyway, and then you can have lunch and tell us—uh, me and Frances—what you got up to last night. If you want."

"Yeah," Maeve said vaguely, still watching Shivani further down the hall. She—she—no! Maybe she didn't know how to deal with the Imogen situation, but she wasn't going to let both of these things weigh on her. She balled up her fists, and stormed after her.

"Hey—can I have that note you got?" she asked as she caught up to Shivani and watched her face flick briefly to irritation. So, she wasn't as fine as she was pretending to be.

"Certainly, if you want." Her voice sounded perfectly even as she reached into her pocket. "Suppose you might like it as an artifact for when you exorcise that ghost?"

Maeve glanced at her for a moment, the question of what exactly she meant by *that* hovering on her tongue before she unfolded the note. A note which was written in impenetrable spidery cursive that reminded Maeve of something. This wasn't Imogen's writing, was it? Her stomach lurched, and she turned away, forgetting whatever Shivani was on about. She must have a sample of Imogen's handwriting somewhere—one of those folios in her room. She headed for her door, let herself in without turning back, and dug to the bottom of her sock drawer.

No, not Imogen's writing—her letters were softer-looking, less dense. The twist of fear and betrayal in her stomach relaxed, though some nervousness remained as she read over the words on the page. There were pieces of Imogen's life tucked away in her room just as some of her possessions had made their way to Imogen. That would be uncomfortable to detangle if... if....

She shook her head and reapplied herself to the problem. Whose writing? Her eyes landed on her sketchbook, and she dove for it, holding it by the spine and shaking it till the paper in question tumbled to the floor. Yes—yes! She held the note and the schematic she had stolen from Camille's office up against each other, and considered the implications with growing worry. Camille knew, of course, that Maeve had been investigating, but how much else did she know? Did she know Imogen was alive?

You may be disheartened to learn that one Sister Maeve of your order has been consorting with poets and mediums in an attempt to solve the murder of the poet Imogen Madrigal. In addition to this, there is reason to believe she may have been associating with the criminal known as the Wraith. We advise looking into these matters as soon as is possible for the protection of your convent's reputation.

So, yes—because Maeve hadn't been seen with the Wraith, since Imogen hadn't used that disguise in a month. She placed the note back into her sketchbook, thinking hard. How had Camille gotten that information? Was the harpoon man involved here? When had she found out, and what else had she been hiding? Maeve's telegraph was in her hand before she noticed it, and her finger was poised to send it when her train of thought screeched to a halt.

Camille knows you're alive—she sent the note to the convent. What does that mean? Wait—could she send this on its own? Without addressing any of what had happened? She read over the words, her mind racing through eight different ways they could be interpreted. Maybe she could. Maybe if she just pretended things were normal, then they would be. But no—no, that was what Shivani was doing. She swore under her breath and rewrote the message. *Camille knows you're alive—she sent the note to the convent. We should meet up again soon.* There—no expectations, no decisions that she had to make now. She sent it, stuffed the telegraph in her sock drawer, and resolved not to look again until that night. She had neglected her duties for too long. Undoubtedly hard work would be therapeutic.

There was no reply by the time Maeve went to bed. Okay—it was okay. Maybe Imogen was busy with Orion or dealing with the vandalism to her mausoleum. Maybe she was still asleep—she'd kept nocturnal hours before. Maeve crawled under the covers, drawing her blanket tight to keep out the chill, and forced herself to sleep.

Nothing by the next morning, either. Maeve woke with a sour taste in her mouth and the clinging anxiety of a dream she couldn't remember. But it would be fine—she just needed to let Imogen have her space and do whatever she was doing. She went downstairs, had flavorless Lenorum Public with flavorless breakfast, faked equanimity to the others, and volunteered for the week's charity cooking as soon as it was offered. Yes. She'd focus on that, and she'd clear her head later that evening by walking over to deliver the meals. That would distract her for the day and tire her out for the night.

Still no response. Maeve returned rain-soaked and chilled from her trip to the soup kitchen and had forced herself not to take a shortcut back through the cemetery. It couldn't be safe; she had no idea who might be there. It had taken longer that way, which had given her plenty of time to think and overthink. And now she was back home, standing over her sock drawer in the glow of the telegraph's tiny screen. She swallowed, then put it away, and knelt by her bed.

Hallowed Mother, bring me peace. Her prayers felt rote, but she said them anyway and crawled under the covers. Maybe if she didn't hope for a reply—maybe if she put all this behind her for good—she would find peace. Imogen had Orion for an ally now, if she said she trusted him, and Maeve had her sisters, same as always. She'd been happy before—maybe, with time and a retreat into what she knew, she would be again. Her mind was agitated, but her eyes couldn't help but drift shut as the rain fell before them. The streetlight glowed hazily outside, and the exhaustion that had sunk into her bones dragged her down into the relief of unconsciousness.

But still the wind howled, as it always did in Lenorum, and in what had to be a dream, she pulled her collar up to shield herself from the cold fingers it slipped down her neck. She hurried along in the glow of the streetlamps, the buildings unfamiliar and foreboding. Turning into the cemetery seemed even more foolish, but she did it anyway; it would be, perhaps, less cruel than some other place. At least then she could be assured that someone would bury the remains.

Now, the bundle tucked into her coat stirred, and blinked ice-blue eyes up at her. A shock of greyish brown hair dusted its pale forehead, but the cheeks were pink with life, and as the gravel crunched under her feet, the baby cooed. She didn't know much about babies; this one couldn't be very old at all.

She sank to a seat on a nearby grave marker, a swirl of emotions tightening her chest. She knew what she was here to do, of course. To abandon someone that had been abandoned already by others; to do the duty requested of her; to retain the life she'd made for herself by hurting someone else. That was what she was considering doing.

The sound of new-fallen snow crunching underfoot approached, and a figure in an overlarge overcoat walked over from the cemetery keeper's hut, sitting down next to her.

"I'm not a baby anymore."

"But you are alone," she whispered, tucking the blanket in closer around the baby's face. It had gone back to sleep, its gummy mouth slightly open.

"This isn't about me." Her companion reached out for her hand. Her arms felt lighter; the baby was gone, and she was colder for it. She looked around and found that they were no longer in the cemetery—no, they were in the chapel, and when Maeve looked back, she found Imogen dressed in a high-collared black suit, an hourglass-shaped pin holding her black silk cravat in place. Her hand was still extended, and as soon as Maeve took it Imogen pulled her in close like they were dancing. "This is about you," she said, and with a twirl they were stood before the same stained-glass window Maeve had given her lecture at the previous week. It had changed; instead of the Blessed Sister it showed a garden in moonlight. Roses covered in dewdrops, the close and cozy composition of a hedgerow behind—the whole thing was luminous even without the glow through the glass, and Maeve knew it was hers. If only she had color to work with. Imogen leaned against the end of the pew and glanced back over her shoulder with a smile. "It could be quite the collaboration, couldn't it?" she said, her voice soft in the echoey room. "I was thinking a verse for each window, but of course it's your choice."

"My choice," Maeve murmured. There was a bronze placard behind Imogen, but she couldn't quite make out the words on it.

"Oh yes. It's your vision—you're the artist."

"But...what if I make a mistake?" She looked back at Imogen, elegant and confident, and she wished it wasn't her choice. That some divine signal or calamity would force her hand. "You...you can't erase in glass. In paint. You can't undo the choices you make."

"Nor in ink." Imogen smiled at her. "You scratch it out, darling. You paint it over. You work it into what you've got. They're not mistakes—they're part of the process."

She knew what she wanted. Of course, she did. The itch in her fingers for her pencils was constant, the desire to record, or—no, to create. To take part in beauty, to bring it home with her and paste it up on her mirror and let it become a part of her reflection. To find the divine in the garden and the sea and herself.

That's why you draw. It's something like praying. And maybe, to find the divine in another.

It wasn't that she didn't know that. It was that she was afraid to admit it to herself—to admit a desire, selfish and against the rules, and to follow that desire into what might be a mistake. Without the Sisterhood she was just Maeve. Did she dare disturb the universe?

"I'm not ready for that."

"I have writer's block sometimes," Imogen said, gazing up at the stained-glass window. "The expanse of the page—I'm afraid to mar it with something that isn't ready yet. Do you know what I do?"

"You scribble." Maeve knew that—she used it herself when she was afraid to waste a page on something that might not be perfect. "Put something, anything down."

Imogen nodded. "I make a mark, just to get started." She stood from where she had been leaning and placed a hand on Maeve's cheek, warm in the drafty chapel. "And I try to find it along the way." The winter winds keened outside like the soughing of some distant organ, and their lips met—

And then a chime shattered the dream, and it was autumn once again.

She woke in her bed shivering, the room pitch-black and her pillow covered in drool. She made a noise of disgust, wiped off her face, and pawed through her sock drawer.

(!) 1 New Message(s).

Yacht docks in half an hour? I know it's late.

Maeve swallowed the sour taste out of her mouth, and tapped a message back, her cheeks burning. She barely hesitated, and that was unquestionably bad.

I'll be there.

The newly occupied rooms on her hallway made sneaking out a more harrowing experience than usual; once, she thought she heard footsteps behind her, but upon looking back found the hall empty. She crept down the stairs and out the side door and made her way to the streetcar stop nearest the convent. It was an expense, but it would probably be for the safest—the harpoon man couldn't shoot her here without causing a scene, if he was out here at all. A corona of gold light from within the streetcar kept the night at bay, and the few other passengers traveling at this late hour spared little notice for her. She rode on, down through the twisting alleys of townhouses and cobblestoned streets, till the curve of the island evened out and they emerged into the open air of the harbor. Maeve checked her watch: twelve-oh-eight. Only a few lights kept sentinel watch over the docks, and the night harbormaster seemed to be dozing when she passed their window.

Her telegraph chimed.

Dock 6. I can see you. She peered out through the darkness and spotted a figure in an anorak waving its hand over its head. Maeve sighed, relieved despite her apprehension; the dark and the lapping of the waves had been starting to make her paranoid. If anyone was coming, she wouldn't be able to hear or see them.

She counted her way down the docks and made her way to Imogen, who crouched down behind a stack of crates and motioned for her to follow. She lit a lantern with a lighter Maeve recognized as Orion's fancy one and pulled down her cowl.

"What happened to you?" Maeve said before she could stop herself. But Imogen looked awful—her skin was even paler than usual, her eyes ringed by dark circles and her lips and nose nearly purple. She looked like she was freezing to death—or had already done so.

Took a swing too hard in the other direction. Imogen rubbed at her eyes with a self-conscious glance at Maeve. *Got unsettled.*

"What happened?"

It's…been a long couple of days. Let me start from the beginning. She held her hands over the lamp, the light highlighting a bluish tinge through her skin. *Like I mentioned back in that cellar—Orion hates Marlene, and I figured I could use that against her. Of course, she's not going to say no to a chance to be cruel to him. I had to wrench his arm a bit, but eventually he agreed. We just went to see her.*

"You met Marlene Warwick with the only person in the city she hates more than you?" Maeve could tell she was being sharp, irritated and defensive for reasons that didn't have to do entirely with Imogen's recklessness. But she couldn't believe it—what kind of death wish did these two have? Why hadn't they called her?

No, no. Imogen made placating gestures. *No, he met with her. She's got a skylight. I eavesdropped.*

"That maneuver almost went very badly for us last time," she reminded Imogen. "If you had gotten yourself killed for real, where would I be?"

Imogen didn't reply for a moment; she looked at Maeve almost guiltily, and then away. *You're probably not going to approve of this either, then.* She held up her hands. *Orion refused to go without the promise of his safety, so we spent the whole two days practicing. I'm not perfect yet, but watch.* She pointed to the lighter beside the lamp, then rested her hands on her knees. Maeve watched, arms crossed, as the lighter twitched, hopped of its own accord, and then jerked up into the air to hover between them. It dropped after a moment, and Imogen let out a sharp breath, her mouth twitching into a grimace. *So, if anyone shoots harpoons at us, we should be good.*

"If you see them coming," Maeve reminded her. She paused, frustration and concern warring inside her, and peered closer at Imogen. "Is that why you're unsettled?"

Imogen shrugged. *To do that, I kind of have to take my hand out of my body and pick it up. And my reach is pretty good, but it takes a little while to go back in.*

"Was that what caused this?" Maeve gestured to Imogen's face, and Imogen shook her head. "What happened at Marlene's?"

Imogen's eyes slid away from Maeve's. *I froze a fountain.*

"You—what—why?!"

Because she was being odious, and Orion was getting distracted, and I thought it would scare them both and it did, and it was really funny, and totally worth it! Imogen blew into her hands and snuck a glare at Maeve. *I'll be fine. It's been like, an hour. I can feel my lips again already.*

"You look like a corpse," Maeve said frankly, the awkwardness diminished by the absurdity of what had happened when she had been out of the loop for two days. A snort of laughter forced its way up her nose. "You'd better be careful doing things like that, or you might hurt yourself."

I'm cursed or immortal or something. Imogen raised her chin, the corners of her lips twitching. *And anyway, we got what we wanted. We confirmed she was there at the masquerade. Orion gave a very touching speech about what I would have wanted for the cemetery. And she*—Imogen's eyes lit up. *She said something very interesting.*

Maeve raised her eyebrows. "About what?"

She said to Orion, "I haven't spoken to you in an entire year, and yet somehow you think I know the name of every little urchin you take a liking to. I honestly cannot remember which of your rabble this Imogen was." And Orion went all stiff—because he hadn't told us about that visit. She told me something he didn't want me to know.

"A year ago? What did he say to her?" Maeve asked. Did Orion actually have helpful information?

He wouldn't say. Imogen bit her lip, a slight frown tweaking her eyebrows. *Which does make me a little suspicious. I tried to get more out of him, but he booted me out of the car as soon as we got back across the bridge.*

"Do you think he was involved?"

No, or I doubt he'd be helping me. Imogen looked up at Maeve. *I think he knows something, but he's too afraid to tell me. He may be the Laureate and have the wealth and fame, but he's afraid of her. Deep down.*

"Maybe she knows his secret."

Imogen's eyebrows rose, and a wicked grin cut across her face. *You know what—I bet you're absolutely right.*

Maeve managed half a smile, pleased with her theory, but she couldn't summon complete satisfaction. Imogen's gaze was more intense than usual—almost too intense to seem entirely healthy. She wondered if there were mental consequences to getting unsettled, too.

"So, next steps?" she prompted.

Imogen blinked and shook herself. *Well, I think there's two ways to tackle it. First is we go gather evidence. The constabulary never knew that I was at that masquerade—we question the people we know were there, see if Marlene ever slipped away. See if Camille was there. We try to wriggle Orion's secrets out.* She laced her fingers together; the cuticles were bitten to the quick, Maeve noticed. *Failing that, I go to this year's masquerade.*

"And try to trigger your memory?"

Imogen nodded. *Who knows? Maybe they'll even try to kill me again.* She must have caught the look on Maeve's face, because she quickly appended another message. *Which I will be careful of, because we don't know if I'm invincible. Even though I can heal rapidly and make things levitate and send messages without touching my telegraph and hold my breath forever—*

"And if I pushed you into the harbor, you'd probably die from salt exposure," Maeve reminded her. "Just be careful."

Imogen rolled her eyes. *I'm not a baby.*

"I—" Maeve blinked rapidly, yanked back to the dream. It felt so comfortable to fall back into the same pattern with Imogen— solving mysteries, tutting at her recklessness, whispering to her in the dark. But what would happen when the mystery was solved? When Imogen's unfinished business was complete? Not just to Imogen, but to Maeve? Would she go back to the convent, and eke out time to draw, and—if Imogen stayed on this side of the veil— go for tea every once in a while? The thought made her stomach feel sour. Or would she make a change?

Had she already changed?

The energy shifted; they both knew the moment had come.

Do you want to talk? Imogen glanced up at Maeve, then looked back out at the sea, at the sailboats in the harbor. *No pressure if not. Say the word and I'll drop it forever.*

Maeve bit her lip and held her breath for a long moment. Where did she fit into Lenorum, if indeed she had changed? Not the Court. Not the convent.

"What was your apartment like?" she said at last.

Imogen blinked a few times, then began to tap.

It was on the top floor of a townhouse—a bedroom with rose wallpaper, and a little library with a fireplace. The curtains were blue-grey. The stove was inoperable, but I ate out most of the time anyway. I had a taxidermy crow, and a writing desk by the window. The streetcar stopped right outside every hour on the hour.

"Will you go back there when you solve this? When you're safe again?"

Imogen hesitated, then shook her head.

*I'd rather build something new. Everything I had in the mausoleum—well, maybe you haven't heard. Someone threw a flaming can of whale oil down into it. The structure was fine, but everything in it, except what Clothilde brought back—*She whistled evocatively.

Maeve forgot the aim of her questions for a moment; she was horrified. "Oh, Imogen—"

Don't worry. I can get more clothes. I'll miss my crow. But all my poetry was with you. She smiled. *Sister Maeve, protecting me and mine.*

She swallowed hard. "So you're staying with Orion for now?"

Imogen nodded. *Until this is over. Then I'll go find somewhere new again. Something fresh. Somewhere with big windows, and...and a view of the harbor!* Her eyes were faraway, the potential smiles of the future ghosting over her lips.

"A window box full of flowers," Maeve suggested.

Oh, absolutely.

"Maybe a little altar to the Hallowed Mother—a few candles?"

Sure. Maybe I'll become more religious after this.

"A drawing table? Would that...fit?"

Imogen's eyes refocused, and her lips parted slightly.

Oh. Wait.

Maeve fought back a blush. "Is there room in...in the future for things like that? Or would you rather—"

*No! Absolutely not! Tell you what—look, I've added a studio and a second armchair and an easel by the window—*She gestured hurriedly as if making space in the aether for Maeve, then paused and looked at her unsteadily. *What about the convent?*

"Well, I'm not leaving," she warned, almost as a reassurance to herself. "That was just...a metaphor, or..." She drummed her fingers on the dock. "I...I..." she swallowed, her words suddenly seeming to leave her. She had known what she wanted in the dream, but it was blurring the longer she was away from it. "I was happy the other night. Being with you made me happy. It makes me happy when you talk about my art with me—it makes me feel like you *know* me. The real me, who I think I've buried so far under trying to put others first that I don't even know her anymore. But I like the me I am when I'm with you." She blushed and gritted her teeth. "If that makes any sense."

Imogen gave her a smile. *I think I get it.*

The color was beginning to return to her cheeks, the dark circles fading, and as she slid her hand over and placed it over Maeve's, she felt her skin to be lukewarm. The gesture was simple, affection and solidarity, and something about it quieted the voice of guilt inside her. *And I like her, too.*

The tension that had been building in her chest the past few days finally snapped, and she let it flood out of her, half a sigh and half a mad laugh of relief. Orion was a bad influence and Imogen was putting herself in danger and Maeve wasn't behaving much better, but it didn't matter—all that mattered was seizing Imogen's hand and yanking her into a kiss and finally, finally letting go. Imogen applauded her for the decision. Her arms were inside Maeve's coat and around her waist before she had even slid all the way over, and her kisses felt as hungry as Maeve knew her own to be. The night of the party had been like a dream—this was cold, windbitten reality, and it was better.

Yours or mine?

Maeve didn't hesitate.

"Mine."

It seemed to take a year to make it back to the convent, and it took all of Maeve's focus to put her key in the lock and turn it. Despite her protests Imogen was hanging close—close enough to smell her jasmine perfume, close enough to feel the renewed warmth coming off her. If anyone looked out the window she was going to get caught. Any normal night it would be stressful—tonight it was nearly exhilarating.

Imogen tried to hold her hand all the way up the stairs and pouted when Maeve swatted it away. She wasn't quite that far gone. Imogen switched to writing in her notebook as they entered her room.

You've an admirable commitment to secrecy.

"Self-control is a virtue," Maeve said archly. Not that she was showing much of it by her standards.

Imogen didn't seem to mind the hypocrisy; her face took on her old smirk, and she sidled over, hooking a finger under one of the buttons of Maeve's coat. She was forced to use both hands to write but replaced them as Maeve read.

Well, how am I supposed to hold out against such sweet temptation?

"I might have said things back at the dock, but if you think pretty words will get me to like you…."

Imogen's smirk grew as she used Maeve's shoulder as a writing desk. *Oh, I don't mind if you don't like me. Just to spend an hour in your divine presence, darling—oh, see, the pretty words are a package deal.*

Maeve scanned the notebook and made a show of rolling her eyes, though she was enjoying the flattery despite herself. "Well, if you must." Imogen had come to the end of Maeve's buttons and helped her out of her coat. Her fingers lingered at Maeve's waist as she turned back around. "Though you're going to have to decide what your highest priority is for your hands."

Imogen raised her eyebrows coyly; Maeve gave her a look that dared her to question the statement. She wasn't going to blush and stammer and hedge about what she was doing. She was making a mark—ending the writer's block, starting something, at least. Imogen clearly got her meaning; she tossed her notebook back over her shoulder. She lifted her left hand to cradle Maeve's cheek, stroking her thumb across her cheekbone, and wrapped the other around her back as she pulled her into another kiss. Her hands wandered from there—to press ticklishly against the side of Maeve's throat, to grasp at her waist, to draw her over to the bed. Maeve hoisted her comforter up around them and leaned into Imogen's touch to keep out the chill. It was drafty and dark and hardly a thing like Orion's apartment here, but that was part of the enjoyment. It was on Maeve's own terms.

It blurred together a bit after that, the world narrowing into Imogen's still-slightly-too-cold hands and indecent mouth. Maeve's breath hitched and her hands sought purchase in Imogen's shirt, her fingers tensing involuntarily at the teasing brush of Imogen's lips along the underside of her jaw. They shifted closer, and closer still, till Maeve's legs were around Imogen's waist and they sank back into the pillows, tangled in each other's arms. Maeve lost her veil and shimmied her dress up to her knees; Imogen popped the last few buttons on her own shirt and buried a hand in Maeve's hair, twisting her fingers in deliciously. The other explored the hem of her skirt, sending a thrill up her spine, and her knees tightened involuntarily over Imogen's hips. Imogen rolled them underneath her, the points of her hip bones digging into her thighs and smiled teasingly. There were a few moments after that where she thought she counted more than ten fingertips pressed into her skin, though it was difficult to focus enough to tell. She snickered out a shaky complaint anyway—"quit...hhh...misusing divine powers"—but Imogen didn't seem inclined to obey in the slightest. Her expression was unutterably smug, half-lidded eyes and half-parted lips, and Maeve couldn't look for longer than a few seconds before want dragged her mouth back up against the latter. The hand in her hair twisted tighter, and the one at her thigh pressed its fingertips in deeper; a cold touch caressed her cheek, and another picked at the buttons at the front of her dress. It was all very heretical, but Maeve supposed she was already a nun sleeping with her girlfriend in her own convent. Atonement for their sins could wait till they finished.

Chapter

XV

The next morning dawned with a dusting of snow on the windowsill, and Maeve drew the comforter up over her shoulders with a sigh of contentment. She felt more relaxed than she had in ages; sure, the murder and the assassin and the note were concerns, but they were outside the covers, and right now she was under them. Her body felt soft and heavy, and the pleasant remnants of sleep cushioned her thoughts. It could stand to be a bit warmer, she supposed—Imogen had cooled off as she slept, and her side of the bed threatened cold tendrils of air. Maeve stretched and sat up, pulling her blanket up over her chest, and surveyed the body beside her. She was lying on her stomach, her face half-buried in the pillows and her mouth slightly open. Every thirty seconds or so her shoulders would rise and fall, marking out her breath at a dirge's tempo. Maeve tried to match it for a few moments, then gave up. Her skin was pale, but not quite as waxy as a corpse's—more like a marble statue, or moonlight on the water. Maeve imagined sketching the curve of her spine, the much-faded tattoo of a lobster on her left bicep, the constellation formed by the mole on her shoulder blade and the trio of freckles in the center of her back. Her hair stuck up crazily, and a love bite had risen purple in the curve of the right side of her throat, at the edge of her wound. She was lovely.

Then the bells in the chapel began to ring, and Maeve was forced to look at her watch instead.

She jumped out of bed with a curse, and Imogen started upright.

"It's okay, it's okay!" she whispered, snatching her undergarments off the floor and yanking her boots on. "Just got to go to service. Be back. Bring you breakfast." Imogen looked at her with wide eyes, the covers clutched to her chest, and for a moment she looked so terribly sweet and surprised that Maeve felt the wild impulse to blow service off and spend the morning the way they had spent the night. She satisfied herself with a kiss, wrestled out of Imogen's sudden attempt to pull her down, and pulled her veil over her head with a scoff of indignance. Imogen grinned and rubbed at her eyes, wiggled her fingers as Maeve opened the door, and dove back under the covers.

She slid into place between Thalia and Shivani just as Mother Superior entered the chapel with the other elders.

"We're on body preparation duty today," Thalia whispered to Maeve. "Consumption. If you're not up for it—"

"It's okay," she whispered back, suddenly remembering her anger at Shivani and wishing she had sat between Thalia and Frances instead. Made a statement. Though, she supposed, she had done that—just in secret. She suddenly felt her skin crawl at that realization, at the knowledge of what exactly she had done. She didn't regret it; she just didn't like keeping secrets.

The stone eyes of the Hallowed Mother's statue gazed down on her, and a prayer beat nervously against the inside of her chest as they all knelt forward. *I'm supposed to live a good life. I deserve as much as I give to others. The rules of this convent are human rules, not divine ones, and they can be changed.*

There was no reply either way—no heavenly chorus or thunderclap of displeasure. Which probably meant her reckoning was to be human, too. She gazed up at the altar as Mother Superior made her way to the podium, and felt guilt settle on her shoulders. Unfortunately, the rules had a face. It would be easier to rebel against people she loved less.

Well, whatever. The hourglass had been set, and sooner or later, her secret would have to surface. But Maeve was a nun, not a poet. She wouldn't let it destroy her.

When she came back to her room that night—the rest of the day spent in the preparation for burial of the body Thalia had mentioned and going over exorcism lessons with the little sisters—she found it still occupied, and somewhat changed from the way she had left it. The oil lamp had been augmented by a lot of candles, the floors were strewn with loose scraps of newspaper, and in the center of the floor sat Imogen, poring over the hurricane. She looked up with a start as Maeve entered, then relaxed and got to her feet, gathering up the clippings.

Going through the alibis again, she wrote in her notebook. *Camille was working in her lab that night according to her professor—at the Academy, but not at the party. Nowhere near that alley where I was found. Marlene was at the party with me but left long after I seem to have. Orion was across town, but not far from the alley.* She gestured in the air. *There's a schedule to it, a dance—where did I go, who did I see, what movements did these players make?*

"Is that what you're trying to make? A schedule?"

Yes. But obviously, there are holes. Imogen huffed. *Solving old murders is hard, especially when there's no record of the victim's movements.*

"We could try automatic writing again," Maeve suggested, unlacing her boots and setting them next to Imogen's beside the door. There was something wildly domestic about it, and it made her stomach thrill. "Want me to ask Frances?"

Imogen made a dismissive face. *I've asked too much of your sisters already in asking them to keep me a secret. I can do this on my own.*

"You don't have to, is what I'm saying."

Perhaps later. Right now, I have opportunities closer to home. But anyway— Imogen finished collating her papers, neatly sidestepping Maeve's chastisement, and reached under the bed for a small, beat-up suitcase. She popped open the latches and placed the clippings inside. Maeve could see her poetry books underneath them, along with the Wraith mask, a few folded sets of clothing and a carefully padded bottle of ink. Was that all she had left? Maeve bit her lip and watched as Imogen latched it back up, then pulled a small box out from deeper under the bed. She opened it and shook Maeve's repaired glasses out into her hand. *Not your dress yet—I realized you might like to pick it out for yourself. We'll go next time you're free.*

"Thank you," Maeve said worriedly, and put the glasses back on. "But don't you need your money now? Now that your stuff is gone?"

Imogen rolled her eyes. *I really don't. I'm living in the spare room of the richest man on the island, and he'll give me a damned allowance if I pout and bat my eyes.* She debuted a sliver of the pout in question. *This and the other things are hardly anything. Let me spoil you.*

"The other things?" Maeve looked at her despairingly.

Imogen caught her expression as she pulled another bag out from under the bed, and burst into silent giggles. *Just some little things. Ten ammonite tops, darling.* The smile on her face was so sweet and delighted that Maeve's desire to protest flagged. Especially when Imogen reached into the bag and withdrew a bouquet of pale pink roses. She folded an arm behind her back and presented it to Maeve with her head bowed.

"Oh, shove off," Maeve said, her face growing hot, and Imogen looked up with a grin.

You started it, darling.

"I started it? You tried to kiss me!"

You gave me a rose, the first time we met! Imogen wiggled her eyebrows. *Quite modern of you. Normally I like a little old-fashioned courtship first, but you just swept me off my feet—*

"That was the least romantic rose in all of recorded history," she laughed, indignant. "Ninety percent for shoving you off the steps of your dead friend's mausoleum and ten percent for mourning." She allowed herself a sniff of the roses—floral and fresh, the stems bowing under the weight of enormous, splayed petals, the pink deepening toward the center of the flower like a blush. "How'd you even get roses this big in October?"

Imogen smiled, and took the bouquet from her hands, crossing to the wardrobe and reaching up to her top shelf for her teapot. *The Court's got a florist growing roses all winter for the Spring Cotillion. I got Orion to pull a few strings—or stems, rather.* She took Maeve's canteen out of her bag and poured it into the teapot, then placed the roses inside and put them on the desk. *Open the tin.*

So, Maeve reached back into the bag, and unwrapped tissue from around a tin that turned out to contain Silver Pearl brand chamomile tea, flavored with what the label claimed to be exotic spices from the faraway south. Imogen sat down beside her, grinning, and drummed her nails on the top of the tin.

I got it for you in bags and everything, so you can make it nice and easy. The best temperature for it is two hundred degrees and two-and-a-half minutes is the time, but really even if you bash the stuff, it'll come out tolerable. A nice beginner's tea.

Maeve glanced over at her teapot, occupied by roses, and narrowed her eyes at Imogen good-humoredly.

"Is this just so you have something drinkable for when you come to visit?"

Perish the thought, her telegraph read, even as Imogen dug around in her suitcase and pulled out a chipped enamel travel tea set. She set the pot up on top of one of the candles with a practiced hand and smiled over at Maeve. *Unless you're busy?*

"Not for the rest of the evening," she said, relenting, and opened the tin, taking a deep breath of the strong spiced scent of the tea. Perhaps Imogen was right—even the smell was relaxing. She passed a pair of bags over to her, and Imogen dropped them in with the rest of Maeve's water.

And this is a good brand—I should know—so if there's any variety that you're particularly fond of, let me know. You struck me as a chamomile.

"Anything but ginger tea." Maeve stuck out her tongue. "Every time I got seasick—any time I got sick, period—'have some ginger tea, Maeve, it'll fix you. Drink more ginger tea. Quit vomiting up that ginger tea.'"

Imogen wrinkled her nose in a grin. *Ugh. That's half of why I couldn't stay a lobster hand. Terrible in rough seas.* She bobbed the tea bags up and down. *Peppermint tea has the same good effects with none of the adolescent trauma.*

"I wasn't even bad in rough seas!" she protested. "I was teaching myself accounting by lamp in my hammock at night—math and writing and the light swinging and ugh! I was trying to get them to let me stay home." She wrinkled her nose "I think the puking did half the convincing, though."

Imogen smiled, then poured out a cup and passed it to Maeve. *I get it. Change your name, keep your name, they say it doesn't matter, but your family always rather expects…* She poured herself a cup and raised it. *Good for you, though, deciding what you wanted and going for it.*

Maeve wasn't sure how to respond to that, so she busied herself with a sip. It hadn't been something she'd wanted; more like leaving something she didn't. She would work twice as hard on land, she had promised, hoping the wrinkles in her mother's brow would iron themselves out. It wouldn't be an inconvenience.

She wondered how Imogen had gotten so confident, to know exactly what she wanted and chase it down so relentlessly.

"Did your guardian want you to become a cemetery keeper?"

Imogen glanced up. *Well...yes and no, I think. They wanted someone to stay and protect the place when they were gone, for certain. They were older—fifty-two when they found me. They knew they wouldn't be there forever, and...*she paused for a moment. *I'm sure it seemed like fate when I showed up to pass things onto. But Oleander hadn't always wanted to be a cemetery keeper. They had had done theater for a while before a bad knee made them retire.*

"Is that where you got the mask?" Maeve asked, gesturing with her chin under the bed. Imogen pulled her suitcase back out with a smile and pulled out her Wraith mask. Silver and porcelain and black, tiny blue flowers spilling from the eye sockets up close. It had been cracked across the forehead and painstakingly repaired with a vein of silver. It was clearly very old, and very beloved.

Oh, yes—it was theirs. I remember the first time they let me wear it—we always made up little plays when I was little, but I was clumsy. All legs, no way was I a dancer. They let me try it on and very carefully walk around when I was thirteen. Immediately spun into a door frame and cracked the damned thing in half. Imogen shook her head in clear embarrassment. *But they weren't mad. And they weren't mad when I left, either. I think they knew what it was like to be young and want to show yourself off.*

"Can't relate," Maeve deadpanned.

Damn shame. Imogen sipped her tea with a coy twitch of her eyebrows. *I'd go to church more if I knew that there were girls this pretty hiding behind the stained-glass windows.*

"If you went to church to seduce nuns," Maeve said dryly, "you'd probably get struck by lightning."

Doesn't the Hallowed Mother want me to be happy? Imogen hooked one of Maeve's curls out of her coif and wrapped it around her finger. *And you gave me that first rose, so....*

"But you seduced me," Maeve returned. She couldn't believe Imogen could so easily do this—slide seamlessly from normal conversation to flirtation. Words had power, sure, but they ought to punish the speaker as much as the listener. Imogen wasn't even blushing. Ugh. Her knee nudged into Imogen's, surely of its own accord. "You took me to see art and got me all alone…" She tried to make it sound like an accusation.

True. Imogen slid closer, looking at her through her eyelashes. *To be fair, I did try to preserve your virtue.*

"Mmm." Maeve gave up. "Good thing virtue doesn't reside exclusively on untouched lips, huh?"

She leaned in to kiss her, but Imogen hissed a curse and held up a finger. She flipped a few pages forward in her notebook, scrawled something down urgently, and then turned back.

Sorry—that was beautiful. Don't want to forget it. Can I use it?

Maeve groaned in exasperation. "Have I mentioned I hate poets?"

Constantly. Imogen shoved her notebook aside and connected the kiss, drowning out Maeve's protests. She was lucky, Maeve thought grumpily, that she was a good kisser, or Maeve would have thrown her out entirely. Sneaking in her window, distracting her, giving her presents and heart attacks. She kissed her back grudgingly, and Imogen took that as forgiveness, maneuvering herself into Maeve's lap without a hint of remorse. It took some doing with her height, but there was something about it that activated Maeve's protective drive in a very pleasant way. Like Imogen felt safe being held by her.

She nearly missed the knock at the door, but some longstanding instinct borne of years of Shivani barging into her room made her leap to her feet before she was really aware of hearing it. She took Imogen half of the way up with her and had to dive to catch her by the arm before she fell flat on her face; it was incredible luck and reflex that got her to swing Imogen behind the door at the very instant Shivani opened it. Thankfully she was stuffing something into her bag as she entered, giving Maeve the chance to slow her breathing and not look guilty.

"Haunted absinthe house. They want it cleared before the evening rush."

Her attitude was pleasant enough but impersonal—none of the excitement from when they had gone out to the mainland. It was a sharp letdown from the events of the few minutes' prior, and for a moment Maeve was at a loss. "Right," she said at last, deciding that she would give Shivani as good as she got. "The one nearby, or…?"

"It's called 'Feyfolk'." Shivani wrinkled her nose and shrugged. "You ready?"

"Yeah—got to pick up fresh salt on the way out, but yeah."

"What's that?"

Maeve looked up from grabbing her bag to see Shivani frowning at her desk. "What's what?"

"Those flowers."

Maeve surveyed the showy bouquet as dispassionately as she could. "Roses."

Shivani looked like she was biting back something sharp. "Where did you get them, I mean. They're not from our greenhouse."

"Oh. Imogen brought them by," she said, a twinge of petty vindictiveness quickly followed by a twinge of guilt hitting her in rapid succession. "Thought I might like them."

Shivani looked down at the pair of teacups on the floor, brushed a strand of hair out of her face, and turned on her heel. "Ah. She doesn't know you. You like purple better."

The streetcar ride to the absinthe house was awkward, as was the walk and the arrival. The place was difficult to miss; a huge neon green sign sat atop the building, the outline of a fairy tapping its magic wand against the F in Feyfolk. An arrow pointed down from the sign to a basement entrance, and through tiny half-opaque windows Maeve could see glowing lights from within. It was misting, and the water in the air gave everything an otherworldly blur. She glanced up the street surreptitiously; the Court sat just a few blocks away, removed from the crush of buildings and tight alleys. She hoped Shivani was right, that it wasn't business hours yet. Otherwise, she might be in unexpected danger of being recognized.

They took the stairs down and opened the door to find the place mostly empty. A few people Maeve assumed were employees were working at cleaning—one polishing the bar and another sweeping under a table, both in street clothes. The goal of the decor was clearly to imply sumptuousness; heavy velvet drapes cascaded from the ceiling, and the booths were upholstered in green satin. The back of the bar was stacked high with absinthe bottles, lit from below and casting a green glow over most of the room. Despite appearances, there was a slight scent of antiseptic in the air, and a closer look revealed the curtains to be somewhat threadbare, some wear on the bar from where it had been cleaned night after night. This was a place dedicated to sustaining fantasy and was beginning to show the strain.

"Ah, perfect." A slightly hoarse voice hailed them and was followed by a woman in her early forties, her hair piled high on top of her head and her eyebrows penciled in in such a way to make her look surprised to see them. "Here to fix our little haunting, no? Madame Lavinia, charmed." She smiled, half-held up a delicate hand, then seemed to recall who they were and returned it to her side.

"Sister Maeve," Maeve put forward, sizing the woman up and trying to determine what they might be about to get into. She couldn't imagine anyone was doing a lot of seances in the middle of visiting an absinthe house, but she wasn't sure what else would trigger a new haunting here. It wasn't like anyone had died recently, was it?

"Sister Shivani," Shivani said, still sounding brusque. She didn't volunteer anything else.

Maeve took the lead, somewhat surprised. Usually, Shivani liked the social aspect. "So, Madame, what exactly have you called us in for?"

Her smile grew wider. "Well, that's what you're here to tell me, isn't it?" She gave a tittering laugh. "I'm not quite sure, but my girls have been complaining—cold drafts, moaning, strange glowing lights. Which I rather thought were normal parts of an absinthe house, but the guests have started to notice, too. Most of the upstairs rooms have had one report or another."

"May we take a look, then?"

"By all means."

Her dress swished as she turned, and Maeve followed her to the back of the room and through a pair of curtains. Not a break room as she had maybe expected—no, it seemed that the rumors were true, for this establishment at least. Shivani was a bit slow in following, but before long the three of them stood in a plushly carpeted hallway staring down a full dozen doors. Maeve took a deep breath—were they all separately haunted?

"Let me know if there's anything you girls need!" Madame Lavinia said with a saccharine smile. "We open in an hour, so do try to be done by then." She disappeared back downstairs and muffled but harsh-sounding orders echoed back up the stairwell.

"Well," Maeve said, glancing around for inspiration. She glanced at Shivani, who was glaring at the floor. "Uh, you take the left and I take the right?"

She nodded shortly, and so Maeve turned into the nearest door and closed it behind her. The walls were painted red with gaudy crown molding—the interior decoration of someone trying to emulate ostentatiousness but taking a swing into tacky. It probably looked better in the dark, which was likely the state it was typically used in if the bed was anything to go by. She crouched to the floor, opened her backpack, and pulled out her planchette, looking around the room for anything unusual. It was a weak haunting, if haunted this room was—no apparent spectral energy except under...She inched closer, lifted the bedskirt, and found the source of the subtle green glow. A single transparent hand, truncated at the wrist, lying curled up like a dead bug. Another fractured haunting.

"Hello there," Maeve said softly, and set down her spirit board, still peering through the planchette. The hand's pinky twitched. "I'm Maeve, and I'm here to help you. Here, I have a tool to help you talk to me. Does that sound good?" The hand uncurled and glitched in and out of sight for a moment. And then it stood directly before the spirit board, using its fingers as legs. Maeve set down the planchette carefully. "Great. What's your name?"

The planchette moved laboriously, as if the hand was working hard to push it around. J-U-L-E-S—

"Jules," she whispered. "Jules, what happened to you? Are you in pain?"

H-O-L-E-I-N-V-E-I-L-F-E-L-L-I-N—The planchette abruptly moved to GOODBYE and stopped moving, and as Maeve picked it up, she saw the hand flicker in, out, back into existence. She set the planchette down again, and it twitched weakly. J-U-L-E-S....

"A hole in the veil?" she prompted.

T-H-R-E-A-D-S-A-R-E-W-A-V-E-S-S-O-M-E-B-A-D-R-I-P-P-L-E-P-U-L-L-E-D-A-L-L-T-H-E-T-H-R-E-A-D-S-O-U-T-A-N-D-I-F-E-L-L-A-N-D-W-A-S-C-U-T-C-U-T-C-U-T—

Maeve frowned—waves? Ripples? "Are you talking about how you got fractured?"

C-U-T-C-U-T-C-U-T—GOODBYE—J-U-L-E-S—

It was struggling, and though Maeve wanted to know more she also didn't want to prolong its suffering. She wrote what it had said—bad ripples, the threads of the veil being pulled out—down, and cleared her throat.

"I'm going to try and exorcise you now, okay? So, you can go back to the other side and heal yourself?" She pulled out her prayer book and began to speak. "Hallowed Mother, preserve this lost soul—" Through the lens of the planchette, the hand immediately flew toward the wall, then disappeared through it, and Maeve got to her feet, following it out into the hall. She frowned; Shivani was still standing there, leaning in a doorway on the left side and staring inside. She lowered the planchette. "Shivani?"

Shivani stood up straighter, and though Maeve couldn't see her face she could tell she felt caught out.

"Sorry, was just thinking. What's—what's the deal with the haunting?"

"Fractured," she said uncertainly, distracted by Shivani's odd behavior. "I was just about to exorcise it—it's not violent or anything, it's just lost."

"Lost," Shivani echoed, and shook herself. She turned around, her expression firmly neutral. "Well, we can help it, I guess."

Maeve found where the hand had gotten to—hiding beneath a small table in the middle of the hallway among dead flower petals—and restarted the exorcism, watching with some horror as other body parts began to scuttle their way into the center of the hallway. Cut, cut, cut indeed—something came from every room in fits and starts and lurches. Shivani read along with her, and slowly through the planchette Maeve could see the puzzle coming together. It was rare to find such a peaceful fractured ghost, and it was the first time Maeve had ever really been able to watch as the pieces rejoined. The seam between an arm and a shoulder glowed bright for a moment, ectoplasm running down the spectral crook of the arm, and dropped into real sight, leaving an acrid smell in the air. It reminded her of how Imogen's throat bled when she was upset and made her wonder if that too was an attempt to heal. To heal the physical wound, or emotional ones? She considered this as the figure of a young woman came together before them, vague and blurred and already beginning to disappear. Her left pinky crooked at Maeve, then faded away, leaving nothing but some ectoplasm on the carpet.

She turned to Shivani. "Well, do you want to bang around a bit, make it sound spooky?" It was a deception, but sometimes one they had found necessary—customers expected spectacle, and tried to wriggle out of paying for a gentler removal.

Shivani swallowed and shook her head. "Let's leave." It may have been Maeve's imagination, but the tension seemed to have gone out of her shoulders. She wasn't sure what it had been re-placed with. Why? Was it something Maeve had done, or was it the unusual exorcism? Was it the frustration of another fractured haunting? Or was it something else?

Should she ask?

Did she want to ask?

"Do...do you want to talk—?"

"No."

A scathing reply leapt to Maeve's lips—fine, *fine!*—but before she could spit it Shivani amended herself.

"Not...right now," she said more gently, and got to her feet. "Come on, it's late. We've got things to do in the morning—almost certainly."

"Aren't you the one always telling me when I'm late for things?" Maeve asked, watching carefully out of the corner of her eye. She didn't know quite what to feel—hope or wariness or annoyance. She didn't like fighting. She also wanted an apology before she let things go back to normal. But she was tired—maybe Shivani was, too. Maybe they needed to aim for neutral first.

Shivani chuckled and scuffed her boot against the carpet. "Well, I'm almost perfect, but...."

Maeve stood as well and followed Shivani down the stairs. It took them a moment to find a distracted Madame Lavinia, clapping urgently and chiding various personages in green lingerie into position.

"Excellent—that'll stop them whining," she muttered, and tersely cut them a check. "Rosalie—I know you can lace that corset tighter, you foolish girl. If I hear you've been off your diet, I swear you'll be out of here—!"

Dire pronouncements followed them out the door, and Maeve raised an eyebrow. "Probably for the best I'm not skinny enough to work at a place like that." Imogen probably would be—but Maeve firmly clamped down on that train of thought before it headed to distracting places. She definitely did not want to think about all the very fancy lingerie Imogen had probably owned before her death—

"Why would you want to?" Shivani wrinkled her nose. "Just people getting drunk and giving into their worst instincts and being vulgar."

Maeve guiltily quit pinching her wrist. "Oh, yeah," she said, swallowing hard. If they were giving into their worst instincts, then what was she doing? "No, I just…I guess I feel bad for the people who work there. Seems tough." She shivered in the mist, and carefully watched where she was putting her feet on the slick cobblestones.

Shivani didn't respond.

Chapter

XVI

I go to get tea. Orion's on the mainland at that point, doing something he won't tell me about. Camille was in her lab. Marlene's with Orion.

"You go back to your apartment. Orion goes back to the Court to prepare for the vote. Camille, lab. Marlene, on the mainland."

I go to the masquerade. Marlene goes to the masquerade. Orion and Camille do not.

"But Camille is at the Academy. Hardly a two-minute walk from the library to the parapsychology department."

But her advisor sees her in her lab at ten o'clock, after I've left the party. Or so the constabulary says.

"And Marlene is at the party."

Orion isn't.

"Orion's at the vote."

Orion's near the alley, though.

"Do you think it's him?"

No. Imogen huffed in frustration and straightened a newspaper clipping. There were dark circles under her eyes—she had been at this since before Maeve had woken up. *Despite him being so wildly suspicious. Even though he's the most likely to be able to overpower me. He just...ugh.*

"But it wasn't overpowering—the constabulary said," Maeve pointed out. "They slit your throat from behind, without a struggle."

Which points to him, too, since I distrust him the least. Unless Camille maybe…but the motive is tenuous. I hadn't rejected her proposal yet. And she's too rational to kill for love.

"Right…" Maeve muttered, looking over the papers spread over the floor and willing them to come together into something sensible. The effort was hampered by the distraction of Imogen sitting beside her, ice cold and carelessly wrapped in a dressing gown she'd brought over to Maeve's room at some point. Maeve considered her from both angles—the curve of her chest disappearing tantalizingly under the robe's collar; the slight dulling of her eyes and the intensity of her stare—and guiltily decided to address the latter. "You look unsettled. Should we take a break?"

I'm fine, Imogen wrote, and of their own accord a few clippings floated up and swapped places. *What if….*

Maeve grumbled in frustration and got up, picking her way through the papers to her dressing table. She wasn't sure if Imogen was just being stubborn or if this was a symptom of her condition, but it was abundantly clear: the more Imogen thought about her murder, the more unsettled she got. She supposed it made sense, if the murder was Imogen's unfinished business, but that raised new concerns. How unsettled could Imogen get? Could she lose control of her body entirely? And what would happen when she completed it?

She drummed her fingers on her prayerbook, wishing for an answer to that, too, but none was forthcoming. She couldn't much focus on the notes in her sketchbook either, but the paper still stuck into it—the notes she'd stolen from Camille's office—sparked half an idea. Waveforms. W-A-V-E-S, the spirit at the absinthe house had said. The Sisterhood didn't study the spirits they helped, but scientists…Scientists had data. And with enough data, you could extrapolate to odd cases.

She turned and opened her mouth, wondering how she should approach this. "Does it worry you, getting unsettled? That you don't really know what's going on with your body?"

I trust you—you're the expert, after all.

Maeve swallowed. "But I don't know what's going on with you. And my expertise is in exorcisms, not in keeping ghosts around." She paced around in front of Imogen as she continued to rearrange her clippings. "I would feel better with a second opinion. Wouldn't you?"

An opinion about what?

She threw up her hands. "All of it! How you heal, why you act like a person and not like a ghost, what's keeping you in your body. Isn't it more important to know what could kill you over who wants to?" She paused for a moment, then plunged ahead. "I think if we looked at it from a scientific perspective...."

That got Imogen's attention—her head snapped up, and the room went even colder. Maeve's telegraph on the windowsill chimed loudly, and she dove to mute it.

I'm not going in to get experimented on—I won't, I've got bodily autonomy, I'm allowed to refuse, I'm not going anywhere near that place—

"Okay, okay," Maeve said quickly. Imogen's shoulders were up around her ears, but relaxed at that. "I just think it might be helpful to go in and talk to...to Professor Chrystos, or someone. I won't mention you—just ask about ghosts in general. I have questions about this fractured haunting thing, anyway, and if I'm..." If she was going around with poets, she might as well throw her lot in with scientists, too, and really disappoint Mother Superior. She winced and refocused on Imogen. "Is that okay?"

Imogen smoothed her hair out of her eyes, and wrote carefully. *Yes, of course. Sorry. I just—* She frowned, scribbled the beginning of the previous line out, and started again. *You know what—if you're going to do that, then I'll go stalk Camille. See if she does anything suspicious. See if I can remember.*

"As long as you be careful," Maeve said, more out of habit than anything. Imogen's vehement reaction had her worried—she looked even more unsettled than she had before. But she nodded and blotted at her throat with a handkerchief. "Anyway, now I'm not asking, I'm telling you—you should take a break. It's almost ten, anyway."

Imogen glanced at the mirror and pursed her lips. She wrote haltingly. *Right. Sorry. I get caught up.*

"No need to apologize—you just need to listen." Maeve gave her a buoying smile. "After all, I'm your expert."

Oh, you're going to use that against me. Imogen picked up her papers, put them away, and gave her a smile. It lit up her face in spite of the livor mortis. *Anyway. Almost ten—am I allowed to know what you have planned yet?*

"Maybe." Maeve got to her feet. "Get your coat and meet me by the front door. I'll be there in a few minutes." Imogen raised an eyebrow, but shrugged Orion's hand-me-down peacoat on as instructed and cracked open the window. Maeve slipped out into the hall, headed down to Frances' door, and knocked. "Frances? Thalia?"

They came to the door. "Give me a second—let me cast off—" Frances said, knitting frantically at a pair of mittens. "Almost done—"

Thalia, holding the ball of yarn with a fond expression, leaned down to Maeve. "I think she wants to impress your friend," she whispered. "She went to the library to see what was fashionable in gloves this year." Indeed, the mittens were a good deal less home-spun than Frances' usual output—rose-colored wool cabled in intricate patterns.

"I do want to impress her, so she knows she can trust us to be cool and fashionable and good friends," Frances said urgently, tearing the end of the yarn with her teeth and throwing the needles back into her room. "And the tops flip down so her fingers are free for sign language—"

"Sign language?" Maeve asked. They began their way down the hall. Frances stuffed the pink mittens into her pockets.

"Oh, yes, Thalia can tell you—"

"When we were at the library, I read about this language they're developing at the Academy—for people who can't hear or speak." Thalia pulled a pamphlet out from under her arm. "Basical-ly, you make signs with your hands to speak. If she wants to learn it, it would work perfectly."

Maeve raised her eyebrows. "Oh, wow, yeah. One second." She stopped at Shivani's door, took a deep breath, and knocked. "Shivani?"

She came to the door after a long moment. "Yeah? Oh, yikes, did I forget something?" She glanced at the other two, who Maeve could feel tense nervously. But she had to offer.

"No, we thought we'd go visit the lighthouse cathedral, and get tea after."

"Oh! That sounds nice." Her mood seemed nearly normal—she stuck her hands in her pockets and gave a small smile.

"Yeah!" Maeve pursed her lips. "And we thought we would take, um, Imogen, because she's never been before. Missionary work, huh?" She forced a laugh.

Shivani's smile grew slightly strained. "You think that'll do anything for a poet?"

"I'm trying to be friendly," Maeve said. She fought the urge to sound sardonic—she meant friendly to Imogen, but she hoped Shivani would take it as an olive branch, too.

"Well, best of luck—I have some stuff to catch up on." It seemed not—Shivani was shutting the door. "I'll see you all later, I suppose."

Maeve gritted her teeth. "Okay."

The three of them made their way down to the front door in awkward silence and met Imogen out on the steps. She raised an eyebrow when she saw them all and looked at Maeve.

"We're taking you out to Lighthouse Cathedral," she said firmly. "And then we're going to get tea. I think it'll be fun, don't you?"

Imogen nodded hastily, though Maeve could see her holding her telegraph behind her back. *Where's your other friend?*

"Shivani was busy, but Frances and Thalia wanted to come!" she said carefully. "They have some things to show you, right?"

That seemed to snap the two of them out of their uncertainty; Frances hurried forward and held up her mittens. "It's getting cold at night," she told Imogen. "And I know you're, well, not feeling the cold so much anymore but still—"

Imogen's mouth opened, then shot into a smile; she quickly reached into her pocket and pulled out her cowl and tugged it on before doing the same with the mittens.

Mother, you didn't have to do this! She wiggled her fingers, grinning broadly. Then she paused, then carefully typed, *thank you very much,* and ducked her head in a somber bow.

Maeve read the message, and Frances smiled, looking relieved. "Well, I wanted to. You're welcome."

"Not to mention we all already have a full set of knitted outerwear. You're fresh meat," Thalia put in, and passed Imogen her pamphlet as the four of them set off toward the streetcar station. "By the way, I did some research and found this—it might be helpful to you...."

By the time they hopped off the streetcar and began the long boardwalk out to the island's point, Maeve had managed to forget her worries about Shivani and enjoy herself. The wind was chilly, but the sun was bright, and the company kept her warm. Imogen, too, looked reasonably happy—which was, of course, her ulterior motive. Damn Orion, but he was right; Imogen needed as many friends as she could get, and she was going to provide them whether Imogen wanted them or not. And she had chosen well—Thalia and Frances were exceedingly polite in waiting for her to write out her half of the conversation. Imogen's shoulders kept tensing and retensing—she seemed to be struggling with the appropriate degree of formality—but she was unquestionably participating. Or trying to, anyway.

The boardwalk wended its way out along the rocks, occasionally spanning a stretch of water brought in by the high tide, and eventually came to its end at the ungainly Lighthouse Cathedral. The name was uncreative; the building had been built to act as both, and mixed its architectural styles into something that had never caught on anywhere else. The spire extended from the seaward side, painted in red and white spirals, and the stained-glass windows sparkled in complimentary shades. "It's still a working lighthouse," Thalia told Imogen as they approached, "and they hold services here on holidays. But the city maintains it now."

Seems an inconvenient location for Sunday services.

"From the island, yes." Thalia skipped up the steps. "Maeve can tell you—it used to be a mariner's church. Whalers would row up."

It took a moment for their eyes to adjust from the bright sun, but the advantage to coming on such a beautiful day was clear—long colorful shadows were cast across the pews, and the place was bustling with life. Maeve smiled and took a deep breath. The smell of brine was soaked into every beam and bit of wood—wood which, as Thalia was telling Imogen, largely came from shipwrecks. The barrel vault of the cathedral was comprised of the whole keel of a ship that had dashed on the rocks here and led them to build a church in this spot. Preserved through the eons and, to Maeve's ear, creaking in response to the waves outside. The place needed a sturdy exorcism each year, so the three of them had been here plenty of times, but it was always a great inspiration. The sea and the afterlife bound in one—practicality and beauty. Her hand itched for her pencil as always, but she hurried to catch up with the others. Thalia was leaning into her role as a docent, and she had probably ought to make sure Imogen wasn't being held against her will.

"And, of course, this pilgrimage would simply be incomplete without a visit to Portia Mate's tomb, darlings. Just this way, if I've done my research—"

Maeve froze, the voice echoing loudly from the entryway unfortunately familiar. No...What were the odds? Was the damned island really that small? She carefully walked up the aisle, making sure to steer away from—right, damn it, the apse that held the tomb of Lenorum's first poet, *damn* it—and sidled up to the others as they toured the stained-glass windows. "Hey," she hissed, and yanked Imogen aside. "Orion's here."

Imogen looked down at her in surprise and scoffed silently as she caught sight of him. *Unbelievable! Is he following me?*

"I don't know." It didn't seem like he had noticed them—and as always, he hadn't exactly dressed to blend in. A slit-sleeved overcoat over the world's most impractically tight fisherman's sweater, and high-heeled riding boots. At least the ensemble wasn't bright green. He'd brought a gaggle of students with him, and they had headed to the poet's sarcophagus without detour, so maybe it was just coincidence. Maeve glanced at Imogen, then back at Frances and Thalia. "Should we...leave?"

Imogen frowned. *No, this is your day out!*

"Yes, but—" She looked at Frances and Thalia again, then hissed in her ear. "Someone's not very good at keeping secrets, is he?" Imogen stiffened with what Maeve thought was worry, until she noticed her staring over her shoulder. She pinched the bridge of her nose. "Is he right behind me?"

On his way over.

"Mother's grave, what are the odds? Good morning, darlings!" Maeve turned unwillingly and received a kiss on the cheek. Ugh—poets. Orion turned and did the same to Imogen, and Imogen rolled her eyes at Maeve. "I apologize for the formal greeting, my dear roommate, but it's been several days since I saw you last." He looked at her through his eyelashes and smiled deviously. "Now wherever could you have been—?"

Imogen drew a finger across her throat, and Maeve shook her head vehemently. She pointed at Frances and Thalia, who had just seemingly noticed Imogen's absence. Orion raised his eyebrows.

"Of course, sweetheart," he whispered. "I get your meaning entirely." He turned on his heel and spread his arms out wide. "And these must be your dear friends—oh, I've heard so much about you all!"

Maeve smacked her forehead—that was absolutely the opposite of her meaning. He seized their hands, planted a kiss on each, and folded his arms behind his back with what he clearly thought was a winning smile. Frances looked vaguely terrified; Thalia was wide-eyed and rapidly turning pink. "I'm one of Imogen's friends. And you are…?"

Maeve glanced at Imogen, then stepped in. "This is Frances, and this is Thalia."

"Nice to meet you," Frances ventured. Thalia nodded mutely.

"Nice to meet you as well! I just love Maeve here—did she tell you how we met? Hilarious, great story. Say, are you all doing anything after this? I'm teaching a little field trip for the next hour, but I'm sure my students can all find their way back to the Court."

"Nothing," Maeve said hurriedly at the same time as Frances said "Tea."

Orion rocked back on his heels easily. "I heard tea. My treat? I'd love to get to know you all better."

You're scaring them, Imogen messaged, but Maeve forgot to read it aloud.

"Of course," Thalia said in a slightly strangled voice. "Looking forward to it."

He beamed. "I as well! Ta!" He spun with a flare of his coat and gave a little wave as he traipsed off.

Frances turned to Maeve as soon as he was out of eyeshot. "Who was that?"

Imogen started wheezing, and Maeve smacked her forehead again. "Mother's grave."

Thalia stared at the lipstick on the back of her hand. "I'm never washing this off."

"You really think he can control himself?" Maeve complained, panting as they reached the top of the stairs.

Imogen shrugged, smiled, and reached into her coat. *If he doesn't, well—* The hilt of her knife glinted in the sun, and Maeve snickered. *I have impressed upon him the importance of easing your sisters into this. That way he sees it less as a secret to keep and more of a fun corrupting influence he gets to be.*

"That really makes me feel better," Maeve said sardonically, but smiled as well, and strolled out along the lighthouse's observation deck. The wind tugged at her skirt and her veil, and the sun dazzled on the waves below. Far off in the distance, she could see boats on the water, lobster boats and whaling ships and freighters and people sailing for fun. She sat down on a bench outside the light chamber, where the flame was extinguished for the day. The smell of whale oil was thick here. She called over to Imogen, who was leaning out over the railing. "Mind if I sit here and draw for a little?"

Not at all. I was going to sit and write.

So, Maeve pulled out her sketchbook. It was getting pretty full, with all the notes and theorizing and writing from Imogen. She flipped to a clean page and looked out across the horizon for a composition that caught her fancy. Maybe the rocks below, or the mainland off in the distance, or—maybe some figure drawing. She considered Imogen, messily trying to refill her fountain pen on the go and smiled to herself with a nod. She framed in the railing and the open sky, waited for Imogen to pull out her journal and start thinking, and then began. She sketched in the lines that described her frame, her hips at an uneven angle, her arms draped over the railing, her head cocked to one side. Then she added volume, sharp shoulders and the long curves of her legs, scribbling a quick tuft of hair. Imogen's back was to Maeve, but her head was turned enough that she could catch her in profile—a long straight nose, a narrow chin, eyelashes caught gold by the sun. And that was it—first try. She blinked, looked between the page and her subject, almost perplexed. It was nothing like that drawing of Shivani, erased through the paper. This had been effortless.

She filled in the background and the details, careful not to overshadow whatever she had managed to capture and glanced at her watch as Imogen finally pulled her journal back over the railing and wrote something down in it.

"We've got five minutes before Orion wants to meet."

Okay. Let me just— she scribbled a few more words, shoved both her pen and notebook back into her pockets, and turned back to face Maeve. *Good to go.*

"What are you writing about?" Maeve asked, as they made their way around the walkway back to the stairs.

Oh, y'know. Imogen glanced around, then quickly pressed a kiss to Maeve's cheek. *The ocean.* Maeve blushed and looked around too, but the observation deck was empty except for them. Imogen waved her on down the stairs. *Let's go die of embarrassment.*

"And it's really quite tragic, because those were my favorite sunglasses." Orion pouted. "She's getting good use out of them, I hope?"

"The inner workings of the little sisters are an enigma," Frances said apologetically. The five of them had been seated on the sidewalk out front of the teahouse, and Orion had immediately ordered a plate of lemon squares for the table and instructed them to get whatever they wanted. Maeve and Frances and Thalia had had a whispered discussion and had eventually landed on a not-too-expensive pot of chai with milk. They were waiting for it now, Maeve sitting ramrod straight and nervous for the barest hint that Orion was going to let something slip. No wonder the whole Court was under his thumb.

"Ah, well. We all have to make sacrifices in times like these." He picked up a lemon square and jabbed it at Frances and Thalia across the table. "Now, I know Maeve here is interested in art—are the two of you similarly inclined? I must say, I thought the Sister-hood of Good Death would be full of a lot of very sad people."

"Oh, no—we try to live happy lives within the strictures of the order." Frances smiled. "But Maeve's the one with the artistic talent."

"I see." Orion smiled and took a bite. "Then what do you two do, for your happy lives?"

Frances smiled uncertainly. "I like to knit."

"Politics," Thalia managed.

Orion raised his eyebrows. "The former makes sense, the latter I was not expecting." He put the rest of the lemon square in his mouth and took a long moment to chew.

What do you think of him, is what he wants to ask, Imogen put in with a grin. *Politically.*

Thalia opened her mouth, evidently thought better of it, and took a lemon square to eat, too.

"So, did you like the cathedral?" Frances asked Imogen.

Imogen nodded. *The view from the top is really something.* Her knee nudged into Maeve's—perhaps accidentally, perhaps not—and Maeve jumped. Orion raised his eyebrows, and Maeve glared at him. She read Imogen's words out very carefully. *Good poem material. I'll have to talk to Adolai and see if he can teach me anything about religious music, see if I can work that in.*

"You could talk to Shivani," Thalia offered, before wincing. "Or, well, I mean—well, she knows loads about music. She plays the organ for us and runs choir and all."

Orion's attention perked up. "Who's Shivani?"

Frances and Maeve glanced at each other.

"Another of our sisters," Maeve told him. "She was…busy."

"Alright, chai and milk?" The server placed their teapot and a stack of cups down for them and laced her fingers together. "Any-thing else I can get you folks?"

"All set, thanks," Orion told her, and fished a gold ammonite out of his pocket for a tip. It easily made up three times the bill.

She blinked, took the coin uncertainly, and then scurried off. Orion leaned back in his chair as Maeve stood to pour for them.

"That's fun to do," he said offhand to Imogen. "Once we get you your laurels proper and your salary, I mean."

Imogen thumbed at the ribbon around her neck and gave a smile. It was an uncertain smile, full of the kind of hope that had long been suppressed. Maeve found a smile of her own on her lips as she watched it, and sat back down, pulling her mug of tea toward her. It smelled delicious. Imogen had pressed a napkin carefully to her throat and took a sip. Orion had his finger in his, which both confused her and struck her as painful. What was the story with that, again? She half remembered a drunken conversation—

Thalia raised her cup to her lips, and lightning-fast, Orion swatted it out of her hand with a gasp. It shattered on the bricks of the sidewalk. Maeve looked at him in shock—had he gone insane? He held up his forefinger—the nail laquer had gone from pink to bright crimson.

They both turned and stared in horror as Imogen took another sip.

Immediately Maeve snatched the cup from her hand, and apologized profusely to the server, who had come over at the sound of the crash. Orion stood up, his chair scraping back, and stuck another finger into the pot of tea, while Frances and Thalia looked at the two of them in absolute bewilderment. Orion pulled his nails out blood red and spun to the server.

"I need to speak to the manager—or whoever made this tea, or whatever. Now!"

"O-okay," she stammered. "Um, one second—"

"What's wrong with you two?" Thalia demanded at last.

Orion wiggled his fingers. "Poison-detecting nail lacquer. Good investment, if people are trying to kill you." Thalia went pale, and Frances pushed her tea away, wide-eyed. Orion rounded on Imogen. "How much did you drink? Imogen?"

Imogen didn't respond—her stare had gone vague and glassy. Maeve rushed forward, pressed a hand to the side of her neck. No pulse, but that was normal. Her lips going blue was less normal. Her mouth moved slightly, her chest heaving like she was trying to suck in a breath, but nothing was coming in or out. Maeve felt her own breath starting to match that tempo and took Imogen's ice-cold hand.

"She'll be okay," she heard herself say from a distance. "She survived that harpoon, she...she...."

Orion said something to Thalia and Frances, who nodded and hurried out of Maeve's rapidly tunneling vision. She became dimly aware of racing down the street, her shoulder bolstered under Imogen's arm, her skin colder than the ambient temperature. The teahouse was built partially on a pier, and they were headed toward its end. She stumbled down a set of rickety stairs, and after Orion threw down his coat, she and Thalia lowered Imogen to the sand of the beach below. Maeve sank down with her, clutching at her hand. Imogen's eyes were open, but nothing was animated behind them. It was frigid—frost formed on the ground around her. Orion knelt, too, and tilted her head back.

"Let me try…" he muttered, and opened her mouth, wiping his hand off on his thigh before sticking his finger down her throat. Maeve watched him, dull and in shock. "Works for alcohol, usually," he said defensively, and pulled his hand out. "Dead people don't gag, though." The rapid movement of his eyes belied similar panic.

"She's not dead," Maeve mumbled. "She's only half dead." She tightened her grip on Imogen's hand. Not dead, not dead.

There was a horrible moment where she doubted.

And then Imogen lurched to a sitting position with a strangled gasp, rolled, and vomited a large quantity of ectoplasm onto the sand. Orion pulled his coat back quickly, and Maeve dove forward, tugging a handkerchief out of her pocket and offering it to Imogen—breathing raggedly, but still breathing. She wiped a few glowing strands from around her mouth, and collapsed into Maeve's lap, panting.

"Told you," she whispered, and fell to coughing. "Cursed or immortal or something."

A sturdy questioning by Orion terrified the staff but brought no answers; the supply of tea was tested and found to be fine, but the pot itself contained a dose of cyanide high enough to kill a whale, if the whale was so foolish as to drink it. The constabulary promised to look into it—after all, it might have killed the Laureate or any of his three young companions. More gold had convinced the staff of that number—three, indeed. Orion called his driver, and snuck Imogen home. He told Maeve and the others he would walk back. He had to think, he said. Frances and Thalia hung closely, protectively around Maeve, which prevented her from saying much.

Which was probably for the best at the moment. Her telegraph chimed twice on the streetcar ride home.

From Orion: *Maeve, darling—you and I should have dinner sometime this week. I've got something we ought to talk about. We'll make a little party of it.*

And from Imogen: *We have to end this, Maeve. That got too close to you.*

They completed the trip to the Academy separately the next day for safety's sake; Maeve walked quickly in street clothes under an umbrella and breathed a sigh of relief once she was off the street and inside the parapsychology department building. It felt a bit more intimidating to enter without Mother Superior's reassuring presence, but it was much better than worrying if the harpoon man or the unknown poisoner were lurking somewhere out of sight. She looked at the note she had taken on the phone—nine in the morning, sharp—and checked her watch, then made her way to that same secretary. From there she was directed to a higher floor of the building—apparently, the professors' offices were given better views than those of the graduate students. Up here, there was a bit more light, though a few odd drafts signaled the presence of spiritual energy. She decided to ignore it for the time being. After all, picking a fight over proper exorcism techniques was a great way to not get her questions answered. She knocked on Professor Chrystos's door and waited.

It was a few moments before it opened, and when it did, she found herself face-to-face with the last person she wanted to see.

"Lost, Sister Maeve?" Camille asked, sarcasm dripping from her voice.

"No, in fact," Maeve said coolly, and drew herself up to her full height. The note to the convent—it had been in Camille's handwriting. What did she know? Was this dangerous? "I have an appointment with Professor Chrystos."

"She always was too free with her valuable time." Camille brushed past Maeve into the hall and knitted her fingers behind her back as she walked. "Do try not to waste it."

"Like you wasted Mother Superior's?" Maeve called, hoping the lie was convincing. "Unfortunately, we're not so strict as you seem to think."

Camille paused, but her back was to Maeve, her reaction obscured.

"I'm sure I don't know what you mean." She kept on.

"And I'm sure I don't know how you talk around that silver spoon," Maeve muttered, petulance oddly satisfying. It was less satisfying when she realized that there was another figure at the door, and she shot an exasperated prayer up to the Hallowed Mother. Point taken—don't be rude. In earshot of other people, anyway.

To her relief, Professor Chrystos seemed not to acknowledge her statement, or indeed recognize her. "I'm sorry, dear, but I have an appointment at this time—"

"Oh, yes—it's with me."

"Oh!" Professor Chrystos adjusted her spectacles and peered at her. "So sorry, I thought you were a student! You look very different without your habit, Sister...er—"

"Maeve." Chrystos opened the door a little wider, and Maeve followed her into an office packed with overfull bookshelves and chalkboards covered in arcane mathematics. She peered at the scrawl, trying to see if anything about waves presented itself, but it was beyond her. Were these the mechanics behind her simple exorcisms? How did the disciplines connect? "And that's the idea, Professor. Trying not to start conflict between our two sides." Ha. Unless it was with Camille.

"Indeed." The professor brushed a stray wisp of hair out of her face and turned on an electric kettle. Maeve grumbled internally—of course the Academy of Sciences got to have electricity. "I was surprised you reached out without Beth—that is, your Mother Superior. Has something happened? Oh, feel free to move any of that—"

Maeve carefully deposited a stack of books on the floor, and took the chair they had been sitting in for herself. "This is for my own personal research, actually. See, we've been seeing some unusual behavior from ghosts in the field, and I wanted to know if you could offer any insights. It's nothing that the Sisterhood has ever seen before, seems like."

There was quiet in the office for a moment; Professor Chrystos looked surprised. The kettle began to whistle, and she snatched it off its hot plate, pouring out a cup of Lenorum Public for each of them and shaking a few biscuits out of a box on her desk onto a plate. She shoved a pile of papers onto the ground and took a seat herself, nibbling at one of the biscuits thoughtfully.

"You want the Academy's opinion?" she said at last.

Maeve nodded cautiously. "I think maybe sometimes we're quick to judge others who do things differently from us. But I imagine we could help each other."

"Yes…" she murmured and tugged at the neck of her turtleneck sweater. "Yes, alright. A civil discussion—not an opportunity I expected to…yes, quite." Her expression refocused, and she trained her thick glasses on Maeve. "What kind of unusual behavior?"

So, Maeve explained the haunting from the absinthe house, and the pattern of seeing fragmented ghosts. At one point, Chrystos got up abruptly and returned with a lab notebook, taking fast and messy notes.

"You see," she muttered, "your Order guards its secrets with what I believe to be an absolutely unsportsmanlike vigor. And since our department is quite young in comparison, it is really difficult to determine what is and what isn't unusual behavior. Our database of readings is hardly statistically significant as it stands."

Maeve winced—hopefully she wasn't giving up too much information—and continued. "I asked the spirit what had happened to it, and it mentioned waves—" She pulled out her sketchbook and showed the transcript of the interaction to Professor Chrystos, whose eyes fairly bulged out of their sockets. "Does that mean anything to you?"

"You actually communicated with this being?" she whispered, tracing her fingers over the letters. "It spoke in intelligible words?"

"Via a spirit board," Maeve said uncomfortably. "Are you not able to get that?"

Chrystos looked up at her wide-eyed. "You've just proved half a dozen theses in one go, Sister Maeve, if this device of yours truly is capturing sapient communication from otherworldly beings." She looked around and seized on Maeve's backpack. "Do you have an example of a—a spirit board with you? Would you allow me to examine it?"

Maeve pushed her backpack under her chair with her foot. "Perhaps later, if you can get me any information about what this spirit was talking about."

She looked disappointed, but quickly perked back up. "I mean, the waveform theory of the spectral is a fairly basic one in parapsychology, which I could explain. Is that relevant to your investigation?"

Maeve thought of the notes she had stolen off Camille's desk. "Absolutely."

Professor Chrystos stood, quickly erased one of the chalkboards, and felt about her person for a piece of chalk. "So—eh—are you in possession of an undergraduate degree? Or any knowledge of mathematics?"

Maeve clicked her tongue. "Ma'am—"

She seemed to think better of the question.

"Okay, a qualitative introduction. Eh. So, light—it arrives to our eyes as a wave." She drew out a waveform on the board, just as Camille had done in her notes. "The closer the peaks, the bluer the light, and the further apart, the redder. Now, there are other waveforms in wavelengths we cannot see—" and here she drew a long, shallow shape below the first. "Radio waves, like the kind that carry signals to wireless telegraphs, are of this sort. There are also higher energy waves that lie on the far side of the blue end of the visible spectrum. We call these infrared and ultraviolet, respectively." She drew out a short wavelength, then turned to Maeve. "Got all that?"

Maeve nodded, and the professor smiled.

"Excellent. Now, this is a drastic oversimplification—really almost a metaphor—but it should serve its purpose. So, we imagine all these wavelengths traveling in the same direction. In real life they can travel however they choose but let us use the spatial dimensions as a metaphor for different energetic dimensions. So, we have all these waves of infrared and visible and ultraviolet light, all traveling in the same plane, and then—" and she drew a new waveform from the top to the bottom of the board, perpendicular to the others. "We have a different form of energy—different waves, traveling in another plane. And these all can have different wave-lengths, too." She drew a few more waves in that same direction. "Very simply put, then, there is a perpendicular direction of energy that cuts through our own and interacts with our energy when it arrives. The two forms of energy weave in and out with each other, forming a sort of—"

"A veil," Maeve said, surprised. She'd all but drawn it on the board, hadn't she? "That's the veil."

Professor Chrystos nodded patiently. "If you want to be a bit poetical about it, certainly. Essentially, that dimension is where spectral energy naturally resides, and when it interacts with our energy, it forms a manifestation."

"But what does that have to do with dead people?" Maeve asked.

Chrystos shook her head. "It doesn't—scientifically speaking, it's impossible to actually prove that any of these odd manifesta-tions are in any way linked to our plane of existence. Likely, it's projection and supersti—" she coughed, and turned away from Maeve— "eh, tradition that makes people ascribe the behaviors of their loved ones to what are essentially random spikes in ener-gy. There is some research—those theses I mentioned—that have begun to understand these manifestations as possibly containing some consciousness, but really it would be an overstatement to link that all the way to the beliefs of religion."

Maeve wondered how many exorcisms Professor Chrystos had actually been to, or whether she simply spent all her time doing math.

"Anyway," she said tactfully, "So these waves—if they act as the threads of the veil, metaphorically speaking—if something disrupted the plane of...of spectral energy, then you might see odd manifestations?"

Professor Chrystos nodded. "These waves have spatial and temporal elements to them, so if the spectral plane were disrupted, you might see ectoplasm manifest all over a room—or in many different times."

"What could disrupt the spectral field, then?" Maeve asked.

"Many things—even excitations in our field. To continue the veil metaphor, if I start pulling threads in the weft, the warp will be disrupted. Holes may even form. And whatever manifestations interact with these disruptions would be affected." She pushed her glasses up the bridge of her nose and steepled her fingers. "It could be anything causing what you're seeing—light, sound, magnetism, electricity—"

Maeve nodded, thinking hard. "Could the telegraph signals do it? Or electrical generators?"

"Oh, no." She laughed to herself. "It would have to be much higher-powered than your everyday energy usage. Such a device would be noticeable."

"Like something being developed in your department?" Maeve pressed.

Chrystos's demeanor closed off slightly. "Student projects are, unfortunately, proprietary. Funding and grants and such—I'm sure you understand."

"I do," Maeve said, setting her jaw and shoving her backpack a little farther back. "What determines where these holes in the veil show up?" She wavered for a moment, then forged on. "Could they move—be attached to an object, or a person?"

Professor Chrystos frowned. "There is anecdotal evidence of manifestations following certain objects, but holes? Not that I'm aware of." She turned to the blackboard, sketched a square, and a lump in the middle of it. "An excitation operates like a mouse under a blanket—it can move around, and you see the effect, but the fabric above it stays in place. A hole—" She drew a small circle— "is a hole." She turned to Maeve. "Why do you ask?"

"Just curiosity," she said hastily. "We've seen so many of these fractured hauntings, it might, er, make sense to start trying to triangulate their source, and if they can't move, then that's easy enough." It was a lie made up on the spot—of course she was asking after Imogen—but now she thought about it, it made sense. Oh no. Was she getting good at lying?

"Perhaps—collecting data is always the first step in understanding things," Chrystos said absently. "Do let me know if you hit upon anything." She shook herself after a moment and blinked at her. "Did you have any further questions?"

"Not right now," Maeve said, shouldering her backpack and preparing to beat a retreat while she was ahead. An interesting new perspective, and certainly helpful on the fractured haunting front, but it was clear—the Sisterhood could still claim expertise, and she was still the best person to help Imogen and the other unusual hauntings. She nodded to herself, then paused at the door and looked back at the professor. "I'll talk to Mother Superior about getting you a spirit board to look at, but a seance parlor planchette might be a good place to start too. Some of them won't do anything—you want manganese glass in the window. Blessed by a priestess less scrupulous than us." Professor Chrystos looked incredulous; Maeve smiled and stepped out into the hall. "Superstition or not, Professor, you've got a few hundred years of knowledge to catch up on. Go ahead and cheat."

Chapter

XVII

There was a knock at the door; it opened before
Maeve could ask for a minute. "You've got to stop doing that,
Shivani," she chided. "You're going to see something you don't
want to see."

"How'd you know it was me?"

"Because Frances and Thalia wait for me to say 'come in'."

"Overrated." Maeve watched Shivani walk by in the mirror and
sit on her bed. She paused for a moment, then continued braiding
her hair up. She supposed Shivani would detail the purpose of her
visit in time, if she wanted to. "What are these?"

She watched in the mirror as Shivani peeked into a file on her
desk.

"Addresses from Mother Superior. The locations of the fractured hauntings. I'm trying to figure out what's going on."

"Ah." Shivani let the file fall closed, evidently satisfied with its
innocence. Her eyes slid sideways. "Where'd you get that dress?"

"It's for Imogen's case—business necessities, you know." Imogen had taken her to replace the harpooned one the other day. She
had vacillated for a while, but eventually settled on a slightly more
daring look than the previous one. Pink cotton lawn gathered at
the sternum and in the front of the skirt. A trail of buttons ran
down the back, and the sleeves gathered at her elbows. She pinned
the completed braid back and tried in vain once more to get that
last button fastened.

Shivani snorted. "Not your usual look."

Maeve gave up and turned, but there was no malice in Shivani's face. "No—I think my usual look is changing a bit."

"There must be better heating where you're hanging out, then." Shivani hiked the cardigan she was wearing over her habit higher and walked over to pluck at the sleeves. "But it looks nice. You—look nice."

"Thank you." Maeve was a little surprised, but she meant it. She smoothed her hands over the fabric self-consciously. "I...liked all the little details. That's the fun thing about art, I always think, and fashion's kind of like art. I could see myself being drawn to it..." She let herself trail off before she made any implications about the source of the money for the dress or her future role in her life.

"Mmm." Shivani leaned against the dressing table, and Maeve started up braiding again. It had been a long time; she wasn't going to the trouble of the full braids her mother favored, but she would at least do something to keep the bulk of her curls out of her face. It had ought to match the formality of the dress and the occasion, at least. "I assume you're headed somewhere in it?"

"I have dinner with Orion Cantor," she said carefully.

A dark shadow passed over Shivani's face before she rearranged it into a sort of wry smile. "She's making you stick your hand into the shark's mouth, huh?"

Maeve shook her head. "It's my choice. And anyway, my blood's good with fish."

"Whales aren't fish, Maevey-wavey."

"I know," she said crossly, and cracked a smile. "Let me have my metaphor."

"Dinner with the Laureate, metaphors—tsk, tsk." Shivani gave a small smile, too. "You're going to need to quarantine for months after this. No poets—only scripture."

Maeve's smile wavered a little, but she fought to stay in the present. "I've got to head over in a minute—did you come in here for something?"

"Hmm." She turned toward the window, then looked back at the floor. Maeve stayed quiet—she had the impression that Shivani was working up to something.

"I just," she said at last, still watching Maeve's rug, "want you to be careful, is all. I, uh—you're tangling with unpleasant people, and I would hate to see any of that spoil the way you see…things. Good life and all, ha. Dunno how well they're sticking to that."

Maeve tried to catch Shivani's eye behind the curtain of her bangs. "They're not as bad as Mother Superior makes them out to be."

"So far as you've seen." Shivani blew out a strained breath. "Orion Cantor has a reputation, Maeve, and for good reason. I know we don't pay much attention to that sort of thing in the convent. And you've been here a long time. But—" The unspoken contrast was plain—that Shivani hadn't been here as long, knew more. Maeve waited, wondering. Shivani had never talked about where she had come from before.

But she stayed silent.

"Imogen hasn't got a reputation like that," Maeve said at last.

"She's his student, isn't she?"

"Yeah, but—"

"She wants something from you. Just be careful." Shivani's tone had shifted, and the window of discussion had closed. For a moment, Maeve felt like demanding more—what, exactly, Shivani was implying about Imogen. What good reason was there for Orion's reputation, and why did Shivani care about it? Why did she hate the poets so much? But her telegraph chimed, and the time on her watch said it was time to go. And anyway, her relationship with Shivani didn't work like that. Making demands would probably drive her away.

"Can you help me with my buttons?"

Shivani did them up wordlessly.

Maeve pulled on her coat and veil and made her way down to the side door. She had insisted that Orion not send his chauffeur, and it seemed like he had stuck to his word—the long black motorcar was nowhere in sight as she made her way to the streetcar stop. That was a relief, and a counterexample to Shivani's dire warnings. If Orion could be prevailed upon to be considerate, then any poet was redeemable.

"My goodness, I thought I was entertaining Sister Maeve, not some cute little socialite!" Orion bent down and gave a stage whisper. "I would have said sexy—better for the alliteration—but your lover's within earshot and she's been nervous all day. Also, I'm too old for you—really, darling. But you look delicious."

"Now I'm both uncomfortable and not hungry!" she declared brightly. "Imogen, come get your mentor, he's making a pass at me!"

The ring of metal sang through the air, and Orion was forced to straighten up by the dagger floating at his throat.

"Do you see what I have to live with?" he complained. "She's positively feral. I fear for my life."

"Well, if it ends you know who to call," Maeve said dryly, and let him lead her into the apartment. He'd shifted the furniture around at some point since her last visit—now what was once the living room was a dining room, complete with chandelier and three ornate chairs around a circular dinner table. Imogen was already occupying one of them, her hand outstretched and her face bearing the marks of intense concentration as the knife followed them into the room and returned to her hand. She had gelled her hair back from her forehead and painted her lips black—her wine-colored tailcoat matched Orion's green one, which Maeve was sure she was unhappy about.

"Macabre," Orion remarked. "You two deserve each other."

Maeve's telegraph chimed as Imogen got to her feet. *You look ravishing, darling, and I love what you've done with your hair.* She placed a prim kiss on each of Maeve's cheeks. *May I place a moratorium on Orion being allowed to call you pet names?*

"You may."

Please tell him that I have done so.

Maeve found herself snickering at the formality of it all as Imogen pulled out her chair for her and burst out into a full laugh as Orion swept back over and placed a silver cloche in front of her.

"Come on," she protested. "This is too fancy."

Orion dropped his wounded act. "I made it all myself—bought the ingredients and everything—so we know it's not poisoned," he told her, and pulled the cover off to reveal a creamy pasta. "Got shafted on the price of shrimp, but that's what you get for wearing laurels to the market."

You could take them off time-to-time, Imogen remarked.

"I have a tan line," he informed her haughtily. "Which you probably wouldn't understand. Try getting some sun sometime."

I'm allergic.

Maeve whispered a quick grace while they argued.

"Smells good, Orion," she piped up before they could cut too deep into each other. "I'm impressed."

He gestured indignantly to Maeve, like Imogen ought to try taking cues from her. "Thank you, Maeve. I've been learning how to cook, and it's been very fulfilling. Shrimp scampi. And I pulled a nice claret from the Court's wine cellar to pair."

"I'm excited to try it," she told him as Imogen trod on her foot under the table.

Kiss-up.

It was surprisingly good cooking from a man who, by his account, had never touched a stove before thirty. Maeve could tell the ingredients were high-quality, and the wine was tasty, if unfamiliar in flavor—she was used to whatever cheap bottle they could sneak in under Mother Superior's nose.

Imogen managed to get her portion down through liberal use of her napkin, and did admit that she enjoyed it, to Orion's triumphant glee. Eventually their bickering died down, and the three of them settled into conversation.

"I think you've been holding out on me, dar—Maeve. Your friend with the freckles mentioned 'artistic talent', not just an interest in art history."

Maeve smiled sheepishly and swirled her wine around. "Well, I didn't want to show my drawings to just anyone."

Orion blotted at his plate with a piece of bread. "Goodness! Can't relate in the slightest!"

"You know people will like your poems—you're a professional." She took a sip and glanced at Imogen. "I don't know. It feels personal, at my level. Which is absolutely not very high."

"Self-deprecation is a bad habit." Orion also looked at Imogen. "Is she good? I imagine you're privy to the inner sanctum."

Yes, she is. She has a very nice soft technique. And a good eye, which you already know. But she only draws in pencil. I think it would look lovely in watercolors.

"I don't know how to use watercolors."

"Well, that's what art classes are for, aren't they?" Orion poured himself more wine. "I always tell my students this, that talent isn't an innate thing. Ugh—hate that idea. You know how much the nobles love that? 'It's in our blood to be better than the peasants, we're born that way, people shouldn't look above their station'. I was a terrible poet when I started."

And he didn't improve much, Imogen teased, carefully sipping from her glass. *But he's right, Maeve. I got a lot better with his help.*

"You had better instincts than me—and better stories," Orion said modestly. "I just helped you with the history and the theory and all. By the way, are you working on anything now?"

Not in earnest. Imogen drummed her nails on the table. *I've got unpublished stuff from…before…but it all seems wrong now. And I'm busy at the moment with, y'know, trying not to get killed again. I have snippets of things started.*

"Makes sense. Well, plenty of time. You say the word and I'll call another vote."

Imogen swallowed painfully and glanced at Maeve. *Okay. Yeah. Just let me solve my murder—after the Masquerade, it's in a week….*

"Do you have to?"

Maeve looked over at Orion in surprise; he was engaged with chasing the last olive from his salad around. Imogen frowned. *Uh, yes?*

"But why? You don't seem to be able to die again. You could just keep watching out for assassination attempts like I do, no big deal…."

Imogen glanced back at Maeve, then away. *Yes, but I'm not the only one in danger here. It's everyone I associate with.*

"A risk that lessens if you come out in public and show yourself to be alive. No one would dare go after you or yours after such a wildly high-profile news story." He finally speared the olive and looked up briefly.

I…I suppose, but…it would still be stressful to live that way.

"What are you going to do when you find out, anyway? What would you get the constabulary to charge them with? They didn't actually manage to kill you."

Look, it's not—I just—

"And will you be able to get proof?"

It's not about the proof! I just have to know! Imogen set her knife down with a clatter and dabbed at her throat. Her wine glass developed a rime of frost as she picked it up and took an unsteady sip. She glanced at Maeve again and set the glass down. *Er—excuse me.* She stood and jogged up the stairs.

Orion watched her go. "Well, closure, I imagine?" he murmured. "But that's not always practical."

"Don't wind her up about it," Maeve chided. "It's not good for her mental state."

He turned toward her. "Oh?"

"Ghosts get fixated on their unfinished business," she told him. "It gets her unsettled to think too much about it, or why she wants it so badly. It's not just about closure—it's about compulsion."

"I'm not trying to wind her up." He looked darkly into his wine glass. "She's digging up old graves. She should know better."

"She can't help it—it's *her* grave," Maeve reminded him.

He managed a crooked smile. "Only hers, you think?"

"What do you mean?" she said sharply.

He didn't answer. "What happens when ghosts complete their unfinished business?"

"They go back to their rest."

"Hmm." He drained his wine and poured another glass. "And it's your job as a Sister of Good Death to make sure that happens?"

She looked at him hard. "To ghosts, yes."

He raised his chin thoughtfully—not quite a nod, but a consideration. He chewed the corner of his lip, then opened his mouth.

"Feeling better, Imogen?"

Maeve glanced over to see Imogen descending the stairs; her cheeks looked a bit hollow, but she gave a thumbs-up and a smile.

If Maeve wanted to learn, could she take classes here?

"Usually, they haven't been open to the public," Orion mused, all traces of his earlier dark mood vanishing. "But perhaps we should change that. People would certainly come to gawk."

"As long as I can stick with landscapes," Maeve put in, striving to make it seem like nothing was amiss. "Your still life compositions would be difficult to take back to the convent and hang up."

Orion instructed them to leave the dishes in the kitchen for Clothilde to deal with in the morning and brought out lemon meringue pie to enjoy in the rearranged parlor.

"Then Imogen, you have to leave."

Okay. Imogen's expression was uncertain, but Maeve gave her a nod. Orion was close to revealing something, it seemed. And if the previous conversation was anything to go by, it was clear why he was wary of revealing too much to Imogen. Was it really just that—trying to protect her? She could hardly believe it, but perhaps she was still thinking too little of Orion.

The pie was good but gone quickly, and Imogen replaced her dinner jacket with her peacoat. *I'll go for a walk around the grounds. Half an hour?*

"Should be enough," Orion said, and waved her out the door with yet another glass of wine. "Don't fall off the cliff!" He shut the door behind her and turned to Maeve. "Now."

She straightened up. "Is this about what you said to Lady Marlene the day before Imogen's death?"

He stared at her. "I said wha—how do you know about that?"

"Imogen saw her talk to you about it! Last week!"

"Mother's grave." He looked at the glass of wine darkly. "I need to lay off this stuff." He took another sip.

Maeve crossed her arms frustratedly. "Then what's this about?"

"Well." He sat back down on the couch across the parlor from her. "I'm continuing in my role as relationship counselor for the two of you and providing you with the sexual education that I have no doubt you are entirely lacking." He said it as if it were the most obvious next step in the world and wound his fingers together. "I'll start small—do you understand where babies come from?"

Maeve stared for a full fifteen seconds, then shut her mouth with effort and got to her feet. "Mmm. No thanks. Good dinner. Bye—"

"Oh, come on, Maeve—this is important!" Orion got up and skidded in front of her. "It's an important part of a relationship and I can't imagine that you learned anything from a bunch of nuns. This is my specialty!"

"Damn it, Orion, I thought you actually had something important to tell me," Maeve groaned, trying to dodge under his arm. He caught her and rebuffed her. "This is what you were thinking about five minutes after Imogen got poisoned? I thought this was a matter of life and death!"

"It could be!" Orion hesitated for a moment, then shook his head. "Okay, maybe not as such, but for the life or death of your relationship, quite possibly!"

"We're fine! Augh! I don't want to talk about this with you!" Anger had overridden shock; she tried to duck under his other arm, but he backed up and plastered himself over the door. "Let me leave!"

"You're fine now—don't you know about the honeymoon phase?" She snatched up an umbrella from the umbrella stand and pointed it at his throat. He looked deeply offended. "You wouldn't want her to get *bored* with you, now, would you?"

The word lanced through Maeve, and her grip on the umbrella wavered. Orion tried to force his face toward seriousness, but she could see the corner of his mouth twitch, and she wanted to stab him all the more for it. "A little overview of some topics, some re-sources," he said primly. "I will be very professional."

She brandished the umbrella closer, and he went cross-eyed looking at it disdainfully. "If I let you get your stupid counseling kicks doing this," she threatened, "then you're going to tell me what you know."

"I don't know what you two think I know, honestly—"

"Save it." He glanced up at her and raised an eyebrow. "Your entire life is built around knowing other peoples' secrets, and you expect me to believe you don't have one of your own?" She set her jaw. "I am trustworthy. I'm keeping my own secrets well enough, and I'll take yours beyond the grave. But we have to figure this out to help protect Imogen, and if you know who did it—"

"I don't." His eyes slid away.

"You know something relevant."

His jaw worked for a few moments; he made eye contact with her, and then held it. "It probably isn't."

"I'd like to judge that for myself."

He curled his lip. "I'll tell you why I can't tell you. Is that enough?"

Maeve swallowed; she wanted to drive a harder bargain, but she was beginning to want the information Orion had offered, too. Shivani had planted the seed of doubt, and now Orion was watering it. What if Imogen changed her mind about Maeve?

"It had better be good," she told him, and dropped the umbrella.

He rolled his shoulders and sighed, eyeing her unhappily. "Because the last time I tried to tell it to someone, she wound up with her throat slit in an alley two blocks from my house." He brushed past her and made his way back to the couch. "May we talk about something happier?"

Maeve paused, trying to slot this new information into her conception of the events as they had transpired. She wasn't sure it was particularly ground-breaking, but maybe Imogen could do something more with it. Maybe it would jog her memory.

She sat down to uphold her part, and let out an extended sigh. "I know how babies are made," she informed him. "Not exactly a pressing concern for the two of us, if I understand correctly."

"That's just the absolute basics. Which of you tops?"

"Come again."

Orion took a deep breath and cracked his knuckles. "Alright."

I'm on my way ba-ack. Coming up to the door. Hide all the secrets.

"And here's my lingerie man—go ahead and put a set on my tab if you like." Orion folded a business card into her hand and checked his watch. "A minute early. Not bad. Got all that?"

"No," Maeve said, unable to move her face. She had understood a lot more than she had wanted to, and in another very real sense had understood nothing at all. None of it had aided with the new insecurities the evening had introduced. She put the card in her pocket guiltily as Imogen opened the door.

She ditched her coat in the closet and sat down on the other end of the couch from Maeve. *Well, is the mystery solved?*

"No. Uh."

"We talked a little about your relationship," Orion said easily. "Maeve is inexperienced, and I wanted to give her a bit of the wisdom I've amassed over the years."

You haven't had a steady relationship in the time I've known you! Imogen turned to Maeve, looking indignant. *Oh, Mother, what did he say?*

"Because that's my goal," he returned. "I like it better that way."

Imogen didn't give that a reply. *Do you want me to walk you home? And unsay all the stupid stuff he unquestionably said?*

Maeve shook herself, and got to her feet. "Sure," she said, coughing up a laugh at the absurdity of it all. "Though you can't stay over—I've got to be up early tomorrow."

I shall hope that's the truth and not some idiotic tactic he's put you up to.

"No, no." She swallowed, found another insane laugh bubbling in her throat, and turned to Orion. "Thank you for the dinner and dessert, and to a lesser extent the advice. I'm sure someday I'll appreciate it."

"Ooh, nice insult." He smiled back and wiggled his fingers. "Anytime, darling."

No pet names.

"Anytime, Maeve," he corrected, and walked them out.

Chapter

XVIII

The next few days were busy—a few hauntings came up at once, and Maeve and the others were hauled out to the far corners of the island before having to rush back to carry off two back-to-back funerals. Her interactions with Shivani were improving, and when they met back up with Frances and Thalia, things seemed nearly back to normal, at least for them. Mother Superior was clearly distracted—she had gone to the Academy every day this week and had inquired after the state of Maeve's research in between.

"Go ahead and put a little more time into it, dear," she told her, scribbling in a ledger and passing it to Sister Priscilla before rushing out the door. "Tell me if you think it has anything to do with that cemetery—you know, the one downtown that we look after? Evidence might be useful in arguing for its preservation." She pinched the bridge of her nose. "We need more sisters by half to keep an eye on all the foolishness in this city…."

So that was a matter of public knowledge, then—the anniversary of Imogen's death was coming up, and with it the expiry of the cemetery's protection. Lady Marlene would have it purchased before long, but there didn't seem to be anything to be done about it. Even Imogen herself seemed to have given up, focusing instead on her plans for the Masquerade.

I don't think you should come with me—I want to try and trigger my memory, and you being there might take me out of it. I'm concerned about your safety, too—Marlene will be there for certain. I don't know if I can watch her and you both.

How about Orion? she messaged back. He hadn't been there last time, but he could be a reinforcement.

No—he said he's got plans, and then gave me this stupid grin. So, either he's got something in the works, or he just doesn't want to see his mother again. I'm betting on the latter.

I still think I should come. You shouldn't do this alone.

You're right, but I'm still not comfortable letting you come into danger with me.

I'll stay on my telegraph, at least, and be ready to come down if you call.

Thank you. I appreciate it.

By the time Maeve sat down with Mother Superior's files to actually study them, it was the night before the Masquerade—a fact she was desperately trying to forget. It wasn't like something *had* to go horribly wrong. The next day didn't have to spell disaster. Of course, it had a very high chance of doing so, and every time she thought about it her stomach jolted.

She very much wanted to demand that Imogen not go, but... Anyway, it was a relief to be off her feet for a while—and that was all she was going to think about. She sorted out all the files that referred to fractured hauntings and began copying down the addresses. It was mindless work, but maybe that was what she needed.

She had to go down to the convent's library for a map of Lenorum to plot the addresses onto, and by the time she got back the light on her telegraph was blinking. It reminded her of all the things she was trying not to think about. She swallowed and picked it up.

What are you up to?

Research, she replied. *That thing I told you about—the fractured hauntings.*

Anything interesting?

Maeve surveyed her pile of papers, sighed, and pinched the bridge of her nose. *Not really into it, to be honest. I thought it would be nice and distracting, but it's too dull.*

Distracting from what?

Her finger hovered uncertainly over the key. *From worrying.* She quickly sent another message. *What are you up to?*

On a walk in your neighborhood. You want a better distraction?

Maeve raised an eyebrow, then got up and walked to the window. A figure loitered in the pool of light cast by one of the streetlights below—a very leggy figure. She shook her head. *I can't believe you're out walking on your own at night. I'm losing count of the murder attempts you've survived.*

Can I come in and hide from the dark, then?

It didn't take long for Imogen to make her way up once Maeve grudgingly acquiesced. She tumbled from the window down to the bed, and immediately set to shedding her boots. Maeve shut the window against the chill she brought with her.

This is a lot of addresses, huh?

Maeve sat down on the edge of her bed with a sigh. "Yes. It's been a real problem for us."

Odd. Imogen took up a pen and Maeve's map and put a mark on it. Maeve was too tired to get up and see what she was doing. *When did they start?*

"Hard to tell." Maeve gave up on work officially, taking off her veil and unbraiding her hair. "They've become especially bad this last year, but there have been intermittent anomalies for a while."

Interesting. Imogen marked down a few more addresses and looked up at Maeve. *You look tired.*

"I am." She hoped that was just a comment on her state as a person and not on her appearance. Mother, did normal people have to worry about that usually? She rubbed her eyes; unbidden, Orion's words came to her. *You wouldn't want her to get bored with you...* Imogen set down the map and made her way over. She didn't look tired at all—the benefits of supernatural untouchability, Maeve imagined, or that huge soft bed back at Orion's. In that beautiful room, in that incredible palace filled with the world's least boring people.

You look like you're thinking too hard, too. Imogen brushed her shoulder against Maeve's and looked through her eyelashes at her. *Can I help?*

No, no—there was one thing Maeve never wanted to be, and that was a burden. Imogen had her own problems, and they were much bigger than whatever silly insecurities Maeve had. She shook her head minutely, and kissed Imogen to distract her from the line of questioning.

It worked for a few minutes—Imogen shifted closer, threading her fingers into Maeve's hair. But that only made Maeve think of all the things Orion had said—how some people were better at this sort of thing than others, that it needed practice—and she hadn't had much practice at all, had she? She swung a leg over Imogen's hips to try to stop herself thinking about that; it didn't work. Mother's grave, no wonder Imogen wasn't afraid of what might happen to her if she solved her murder—at least she'd be free of Maeve's incompetence again. She probably wanted to cross Camille off the list of suspects, so she could stop screwing around and go back to someone interesting....

Imogen sat up suddenly and pushed her telegraph into Maeve's hands. *Hey! Slow down—are you sure you're okay?* She crossed her arms. *You never ignore my messages.*

Maeve scrolled back up the messages, cringing. She had missed a couple. "Sorry."

Imogen's frustrated expression wavered. *Look, I know I can't, but...you have to talk to me.* If Maeve didn't know better, she'd have thought Imogen was the one who looked uncertain. *Reading minds isn't one of my ghost powers, unfortunately. And communication is necessarily...slow for me.*

Maeve swallowed hard, and before she could stop herself, she was spitting it out. "You're going to get bored of me at some point, right?"

Imogen's expression went blank. *What?*

Maeve waved her hands uncertainly. "I mean, you, you can't possibly find my life interesting. You loved Camille, and she's a scientist, and has a car and I assume some kind of impressive life, and I'm just a nun with, like, a suitcase to my name and don't do anything besides talk to dead people. And once we've solved your murder, I won't have anything to give you anymore." She didn't say the other worry—the one that had her interviewing scientists and pawing through old library records. She didn't want to put voice to it—words had power, after all. "And the Court is so fashionable and forward and this convent hasn't changed in a hundred years except to get smaller, and I don't know anything about romance or sex or any of it and there's no way I'm good at it, and Orion said—"

"Orion," Imogen hissed in a murderous whisper, and stopped Maeve's hands in their agitated gestures. The key on her telegraph began rattling rapidly, such that Maeve could barely read the text as it spat out across the screen of her own. The torrent subsided after a moment, and Imogen released Maeve's wrists, picking up Maeve's telegraph again and folding Maeve's hands around it. Her expression was hard to read. Maeve bit her lip and scrolled back up to the top.

I don't know what Orion said to you, darling, but he should not *be the person from whom you take relationship advice. He is a good friend and at times can be kind, but he is also the most capricious, fickle, fair-weather son of a bitch on this island. He does not like to work—he does not like to struggle. He's tried it once or twice and decided it wasn't for him. I am* not *like that. And for that matter, you're nothing like Camille! Thank the Blessed Mother! You don't try to change me or twist my meaning or tear me down or hold your affection out of reach. You're not poisoning me alive. I don't feel like any little inconvenience will snap me in half anymore, even if things are harder for me than they were before, and I can't believe I didn't realize before what it was putting me at the bottom of those bottles! Mother's grave,* never *compare yourself to her, or to what Orion's told you that you need to be, or any of it! You are the greatest delight, the easiest person to love I have ever met—just by being you—and if I haven't made that abundantly clear, then it's the fault of this* accursed *injury and my* stupid *voice and the fact that I can't. Fucking! TALK.*

I used to talk so much, Maeve—I wouldn't shut up. Every thought in my head—it was so easy to just open my mouth and say it and have it sound good. *I was good at talking—I was a good damn poet. And I don't know if it's the Hallowed Mother cursing me for my hubris or some freak accident that doesn't mean a thing, and I don't know which would be worse. But the fact remains that every thought I have to type out. Slow. Painful. With proper punctuation and sentence structure. The music of it is gone. I could open my mouth and love songs would fall out of it and you would* know*, Maeve, how much I care about you. How much I admire your kindness and your resilience and your bravery, how much I've learned from you about family and friendship, how impossibly interesting I find your work and your art and your viewpoint on life, and how desperately I fantasize about stealing you away from here for myself. I could whisper in your ear on the streetcar and sigh to you in bed* *and sing to you in our kitchen and shout it to the sea and you wouldn't wonder! You wouldn't doubt!*

I'm not just here for your help, or, or what you can give me. I haven't been since that day at the Court. I haven't been since the day you gave me that rose. You don't have to...to earn your keep or keep me entertained. If anything, I'm hard to love. All...broken glass, fucked-up, washed-up shards of who I was. But please don't mistake my silence for disinterest. Please give me a chance to keep you. I could never be bored of you.

When Maeve looked up, blushing from all the compliments, she found tear trails of ectoplasm on Imogen's cheeks and a fierce look in her eyes. It kicked her in the gut, that look, and made any doubt she might have had in Imogen's flowery words evaporate.

"You're not hard to love at all," she stammered, "a-and I'm sorry. Grief is a terrible thing."

Imogen's eyes went wide, and then filled with glowing tears again. *Grief.* She hesitated for a moment, scrubbed at her cheeks. *Yes. Well. But that's not my point right now. I can be sad on my own. I want to be happy with you. For devil's sake, don't listen to Orion.* She took Maeve's hand, interlaced their fingers with such intensity and care that Maeve half-wondered why she had worried. *Bored of you—he's ridiculous.*

Maeve managed a smile. "Well, that was my own worry. He just blackmailed me with it. But point taken."

Imogen squeezed her hand and huffed a small laugh. *Blackmail?*

"Well, his idea of how to keep you from getting bored with me was, uh," Maeve felt her face get hot, and she laughed, "taking tips from him, bedroom-wise."

Imogen dropped her hand; she reeled back like she'd been shot and buried her face in Maeve's pillow. *Aaaaaaaaaaaaahhhhhhhh!* read her telegraph for several consecutive messages. *I'm going to die again! My soul is leaving my body! Horror of horrors!* She flailed in anguish for a while more, then went petulantly limp. Maeve's telegraph chimed after a few moments. *What did he say?*

Maeve bit her lip to keep from laughing and forced herself to comb through memories she had previously marked for repression.

"That you're not as much of a dom as you think you are, that you have a thing for hand kisses, and that you probably have fantasies about being a brooding ship's captain rescuing half-drowned maidens."

A few more screams appeared on Maeve's telegraph, and Imogen sat up abruptly, jabbing a finger into Maeve's face.

He only thinks that because I wrote a poem about that once. First rule of art, it doesn't necessarily reflect the artist's personal feelings, I'm EXPLORING THEMES and just because HE thinks that the pirate captain is hot—he doesn't get what the point—the flowy open shirts are about VULNERABILITY, not whatever HE'S projecting, and—and he's just misinterpreting—

She was blushing hard. Maeve raised her eyebrows, made a mental note to retract her insults to Orion, and pushed Imogen's finger out of her face with a grin.

"What about the other two things?"

Imogen snatched up the pillow and pulled the pillowcase over her head, crossing her arms.

I've reached my daily limit for sincerity. All further conversations will be smirky and disingenuous.

"Well, he diagnosed me with a praise kink, which sounds like something I should probably get checked by a doctor," Maeve consoled, suppressing a giggle. "Hand kisses are very romantic."

Bite me, Sister Maeve.

"You know, he mentioned that you might be into that, too."

Ah. Excellent. I've changed my mind. I'm not going to die—I'm going to kill him. She took the pillow off her head; her face was flushed, and her eyes met Maeve's sideways. *In fact, I ought to go do that now. So, it's a crime of passion, you know.*

Maeve nodded along contritely. She would have protested more if she thought Imogen really planned to waste the evening on murdering Orion. "By all means, if you really want to go," she said, and took Imogen's hand. "Here, let me see you out—"

I swear to the Hallowed Mother, if you kiss my cursed hand—"

So, of course, Maeve did, mentally cursing herself for following Orion's instructions in seductive half-lidded gazes. And, of course, Imogen jumped her, only half in outrage. Maeve went down choking back laughs and held a finger to her lips indignantly. Imogen pointed to her throat, then narrowed her own eyes, and yanked Maeve's dress down around her shoulders as the buttons opened of their own accord. She applied her mouth to the most ticklish parts of Maeve's throat with vengeful eagerness, and Maeve gasped, fighting to keep silent. She fought Imogen off with the hysterical strength that comes from trying to avoid being tickled—rolled her over, wrestled Imogen's hands away from her, pinned them safely over her head.

"I said quiet!" she mouthed.

Imogen just smirked, her chest heaving at a rate that undercut her nonchalance. Her face was flushed purple again; she glanced up at Maeve's hand restraining her wrists and worked her jaw in mixed amusement and annoyance. "Orion…is an idiot…but…I admit—" She swallowed with a grimace and forced it into a grin. "You…taking what you want…is…rather hot."

And it seemed insensitive to say, but there was something about Imogen's whispers—drawled, ragged and low—that was rather hot in itself.

"Don't talk if it hurts," Maeve heard herself murmur; selfish and unselfish both, she hoped it didn't.

"Oh, but…suffering for love…so capital-R Romantic…" Imogen sighed, and wriggled deeper into the comforter underneath Maeve. The movement of her hips was distracting, as were the phantom touches urging her down, but Maeve held out a moment longer. Imogen's voice was hardly louder than the rustle of the fabric, and she wanted to catch every word. "And if…you kiss me…I'm sure…I'll…feel all better…."

So, Maeve did as she was told and placed a prim kiss on Imogen's lips, stifling a laugh of surprise as more ghostly hands seized her and pulled her down, reversing their positions. It was cheating, if Imogen's aim was to let Maeve take what she wanted, but Maeve would let her. Hands worked into her hair and caressed her cheeks and plucked at the remaining buttons of her dress, and instead of worrying over sin and sacrilege, she kissed Imogen and let herself be kissed. That was what she wanted, to be close and held and wanted back. When she pulled back to catch a breath, she could see Imogen grinning at her crookedly, her irises pushed back into thin rings of blue around dilated pupils, her hair mussed and her shirt trailing off her shoulders, and the ache low in her stomach that she had come to identify as pleasure rolled in lazily.

"All better?" she whispered teasingly.

"Divine," Imogen murmured back, and drew Maeve into an open-mouthed kiss, tugging at her lower lip with her teeth each time they broke apart for breath. Maeve pulled her dress off over her head and leaned back in. Imogen shrugged her arms out of her shirt and found a spot for her hands in the bare strip of thigh between Maeve's shift and stockings. Her fingertips pressed in, deliciously insistent. Imogen was never anything but insistent, of course, but there was something that set Maeve's breath catching about it now, as Imogen rolled her hips against Maeve's and kissed her back into the pillows—her mouth, her throat, down her chest. She thought that was it—the attention, the fact that someone wanted to put her first for a change.

"Is that okay?"

"Is...what...darling?"

"Er—do you want me to—"

"No," Imogen breathed, smiled, leaned up and claimed her mouth in an emphatic kiss. "I...just...want...you."

So, Maeve twisted her fingers into the fabric of the comforter, and abdicated responsibility.

"We'll be back soon," Thalia said firmly, collating a set of papers into a moth-nibbled briefcase. "And we're coming with you—so, no trying to go this alone, okay?"

"Yeah, yeah." Appreciation and frustration warred inside Maeve; why wouldn't Imogen listen to the same logic? She had unconditionally refused to let Maeve attend the Masquerade with her, forcing her to offer support from the nearby teahouse as a compromise. "I'll just sit there and if something goes wrong, I'll call the constabulary." Fat chance of that—if Maeve didn't hear back, she was going in herself.

But Imogen had believed her and reluctantly agreed; Maeve had been forced to do the same when Frances and Thalia offered to go with her.

"We'll drag Shivani, and it will be a positive bonding experience," Frances had said, an edge to her voice. "And we'll *help* you if something goes wrong."

Maeve had rather expected to wriggle out of it once Shivani declined, but to her surprise she had accepted.

"It's been a while," Shivani teased with a trace of her usual good humor, "and if this is the last of it then I'm certainly not letting you get killed this late. We don't work alone, Maevey-Wavey."

So once Frances and Thalia got back, Imogen and the four of them would head for the Academy. Frances and Thalia had been selected as Mother Superior's backup today—a last-ditch attempt, a meeting with the City Council on the topic of the ownership of the cemetery. There was little chance of it working; Lady Marlene had even declined to attend. But if anyone could argue it, it would be the three of them—Thalia lawyering and Frances worrying and Mother Superior preaching. Words had power; she hoped that they might work for the sisters as well as they did for the poets.

Thalia finished packing, and Maeve walked her and Frances to the door, anxiety percolating around her stomach. Even now it was frustrating to be on the sidelines; she couldn't imagine how frustrated she was going to feel tonight. Waiting, worrying, trying to have faith that Imogen would find what she needed. What was it Shivani had said about faith?

"Faith just means waiting. And things don't always work out by waiting."

She waved the two of them and Mother Superior off into a crisp autumn afternoon, then walked vaguely to the chapel and sat down. She would try to have faith, about all of it.

Hallowed Mother, please, help them make the Council see what a mistake they're making. Protect Imogen and help her find what she needs to find to set her free. She paused, clasped her hands tighter, and bowed her head. *Please, give me the grace to accept whatever happens. Your will be done.*

She looked up once more, at the statue of the Blessed Sister Artemisia—who had had the Hallowed Mother's ear, who had founded all this, who had decided in the first place that sisters should be apart and alone from the rest of society. She was too afraid to admit to herself that she didn't agree anymore. Because what did that mean for her future? And if Imogen...if the Hallowed Mother's will was done, if that will was what Maeve was so afraid of, then what would that mean? Maeve had been selfish—she had followed Imogen to freedom and pushed the blame off on her every step of the way. If she lost the crutch that Imogen had become—though Imogen wouldn't think of it that way. She wouldn't see it as Maeve taking advantage of her kindness; she would just insist on doing it. Maeve could understand that, she supposed. She did the same for her sisters—checking on Shivani's emotional state and reassuring Frances and lending Thalia a listening ear. And she did it for Imogen now, too. She didn't expect anything back; she loved them, and so she'd do anything for them.

She just supposed she hadn't expected anyone to feel, so clearly and ardently, the same way about her.

She frowned, clasped her hands, looked up at the altar, and said a final, rushed prayer.

And if your will could be that Imogen can stay here with me, then I would appreciate that very much. Amen.

The afternoon was an agony of waiting; Maeve spent a while in the garden kneeling in the flowerbeds and staring off into space, and then went down to the kitchen to polish the same teacup for about twenty minutes. She only realized it had been that long when Shivani told her so.

"I admire your commitment," she teased, "but Eleanor needs water to boil noodles."

Maeve blinked with a start and moved aside to permit a concerned-looking Eleanor access to the sink. "Sorry, just thinking."

"Clearly." Shivani smiled and socked her lightly in the arm. "Go ahead and have a lie down or something. Skive off—I won't tell Mother Superior."

"But I—" Maeve looked around, at the army of little sisters working in surprising harmony to make dinner and sighed. They probably needed her to get out of the way more than they needed her help.

Shivani put her arm around Maeve's shoulders and steered her toward the stairs. "I'll come up later with some tea, and we can chat until it's time to leave."

"Okay," Maeve said, her voice smaller than she'd hoped it would be. "Thank you."

"'Course, Maeve."

Maeve made her way up the staircase and down the deserted hall and finally turned into her room. She laid out on the bed, already bored, then sat up and opened the window. The sun was beginning to kiss the tops of the buildings, though it still had a long way to go before it hit the sea. She sat and stared for a while, watching passersby walk along the street and autumn-orange leaves rustle on the tree outside her window. In the light of the golden hour, it was lovely.

So, she did as she always did, and sketched it. The jitters gave way to smooth, confident lines, and her mind turned to the gentle puzzling of perspective. By the time she heard movement on the fire escape and looked down to find Imogen on her way up, she had found it within herself to smile.

What a welcome, the window already open! Imogen tossed a pair of tall, embroidered boots and a small bag in through the window, and then rolled the rest of herself in over the sill, onto the bed, and into Maeve's lap. She smiled and twitched her fingers until the telegraph chimed again. *Good evening, Maeve.*

There was a ghost of a bruise under each of her eyes, but otherwise Imogen looked comfortably settled, her hair brushed back off her forehead and her eyes far more blue than purple. She was already dressed up for the party. A mutton-sleeved bolero and high-waisted trousers made up the suit, richly embroidered in blue and purple and hints of green, with a crisp white shirt beneath and her velvet ribbon tied in its bow around her neck. Maeve recognized the costume from the play at the Court—had it been the lover or the assassin? She supposed it didn't matter—likely, there would be lots of people dressed like this. No one would notice that one of them was the Wraith, and no one would connect that to Imogen. She hoped.

"Good evening, Imogen," she replied, overly polite, and offered a hand to help Imogen up. Imogen kissed it, which elicited a laugh from both of them, and then got to her feet, pulling her boots back on and replacing her knife inside the calf of one of them. She pulled something out of the bag—her Wraith mask—and put it on, then spun on her heels and wiggled her fingers in demonstration.

How do I look?

"Mysterious," Maeve told her. It was true—with only her eyes visible behind the porcelain mask, Imogen could have been anyone, or anyone if Maeve didn't recognize her swagger by now. She felt slightly buoyed by this. "Let's hope you attract clues."

I plan to. She bounced on the balls of her feet and took the mask off. *And I'll keep in touch throughout, let you know how things are going, keep you from having to worry.* She smiled and sat down beside Maeve, tucking her hip up against hers. *It'll work. And if it doesn't, I'll catch Orion when I get back. He's having*—she shuddered—*a personal get-together tonight.*

"That sounds ominous." Maeve leaned over on one arm, so it lay against Imogen's back.

Mmm. He never let me come to one, so it's got to be even worse than a bacchanal. She grinned, and her nose wrinkled cutely. Maeve suppressed the urge to kiss it. *But he'll be drunk, unquestionably, and he's a bit chattier when he's drunk. Maybe if I pin him between his little party and a question, I can do a little vivisecting.* She drummed her fingers in anticipation, her eyes lighting up like a mad scientist's.

"Be careful," Maeve said slowly, the conversation jogging the memory of a conversation that had been all but buried under the horror of Orion's romantic advice. "I managed to get something out of him the other night. Before the…conversation I got roped into."

Imogen frowned. *Is it important?*

"No—well, maybe." Maeve relayed what she had found—that Orion did have something to hide, that he had tried to tell it to Imogen before, that he believed it to have been connected with her death. Imogen's eyebrows rose, then knit together.

Damn—I should have leaned harder on him. She stood, paced around the floor a few times, then sat again. *Okay. Doesn't change anything now. Mother, I wish I knew what it was but—maybe I do know it.* She ran a hand through her hair, then gripped it tight for a moment, as if she could pull the memory out by the roots.

"Maybe you shouldn't try to remember it," Maeve said softly. Imogen looked at her for a moment, and she stammered, trying to decide whether to backtrack. "Maybe—er—knowing it is dangerous. Maybe that's why Orion gets so many assassination attempts or whatever. I just—er—I don't want—" She shook her head, and her hourglass necklace shook with it. She lifted it and gazed at it for a moment, then took it off over her head and looped it over Imogen's. "I want you to come back," she said sternly.

Imogen cradled the pendant in her hand, looking shocked. She looked up, slight panic in her eyes. *I don't know what this means, darling.*

"I don't either—it's nothing. Or it's something. I'm making it up." Maeve blushed but forced herself on. "She owes you and me both, and She's going to protect you. I've decided."

Imogen's face went slightly flushed as well, and a tiny smile twitched at the corner of her mouth.

Well, if She'll listen to anyone, it ought to be you. She looked at the pendant once more, then tucked it into her shirt and held a hand over it. "I promise…" she whispered and raised a hand to Maeve's cheek. "I'll…come back."

It was impossible to stay worried long with Imogen's strength of conviction, and harder still to stay away from her. Their lips brushed, then connected, and Imogen twisted her hands into the front of Maeve's habit, her touch desperate and hungry. Mother's grave, it felt good—to be wanted, to be someone's person. To be Imogen's, with her dangerous words and her uncertain smiles. She kissed Imogen gently, a reassurance—steadying, she hoped. Imogen's hands loosened by a fraction, and she gave a sigh. It obscured the sound of the door opening, and before Maeve realized that it had, she felt relief.

But the shatter of ceramic on the hard stone floor was hard to miss.

"Oh, you fucking whore!" And Shivani's shout was damn near impossible.

Imogen pulled back in a fraction of a second and tried to look innocent, but the damage was done. Maeve was too shocked by the vitriol in Shivani's voice to move—vitriol that was directed, not at her, but at Imogen, who Shivani was looking at with violence trembling through her person as she stepped forward through the shards of the teacup.

"I fucking knew you would, you wicked bitch! You can't help yourselves, you goddamned disgusting *poets*." She spat the word like Camille spat the word "artist". Imogen hesitated, looking first at Maeve and then down at her own telegraph. She tried to hold it out, but Shivani slapped it out of her hand. There was a shattering of glass to match the ceramic, and for a moment they stood frozen. Imogen's eyebrows knit together, and for a moment she looked as scary as Orion. Shivani's eyes darted down to Maeve's desk.

And before Maeve could act, before Imogen could find another way to explain, Shivani picked up the prayerbook. Her eyes burned with anger as she looked at Maeve. "Hallowed Mother, preserve this lost soul—"

And Imogen clutched at her throat and fell.

Chapter

XIX

That shocked Maeve to motion; she dove to the floor, and seized Imogen's arm. No pulse in her wrist, and no response besides.

"Shivani, stop!" she shouted, then dropped Imogen's arm with a gasp. Her skin was so cold it burned.

Shivani didn't respond; she just kept on reading, cold and steady. There were tears in her eyes, glimmering in the sunlight from the window, but she wasn't stopping.

A blast of cold air rushed by Maeve, tearing drawings from her mirror with the force of a gale, and she saw Shivani fumble the book, then nearly lose it entirely. She felt Imogen twitch beside her, and looked down to find her arm flopped over, weakly extended toward Shivani.

It broke Maeve out of her terror. Yes—yes, Shivani didn't have her exorcisms memorized, if Maeve could just—She leapt to her feet and rushed over, snatching at the prayerbook. Shivani was prepared for that, but it broke her concentration.

"Fuck *off*, Maeve, I'm doing what's best for you!"

"You don't get to decide that!"

Imogen sucked in a ragged gasp, and it distracted Maeve enough that Shivani was able to shove her away. But Imogen's eyes opened properly, her chest heaving, and she lifted a hand, something skittering along the floor with it. Maeve just managed to duck the useless shell of the telegraph as it shot toward Shivani.

Shivani batted it down with her prayerbook and pinned it under her heel.

"I've dealt with nuisances smarter than you," she snarled and snatched something out of her pocket as Imogen hauled herself to her feet. A sachet of salt—it almost looked comical as a weapon, but Shivani brandished it like a dagger and Imogen was forced to arrest her lunge. Her throat and nose were bleeding ectoplasm, her eyes glowing a livid purple, and her hand hovered at her side, twitching toward the knife. But Shivani started reading again, and she crumpled like she'd been shot. Shivani had Imogen out-gunned—it was, of course, what Sisters of Good Death were trained to do.

But they didn't have any particular defense against each other.

Maeve was in motion again, no idea in her head what she was going to do, but certain that if she didn't do something that Imogen would die—die for real. And if Shivani wouldn't stop, then she was going to stop her. She seized the prayerbook again, Shivani holding on and reading in spite of her, and wrestled and wrenched and fought against her. There was a detached part of her mind that said that this was absolutely absurd, that they could talk this out and resolve it like grown adults, that this was perhaps the most undignified manner in which a murder had ever been prevented; another part of her mind, long dormant since her brother had gotten taller than her and she had gone onto more solemn things, reminded her that this was exactly how one dealt with a sibling that was pissing you off.

She managed to get the book off Shivani and whipped it toward the window; it missed and fell into the crack between the bed and the wall, but while Shivani was distracted by that Maeve managed to kick her leg out from under her and throw her to the ground. She went down with a yelp not far from Imogen and Maeve managed to wrestle her onto her back, forcing her into a pin.

"What are you…doing?!" Shivani gasped, struggling against her weight.

"What are *you* doing?!" Maeve snarled back and shoved the telegraph from where it had fallen out of Shivani's reach. "I'll tell you what you're doing—you're going to stop right now, and I'm going to check on Imogen, and you're not going to do anything about it!" Shivani's eyes slid away mutinously, and Maeve gritted her teeth and forced her face in front of her. "Listen to me, damn it!"

"Yeah, sure, let's go check on the corpse girl," Shivani said in a mocking voice, trying to wriggle out from under Maeve. "We're Sisters of Good fucking Death! And you're just ignoring all those vows, just for some awful—"

"She's not dead, Shivani!"

"She ought to be!"

Maeve had forgotten checking on Imogen; she started get to her feet, her temper lost. "You—you—you just hate her! For no good reason! You never once listened to what she had to say!"

"I didn't have to—you don't really think she's telling you anything true, do you?" Shivani sat up and laughed mirthlessly. "Oh, Maeve, you're so special or whatever. I've never cared about anyone else so much! By the way, unrelated, but will you put your life in danger to help me? I'll pay you back in hollow compliments!"

"Fuck off!" Maeve hardly ever swore. "Like you never string me along with compliments to get me to do things for you. At least she cares about what I want back!"

"Oh, what's this, then? What's this if not caring about you?"

"It's fucking jealousy!"

"You think I'd be jealous of a fucking *poet*?"

"What...did you...call me?"

Maeve rounded, and found Imogen clutching at her head, her arms trembling as she tried to push herself up to sitting. She aimed a glare back at Shivani, then knelt at Imogen's side.

"Are you okay? Imogen?"

Imogen shook her head like she had water in her ears; her eyes focused on Maeve for a moment, then rolled back; her whole body spasmed, and Maeve dove to catch her before she struck her head against the floor. She rallied, and sat up with a start, her lips moving quickly and unintelligibly before she realized nothing was coming out. Something was unquestionably wrong—she looked disoriented and afraid, and swung her head back and forth quickly before jumping to her feet and casting about her person. She seized on the dagger before Maeve could take it from her and held it out defensively. Her lips formed a phrase:

"Who are you?"

"Imogen, it's—it's me, it's Maeve," she said, horror creeping up her spine. "You're at the Sisterhood of Good Death."

"I don't know any nuns…" she hissed, then paused, and shook her head, and looked at Maeve, the vague look in her eyes clearing. "Maeve…" She hesitated for a moment, then started forward toward Shivani, who scrambled to her feet and backed up against the wall.

"See? She's unstable," she snarled at Maeve. "I'm getting Mother Superior."

"Mother Superior's out," Maeve shot back, moving to intercept Imogen. "Imogen, Imogen, it's okay, it's okay. Shivani's not going to hurt you further. I won't let her."

That glassy-eyed look had come back over Imogen, and she smiled down at her.

"I can…take care…of myself…Camille."

Maeve felt like the wind had been knocked out of her; Shivani spoke up bitterly. "See? Some other woman, Maeve—you can't trust poets."

"Shut up!" She patted Imogen's face. "Not Camille, Maeve. I'm Maeve, Imogen, come on."

"Camille…" Imogen's expression cleared, and she startled out of Maeve's grasp. "Camille…Marlene…ohhhhhh…" She staggered, held her face in her hands, then straightened. "It's the Masquerade." Her voice tore painfully. "One of the two."

"Imogen, I think maybe you shouldn't go to the Masquerade now," Maeve put forward in a small voice; she didn't like the line of Imogen's shoulders. "You don't seem to be quite…right."

Imogen didn't respond. She lifted her head and recovered her mask from the bed; with it on, Maeve couldn't see her expression.

"No, no," she said quickly, as Imogen backed toward the window. "No, no, Imogen, talk to me, don't go, you can't go like this, no!" But Imogen didn't seem to heed her; moving vaguely, dreamlike, she replaced her dagger in her boot and stepped out the window, dropped onto the fire escape. Maeve was too slow to catch the back of her jacket; she jumped down to the street and began to walk. Slow, swaggering as usual, with an occasional sickening sway. Maeve watched her go, her stomach lurching in tandem.

She turned. Shivani was still against the wall, looking murderously sullen. Maeve had had it.

"Spill."

"What?"

"What," she said, firmly, without malice but without quarter, "is your problem with poets? You're the rebellious one. You're the one who's always trying to wriggle out of the rules. But this is one you've just decided you're going to follow to the point of murder? I'm walking out of this room in five minutes to go find her. You can tell me what's wrong and we'll stay friends, or you can stay silent, and we won't."

For a moment it seemed as though Shivani was going to take the latter option. She looked down at her feet, her veil askew and her eyes rimmed red. She muttered something, and Maeve sighed and pulled out the chair at her desk.

"What?"

"I said why do you even like her?"

Maeve crossed her arms.

"I asked you first." But Shivani offered nothing else. She sighed. "Because she's clever and kind and encouraging to me, and...yeah, Shivani. There's no dark conspiracy."

"You've kissed her before, huh."

"I think I won't answer that before I know whether you're going to call me a fucking whore," Maeve replied, guarded. "But I went into that of my own free will, if that's the question."

Shivani's cheeks had grown a bit flushed, and she sank to the ground, lowering her face into her hands. "I—no, I—I—she... fuck." The curse sounded defeated, and her shoulders rolled in. It was a long moment before she spoke up again.

"I...was pretty poor growing up," she said, muffled. "Poorer than whalers for sure. My, um, my mother did laundry. And I would help her, and see all these beautiful clothes that ladies and merchants and stuff had, and I...I wanted that. The glamour. The escape from that miserable damp little apartment. I don't know." She looked up and glared furiously at Maeve. "So don't you dare judge me because I did what I had to do to get what I wanted. Not all of us got comfortably swept up by the convent."

That rankled slightly—Maeve wouldn't describe her deathbed vigil for Tia as comfortable—but she held her tongue. She was almost certain Shivani was just lashing out, going on offense to preempt whatever she thought Maeve was going to say. So, she'd keep quiet. "I won't," she prompted gently.

Shivani held her glare for a moment more, then clicked her tongue and gestured irritably. "I was an absinthe girl. Go ahead, be horrified."

Maeve drummed her fingers on the desk uncertainly. Of course, she was a bit surprised, but...was she supposed to find it some breach of purity or something? Imogen's words to her on their second meeting floated through her mind. *Sex isn't a heresy, darling.* Maybe the Sisters had a reputation. She swallowed. "Why would I be horrified?"

Shivani raised an eyebrow, then scoffed and rolled her eyes. "Of course. You're too much of a perfect Sister to even know. It's shameful, Maeve. It's the kind of thing that respectable families have nightmares about their children doing. The only thing worse than getting caught going to an absinthe house is working at one."

Maeve tried to reconsider the night at the Court in all its smirking, knowing debauchery. "The poets don't seem to think—"

Shivani raised her chin. "And what in the world made you think they're any better? Sure, maybe you don't know the whole reputation absinthe houses have, but we get a lecture every week on the poets! The only reason they get any more respect is that they've got money!"

"I..." What was Maeve going to say? That she hadn't seen the poets do anything so awful? That she was beginning to disagree with Mother Superior? That when Orion Cantor had sat across the table from her with a matching hangover and informed her that he wasn't ashamed in the slightest, that Maeve had wondered which of them was reacting properly? "So, explain. You were an absinthe girl. That doesn't explain completely why you hate the poets. That woman at that place we went to do the exorcism seemed much worse."

Shivani curled her lip. "That hag. You're not wrong. That's the one I worked at, in fact. Did you see, she didn't even recognize me? Wouldn't care if a girl dropped dead of starvation, only that her slot would be empty." She waved a hand with some violence. "But she was consistent; I'll give her that. The poets..." She got to her feet, suddenly, and took to pacing. "It's all a performance. And that was the only comfort, to me. The customers had to go be honest and admit to themselves that they wanted all that. But the poets…" Her expression was bitter. "Well, they love to perform, too, don't they? And they're damned persuasive."

"I…don't understand."

"They liked to pretend they'd fallen in love. Out of malice or idiocy or whatever, I've no idea. But you'd walk into dressing rooms and find huge bouquets sent by poets to particular girls. Love letters. They'd come back to you night after night or be nice or ask about *you*, not the character you played. And if you were foolish—if you were young and dumb and naïve and you *believed* one of these poets might actually want you…" Shivani scoffed. "I remember the first time I met him. I was eighteen and he was older, and Mother's grave, I was dazzled by the attention. Got to sit next to him for an hour while he put away our most expensive champagne and asked me about myself. He gave me a taste of it—it was delicious, and I felt so, so lightheaded for the rest of the night, and he tipped me a whole gold ammonite and I hid it in my bra and bought a stupid fancy coat with it. Thought maybe I could climb up and be a lady, if he could climb down and not be a lord."

A sick feeling curled into Maeve's stomach at that. "Who?" she whispered.

"Orion Cantor." Shivani spat his name on the floor. "Obviously."

"What did he do?" Maeve blurted before she could stop herself. She didn't want it to be true, for Orion to be the villain, but she had said that she would listen.

Shivani curled her lip. "I told you," she said, "that he has a reputation. For being merciless—two-faced. And I was young. Words have power—" she said it sing-song, mocking, "so of course you believe the poet when he strings them together for you night after night. 'You and I get each other, you're clever and beautiful, we could run away together.'" Her voice grew ragged. "Of course he wasn't going anywhere. He was running for Laureate—why would he go anywhere?" She wrapped her arms around herself. "My fault for being stupid. His fault for leading me off the edge of a cliff. I made the jump, and he wasn't there to catch me. Lavinia replaced me without a thought. I had nothing. And if I hadn't swallowed my pride and knocked on the convent's door, well…

that coat I bought looked nice, but it sure didn't keep me warm. Winter was coming."

Maeve remembered that winter, and she remembered Shivani— an elegant nineteen to Maeve's insecure seventeen. Maeve had thought her impossibly worldly and glamorous. It took till now to recall how skinny Shivani had been, how sullen, how shattered. Grief was familiar to her, but Maeve hadn't met heartbreak for herself until she'd met Imogen. "I'm sorry, Shivani," she said at last, Imogen's absence rushing back in upon her at the thought. "Really, I am. I understand—well, I can't understand exactly what you went through. I understand why you hate him. But—"

"But Imogen isn't like that?" Shivani pursed her lips and leaned against Maeve's desk. "You don't know that. She's his student—his darling. She wants something from you, same as all those poets wanted things from me. The flirting along the way, it's just sport, for them. They'll lure you in and let you fall."

Except Imogen had offered Maeve an out, at the beginning of all this. She swallowed and got to her feet.

"I don't think she will, Shivani. She's been honest when she didn't need to be." The night at the library, the conversation over tea. Imogen had trusted her grief and her heart in Maeve's hands.

"And how do you *know* it was honesty?" Shivani crossed her arms. "They trade in vulnerability. Their job is to splash their blood on a page. They aren't afraid like the rest of us, and that's a bad thing. It makes them dangerous, Maeve."

"Why is it a bad thing?" Maeve challenged, anxious. "Sometimes being afraid just stops us from doing the things that we should!"

"And sometimes it keeps you from throwing yourself into harm's way!" Shivani took Maeve's hand. "You're naïve, Maeve, and it's your best trait! You're kind and sweet and you think the best of people. You like to help, you put others first. But you don't know what the world is like! If you let her, she'll corrupt you. She'll drag you down with her."

Maeve frowned and twitched her hand away. "I'm...I'm not naive, Shivani."

"You've been living in this convent for ten years! You've only ever known this place. You're a perfect Sister—and I'm so, so jealous of that, wish I could be like you! You don't know how good it is here, how good you are. Don't let her change that!" Shivani reached for her hand again.

But Maeve hadn't only ever known the convent. She had been a whaler—she had fired harpoons and kept meticulous accounting books and walked around museums with her grandmother. She had sketched, and gone to a poet's bacchanal, and analyzed data with scientists and fallen in love. She had taught and gardened and exorcised ghosts and tried to solve mysteries. She looked down at her desk, at the map where Imogen had marked down the addresses of the fractured hauntings before they had gone to bed together last night, the farthest possible thing from perfect Sisters of Good Death.

Now that she looked, the markings formed a pattern—lines, radiating out across the island, like fractures across the land. Threads plucked from the veil, yanked out from a single, central shatterpoint. The Academy. Where Imogen, the strangest anomaly yet and the woman she desperately wanted the chance to love, had last been seen before her death. Where she was heading now.

"She's not corrupting me," Maeve told Shivani, and took up her boots from the floor. "I made my own choice to help her, and she does love me." She meant to say more, but Shivani's hands on her face interrupted the lacing of her boots, and she looked up just as Shivani pulled her in and kissed her, too.

"I loved you first," she said bitterly.

Maeve swallowed.

You draw her like you love her.

And maybe she had, once, but....

She pulled away, Shivani still holding onto her, and squeezed her arm. "No, you don't," she said, with bittersweet clarity. "You love who you think I am. But even if I ever was her, Shivani, I've changed." She tucked a loose strand of hair into Shivani's coif for her and pulled Shivani's hands away from her face. Shivani didn't respond. "I've got to go. I'm...going to get help. From him." She surprised herself as she said it, but it felt right in her stomach. Felt like the right place to go. Felt like the right way to make this break. And indeed, Shivani nodded, stepped away, and put her hands in her pockets. "You...don't have to help," Maeve said. "But if you could tell Frances and Thalia where I've gone when they get back. Just so...so people know where I am."

Shivani turned away slightly, her veil hiding her face.

"I will. Be safe. And come back."

Maeve knotted the last of her laces, pulled on her coat, and nodded, watching her with sorrow sitting heavy in her stomach.

"I promise I will."

The sun had set completely now, the chills running up and down Maeve's spine only partially caused by the temperature. She looked back, but the convent had already been blotted out by a light shower of flurries dancing in the streetlights. She muttered a curse under her breath. She had to focus, had to put Shivani from her mind, cruel and painful as it felt to do. At least she was safe, her secrets put to as much of a rest as they could be right now. Orion's secrets were still outstanding—Orion, who had so much capacity for kindness and cruelty. Her fingernails bit into her palms, and she forced herself to consider the other revelation—the shatterpoint at the Academy. The fractured hauntings...Professor Chrystos had shut her down when Maeve had suggested a student project might have something to do with them. But those anomalies...Imogen's anomaly, and her connection to Camille...what could Orion possibly know about that?

She stormed up the gravel drive and around to the entrance to Orion's apartment, noting as she went the golden light blazing through the curtains. Ugh—Imogen had said he was hosting something or other. Maeve gritted her teeth, and hammered on the doorbell, praying that he wouldn't be too drunk or stoned to pay attention. There was some tittering from within—a loud burst of laughter, and then some thumping on the other side of the door. It resolved into an attempt to open it, and finally Orion managed to trip through the door, leaning on the door frame for support. A mostly-empty bottle of wine occupied his hand, and it was clear that the robe he was wearing had been hastily thrown on and knotted without dexterity.

"Maeve!" he managed and gave a grin and a shiver. "You are absholuuuutely *not* invited to this party."

"Orion, Imogen's in trouble," she said sharply, snatching the wine away from him. "You have to tell me what you know and come with me right now. She's gone to the Masquerade alone."

His face fell for a moment, but he quickly rallied and grasped ineffectively for the bottle. "She can take care of herself. She's got a knife n' all."

"She's..." Maeve grasped for words. "Sick, I don't know. Shivani tried to exorcise her. Something's wrong—she keeps flashing back to last year."

Orion's frown deepened. "Well, whaddaya want me to do about it?" he said sullenly and slid down the door frame a bit. "I'm a terrible medium." He canted his head for a moment, then stuck a finger towards Maeve's lips. "Shhh. Don't tell anyone I told you that. They'll laugh at me."

"I want—" Maeve tried, batting his hand away, but she was interrupted by voices from inside.

"Oriooooon!"

"Come back, babe, what's going on?"

"Shut the door, I'm catching a chill!"

Orion rolled his eyes exaggeratedly, and kicked the door shut behind him. "I swear, if he didn't give such divine—"

"Don't want to hear about it," Maeve said angrily, cutting him off. "I want to know what you're keeping secret. What you think got Imogen killed last time. We have to know—we have to solve this, or she's going to do something rash and get herself in trouble!"

He snatched back the bottle of wine and pouted. "I don't know who did it."

"Yes, but if we combine what I know with what you know—"

"She never knew it, though, so it's irrel—illerr—not important!"

"You said you tried to tell her!"

"But I didn't!"

"But if you did now—please, Orion—"

"No! It's dangerous!"

"Please—"

"I *won't*!" he finally shouted, and threw the bottle down on the step, shattering it. He was sober in an instant. "What good does it do to dig up old graves and disturb the dead? You should know better—some things should be left to lie! Sometimes people do terrible, terrible things because they don't know what else to do, because they have no other choice, because they're too afraid to make the other choice, and haven't I paid enough penance? Haven't I lain awake with the guilt of it for two decades? Hasn't it all turned out well enough anyway, better, really, than if it hadn't happened at all?" He balled up his fists at his temples and screwed his eyes shut. "You can't make me confess it if it's not a sin, Sister, and I *won't* tell her! She would hate me, I know it!"

That was it—he wasn't going to block her way *and* try to paint some pious veneer over it to make himself feel better.

"You *will* tell me," she shouted, "or I'll tell her all that, and she'll drop you anyway! What could be worse than what she can imagine, Orion?"

He swallowed, and Maeve could see his eyes shift nervously even under the glower he was trying to muster.

"You are sailing dangerously close to the wind, darling. I could annihilate you. I could buy your little convent out from under you and turn you out onto the street. I need only make a press release and your whole exorcism business could go under." He bared his teeth. "Words have power, darling, and mine more than most."

She wasn't cowed—it might have scared her more before, but she was angry on Shivani's behalf, and that feeling that she had come to the right place was still sitting insistently in her chest.

"My apologies, Young Lord Warwick," she shot back, imitating Imogen in the most acidic tone she could muster. "I didn't take you for such a Mother-damned aristocrat."

And it seemed that her words weren't entirely devoid of power themselves, because the instant the word "Warwick" passed her lips his face went white, and by the time she finished he had slid down the door frame to her feet.

"I'm sorry," he murmured, and wiped his eyes with her skirt. "You're right, I'm sorry. I...I..." He cleared his throat. "I'm a coward, Maeve. I can't go with you. My mother..." His eyes flicked back and forth calculatingly, but they were filling with tears again. "I think if I was there, it would make it worse. Make it more dangerous. She hates me, she really does, and if she thinks I'm—working with Imogen, then I worry it'll put you both in more danger." He hiccuped and looked at the remains of the wine bottle sadly. "You'll need a costume. To sneak into the Masquerade. Naomi, she can—" He pulled himself haltingly to his feet. "She can give you something. And I...I can tell you this. Camille Sinclair—Imogen's ex-girlfriend—she's Marlene's goddaughter. Which means that Marlene is responsible for mentoring her. Noble idiocy." He spat off the step and seized her hand too hard. "The Masquerade is at the Academy, right? So, I don't know. Maybe..."

"They're working together," Maeve finished his sentence, and let him pull her inside. Maybe they didn't need to know the whole secret—and doubtless, in this state, he would just slow her down. Maybe it was enough to know that Orion had somehow wronged Imogen, that he had gone to Marlene a year ago and...Maeve heard irritated conversation coming from the parlor as she sat in the kitchen, pieces starting to come together. He had told...Marlene, perhaps, that he meant to tell Imogen. Maybe it was some piece of knowledge that could keep Marlene from buying the cemetery. Maybe Marlene had panicked—though, from what Maeve knew, she didn't seem the panicking sort—and ordered Imogen killed. Or maybe it had something to do with Camille, and the proposal, and Orion's apparent dislike of her. Was it just because she was a noble? Was it something more?

She barely noticed being dragged upstairs and having ballgowns held up to her, but when someone went fumbling at the buttons of her habit, she started paying attention again.

"I've got it," she said hastily, and undressed as someone pulled a velvet dress with huge tulle underskirts over her head.

"I don't know what you've done to get Orion so violently in your corner," Naomi grumbled in her ear—she, too, was in a state of undress, the smell of absinthe on her breath. "But I had better get a kickback from it."

"I won't be coming back here tonight," Maeve told her, that feeling in her chest already starting to wander toward the Academy. Whatever divine intuition she was following said she had gotten everything she needed here. "So do...whatever it is you wanted to do, and maybe you can shame him into something extra."

Naomi nodded approvingly, and passed Maeve a porcelain mask. "Oh, I plan on it." Pink roses on the cheeks and fine filigree brows. "Best of luck, *Donna*. You seem to be the lady of this house, anyhow."

Maeve pulled on her coat and stamped down the stairs in her boots, brushed past the other guests and Orion still looking sloshed and watery, and opened the door. Back out into the chill of the night, for answers.

Chapter

XX

By the time Maeve reached the Academy, it was
clear that no one was checking tickets anymore. Compared to the
bacchanal, it seemed tame—couples strolled around the Academy's
greens and a few students were whooping and hollering, sprinting
down snow-dusted footpaths in masks and fancy dress, but until
Maeve saw someone half-naked and smoking opium, she was going to feel relatively unimpressed. She looked around, just in case,
but didn't recognize Imogen's mask anywhere. She had planned to
be in the library, where the main party was taking place, so that
was where Maeve would search for her. She went to put on her own
mask, then realized her spectacles were in the way, and bit her lip.
This might be more difficult than she thought.

She tucked them into the waistband of her dress and dove into
a room full of warm light and movement. It was hard to get clearer than that, even if she squinted, so she did her best to hold the
glasses before her eyes. Oh, opera glasses—that was what she saw
others using, and what she should've had. She grumbled, and did
her best, taking in a hugely vaulted library with wooden beams
and stacks upon stacks of books. Patrons of the Masquerade were
milling about, many holding champagne flutes and chatting, others making use of the dance floor set up before an elegantly masked
string quartet. She turned a few times in place, noting the lofted
second floor and beginning to despair. With all the shelves and
nooks, it was going to be difficult to get a survey of the place, much
less to find one anonymous figure among the crush of the crowd.

She just hoped that if Imogen was trying to do the same, that she was having the same difficulty too.

So, she dove into the throng, listening hard for mention of any strange happenings or either of their suspects. Marlene was to be here, she knew—likely celebrating her purchase of the cemetery. With her goddaughter? She slipped between a pair of conversing groups and found herself next to a wrought-iron spiral staircase. Perfect—she mounted it and made her way up to the second floor. The crowd was thinner up here, and Maeve was able to divest of her mask for a moment, putting her glasses on and peering hard.

Well, the group up at the front behind the string quartet looked important—perhaps one of them was Marlene. The woman in green? Orion had a fondness for the color, so perhaps not. Where would Imogen go? A familiar jacket caught her eye for just a moment, but before she could pick the figure back out, an even-more-familiar voice caught her ear, and she put her mask back on in a hurry. She pressed her back to the nearest bookcase as the speaker passed by.

"I'm fine, Professor. Just watching for someone, that's all."

"Oh, a friend?" Now that Maeve was listening, she could pick out Professor Chrystos's voice, too, and recognized her wispy grey hair behind a mask decorated in geometric designs.

"No." Camille had shed her usual lab apron and looked extremely expensive in her ballgown. Maeve was comforted by the fact that she had probably borrowed an equally expensive one off the poets, but she still wrinkled her nose. Nobles.

"Oh." The professor sounded slightly discomfited. "Well, dear, try not to focus too much on unpleasant things tonight. It's supposed to be a happy time, even if you're not quite done with your degree work, yet."

"I know." Camille's voice grew closer, and Maeve ducked to the end of the aisle just as Camille peered down it. "That's why I'm looking for her."

"Oh, a collaborator." Chrystos sounded relieved.

"Something like that."

"Well, don't work too hard." Her voice drifted off, and Maeve started walking the other way, trying her very best not to draw attention. Camille had only seen her once without a veil, so that might work in her favor. She hurried back down the stairs while she still had the chance and glanced back to make sure she wasn't being followed. Which caused her to bump into someone.

Someone who happened to be Imogen.

Maeve gasped and quickly grabbed Imogen's hand to steady her.

"Oh, Mother, I've been looking everywhere for you. Are you alright?"

If Imogen responded her whisper was lost in the crowd, and Maeve touched her forehead in frustration.

"Sorry, sorry." She withdrew the notebook and pencil she'd grabbed from her desk from their hiding place in her boot and gave them to Imogen quickly. She took them hesitantly but put the notebook up against Maeve's shoulder to write, which Maeve took as a good sign. She'd done that before.

Well, I'm not sure who exactly you are, but I'd like to say I've been looking for you too, darling. Love your dress—you look stunning. Any chance you'd let me get a peek under that mask?

"Imogen, it's Maeve," she said urgently, even as Imogen started to drift slightly through the crowd. "You remember me—you have to remember me. I've been helping you solve your murder for months."

Imogen shook her head slightly and took back the notebook as Maeve offered it. *I...yes. It's all...yes, I'm sorry. Maeve. It's all happening at once, Maeve. I'm supposed to tell you that I've thought about the proposal and decided that I want to focus on my career, right? I'm very sorry.*

"No, no, that's Camille," Maeve said. "But Imogen, you said before she wasn't at the last Masquerade."

Well, no. You're stopping in. You're busy in the lab. But you tell me we should have tea anyway. Stay friends. She shook her head. *Though that's a bit out of character for you, isn't it? Maeve would be nice and have me up for tea, not you. Though she would drink that Lenorum Public swill.*

"Imogen, I'm Maeve," she pressed. "What else do you remember?"

Well, I remember Maeve waited for me at that tea shop. With the others from the convent. Or she was going to, before I got murdered.

"By whom?"

Shivani, I think. She hated me. Imogen had continued to stroll and scrawl in the notebook even as Maeve tried to get her to stop, and now they were approaching the edge of the dance floor. *She loved Maeve, too. I could tell.*

"That's not—" Maeve hesitated, then stepped onto the dance floor and held out her hand. At least she could keep a better hold on Imogen here. "So, what's going to happen tonight?"

Imogen took her hand—ice cold—and tilted her head in such a way that Maeve could tell she was smirking underneath her mask. She stepped out and wrapped her arm around Maeve's waist, drawing their hips together, and despite the stress of the moment and the fear of who might be watching, Maeve felt a little thrill within her. This would be delicious if she wasn't terrified that Imogen had permanently lost her mind.

Writing and dancing will be tricky, darling.

"Can you control a telegraph without having your own to type on?" Maeve asked, withdrawing her own from the dress's single tiny pocket. "I can hold it."

I don't know how to do any such thing, the telegraph read. *And dancing takes two hands.*

"You lead."

Imogen's head tilted again, and she slid her hand down Maeve's arm to her bare shoulder. She shivered. *You never let me lead, Camille.*

"I insist."

Oh, don't ask twice. And with a hand at her shoulder and the other at her back Imogen guided Maeve into a waltz, only occasionally marred by an unsteady step on both parts.

"So, what's next?" Maeve prompted, focusing more on squinting at the telegraph than her lack of dancing skills.

Well, Maeve and I must have danced, because you and I just went right back to the lab. Imogen looked down. *Maeve and I...are dancing. So, you're Maeve. See, Maeve, I told you you should wear lower-cut dresses. There are an awful lot of unused study rooms in this library, did you know?*

"Focus," Maeve told her sternly, even though the recognition and the flirtation both gave her hope. "You were remembering the last Masquerade. You went to Camille's lab. What happened there?"

I...I'm not entirely sure. Imogen blinked hard behind her mask. *Did we dance?* She spun Maeve around in a twirl of skirts and dipped her low. Maeve felt her heartbeat quicken, but she fought the rush of blood to her cheeks and focused on the hand holding the telegraph over the hand on Imogen's arm. *I do like dancing. Do you think Maeve did?*

"Yes, very much." They wheeled toward the stage, toward the chamber musicians and the knot of important-looking people sitting higher up and surveying the crowd. The woman in the green dress caught her attention again—her posture perfect, her hair black but for a streak of grey, like Orion's. Her mask was undecorated, cold and white in its expanse. Maeve felt a chill roll down her spine. The ice queen, Imogen had called her. She took a nervous breath. "Did Camille like dancing? Was that why she came to the Masquerade?"

Imogen seemed oblivious to the proximity of her enemy. *No, no. You wanted my answer, and to show me your project.* Imogen's hand tightened on her shoulder. *But I don't like labs. Something bad happened to me in a lab once. Maeve...or Camille, no.....*

"What happened?" Maeve prompted. Memories surfaced, of Imogen ever-so-occasionally working herself into a panic.

You're not going to experiment on me and try to figure out what's wrong with me, are you? she had asked, and protested. *I'm not going in to get experimented on—I won't, I've got bodily autonomy, I'm allowed to refuse, I'm not going anywhere near that place*—It had happened when Maeve had mentioned talking to the Academy.

She looked up in slow-dawning horror. "Imogen, did Camille...experiment on you? Is *that* why you—?"

A stinging sensation in her arm drew her attention away, and as she turned, Maeve felt the room smear. Something was...off, all of a sudden. She managed to recognize Camille behind her— Camille, whose mask as looked cruel and cold as Marlene's above.

"Takes one to know one," she said sweetly. "Though I love what you've done with her. Very docile."

"What I—what?" The words seemed to drip into Maeve's brain as if she had honey in her ears, and she couldn't parse what she was seeing as Camille placed an empty syringe into her clutch and took Maeve by the upper arm. "Come on, ladies. Imogen—you were coming to tour my lab."

"N—no, that's not—" Maeve tried weakly to turn to Imogen, to tell her that that was the other Masquerade, but her body felt too heavy to do anything but let Camille drag her along. "Imogen, don't—listen to...."

But the black swallowed her vision, and she faded.

When she surfaced again, she was freezing—her back up against cold tile, placed unceremoniously in the corner of some inhospitable basement. There was something eye-achingly bright before her, and when she reached for her glasses, she found her hands bound. Her ankles seemed to be tied as well. She fumbled the glasses on as best she could, and the brightness resolved itself into some sort of screen, like the one on her telegraph but much bigger. Her telegraph! She tried to surreptitiously reach into her pocket, to tap something out to Orion, anybody—

"Looking for this?" Her eyes adjusted to the shadows in the room, and now Maeve could see Camille on the far side of the screen, peering at some other monitor. She drummed her fingers on Maeve's telegraph—the power cell removed—but didn't look up from her work. "What in Mother's name did you do to her? You've introduced a harmonic, somehow."

Maeve tried to force her brain to make sense of those words. "A...harmonic?" Or that was what she tried to say, anyway—it was then that she found there was a gag in her mouth.

She must have been at least somewhat intelligible because Camille made a noise of annoyance and spun the other monitor around to face Maeve, stalking over to the other side of the room. "Yes. It's not a steady wavelength anymore, see? I'm getting two sets of readings. You've destabilized the rift." Maeve squinted at the screen, where she could see two waves of two different frequencies pulsing across a grid. Looking at it made her eyes hurt. She shifted her attention over to what Camille was doing, worry sending discomfiting spikes through the fog of whatever she had been drugged with. Readings from what?

That was answered easily enough; leaning forward put her in eyeline of a gurney with a set of leather straps, upon which Imogen was currently perched, electrodes taped to her temples and wrists. The wires ran back to a bank of machinery that ran around the entire room, full of blinking lights and readout screens. One displayed a map of Lenorum with red spots overlaid, just where Maeve had noted down her fractured hauntings. Imogen didn't seem surprised about any of this. She was writing something, looking gently confused, and passed the notebook to Camille as Maeve watched. Camille read for a moment, then took Imogen by the shoulders and urged her down onto the gurney.

"It's just for your safety, Imogen. Don't worry."

Maeve sat up fast, and tried to warn Imogen, to make any sort of comprehensible sound. But Imogen laid down, unresisting, and Camille strapped her in, tilting the gurney upright and retrieving an electrode-studded headband from the machine.

"You'll tell me what you did to get her in this state in a minute. But I believe if we…" She tightened it around Imogen's head, turned back to the main monitor, pressed a few buttons, and, after pulling a pair of goggles over her eyes, turned a dial. Sparks flew, and immediately Imogen's body seized, the smell of lightning in the air. Maeve shut her eyes, the light searingly bright, and squinted as both of the waveforms on the monitor vibrated frantically. Impassive, Camille turned the dial up a bit higher for a few seconds, and then turned it back to its starting position. The second waveform had synced and merged with the first. And on cue, the room went cold.

Maeve turned back as fast as she could to look at Imogen, whose head was down, smoke wafting up from it. She picked it up after a moment. No more vagueness in her eyes; she looked up with naked fear in her face, sighted Maeve, and shot immediately to fury. A gust of wind rushed through the room, tearing at Maeve's hair and clothes. Camille, however, looked unimpressed—not to mention, untouched by the wind—and gestured to a yellow and black strip of tape across the ground.

"Salt barrier, Imogen. Now, behave yourself, or I'll kill your little friend." She pulled on a rubber glove and took up what Maeve realized was Imogen's knife from the desk beside her. All the contents of their pockets were arranged there neatly, including Maeve's hourglass necklace. She swallowed hard.

Imogen's jaw set pugnaciously, and a flicker shot across one of the monitors outside the salt line.

What did you do to me? the output now read.

Camille raised an eyebrow.

"That's an interesting effect. Did you do that mechanically, or by manipulating the electrical currents?"

Not in the mood for scientific theory, darling. Imogen looked at Maeve, her chest rising and falling rapidly. *Maeve, are you alright? If she's laid a finger on you....*

"Unfortunately, I *am* in the mood for scientific theory," Camille interrupted, and strolled over, holding the knife to Maeve's throat as she removed the gag. "If you scream I'll end you right here. Now, how did you introduce that harmonic to the rift?"

Maeve took a deep breath and blinked a few times. The gag being gone was nice, but the cold steel against her neck did nothing to help her relax. "She was partially exorcised. Or at least that's when she started acting oddly."

Camille raised an eyebrow. "And what exactly does that entail?"

A tremor of indignation cut through Maeve's fear. "You've been to one of our exorcisms!"

"You locked me outside the room," Camille replied coolly. "And in any case, I presumed your Order was the front for a scam. But you're saying you actually have some way of affecting the spiritual plane?"

Maeve raised her chin irritably. "Yes! Of course! How did you think this island's been talking to ghosts for the last thousand years?"

"Don't get snippy," Camille warned. "Who knows how to do this exorcism ritual?"

Maeve wanted very much to tell her to ask the bottom of the harbor, but the knife really was persuasive. She bit her lip and glanced at Imogen. "It's the point of the Sisterhood of Good Death, obviously."

"But no one else?"

"Not that I know of."

"Well, good." Camille pulled back and paced back to her monitors. "That problem should resolve itself, shouldn't it? As far as I've heard, you're going extinct."

"Not if I have anything to say about it," Maeve snapped.

"You don't. Have any say, I mean," Camille said dismissively, scrawling something down into a lab notebook and taking it up. "Now, Imogen. You're going to answer my questions, but I don't think this knife will work on you, will it? Don't do that irritating pout of yours or Sister Maeve will suffer for it."

Imogen arrested herself mid-pout and arranged her face into something pleasanter. *Of course. I've got all night, darling.*

"Don't call me that," Camille snapped. "Tell me about the harpoon attack. Did you go unconscious when it happened, or were you awake for all of it? Can you feel pain in your current state?"

"That was you?" Maeve would have started to her feet if she hadn't been restrained. "Was the poison you, too?"

Camille glanced down at her, irritated. "I'm trying to collect data, so if you'll kindly be silent—"

"What's the point of all this? What did Imogen ever do to deserve this? What purpose could it possibly serve?" Maeve demanded.

"I said be silent!" Camille flashed the dagger, and Maeve held her tongue. "I've limited time. You can ask as many inane questions as you want later, but right now I am trying to work." She flexed her free hand angrily, then ran her fingers through her hair, and turned back to Imogen. "Pain, Imogen? With the harpoon or the poison?"

Imogen bared her teeth in a grin. *Excruciating, darling. The kind of pain that saints call ecstasy. A bit sexy, really, if I had masochistic tendencies—*

"Can you not be disgusting for five minutes?" Maeve wasn't sure if Imogen was trying to rile Camille on purpose, but it was working with impressive efficacy. It didn't seem to line up with Imogen's story of their relationship—where Camille had pursued her aggressively. Clearly, they loathed each other. So, why had Camille proposed? "And the throat wound, unhealed? Still painful?"

Less so. Only when I try to talk. And perfectly unhealed. Who do I have to thank for their handiwork?

That seemed to give Camille pause. She turned from the monitor to look at Imogen and narrowed her eyes.

"You don't remember?"

Imogen shook her head. *I thought I had it for a moment there, back when everything was happening at once. But it's slipped away again, like the rest of the day I died. Which is a very clever way of covering your tracks, if indeed I have you to blame.*

For a moment, Maeve was struck with fear—fear that Camille would indeed reveal herself as the murderer, and that Imogen would...but Camille waved a hand dismissively.

"I think perhaps I'll leave that a mystery for you, actually. Suffice it to say it's a very handy side effect." She made a note in the lab book. "Speaking of—these abilities of yours. I've got to admit, I didn't expect those. Tell me—what exactly can you do?"

Make the room colder. Blow a lot of wind around. Move quietly and climb more easily. I'm lighter on my feet. I can mess with screens and things. I can survive everything you've managed, so far. Her lip twitched, and Maeve noticed the lie. It wasn't messing with screens—it was manipulating physical objects, like telegraph keys, and knives. And, perhaps, bindings. *And I'm a lot less naïve than I was.*

"Indeed," Camille said, her voice dripping with sarcasm. She looked back at the monitor with the waveforms oscillating across it. "Well, I'll need bloodwork to tell if your body is continuing to age, but..." She flipped back to the beginning of her lab notebook, her expression growing lighter and lighter as she moved down the page, ticking boxes. "Resistance to trauma, full mental function, not to mention the extras—it seems to have worked." She looked rather awed by the prospect. "I did it."

"Did what?" Maeve demanded. "You've got your data, now I want answers."

Camille smiled.

"According to my metrics, I've obsoleted death."

That pronouncement sat heavily in the room for a long moment before a ringing sound shattered the silence. The cheerful expression slid off Camille's face, and she strode over to the wall, picking up the phone irritably....

"What? Oh, come on—I've got bloodwork to do. No one— ugh—yes, ma'am, you don't have to remind—okay, fine, I'm coming." She slammed the phone back down on the receiver, and strode back over to Maeve, untying the rope around her ankles. "Alright. Up. We're going."

"I'm not going anywhere!" Maeve shot back indignantly. "Not without Imogen and certainly not with you!"

"Need I remind you you haven't got a choice?" Camille hauled her up by the rope around her hands and pressed the dagger in under her ribs. "I really would rather keep your guts off my lab floor, but if I must, I must."

"What happened to obsoleting death?" Maeve tried to taunt her, but it came out sounding a little weak. She probably wasn't supposed to see this lab or learn what Camille's part in Imogen's death was. Which meant that Camille probably didn't intend to let her go. She swallowed, beginning to feel sick, and let Camille usher her towards the door. Her eyes grazed over her hourglass pendant on the way, flicked around for somewhere to flee to, landed on Imogen's face. Imogen's eyes bored into hers, and she mouthed something as Maeve passed by.

I'll come for you. Maeve closed her eyes. Yes. Maybe if Imogen could take her bindings off, get out, figure out where Camille was taking Maeve....

"And just so you don't get any ideas—" Camille paused by the door, then reached back, and turned the dial up again. The waveforms on the screen spiked, and Imogen's body spasmed, her eyes filling with ectoplasmic tears as she stared at Maeve. Maeve sucked in a breath, her own throat beginning to feel raw, but the press of the knife to her stomach forced her on. No, no, no. "I won't be an hour, Imogen. Let's see if you can survive this, too."

Maeve turned away so Imogen couldn't see her tears and prayed.

Camille led her through deserted back corridors to a door that opened onto the street outside the Academy. No bystanders—it had to be quite late by now. Had she been missed back at the convent? The others couldn't find that lab; Maeve herself had gotten hopelessly lost on the way up, and now she wasn't even sure which direction they were facing. Some whaler was she, lost without a compass. Camille shoved her down the curb to where a white motorcar was parked and shifted the knife to her back.

"Get in."

Maeve had no choice at this point; she slid in, and Camille climbed in after.

"The rendezvous," she snapped, and the car pulled away from the curb. Maeve squinted at the driver—surely Camille didn't pay him enough to keep quiet about murder. They passed under a streetlight, and the glow glinted off an object in the passengers' seat. A harpoon gun. Oh. Maeve shut her eyes.

"What did you mean, you obsoleted death?" she asked, opening her eyes to find the knife aimed at her abdomen once again. "Is it something you did that made Imogen half-alive?"

Camille watched her narrowly for a moment, then shrugged. "My research needed human participants to progress. Imogen presented a convenient option."

Maeve nodded. "You killed her."

"Depends on what you mean by killed," Camille said coolly. "She's alive, isn't she?"

"She wasn't, for a year."

"Yes. That was disappointing, to be sure." She looked out the window. "I'll have to find a way to shorten that transitional period."

Maeve sighed and looked up to the roof of the car. "You do understand that death is a part of the natural order of things, and that preventing people from dying could have unintended consequences? You of all people should understand how the energy of the living and dead is interwoven."

"I do," Camille replied.

"You've seen the fractured hauntings? You understand that they're being caused by whatever machinery you have going down in that lab, by whatever you did to Imogen? You get that that will happen a million times over if you do this?"

"You misunderstand my intentions. I agree—I don't know enough yet to determine whether the resurrection procedure would cause problems on a large scale. So, I don't intend to perform it on a large scale. Not with what I had to do to develop it. And if everyone lives forever, what's the point?" She inspected her nails. "A few high-paying clients desperate enough to look the other way should be enough to get started with."

Maeve's jaw worked of its own accord for a few moments, looking for the right words to describe just how irritating it was that Camille's brand of evil didn't even have the decency to be idealistic.

"Fucking nobles," she muttered at last.

There was quiet in the car for a few minutes, Maeve's thoughts returning to Imogen, being tortured alone in that basement laboratory.

"Does Professor Chrystos know about this?"

"My thesis drafts are vague." Camille curled her lip. "House Sinclair's a little cash-poor these days. The Academy has ample funding, so long as you can string together some sort of research proposal."

If the professor went to Camille's lab, she wouldn't like what she saw. A tiny sliver of hope formed in Maeve's chest, and she prayed at it with all her might. Imogen didn't deserve any of this, caught in the machinations of something bigger than herself and chewed up by the gears. She had only gotten into this mess because she had been too quick to love. To enjoy life. So, if Maeve couldn't protect her, then the Hallowed Mother sure as blazes ought to.

"Did you even ever care about her at all?" Maeve hadn't quite meant to say that aloud. Camille raised an eyebrow, but she pushed forward. "Or was it just a cash-grab—like you said? Because Imogen had money?"

The corner of Camille's mouth rose, and she looked back out the window. "Oh, no. It wasn't that."

"Then what was it?"

"It's a complicated story. And I don't have time to explain it all." She smoothed down her skirt and glanced at Maeve out of the corner of her eye, the other side of her mouth raising into a smirk. "If it makes you feel better, no—I didn't care. Sentimentality…it's a weakness. One that you and she share."

Maeve was about to retort, but just then the car pulled to a stop, and Camille got out.

"Alright. Get out."

It occurred to Maeve that she had a door on her own side, and that Camille might not notice that she was disobeying until it was too late. So, she fumbled the door open with her bound hands, hiked up her skirts, and without a glance back, ran.

She made it half the block before strong arms caught her in a vicelike grip, and she was spun around to face the harpoon man. He looked no less intimidating up close—stubble ghosted his cheeks, and his eyes under his hat were a cold grey.

"Now, don't be causing trouble," he said sternly, and hauled her back to the car by the upper arm. No anger, no cruelty. And that scared her more than any of Camille's sadism. This was a man who would kill her without thinking.

Camille's shoulders were up around her ears when they got back; she was seething with anger. "No more stunts like that, or I'll kill you right here," she hissed, brandishing the dagger.

"You're just going to kill me anyway," Maeve retorted, trying to sound braver than she felt. "Why should I make it convenient for you?"

Camille didn't answer and turned on her heel.

"Let's go. We're late already."

"For what?" Maeve glanced around and noted with a shock that this block was intimately familiar to her. They were at the cemetery—Imogen's cemetery. The flurries that had been falling all night had thickened into snow that stuck to the grave markers. Winter was on its way. "Surely you don't have a timetable for my murder."

They passed through the gates, and Camille tossed a glare over her shoulder. "You're an afterthought. I'm here to meet with my first client."

Chapter

XXI

Maeve had been to this cemetery many times in the dark now and yet never had she been quite so aware of the bodies beneath her feet. She could join them if she made a wrong move—just like Imogen had a year ago. It was starting to come together: Imogen at the Masquerade, Camille popping over just for a few minutes. Imogen rejecting the proposal, and Camille—calculating, cold—inviting her down to the lab for tea anyway, to stay friends. The tea unquestionably drugged, just as it had been poisoned that day at the teahouse. And then—a murder, then and there? She didn't know the specifics of Camille's so-called resurrection process, but she wasn't sure it mattered. At some point that night Imogen had been disposed of.

But why? Why had Camille pursued Imogen specifically? She'd all but said experimenting on Imogen was a choice of convenience. And why abandon her out on the docks, when she had gone to so much trouble to get her back for data collection tonight? And what did Orion have to do with all this? For a certainty sat in Maeve's stomach that his part was important, whatever it was. She had to understand the whole of it if she was to put this all to rest.

If she had time left enough to do so.

They made their way along one of the gravel paths to the center of the cemetery, where a lone figure stood with their arms crossed. It was dark, but the light from a full moon and the streetlights outside gave Maeve enough light to recognize her. Lady Marlene Warwick, looking aged from the portrait Maeve had once seen of her in the library, but no less forbidding. High cheekbones like Orion; pale, ice-blue eyes and the ghost of displeasure on her thin lips. She held a pocket watch in one of her hands, drumming her long nails against its exterior.

"You're late, Camille."

"Sorry, ma'am," Camille muttered, her eyes downcast, and Maeve stared. She had never heard Camille speak to anyone in a tone that respectful. "But we had a bit of a complication, as you can see. Imogen's secured. But I figured leaving them together would be a liability."

Lady Marlene arched one of her eyebrows. "Yes, I see." She closed the pocket watch. "Remind me who this one is?"

"Some death nun. She's been helping Imogen."

"A nun?" She paced a few steps closer, eyeing Maeve coolly. She was tall—at least Imogen's height. Maeve raised herself up and tried to glare at her. "These Sisters of Good Death are getting to be quite annoying." She didn't even deign to make eye contact with Maeve. "What's your plan for her?"

Camille pulled out Imogen's knife. "Frame the Wraith. She was walking alone in the cemetery and got her throat slit."

A tiny twitch of approval came into Marlene's face. "Recontextualizes Imogen's death, too. Very tidy."

Camille looked like she was suppressing a smile. "Thank you, ma'am."

"Pardon me," Maeve said, pushing away the horror of what Camille had just said with effort, "but as a Sister of Good Death, I think it's my duty to mention that if you kill me now my spirit will likely count being avenged as my unfinished business. And I'll do my very best to drive down the value of this property, ma'am."

The two of them looked at her like they hadn't been thinking of her as anything more than inconvenient scenery. Maeve set her jaw.

"I at least want answers. What did Orion say to you the day of the Masquerade last year?"

Marlene stiffened slightly, and she turned to Camille. "You didn't tell me *he* was involved with all this."

Camille's lips pressed together. "He hasn't been—or not as far as I've seen. Beyond that time at the teahouse."

"Indeed." Marlene folded her arms once more. "Which might have removed the issue entirely had you not failed."

"It wasn't a failure," Camille muttered and looked up nervously. "I obtained important data about what Imogen could stand up to. Cantor and the others were secondary."

"And yet now we have this one on our doorstep, and we've not the slightest idea where *he* might be." Marlene looked down her nose at Camille. "Your interest in science is proving something of a distraction for you, Camille. There were easier ways for you to secure your future, and you've introduced a great deal of complexity to the situation by being difficult. I do not appreciate it when my wards are difficult."

"Well, I wouldn't have had to be if—"

"That's enough." Marlene's voice was sharp, and Camille held her tongue. Maeve was infuriated by the interruption. If what? "You were impatient—it would not have been a permanent situation. But that's in the past. Now we must deal with the hand we have and make everyone who knows about this a priority. Mr. Butcher?" She spoke to the harpoon man—a brutally apt profession, Maeve thought—for the first time, and he stood to attention. "We shall need to discuss a few more contracts after this evening. I trust you can be more effective than my goddaughter?"

The harpoon man inclined his head. "Yes'm, and begging your pardon, miss. It's easier to get out of a poisoning than it is out of a well-aimed bullet."

Camille's expression was taut. "Quite." She turned to Lady Marlene. "But ma'am, speaking of the data—I've finished my analysis, and I really do think it's promising. Imogen retains all of her previous faculties—such as they were—and has additional abilities that even I didn't expect. And she *did* drink that poisoned tea and survive. Pending a few more results and all, this could be a far better way to preserve the Warwick line than—"

"Camille." Marlene's voice was slightly less reproachful than before. "It's bad practice to discuss secrets in front of the help." Maeve glanced sideways at the harpoon man, who happened to be rolling his eyes behind the brim of his hat. She suppressed an insane laugh. "You may present your results to me once we resolve the loose ends of the previous project." She turned, and Maeve was surprised to find her addressing her this time. "Who have you told about your involvement in all of this?"

The discussion of contracts from a moment before suddenly took on hideous significance, and Maeve hoped the brave expression she put on hid the sick feeling in her stomach. Camille's business had been dealt with, and she was running out of material to stall with—stall for what? She felt a resurgence of that warmth she'd felt on the way to Orion's, that strange confidence that had told her she needed to figure all this out, like a comforting touch on the shoulder. Was it her own survival instincts? Was it something more—divine guidance when she needed it most? Even at the lowest point of her sisterdom, wearing a scandalous ballgown that wasn't hers and lying and cheating to save a half-ghost lover she wasn't supposed to have? A lump rose to her throat that had nothing to do with her fear, and she obeyed the feeling.

"I didn't tell anyone."

"She's lying," Camille snapped. "She told the abbess of her convent, at least. She gave that away earlier."

"I did no such thing," Maeve responded, trying to keep an even tone. An argument would waste time. "I simply told you that the convent was more flexible than you thought."

"After I sent a letter to your abbess!"

"You did what?" Marlene looked up from her pocket watch. "You gave them *evidence*?" Her expression darkened instantly.

Perfect. Maeve grinned. "She wrote Mother Superior a lovely note saying I was consorting with poets and criminals. In her own hand and everything. Led me right to her, in fact."

"It wasn't incriminating!" Camille rounded on Maeve. "It was meant to get you to leave well enough alone, you nosy little bitch. Maybe if your convent had turned you out on the street it would have taught you a lesson about sticking your nose where it doesn't belong."

Maeve smirked, trying her very best to imitate Imogen. "Mother, what a cliché. I'm sorry to say I'm not threatened in the slightest by an insult that poorly worded."

"Silence, both of you." Marlene pinched the bridge of her nose. "Where is this note now?"

"Well, I could find it." Maeve clicked her tongue. "I'm not sure where I left it. Might have been at the convent, or at Orion's place—I think he wanted a look at it, actually. But I might have given it to Imogen, too. Would you like me to go have a look?"

Marlene didn't respond. "You'll do nothing more with this science project of yours before you find that note, Camille. Deal with this girl and then go to it. Tonight."

"What? But I have more testing to do—and Imogen will find some way to damage herself if I leave her too long! Just to spite me," she spat.

"Dispose of her, too!" Marlene waved a dismissive hand. "I've been more than generous allowing you time to play around with her. But she's the worst liability we have. Find some stray dog or vagrant and finish up your testing some other way. I truly do not care and will not be involved." Her eyes narrowed. "If you want a cent of what I've promised you you'll deal with them both tonight."

Camille had opened her mouth, but that threat seemed to cut her off. Her jaw clenched as Marlene turned her back. She rounded on Maeve.

"Tell me, now, where you put that note, or I'll cut your ear off."

Maeve blinked a bit, her faith in the guiding instinct quailing in the face of the actual threat. "Which one?"

"Which—you idiot, does it matter? I can kill you quickly or I can make it painful. And wouldn't you rather your little friends at the convent not have to see you mutilated?" Camille took a step forward, and Maeve took one back. She could feel the harpoon man behind her, ready to prevent her from running. But she wouldn't be running backwards if it came to that.

"They've seen worse," she said conversationally, her eyes flicking around Camille's person for a weak point. Probably the shin— she'd seen Imogen take Orion down that way, and she was still wearing her heavy boots. She'd get cut a bit on the arms, probably, but if she could get the knife near the rope—maybe even grab it for herself— "Drownings and consumption and murders, yes—we've seen murders. Death doesn't scare me, Camille. It's my job to face it."

"How about pain?" Camille took another step forward, and now Maeve was out of room to retreat. She took a breath, began to step forward, and was arrested—too close to the harpoon man, close enough to grab, and as he held her arms down in a bear hug,

Camille lifted the knife in a scalpel grip and seized her ear and made the first cut—

"Pain, darling? Life's too short!" Maeve bit back a scream, but she could hear that even through the blood trickling into her ear. Camille pulled back with a start, and facing away from them, Lady Marlene stiffened. She clearly recognized the voice—as did Maeve. "Now, pleasure—" said Orion, and strolled down the hill. "That's worth bleeding for. But Maeve, sweetheart, you don't seem to be enjoying yourself."

"I'm not," she managed to squeak, even as the effort of moving her jaw aggravated the wound further. Orion didn't seem to be enjoying himself either—he was carrying a walking stick which he seemed to be leaning on slightly, and his boots had the shortest heel Maeve had ever seen him wear. She wasn't certain he was sober, but she wasn't about to care. His eyebrows were low and angry, and that was what she needed on her side.

He came to a stop and planted his walking stick in the gravel of the path.

"Hello, Mother."

Finally, she turned. "Orion."

He leaned in and bared his teeth. "You know I love our little chats, and I did have lots of good witty banter planned out for you to stonewall, but I'm afraid it's going to have to wait. I think I need to take Maeve to the hospital."

"And why in the world should I let you do that?" Marlene didn't react beyond allowing the slightest hint of disdain into her face.

"Because," Orion said, and raised his chin, "I'm a witness to Maeve's murder otherwise. And unlike hers, my death would be very much scrutinized. I keep a letter in my desk drawer telling them to check on your movements in the case of my untimely demise, in fact. And," he stood to his full height, took a few steps toward Camille, and smiled at her. "If you were going to kill me, you'd have done it by now. Because unlike Little Miss Sinclair, I could come and take the name back up. And you're not willing to risk getting rid of an heir, even one so traitorous."

Lady Marlene was quiet for a long moment as the two of them sized each other up. There was electricity in the air, long-suffered hatred that neither of them could quite contain.

"Camille," she said at last, never taking her eyes from Orion. "How certain are you in the efficacy of your treatment?"

"One hundred percent," Camille breathed.

"Then it should seem I no longer need an heir." Marlene turned to the harpoon man as the smile dropped from Orion's face. "Mr. Butcher, would you be so kind as to shoot my son?"

"No!" Maeve shouted as the harpoon man dropped her, swinging his gun up into position as Orion began to back away, too slow by half. The trigger clicked, the bang deafened her, and the harpoon left the barrel.

And then it stopped, shuddered in midair, and clattered to the gravel path. Orion opened one of his eyes, looking surprised to be alive.

"That's...not...possible..." Camille said in a strangled voice, looking over Maeve's shoulder like she'd seen a ghost.

For, of course, she had—a ghost lugging around a body rumpled and charred and smirking gloriously, her hand outstretched as if to catch the harpoon. Imogen turned the palm to face herself and folded three of her fingers down. And that gesture was nearly as eloquent as Orion's entrance speech.

A number of things happened in the following moment. Maeve felt a gust of frigid wind nudge her out of the way as an unseen force wrenched the knife from Camille's hand, and as it flew back to Imogen Camille cursed and dove into her pocket. She withdrew what looked like a modified telegraph just as Imogen wound back up with the knife, and in the instant Imogen threw it at Marlene, Camille turned up a dial. The device emitted an earsplitting high-pitched noise, and immediately the knife lost its trajectory. Imogen bent double. Orion dove forward to recover the harpoon from the ground, and Maeve ran toward Imogen. Imogen held up a hand to ward her off, the other pressed to her throat as fresh ectoplasm spurted from the wound. She made a violent twisting motion with her hand and straightened up, diving forward for the knife once more and running toward Marlene. But Camille wrenched the dial on her device again and once more Imogen staggered. Whatever it was, the sound—the waves from the sound?—was disrupting her powers, disrupting her. Maeve spun on her heel, spots swimming in her vision as her ear protested the sudden movement and ran back towards Camille. Orion was engaged with the harpoon man, fending him off with his walking stick, and she dodged the back-swing as he took a vicious swipe at his adversary. Camille tried to duck her, keeping the whining device aimed at Imogen, but Maeve got her hands on it and yanked. Camille held fast—Maeve wasn't going to be able to overpower her, not in this state. They needed some other advantage, and fast. She shouted, "Orion!"

"Yes?!" He sounded out of breath, though she couldn't turn to look at him. Camille kicked at her shin, and she winced in pain.

"Tell Imogen your secret! *Now!*"

"What—now? Maeve, I'm—ah—I'm a little busy!" She kicked Camille back and chanced a glance over her shoulder—Orion was grappling with the harpoon man for control of his gun. It didn't look like an even fight; Orion was shorter and slighter than him, and his walking stick lay on the ground.

"You want to die instead? This is what you were supposed to come here for—to tell her!"

Imogen paused in her tracks, looking wide-eyed at the pair of them. Orion glanced over at her and cursed.

"Fine! You know what—fine!" He broke away, running to-wards Imogen. "I'm going down, but I'm taking her with me!" He wasn't talking about Imogen—he was looking at Marlene, whose face immediately went livid.

"You wouldn't dare—you're as complicit—"

"I would! Hang it! I would and I will!" Camille wrenched at the device, and Maeve had to turn away to fight her, but Orion's words were still flowing, nearly there.

"Give it up," Maeve hissed at Camille.

But Camille wasn't looking at her—she was looking at some-thing happening over Maeve's shoulder. A cruel grin flashed across her face, and she looked back at Maeve. "If you insist." She let the device go, and Maeve stumbled and fell.

"Imogen, you're my—"

She scrambled back up to sitting, turning the dial on the de-vice down and looking around fearfully. What was Camille—? Another bang sounded.

She turned in time to watch Orion fall to his knees, a second harpoon sticking out of his back.

Maeve felt a scream rip from her throat, and just as she had fallen in that detached way to Imogen's side at the teahouse, she ran and fell to Orion's now. His eyes were wide, almost offended—he lay slumped to the ground, blood beginning to seep out around the wound. No, no—he couldn't be dead; he was Orion Cantor! He bragged constantly about all the assassination attempts he'd survived—he lived harder than anyone she'd ever met! She shook him, felt shakily for a pulse.

"No, no, Orion, please—" It was there, but any second it would fade. This was her fault. She forced herself to look at the wound, her mind already running well-worn tracks of disaster and death. They'd stuff his chest with cotton and dress him in a fine suit and place flowers to hide the wounds. Make his face up to a living flush and tell stories of a life cut short too soon. It was all her fault. She heard Imogen's feet sprinting towards them, Marlene forgotten.

"Oh, Imogen!" Camille's voice. Maeve looked up; Camille glanced down at her with another sadistic smile, and then shouted again. "You want very badly to know who killed you, right? Enough to come back from the dead for it?" Imogen's footsteps had stopped. Maeve started to her feet, but it was too late—she couldn't stop Camille, couldn't stop Imogen from hearing. "I did. I slit your Mother-damned throat."

The gravel crunched as Imogen, too, fell.

Maeve's mind went blank—she was in even more danger than she had been in before, and now she was well and truly alone. Camille strode forward, bent over Imogen, and recovered the knife. The harpoon man was beginning to edge towards her, and when she looked at Marlene she found the ghost of a smile on her face. *Run,* said the instinct that had warmed her chest before. It had gone cold now. *Run, now.*

Her heart cried out in protest, but her legs were moving. She turned her back on her friends' bodies and ran deeper into the cemetery.

She had surprised the harpoon man and Camille; she could hear them following at a distance, but she had put enough tall mausoleums between her and them that she wasn't in immediate danger of being shot. Where was she going? Where was safe, without Imogen? Was this cowardice? Was it faith? She looked toward the exits—but no, no, that wasn't it. Deeper in, towards the back, the dark, the burned-out remains of the groundskeeper's hut. Maybe she was supposed to hide in the cellar—but that couldn't work on the harpoon man twice. The bare branches of weeping willows brushed past her and caressed the tears from her face, and she pressed a fist to her mouth to keep from sobbing aloud. She didn't understand. She knew who killed Imogen, she even had parts of why. But it hadn't been enough to save her a second time.

She tripped, stumbled, and fell to her knees. Her head was ringing now with the pain of her injury, and she could barely make out the object she had fallen over. A small marble grave marker, nearly hidden in the unkempt grass around it. It had been missed, it seemed, in the sisters' cleanup, and unthinkingly she rubbed at its face with the ball of her hand. What else could she do? The name came out from under its coat of frost quickly.

OLEANDER GRAVE.

Maeve sucked in a shaky breath, wondering what had led her to this spot. The grave of Imogen's guardian—it was as good a place as any to die, but all of a sudden, she felt like she wasn't going to accept that yet. Why Imogen's guardian? The previous caretaker of the cemetery, before her and her sisters. They had been in theater, a dancer—an artist, like Imogen. Or like Maeve. They had died, like Imogen. Like Maeve probably would.

They had…died.

Maeve felt the hairs on the back of her neck stand up on end. She had never asked how Oleander had died. Surely Imogen would have mentioned if anything was strange—and yet, Maeve knew death in a way Imogen didn't. Sickness could come in many forms. From many causes. Oleander had to have died unexpectedly, or else they would have trained an apprentice. They had died and left the cemetery unprotected, for Marlene to purchase.

Imogen had been the loudest critic of Marlene's bid to buy the cemetery, and she had died. Marlene had just killed her again, killed Orion, too. She was desperate—impatient, just like she accused Camille of being. She had no qualms about using murder to get her way.

Could Oleander have gotten in her way?

That feeling of fate, of faith, swelled into her throat, and without really knowing why she was doing it Maeve clasped her hands together, and bowed her head. She was out of living allies and out of time—she could hear footsteps running up the gravel path behind her, and behind that, the slow tempo of someone walking, unhurried, to watch the spectacle. Oh, she'd get a spectacle—she knew that as surely as she knew to open her mouth and speak. As surely as she knew what words to say.

"Hallowed Mother, raise this wronged soul...."

Maeve's typical experience of an exorcism was one of calm—of projecting restful energies, of bringing peace. This felt...different. The words buzzed and burned her tongue as they fell from her mouth, and her heart started hammering in alarm. A Sister should not be doing this—should not have been able to do this. But it felt *right*. Adrenaline surged through her body, and she got to her feet—and as she did, as she pulled her hands apart and raised them shudderingly, something rose with her. The silver-green specter of a tall person, their figure largely hidden by the broad hat and over-large overcoat that whipped about them in the icy wind. Visible, without a planchette. She panted for breath, looking up at them and ignoring the footsteps she heard halt and backtrack behind her.

"Oleander?" she said raggedly.

The hat inclined slightly.

"Were you murdered?"

Another nod.

"By Marlene Warwick?"

The air grew colder, and Maeve took a deep bracing breath.

"She's here. She bought the cemetery. She killed your daughter to get it."

The hat cocked to the side, and before Maeve could move the specter floated through her—chilling her to the bone, taking her breath away. She spun, and as she did, she watched Oleander pass by Camille, pass through the harpoon man, leaving him trembling, and come to rest in front of Marlene. They turned briefly, looked back at her, and tipped their hat. And then, they raised their own hands, and the wind began to stir.

Slightly at first, then quickening and chilling, making the few remaining leaves of the cemetery's trees rustle and sough—a whisper that only grew in volume from there. For the first time Marlene looked unnerved, staring down the ghost in front of her. She seemed to have the good sense not to speak; Camille did not.

"Go back to rotting," she muttered, raising her device and turning the dial up. For a moment, Oleander's figure shivered; in the next moment, Camille cried out in pain and dropped it, the metal hull riming over with ice and the glass of its display splintering. The wind joined her in a wail, and as it screeched and tore at Maeve's dress, she saw far off in the cemetery a glow beginning to arise through the snow. Green—ghostly green. The glow resolved into a fog, and the fog into pillars, and the pillars into figures, and Maeve gasped, finally understanding what Oleander was doing. They had been the cemetery keeper. In life, they had protected this cemetery, and the people buried there.

Now the ghosts of the cemetery were repaying the favor.

Her arm went numb, and she stepped out of the way as a spectral figure in a centuries-old dress passed; another limped after, dressed in the coat and missing the limbs of a whaling captain. A little girl, an old man, a figure so blurred and ancient she couldn't make out features at all. They all ignored her and Camille and the harpoon man, and made their somber, silent way to Oleander, Marlene nearly obscured by the translucent crowd forming around the two of them. There were hundreds of them. Maeve had never seen anything like it.

The ghosts came to a stop, hovering silent and still. Marlene took a step back but was rebuffed by a gust of wind. She looked back, then faced Oleander and raised her chin. Oleander hovered in place for a long moment, and then the wind began to blow again, gentler this time, setting the leaves whispering again. It sounded uncannily like voices, hundreds, repeating a single word.

Confess.

It wasn't just Maeve's imagination—Camille and the harpoon man looked around nervously. Marlene's lips pressed together into a thin line.

"I confess," she said, even and dispassionate, "that I have no idea who you are."

The murmuring swelled, and Oleander turned and spread their hands in a calming gesture. They turned back to Marlene, and the trees whispered again, the many voices overlapping.

Repent.

The voices trailed off, and there was a moment of silence. Maeve wasn't sure if she imagined it—a flicker of uncertainty, a muscle twitching in Marlene's jaw. Or maybe she misinterpreted it.

"Repent," Marlene said, and her voice sounded tight, like some emotion was coiled tight inside her. Her lip curled, and then Maeve knew what it was. Disdain. "For what."

It wasn't a question—it was a statement, a self-absolution. And a self-damnation too. The wind rose again, the cemetery's voices hissing and spitting and cursing, chaotic and cacophonous.

A thousand cruelties—
Cold, so cold—
The ice queen, the ice queen—
Abuser—murderess—thief—
Retribution, justice, judgment—
Peace, peace across the veil—
Holes across the veil—
Rest in peace—
Rest—rest, yes, rest, rest, rest—

The voices converged, and as they did so did the assembled figures, pressing in closer until the glow in the center was nearly as bright as day. Maeve squinted against the glare and the howling wind, and saw Marlene silhouetted among the ghosts. They were grasping at her, pulling at her skirt and her hair and her arms, pulling down. Maeve had been grabbed by ghosts before; they usually couldn't do more than rustle clothing. Or they couldn't, alone. But hundreds of hands were reaching for Marlene now, passing through her and every so often catching, and within seconds Marlene had fallen to her knees. Within a few more seconds, the ghosts had pulled hard enough to make headway against the ground itself; in an instant more Marlene was beginning to sink. She stayed silent, or maybe the deafening sound of the wind hid whatever she may have tried to scream. Her hands clawed against the tide of the earth and found no purchase. The ghosts went down with her, save Oleander—dozens of hands reached up and seized her wrists, and gave one last pull.

Lady Marlene had dug her own grave. Imogen, Maeve thought, would protest the cliché.

Her musing, detached and not a little horrified at how guiltless she felt, didn't last long. A wordless shout of shock and fear and rage cut through the dying wind, and Camille rounded on Maeve.

"You—you—!" She threw her device to the ground and started forward, her fingers tensed like claws, reaching up with the clear intent to strangle Maeve. Maeve backed up—too slow, too numb, too overawed—and Camille fastened her hands around her throat and squeezed—

And fell with a resounding crack.

"Little sister," Orion panted, and lowered the walking stick to his side.

Maeve could only stare. Orion, in the flesh. Not dead. Not dead at all.

"What?" she heard herself croak.

Orion pinched the bridge of his nose. "Damn it all, that sounded a lot sexier in my head—continuing what I was about to say before I got shot, taking out this brat." He nudged her with his foot, talking a little too quickly to pull off any impression of suaveness. "But you had to go and be a better medium than I've ever been and steal all my glory and raise a whole army of ghosts from the dead and did I see that right? Hundreds and hundreds of—all that 'confess' and 'repent' and—she, she's, she's—?"

Maeve seized him around the middle and hugged him as tight as she could.

"Oh—!" Orion didn't say anything more after that. Uneasily, his arms settled around her.

"How—how are you not dead?" she mumbled into his shirt, feeling herself start to cry with relief. At least she had him, the bastard. At the very least. She could face whatever had happened to Imogen, maybe….

"I told you," he said softly, and gently pushed her back. "Lingerie is extremely important." He pulled the neck of his shirt open slightly to reveal the most lacy, ornate, ridiculous corset Maeve had ever seen in her life. Steel-boned. "That being said, I did still get a pretty good scratch—" and now Maeve saw her hands had come away bloody from his back— "so, um, we should—where's Imogen?"

And then what Orion had said, two halves split apart, finally came together in her head.

"Imogen, you're my—little sister." She gasped, her hand to her mouth. "She's your—? How—?" She shook her head, seized his hand, and took off running—back up the hill, to where Imogen had fallen. Maybe, if Orion could come back—Imogen hadn't known the whole story—maybe it wasn't too late—

They had been beaten to Imogen's side, however. The green glow was fading, the specter within growing less defined, but as Maeve crested the hill and looked down, she could see Oleander taking a knee in the snow next to Imogen's body.

"No," she murmured, and closed the rest of the distance as she watched a dimmer spirit, the unusual purple of Imogen's ectoplasm, sit up from the body. The two spirits looked at each other for a long moment.

And then, Imogen's ghost began to talk—or at least it looked like she was speaking. She looked around and her lips moved, slightly at first and then with more animation, and as she turned back to her guardian she began to gesticulate urgently. Was she telling Oleander what had happened to her? Was Oleander telling her what had happened to them? Then, suddenly, they both stopped speaking, and slowly, Oleander got to their feet. They extended a hand, and Maeve felt her throat get tight. She couldn't bring herself to interfere, and yet—

Imogen gazed up at her guardian for a long moment, then looked down at her ghostly hands, at her body, and then up at Maeve. Maeve's breath caught—it was the most tender possible look, bittersweet and uncertain and…Hallowed Mother, her spirit was beautiful. Graceful, radiant, and unquestionably undrawable. A divine mystery. Maeve smiled at her, tears pricking her eyes, and gave a wave.

"Go ahead," she mouthed. "I understand."

But Imogen shook her head, just a little, and then turned to her guardian and shook it more vehemently. She was speaking again, fast and fluid, and Oleander's shoulders sagged slightly. But they nodded and knelt once more, stiff—their bad knee—and took Imogen's ghostly face in their hands. They kissed her forehead, and then they laid her down, like a parent putting a child to bed. Imogen's ghost faded. And with a great deal less dignity than her spirit had shown, her body spasmed, jolted upright, and took in a ragged breath. She turned wide-eyed to Maeve and Orion, then looked up at Oleander, and raised a hand to her forehead.

"Mother's grave," she breathed.

Maeve was already running, tackling Imogen back to the ground and kissing every inch of her face she could get to, sobbing and laughing. Imogen squeezed her back, grinning for all she was worth, and then scrambled to her feet, lifting Maeve with her and gesturing frantically to Orion.

"Meet my guardian," she whispered, and yanked them both over to Oleander's spirit, which had begun to drift away. "Maeve," she told them, and Maeve shook her head incredulously, wiggling her fingers. "And Orion."

"We've met," Orion said softly, and Oleander nodded. Imogen looked surprised by this; she looked at Maeve in confusion as Oleander attempted to pat Orion on the shoulder but passed through him and left him shuddering. They shook their head lightly, then gave Orion a careful nod, and waved back to Maeve. And then, as if the wind moved from the living side of the veil to the dead, their glow dispersed, and they disappeared.

Imogen turned to Orion, and the hush of her voice fit how Maeve felt. "How?"

He ran a hand through his hair and swayed slightly. "May I... sit down before I explain? Got the worst bed spins."

Imogen rolled her eyes, then started and turned him around, raising a hand to her lips. Words had power but calling that a small scratch was a flat-out lie.

"The convent," Maeve offered, not feeling great herself now that the adrenaline had worn off. "We have medical supplies. For sewing up corpses, but they'll do." She looked back over her shoulder, toward where she could see Camille's figure lying slumped and diminished. "What about...?"

Reluctantly they made their way down the hill and found her breathing, uninjured but for a growing lump on the back of her head. Orion recovered his walking stick and leaned on it hard.

"Leave...her." Imogen winced, and tugged her journal, recovered, from her pocket. *She'll find her comeuppance when she goes back to the Academy.* Maeve looked at her quizzically as she pulled Camille up to a sitting position and propped her against a headstone. *That advisor of hers—Chrystos—may be a bit behind the times with ghosts, but she got quite vehement about the rights of the living. Correctly deduced that I was.*

"She let you out?"

Imogen nodded and looked around. *What happened to the assassin?*

Now they all looked around, but save Camille, the cemetery was empty. The harpoon man was gone.

"Let's..." Maeve said after a moment, wishing she too had a walking stick, "take his lead." Her and Orion's eyes connected, and she exhaled a weak laugh. "Er—bed spins."

Imogen shook herself and nodded firmly, threading one arm around her waist, and proffering the other for support. Maeve took it, and found her strong and steady and, blessedly, solid. Imogen beckoned Orion on, taking an accommodating pace down the gravel paths, and led the three of them from the cemetery to the city of the living.

When they got back to the convent, Maeve was surprised to find all the windows lit. She fumbled in her pocket for her keys, realized Camille had taken them, and gave up, rapping the knocker against the front door. It opened nearly instantly to a snappy voice's rebuke.

"Can't you see what time of night it is? We've got extremely pressing matters so if your grandmother could just hold on until—" Shivani caught herself in the middle of her sentence, shoving a canister of salt into the backpack dangling off one of her arms, and stared at Maeve. "You're back," she whispered, and then turned and shouted. "She's back! She's hurt! Out of my way!"

A commotion erupted inside, and before Maeve knew it, she found herself being pulled by many hands into the entryway, through the cloisters, into the chapel. Things had been dragged up from the preparation room in the basement—a couple of gurneys, a makeshift cart of medical supplies—and when Shivani led the procession down the aisle Sister Priscilla jumped to her feet.

"What's wrong? You haven't even left yet!"

"She made it back on her own!" Maeve was forced to sit on one of the gurneys, familiar faces flashing before her eyes as about six different people checked on her. "She's injured—still bleeding a little, looks like—oh, whoever did this—" The last was Thalia, cracking her knuckles as more of a nervous gesture than anything, her eyes ringed with red. Frances pulled her out of the way, and Sister Priscilla descended with a gauze pad soaked in alcohol.

Maeve hissed in pain as it was applied. "I'm fine," she tried to protest, as someone else wrapped her in a heavy wool blanket and yet another sister started unlacing her shoes. "Orion got shot—someone help him."

But she needn't have asked—she turned her head, to Priscilla's protest, and found that at least as many sisters were gathered around Orion's gurney, Shivani leading the charge in the uncomfortable matter of taking off his shirt.

"I would—ah—make a joke about nuns," he said, wincing as he extended his arms for her, "but I think it would be rude."

"Good instincts," Shivani said dryly, throwing the shirt to the ground with a little more force than necessary. She curled her lip for a moment, set to unlacing the corset, and then groaned. "Why am I not surprised at all? Could you have dressed any worse for this occasion?"

Orion looked at her through narrowed eyes, then opened them wide. He swallowed and looked away. "I'm not exactly a church person—as you...may know."

"Indeed." Orion sucked in a breath through his teeth as Shivani pulled the dented stays away from the wound in his back, and crossed his arms over his chest. Imogen, who caught Maeve's eye from an out-of-the-way pew, mouthed: *the piercings?* Maeve choked on a laugh and glanced around in slight horror. A number of the elder sisters were clustered a distance away, conferring among themselves and eyeing Orion—she wasn't sure if it was disapproval of a shirtless man in the chapel or...other opinions. At least he was taking the attention off Imogen, even if they did recognize him.

"Pack that wound with gauze," Priscilla ordered, applying pressure to Maeve's ear. "Not too tight, but make sure you get all the way to the back."

"Mmhmm." Shivani crossed behind Orion and wadded up a pad of gauze with a grim expression. "Sorry in advance."

"I have a pretty high pain toler—" He choked off into a groan of what sounded pretty well like agony. "Mm. I deserved that," he managed under his breath.

Shivani looked just about ready to garrote him with a bandage for even coming close to implying their history, but before Maeve had to step in and prevent another murder there was an interruption. "Did I hear right?" came a stentorian voice from the side door of the chapel, and near all eyes turned toward its source. "Maeve's back? Unharmed?"

"Yes to the first, no to the second," Priscilla told Mother Superior, holding Maeve's head in place and not looking up. She was focused on probing Maeve's wound, murmuring platitudes softly as she disposed of another soaked pad of gauze. "She needs stitches. I can do them. Also, we have company."

Mother Superior strode over into Maeve's field of view, a number of the littlest sisters orbiting around her skirt and an ancient hunting rifle in her hands. It seemed everyone was up, then.

"Maeve, dear. Are you alright?"

She tried to nod before Priscilla protested and cleared her throat instead. "Yes, mostly."

"Right. Well, I suppose what happened can wait..." Her eyes slid to her left, and she took in for the first time the company. Her mouth opened slightly, then closed again, then reopened. "Ah." Her hands tightened slightly on the rifle. "Actually, scratch that, I think I do need to know at least—Shivani, dear, come here for a moment? Thalia, take over."

Shivani glanced up nervously, and passed the tape she was using to attach a bandage over the wound to Thalia. To her credit, Thalia only turned a modest shade of pink, and spoke without stuttering as she told Orion to raise his arms up a bit.

Mother Superior and Shivani conferred for a short moment, breaking apart to look as Shivani pointed out Imogen. She looked at Imogen for a long moment, a frown wrinkling her forehead, and then bent back down to listen to the rest of the story. At length she straightened, set down the rifle, and made her way with her coterie of little sisters back to Orion's gurney. Amal was among them; Maeve thought she caught her give Orion a solemn wink.

"I will...not ask you, either, Mr. Cantor, to explain what exactly Maeve has been getting herself into—tonight. If you wish, we can make a room ready for you to stay over."

"We will," Priscilla put in, stepping over from Maeve to him briefly. "If I'm right and that's a harpoon wound—" she raised a hand and pressed it briefly to his back, and he hissed— "mm. Cracked ribs. You shouldn't be going anywhere."

"I'd hate to impose," he managed, levying a bit of a glare at Priscilla's back before catching himself.

"It's no imposition—we have plenty of space." Mother Superior tugged her skirt out of the little ones' grips and knelt down to them. "Una and Lavender—get a set of sheets and a blanket from the closet and make up a bed at the end of the second-floor hall. Amal, do you feel comfortable turning on the stove to make a pot of tea?"

"I'm twelve," she grumbled, gravely insulted, and rushed off with the others to fulfill her duties.

Orion watched them go and managed a strained smile. "Well, I've never been one to turn down a nice cup of tea. Thank you, er—"

"Mother Superior."

He nodded and straightened up with a wince. "I apologize for the disturbance, Mother Superior. And I offer my strongest possible thanks to your remarkable organization. Your sisters here have been wise and kind and deeply diligent every time I've had the fortune of meeting them, and Maeve has gone miles above and beyond the demands of her position. She deserves nothing less than the highest award you have to give her, and also every art class I have to offer her at the Court." He caught Maeve drawing a finger across her throat, and quickly added, "If such a thing could be allowed."

Maeve closed her eyes in frustration—the issue wasn't that he was inviting her to art classes as much as it was that he was showing he knew her well enough to offer them. Which Mother Superior would unquestionably pick up on, which—ugh. Whatever. She was already definitely in trouble. If Orion could rehabilitate his image with politeness and compliments, perhaps being associated with him wouldn't be as bad in Mother Superior's eyes.

Indeed, a smile had risen to Mother Superior's lips, though it looked a little tense. "That's good to hear, and I look forward to hearing the full story when we've all had a good night's rest. Speaking of—" the little sisters had returned, Amal carrying a kettle and a few mugs tucked precariously under one arm. "Excellent. Now, can you show Mr. Cantor to his room?"

"Orion's fine, ma'am," he said awkwardly, and got down from the gurney with much wincing. "Ah—Imogen, you can go. Key's under the marble peacock statue in the garden. I'll call you in the morning." Imogen took the hint, glancing at Maeve and pointing towards the door with a nervous smile, and started down the aisle.

"Oh, she ought to stay with us, too, if she wants," Mother Superior said, and turned to Maeve. "Though, dear, that was our last spare room. Would you mind if we set a cot up for her in your room, while you get your stitches?"

Imogen froze, and Maeve fought to keep her face even, searching Mother Superior's. That was in no way their last spare room. There was a bit of a knowing tilt to her smile, but no malice. Maeve felt sick anyway. "Of course."

"Excellent." Mother Superior clapped her hands together. "Everyone who isn't doing first aid, back to bed. Orion, the girls will show you to your room, and—Imogen, was it?—follow me. I'll set you up with Maeve." Imogen made her way hesitantly up the aisle as Orion followed the girls out of the chapel. As soon as he was out of sight Mother Superior turned back to Frances. "And Frances? You have extra sweaters, don't you? Could you *please* find that gentleman a shirt?"

Chapter

XXII

There was a knock at Maeve's door, just as she was turning down the lamp, and as she opened the door, she heard quiet organ music drifting down the hall. Most everyone else had gone to bed once the commotion was over, but it seemed a few denizens of the convent were still lurking.

The one at her door turned out to be Orion, ensconced in an overlarge sweater and for the first time she had seen, not wearing his laurels.

"Do you need something?" she asked, yawning and rubbing her eyes. Sister Priscilla had given her—and she'd thought, him—a sturdy dose of laudanum, and with the pain in her ear lessened, she had been nearing sleep.

"Before I..." He worried his lower lip and tried again. "It's a story I...would rather tell now. Before I can talk myself out of it or leave it to you."

Maeve rubbed her eyes again, and let him in. The embarrassment she had felt the first time she had let Imogen into her room was having a hard time fighting its way through the medicine as Orion looked around.

"Lovely," he said. "I ought to get an organ for my apartment."

"Mmm. It's Shivani playing." She tried to give him a look, but a yawn undercut it.

"Your opium tolerance is really embarrassing, darling." He gave a melancholy chuckle and looked back toward the door.

"You should apologize to her."

"I will." He winced and placed a hand on his ribs. "One sin at a time, Sister."

Maeve sat on the edge of the cot. Imogen had insisted on taking it to keep Maeve's ear from getting bumped or crowded and seemed to have pulled her usual trick of falling asleep the instant her head touched the pillow. She stirred when Maeve touched her shoulder, then sat bolt upright and groped around for her journal.

Do you need more medicine? Water? she scrawled with her eyes closed. *I wasn't asleep.*

"I'm okay," Maeve assured her, and let herself lean in as Imogen slid up next to her. "Orion has something to tell you."

Her eyes popped open at that, and she raised a questioning eyebrow at him. He glanced around again, then pulled out Maeve's desk chair and sat perched on its edge. "Right. Er. Imogen, you... you have a right to know why what happened to you did. And, er, what my part in it was. I thought, maybe, it didn't matter, but..." he swallowed. "Your murder had far longer roots than I knew." He held up a hand. "I didn't tell you what I knew—or I told myself I didn't tell you—because it was the safest course to keep you in the dark. But also because...well, I'm a coward." He gave a weary smile. "I hope you'll understand why I did it, and if I can be even more wildly selfish than I usually am, then I hope you'll forgive me. But I did something terrible, and the long and short of it was that I didn't want you to hate me."

An auspicious start, Imogen wrote. Her words were sarcastic, but her eyes were wide. She was hanging on his every word.

Orion laughed softly, and laced his fingers together behind his head. "Right. So, when I was thirteen, *she*—" a 'she' laced with terrible dread, even after the events of the night, and Maeve finally thought she could see the shape of Orion's fear— "had a baby. Which was, of course, odd, given that my father had been on a Warwick Company mission surveying tea fields in the south for the last year. I didn't quite understand how those things worked yet, but the servants muttered. I was a terrible eavesdropper as a child."

"Anyway. One day, *she* brought me upstairs, and told me that I was the heir to the Warwick title and estate." Leaning against Imogen in the twilight of her bedroom, Maeve was beginning to drowse under the influence of laudanum and soft music and Orion's quiet story. It was told with none of his usual aplomb and seemed all the more real and powerful for it. Maeve could almost see the dark old manor with its twisted hedges, the teenage Orion—just Amal's age—called into some room with moldering velvet drapes, reminded that it would all be his. He spoke on. "Which I knew, obviously—it had only been hammered into me for the last thirteen years. And she told me that…that this baby was a threat to that. That through some quirk of inheritance law, bastards could claim noble lineages, and if they could prove it, they could claim a share of the estate. My mother told me that she wouldn't see the estate split up, and so to prove my worthiness to inherit such a lofty title, I had to…remove my competition, or be removed myself."

"I took the baby," Orion continued, his voice growing more constricted by each word. "It was winter. I figured maybe I could just leave it somewhere and it would go to sleep and not wake back up. I tucked it up in my coat and brought it across the bridge to the island," and Maeve pictured that long, harrowing trek in the dark, "and wandered till I found a cemetery, which seemed right somehow. But when I went in and found a nice-looking slab and was about to put the baby down, I…I looked up, and there was this little hut, with light in the windows."

"I…didn't think very hard. I tried not to—to ignore my mother's voice in my head. I meant to just drop the baby on the doorstep and go. But the groundskeeper must have seen me lurking around or something, because they opened the door the instant, I put the baby down on the step. I couldn't—couldn't speak, at all." Orion coughed, and Maeve could see him bathed in the warm light from within the hut as Oleander gazed down at him. Did he know, then, that this was a better home than his own? Did he think about staying? Could he have done so, escaped Marlene's long reach, or had he known even then that he was trapped as long as she lived? "I just stood there frozen, guilty, and watched the groundskeeper take her inside. They never said anything to me—just looked. I ran as soon as they were gone."

"My mother seemed impressed. I made it three more years on that, before my father died and she tried to marry me off to that Heathcliffe girl and it all became too much. I could never stand up to her alone. I ran again—I've always been a coward, you know—and I began again. There was only one way to be free of her, I thought, which was to meet her at her level, or as close as I could get to it. To find my own source of power and surround myself so that if I did have to face her, I'd never have to do it alone." He laughed a bit. "I'm not a poet of finesse, as you must know by now, Imogen. I've seen you write wanderlust and bittersweet and anger and love into your pages, but me? I forced my way onto the Court with desperation alone. There's power in that, but not honesty. It's desperate charisma—a man with his neck under the guillotine, staying it with whatever last words appeal to the crowd."

There was the slight scratching of pen on paper, and Orion paused for a moment, then spoke with a smile in his voice.

"I promise you, Imogen, no. That night wracked me with guilt for years—two full decades—and I had never gone back to the cemetery. I started my school with some notion of teaching that brute force sort of poetry I had gotten good at, and maybe making a few allies beside. I liked your work because it had a bit of that hunger. You were running towards something instead of away; I recognized it. I didn't recognize you."

More scratching, and Maeve imagined what that meeting had been like—Imogen getting her crack at the Court and taking an apprenticeship with the Laureate. In that painting room, perhaps, with the hardwood floors and the wide, white-curtained windows. Orion with his air of glamorous unconcern, and Imogen hungry to prove herself. How long had it taken for them to go from teacher and student to friends? Or had it taken Imogen's death for that barrier to break down?

"A year or so after you joined my school—once it was only the three or four of you left. You were outstripping them; you know you were. I was harder on you than them! If there's one thing I abhor it's all that gilded noble nepotism. But yes, you had come back from visiting your guardian, and you were all bent out of shape about a cemetery getting sold. Finally, I put it together—I never met the father of that baby, so I had no idea what my half-sibling would look like. But unfortunately, you did get that Warwick nose. My condolences."

There was a pause in which Maeve would typically expect Imogen to kick Orion in the shins for such a comment, but when none was forthcoming, she managed to pry her eyes open and look up at Imogen. She seemed lost in thought, her pale blue eyes unfocused.

They were the same eyes that looked so striking on Orion and so icy on Marlene. The resemblance between the two half-siblings was imperfect, but with Marlene placed between them it might have been quite apparent.

"Did Marlene figure it out?" she asked, and Orion shifted his gaze to her.

"Oh, yes. I could hardly stop Imogen from defending her home, and secretly, I wanted to see if she could stand up where I failed. But she must have figured it out at some point, because Camille showed up."

"Marlene's goddaughter."

Orion nodded, his lips pressed together. "To act, I imagine, as a sort of handler for Imogen—to bring her back as an heir and get Camille married into the family. I didn't see it coming until the last—when Imogen came to me and told me about her trouble with her girlfriend's proposal. I hadn't known who it was, until that last week. And immediately I knew something was going on."

"So, you went to the mainland—"

"And threatened to tell Imogen my and my mother's secret if Camille didn't leave her be."

And she couldn't let me know because I was far too troublesome as an heir. Imogen picked her head up. *Camille tried very hard, but she couldn't quite break me.*

"She hated you," Maeve said with a yawn, "and she couldn't bear to marry you, even for a little while. That's what she meant in the cemetery. And so, she offered Marlene the alternative—"

Her crazy science project. Imogen looked at her hands. *No need for an heir if you're immortal. But it didn't work, not like she thought it would.*

Maeve perked up. "No?"

Imogen shook her head and pawed through her hair till in the gloomy lamplight Maeve could see a trio of grey hairs. They were just in the same place as Orion's grey streak, and as Marlene's. *New. I noticed them when we did my hair for the bacchanal.*

Well, that was a small but real comfort—Camille's talk of immortality had begun to worry Maeve slightly. That, surely, was against the vows of the Sisterhood to allow—though, summoning and dating and going to masquerades and bacchanals in daring dresses were also against those vows. A twinge of guilt forced its way through the laudanum, and Maeve shut her eyes tiredly against it. The mystery was solved—Imogen had died in a tangled web of family ties and inheritances and secrets, and had returned through a rift in the veil that Camille had somehow torn in her experiments. She had finished her unfinished business, and she had managed to stay alive anyway. She was going to be okay.

Maeve just wasn't sure where that left her, now.

"So," Orion said, and got to his feet with some effort. He looked especially tired tonight, out from under his makeup and his fancy clothes and his usual studied nonchalance. "I cannot fully apologize, or make up for, what I took from you. You could have been a lady if I hadn't been a coward. Things could have been easier for you." He bit his lip, looked at his feet, then looked back up. "I'm sorry, Imogen. For setting this all in motion, and for not being brave enough to stop it."

Imogen was quiet for a long moment. Then she uncapped her pen and wrote for a bit. She scratched out some parts, started over, scratched out the rest, and passed over something that couldn't be very long at all. She handed it to Orion, and stood, and once he had finished reading it and set it aside, she pressed a kiss to his cheek and seized him in a hug.

I have a lot to think about, and I can't comprehend it all right now, the journal read from where Maeve was trying not to snoop. *But it seems to me that you acted in kindness, then and now. Oleander was always my parent, and...I'll hold to that. But I always wanted a sibling, and—* there was a lot of crossing-out here, half-obscured pet names Maeve could tell were designed to aggravate. She could see Imogen grinning over Orion's shoulder now. *I think the worst possible option is my slutty old poetry teacher.*

"Your slutty mid-thirties poetry teacher," Orion corrected, a catch in his throat. "I'm...I'm only crying because you think I'm old. Wait till you turn thirty."

Imogen pulled back and turned and smiled at Maeve. She was crying, too—still ectoplasm, but that was okay. "Can't wait... brother dear."

324

When Maeve awoke in the morning, it was only because her pain medication had worn off and there was loud conversation out in the hall. She could have slept for days otherwise, hiding under the covers from the complications that were left to sort out. But her ear was aching too much for her to fall back asleep, and when she picked her head up to look for the bottle of medicine, she found Imogen's cot empty. That woke her all the way up, and she sat up with a start. According to Sister Priscilla she had lost a lot of blood, and it rather felt like it as she blinked spots out of her vision and groped around for her glasses.

She dressed as quickly as she could and rushed into the hall to find that the argument was in fact echoing all the way up the stairs from the entryway. She considered sliding down the banister, thought better of it, and hurried down them. The subject of the shouting—and the identity of the combatants—was becoming clearer as she approached, and she had probably ought to take her post.

"You cannot come to my department and condemn me for experimenting with what you presume to be human—"

"Professor—"

"—and in the same breath take this woman, unquestionably human, and—and—subject her to whatever sort of rituals—"

"Really, Professor Chrystos, that's quite out of—"

"She's been through enough! Would you like me to describe the actual quantitative value of 'enough'? A sustained ten milliamp shock for at least ten minutes, for one, and the psychological trauma of being *murdered*—"

It was at this moment Maeve came around the corner, to find that perhaps the situation was less dire than she expected. Professor Chrystos stood across from Mother Superior, shaking a lab notebook—Camille's lab notebook—with some violence. A number of sisters had crept in along the sides of the entryway, watching the match go down with interest, and among them, looking slightly frustrated and holding a box from the bakery down the street under one arm, was Imogen. Not in any immediate danger of exorcism, it seemed, but Professor Chrystos wasn't conceding that. She rushed over, and seized Maeve's forearm.

"Excellent—the only one of you with any sense! Sister Maeve, I insist you talk to Bethel before she does something rash to this poor woman!" She pointed at Imogen and lowered her voice. "One of my students—Camille Sinclair, who I believe you're acquainted with—she's..." Her words failed her for a moment, and she gestured angrily. "Committed some severe ethical violations!"

"Nadia!" Mother Superior had marched over now and detached the professor's hand from Maeve's arm. "I would appreciate it if you released Maeve, and if you would calm down and listen! We're not going to do anything rashly, or without Imogen's input!"

Professor Chrystos raised her chin and took a few steps back. "And who, exactly, is this Imogen—"

"She's someone neither of you are listening to, darlings," came a voice from behind Maeve. Orion strolled out and leaned against the door frame. "Pardon my interruption, but I think she's trying to do so."

"Mr. Cantor," Mother Superior said with a slight edge of aggravation, and Professor Chrystos stared at him. Imogen took this opportunity to dash across the hall, place the box in Maeve's hands, then cross to Orion and mime tapping at a telegraph. He handed his over, and Imogen began to tap as she made her way back across to the two women in the center of the hall. Maeve snuck a peek inside the box, and found a pair of chocolate croissants, still warm.

"Imogen Madrigal—I see," said Professor Chrystos, looking up from the telegraph. "I apologize. Camille refers to you only as 'the subject' in her notes. I've read them—they're comprehensive."

Imogen's eyebrows quirked in irritation, and she looked at Mother Superior. "I know a reasonable amount of it, I hope," Mother Superior said. "But as I was *trying* to say, given the unusual nature of the situation, I—" She glanced around, seemingly just noticing the audience they had attracted, and levied a stern look around the room. "I will discuss it with all the involved parties in my office. And everyone *else* should go back to enjoying the lovely day."

The hint was taken; the little sisters fled, whispering, and the elders did so in a manner only slightly more dignified. Except for Thalia and Frances, who both mimed for Maeve to wait and then took off running toward the chapel. Mother Superior beckoned her and Orion forward to join the group properly.

"Come. We'll get this all—"

"Not without us!" Shivani shouted, appearing in the doorway again with Thalia and Frances. "We're involved parties!"

Mother Superior glanced between the three of them, looking exasperated. "All three of you? Mother preserve me, does the whole island know?"

Shivani strode forward with the other two and crossed her arms. "We're supposed to be sisters, aren't we?" She stood shoulder-to-shoulder with Maeve, and Maeve noticed Frances move her elbow slightly, ever-so-slightly, and nudge Imogen too. "We stick together."

Mother Superior pinched the bridge of her nose, sighed, and beckoned them on as well. "Fine. Come along, then. Let's put this to rest."

Maeve's opinion on science was starting to shift as Professor Chrystos argued for a full twenty minutes on the nature of Imogen's condition, the damage Camille's machine had wrought to the veil, and why, despite all of that, Imogen should be allowed to remain. It had taken Maeve and Imogen months to figure a fraction of this out, and in the few short hours Chrystos had to read Camille's notebooks, it seemed she grasped it entirely.

"Artificial bursts of energy, as I explained to Maeve previously, can disrupt the prevailing flow of energy, in both our direction and in the direction of the paranormal. And the energy bursts generated by my student's experimentation," she pursed her lips, "were unusually strong. The abnormal manifestations that Maeve reports—the 'fractured spirits', as she calls them—are products of these disruptions. The waveforms that they come from are spatial in nature, and due to the great prevailing currents of spacetime, I believe they should heal in due course as long as no further aggravation occurs. But Ms. Madrigal is a different case."

Maeve glanced around, trying to gauge everyone else's comprehension. She wasn't exactly sure of what the currents of spacetime might be, and Frances seemed similarly confused. Thalia and Imogen both were frowning tremendously, Imogen scratching down notes, and Orion and Shivani both wore entertainingly identical expressions of disdain on opposite sides of the room. Mother

Superior sat in front of Maeve, so she couldn't tell how she was taking this.

"Continue, Professor."

Professor Chrystos wove her fingers together. "There are a number of different kinds of energy that govern and make up our world—light and sound and the spatial sort that I mentioned before, that makes up the matter we touch. But my student seems to have hypothesized—and proven—that *emotion*, too, is a form of energy that can impact the real world. And that, given proper motivation, that it can affect the spiritual realm, too. That a nun's prayer, if believed sincerely enough, could dampen the vibrations of the spiritual plane, and counteract any manifestations arising in our world. That, symmetrically, a medium could excite the same vibrations and cause a manifestation by force of will. That, scientifically, a poet's words could have power." Maeve snuck a glance at Orion; he was still leaning back, but his eyes had narrowed. "Her eventual conclusion was that, by the power of some violent and ongoing feeling, a permanent disruption could be made to follow the person feeling it around—that, in her words, a spirit could be brought back and reattached to its body."

"Where is Camille?" Maeve voiced at last. She couldn't imagine that Professor Chrystos had been kindly lent that lab notebook.

Professor Chrystos leveled an impassive look at her. "She is, for the time being, removed to Edgewood Heights Sanatorium for the Mentally Uncertain. A name that is perhaps not entirely appropriate, for she seemed quite certain in a number of violent intentions toward the people in this room." She shifted slightly. "I promise, the Academy takes ethics seriously. I excused the inconsistencies in Camille's proposals as a student's mistakes, and I now see I should not have underestimated her. But I will try my best, Ms. Madrigal, to make sure all possible reparations can be made to you."

Imogen waved a dismissive hand, and held out her journal. *So, essentially, Camille tore a hole in the veil by torturing me and then amplifying my feelings enough to disrupt the currents of the paranormal?*

Professor Chrystos nodded sadly. "And as I understand it, the rift was then left in an ambiguous state once you were killed. It remained partially open until your spirit could reform enough to have emotions again—to, as the Sisters say, I believe, recognize its unfinished business. That was when you likely would have awakened—which, I assume, is why you were assumed dead for the better part of a year."

Imogen nodded and sat back. She wrote for long time, then passed the journal to Orion, who laughed slightly.

"She's written 'be convincing'," he informed the assembled group, and cleared his throat. "I understand, Mother Superior, the purpose of your order and what should probably be my fate here. Maeve has been very tactful in not mentioning her reservations in allowing me to stay on this side of the veil; I imagine the rest of you hold similar concerns." Imogen was looking at Mother Superior, but her eyes flicked briefly to Shivani as Orion said this part. "I know I died, and though I would like to beg on the merits of it being an untimely murder, I know that the world is not so kind to others who have found similar fates. I also have no grounds on the merit of wanting to stay alive; Maeve has told me about her work with the fractured hauntings, and with other ghosts who wanted to keep meddling in the affairs of the living who were given no such clemency. I understand the importance of life and death—I was raised by the keeper of the cemetery which you and Frances and Thalia just fought so hard to protect, and both they and I died in its service. My only argument is this, and I hope you won't think I'm playing on your sympathies to mention it. *Something* kept me from passing over completely in that year I lay in my mausoleum."

Orion paused, and glanced up, then kept going.

"I don't know what it was—I don't know enough to say. I'm not a scientist, I'm not religious. Was it a quirk of Camille's process, or...what I would like to believe, what I think might merit leaving me around...was it divine intervention? Was it a second chance from fate? I've been living like it was for these few months, and I would like to continue to do so." Imogen spread her hands out wide, and unconsciously Orion mirrored her. "I don't have one piece of unfinished business anymore. I have a whole, wide, unfinished second chance, and I'd like to take it, if you all will let me."

Professor Chrystos turned and looked hard at Mother Superior, and Mother Superior glanced around the room. Maeve nodded encouragingly as her eyes fell on her.

"Well," she said at last, and pressed her hands together. "I am not so gifted with words as you poets, but...I will say, as much as I would like to pretend otherwise, organizations are made from people, and people are fallible. I will not pretend to be perfect. I will admit that I was not sure I would be able to bring myself to order an exorcism in this case. The rules state that the dead belong on the far side of the veil, but I could not manage to convince myself that you were among them. But what you all have done for me is given me peace with the decision. Your explanation, Nadia, gives me hope that when the time comes—for come it must—" she said sternly—"that Imogen will be able to find her rest. And Imogen: you say you're not religious, but I am impressed by your faith, nonetheless. I agree. Science can get us far, but—" she smiled askance at Professor Chrystos, and tilted her hands down. "There is still room for a few divine mysteries. So, yes."

"Yes?" Imogen whispered.

Mother Superior inclined her head. "We're exorcists, not executioners. As long as my sisters are in accordance with my interpretation—" and Maeve nodded furiously, feeling the others do so with varying degrees of surety behind her—"then yes. Take your second chance. Live a good life, and in a long time, when I'm long gone, die a good death." She smiled. "Is that good enough for you, Nadia?"

Professor Chrystos stood, and collated her notes messily, extending a hand to Mother Superior. "Indeed, Bethel. Ms. Madrigal—" She turned, then spun back to Mother Superior's desk and snatched up a scrap of note paper. Mother Superior raised an eyebrow. "I'll continue to work on this and see if I can improve your quality of life in your state. I may contact you for further data—this is my telegraph number."

Imogen took it hesitantly. "I won't…need to go…back to the lab…?"

Professor Chrystos looked perplexed for a moment before comprehension dawned. "Ah. Yes. I can make a house call."

She left, and after a few pleasantries and assurances, Orion did as well.

"We can discuss…well, plans, back at the Court," he told Imogen with a kiss on the cheek, and gave Maeve one as well, then nodded to the rest of the sisters. "Thank you for your hospitality and also for this lovely sweater, dear. I'm sure we'll see more of each other soon." Maeve could tell Mother Superior didn't like that or the knowing smile he levied their way on his way out.

"Did you give him that sweater or did he just assume—?" she asked Frances.

"The former," she assured Maeve. "I have a whole closet full of them. It's a problem."

"Start selling them," Shivani advised. "You just gave the richest man on the island something for free."

Mother Superior cleared her throat. "In the interest of dealing with all of this at once, girls, would you give me a minute with Maeve? Alone," she added in Imogen's direction.

Maeve took a deep breath and watched as the others filed out of the office, dragging their heels. Imogen was the last to go and shut the door behind her with trepidation. Maeve tried to give her an encouraging look. Then she turned, and sat in front of Mother Superior's desk, and said a small prayer in her mind.

"You look scared, dear," Mother Superior said, a slight note of amusement in her voice.

"I never wanted it to get so…twisted," Maeve told her miserably. "I hate lying. I hate secrets. But it…it just got…" She sighed. "What do you want to know?"

Mother Superior tilted her head thoughtfully. "Well, I don't quite know how this all began in the first place."

So, Maeve told her. No more secrets. About meeting Imogen on the steps of the mausoleum, and the Wraith, and their devil's bargain.

"I only wanted to save the convent," she said softly. "I felt like… waiting wasn't enough."

Mother Superior inclined her head. "And Imogen. The two of you…I apologize, but I did see your light on once or twice a touch late. And Shivani, when she explained where you had gone, seemed quite upset. I won't pry, but…you seem very close."

Maeve nodded miserably. No more secrets, even if the telling made her feel sick with guilt. *It shouldn't have to be this way*, whispered the seed of rebellion that had lain in her heart for so long now. *Orion doesn't feel guilt like this. Imogen doesn't.*

Mother Superior nodded again and sighed. "I've already broken rules today, Maeve, but I feel like perhaps this is the less monumental of the two. I know that living like this, with only your sisters for companionship, is different. It is difficult. It, quite frankly, removes a number of people who might like to join the Sisterhood from contention. It's an important check on the power we wield, but if there's no one left to wield that power, then does it matter?" It became obvious after a moment that she was actually asking—it wasn't clear if she had an answer in mind.

"You told me that things die, and that we shouldn't stand in their way of doing so," Maeve said. She would voice her opinion, she supposed, and let things fall how they might. "But I think also we can't stand in the way of letting them live."

"So, you're in favor of change?" Mother Superior was watching her closely, Maeve found when she looked up. She swallowed.

"I think it's change or die," she said. "And, um, I've done a lot of changing lately and it's not so bad."

Mother Superior nodded to herself and was silent for a long moment. At length she shook herself and stood.

"Well, thank you, Maeve. I believe your cohort is making dinner tonight. Try not to overexert yourself until then, if you can help it. Or Priscilla will get angry with me." She smiled.

Maeve stood too, wary. "That's...all?"

Mother Superior smiled wryly. "Like I said, Maeve—the Sisterhood is made up of people. And people are fallible. You've done good service for Ms. Madrigal, and I believe there's truth to what you said, about change." She sighed. "It is an unusual situation. Perhaps there will need to be more discussion later. But I want to follow my instincts, Maeve, and my instincts tell me that punishing you for doing good is exactly the way to destroy this convent entirely."

Maeve considered that for a moment, hovering on the precipice of accepting it. But she hadn't told Mother Superior everything yet, had she? "There's...one more thing," she said at last. "What happened in the cemetery."

Mother Superior listened quietly, though her eyebrows rose, and her eyes widened at some points. At last Maeve came to the end of it, leaving out the part where Oleander and Imogen had talked. That felt like Imogen's story to tell, not hers.

"So, I've developed attachments outside the convent, I've kept a ghost around out of my own selfish desire, and I raised about a hundred ghosts from the dead," she said in a rush. "I've broken every possible rule. And I'd like to say I'm sorry, but I want to be honest! It felt like the right thing to do at the time!" She felt herself starting to get worked up, the guilt and rebelliousness warring inside her, and she clenched her fists. "That's it. That's all of it."

"I see." Mother Superior was silent for a few moments. "This voice, this instinct you felt, that told you how to raise the spirits—you think it was divine in nature?"

Maeve hesitated, then nodded. "It's not an excuse. I know what I did is against the rules. But it felt like...like someone thought I ought to—"

"I believe you," Mother Superior said, and pressed her fingertips together. She gave Maeve a strained smile. "This doesn't change my decision, dear. If anything, it makes me feel better about it. You followed your faith—isn't that all any of us can do?"

Maeve knew she should agree, but for some reason Mother Superior's clemency irked her. She didn't want to get away with it all—she felt guilty, she ought to be punished, and finding that all the rules she'd structured her life by had the strength of wet tissue paper was frustrating! Why had she needed to feel so guilty in the first place? She'd grown and changed so much, and now she was just going to be allowed to slot back into her box? A box made slightly roomier, with walls that might not be as strong as she had thought. But she'd been outside of her box, now, and thinking that the way back was barred had empowered her to move forward.

If she went back in now, she'd be a nun—a very good nun, granted, who had experienced divine guidance and given a hundred ghosts their shot at justice—but a nun, forever. She would always be Sister Maeve. She couldn't be Maeve the unlabeled, Maeve the still-figuring-it-out. Maeve the someday-artist.

But Imogen, and Imogen's way of living, let her have that and more.

"You don't agree?" Mother Superior was looking closely at Maeve; she was sure that her inner turmoil was roiling on her face. "Do you *want* to be in trouble?"

Maeve swallowed, took a deep breath, and closed her eyes.

"Mother Superior, I think I want to leave the convent."

She cracked open an eye; Mother Superior looked shocked, and about ten years older to boot. The guilt rose up again inside her—*look what you've done, this woman who's been so kind to you all your life, you gut her*—and she would've killed to take it back in that moment. But it was too late now.

"I see." Mother Superior folded her hands and looked up at Maeve. "I can't pretend that I—I don't want to make you feel badly about this but—oh, why, dear?" Her usual impassivity had lapsed somewhat, and Maeve could tell she was stricken with sadness.

"I...oh, Mother Superior, please don't take this the wrong way. Please don't be hurt." She fell back into her chair and put her face in her hands. "I'm just different now. I want different things. And I don't want to feel guilty for enjoying those things. I feel so...guilty, all the time, about everything I've done these last few months, but I don't want to go back to a life without them! I'm supposed to live a good life—how can I, if everything I've found that I love is something that you'd call frivolous?" The words came to her easily—too easily for a nun used to rote and too close to poetry. "You said you didn't want us to become sheltered—and these last few months, I've done just the opposite. I haven't found the divine in these walls—it's been out there, at the sea and the Court and the tea shop and in *living*, not just waiting to die! I don't want to leave my faith! I'm running towards it, if anything! I just...."

"Oh, Maeve..." She looked up and found Mother Superior looking at her in anguish. "I didn't know you felt that way."

"I felt like I had to be a good little sister," she said miserably. "Because I...I don't know, I just feel like I'm no use to anyone unless I can be useful. Helpful. And, ugh, these are my problems and they're not important for you to know and I don't want to hurt anyone but—but—"

"Maeve, they are important." Mother Superior stood, crossed to Maeve's side of the desk, and knelt beside her. "Dearest, I...I'm sorry. I see why you feel that way, and why the Sisterhood's teachings haven't been the right thing for you. I'm sorry I didn't see it earlier."

"I didn't know earlier," Maeve said, fighting back tears as Mother Superior gathered her into a hug. "But, but now I think I do. At least a little better."

"Shh, shh. I understand." Mother Superior patted her back and leaned back out to face her. "I'm torn, dearest. As your abbess and as your guardian—I want you here. I want to keep you close and try to repair this. But it sounds like you've found something out there. As much as I want to hold you, I'd only be holding you back from it." And that finally broke Maeve, and she started to cry.

"Go. Go with every honor and accolade I can give you, like Mr. Cantor said. Take as much time as you need to find someplace new and come back as frequently as you like to visit. And if ever you find what you're looking for and you want to come back for good—well, change can be good. Like you said. Perhaps it will be a better Sisterhood you come back to."

Maeve couldn't rally enough to respond; she just sat and hugged Mother Superior and sobbed into her habit until she was sure she had fully soaked her shoulder. But at length she sat up, and accepted a tissue, and stood and held her box of croissants tight against her chest. It felt like she had thrown something precious away. It would be a long time till she knew whether she had made the right decision, she could tell.

"Thank you, Mother Superior," she managed, and backed toward the door.

"Bethel, now, if you like," she said, and gave Maeve a small smile. "Enjoy those. And at least come back for dinner."

Maeve nodded tearfully and stepped into the hall. She found Imogen still there, leaning against the wall in a good show of nonchalance.

"Were you eavesdropping?" she whispered, managing a watery smile.

Imogen opened her mouth, then shook her head vehemently and fished her notebook back out of her pocket.

I was just making sure you were okay! I stopped listening when— She hadn't finished the sentence; when Maeve looked up she found Imogen looking rather teary, too. *Did you just leave the convent for me? Because I swear to the Hallowed Mother on high, Maeve, if this is another one of your stupid sacrifices—*

"No," Maeve said, and was forced to laugh at Imogen's indignant expression. "No, this is the first selfish thing I've done in my life. Hey, Selfish Thing Two—do you think Orion will let me take him up on those art classes? Oh, three—can I sleep on your couch until I get…oh, Mother—a job?"

Imogen's mouth was hanging slightly open, but when Maeve said that, she snatched her journal back and wrote angrily. *You don't have to get a job! I owe you my entire life like three times over, and I'm rich! I'm the Mother-damned Young Lady Warwick! You're becoming an artist, or whatever you want to become, and you're not waiting another second!* She tossed the journal back at Maeve, crossing her arms, and then snatched it back. *I'm so proud of you. Augh. You scared me half to death. Or at least three-quarters to death.*

Maeve giggled. "Sorry."

Don't apologize! You're on a roll, taking what you want! Imogen let out a huff and ran her fingers through her hair. *This morning was supposed to be nice, before people had to go ruining it with making me plead for my life and making you cry. I was going to bring you croissants in bed, and nice tea.*

"Well," Maeve said, hugging the box, "we could go have tea at that teahouse by the lobster docks. You know, where you threatened me with a knife?" She smiled. "I want to go sketch the boats."

Absolutely. Imogen took the box of croissants to carry for her, and after a quick detour upstairs to recover Maeve's sketchbook, the two of them emerged into a cool November day. They turned the corner of the block, and Imogen slipped her free hand into Maeve's, and Maeve felt a knot tied tight in her chest begin to unfurl. Things were changing, but that was okay. There was a new normal on the horizon, if only she could keep afloat.

Chapter

XXIII

For the entire winter, the only question in any Lenorum newspaper was not whether Orion Cantor had finally snapped and killed his mother, but how he had done it without leaving a shred of evidence.

It had taken some time for her to be noticed missing—her servants evidently reluctant to perform a full search of the Warwick manor's many private chambers—but once she had, the constabulary mobilized with a vengeance not often seen on the island. The prime suspect, of course, was her main public enemy, though no one could place him at the scene of the crime. No crime scene, it turned out, could be established—the woman's body could not be found, even on a tip from a young noblewoman who produced raving testimony from within the custody of Edgewood Heights Sanatorium. The old cemetery in the center of the city—which Lady Warwick had recently taken possession of, and which now floated in legal limbo—was overturned looking for a body, resulting in a number of unintended hauntings. These were dealt with by the Sisterhood of Good Death, who offered to continue tending its graves until the legal complications could be resolved. No evidence was found, and no one could offer a single suspicious action Orion Cantor had undertaken that night. Testimony from four separate witnesses placed him in his Court apartment throughout the evening, and under hours of strict questioning the Laureate remained unconcerned by the accusations, if unpleasantly irreverent toward his disappeared mother.

And yet, unquestionably, it was fixed in the public mind that he had done it; opinions varied on whether he should be applauded or reviled. The printing presses had worn out their type in the letters of his name by the time another scandal rolled around, and once it had, a strange sort of mythology formed around the two events—one a disappearance, one a reappearance. Some were happy to turn to pleasanter matters; others whispered about the Court's experiments with seancecraft and ignored the official story of the botched assassination, the faked death, and the year away in the southern isles.

Perhaps some things were better left as mysteries; perhaps words could have too much power and poking into the business of the Court and its Laureate was an errand for the foolish. It was time for supper, anyway, and if Imogen Madrigal had indeed come back from the dead, then she ought to be left well enough alone. It was clear she had powerful friends.

Spring had arrived, and with it the lengthening of days—the sun reclined for what felt like hours just above the horizon, casting the sky in gold and scattering coins of light out across the water. A few tumbled in the window and came to rest on the worn hardwood floors of a studio, paced through by bare feet and sparkling off the bronze diadem their owner wore. She crossed silently to the window, where the artist bent over her work, and gave a tiny whistle through her teeth.

Maeve jumped and shot Imogen a glare. "I'm going to put a bell on you!"

Imogen smiled and set the cup of tea on the corner of Maeve's worktable before leaning in for a closer look. Maeve took the cup up with a grumble and fished her telegraph out of her pocket just as it started to chime.

I've no idea how you create depth like that, darling—I could drown in it. I want to drown in it! Like breathing light….

Maeve looked at the painting wryly—she wasn't sure it was quite worthy of Imogen's praise yet. A gold misty morning at the whaling docks, intended for an assignment from one of Orion's classes, though whispers had been going around that Adolai Anchorman was in the market for an anthology cover. She had been working on capturing the translucence of the fog, dozens of wet-into-wet washes that had taken the day to perfect—yellow was complicated, and the experimental swatches littering the desk were testament to the fact.

But Orion had gotten on her case last week about using blue as a crutch, and here they were. She sipped the tea—herbal, like she preferred after noon, with an iced lemon cookie on the side of the saucer—and surveyed the studies littering the floor behind her. The sea and the hour just after sundown, the weather-beaten siding of their apartment, shadows leaning into the chapel, the blues sliding into purple for Imogen's portraits and back toward green for the spectral studies. She had enjoyed these the most, working from photographs Shivani had brought her back from exorcisms. Working in the dark was familiar. Bringing things out into the light was new.

"He'll call the composition trite," she told Imogen, and dropped her brush into the water as she turned back to the gold-flecked waves on her workbench.

And what will Hubert say? Orion's a poet, not a painter.

A smile rose to Maeve's lips in spite of herself. Hubert Carver had been Orion's one concession to otherwise iron control of his art classes; while he insisted that medium was irrelevant to developing creative sense, it was undeniable that technique played a role. So, while Orion stomped around in his heels and made gory pronouncements about ripping one's heart out and smearing it on the canvas, little old besweatered Hubert peered at their paintings and gave pointers about brushes and pigments. Maeve was growing increasingly fond of the old printmaker.

"He'll commend me for going outside my comfort zone and give me a hard candy."

Indeed. And then he'll take you on as an apprentice and you'll corner the whole illustration business and force Orion to send his books to the curb with plain white covers. Imogen grinned, and turned back to the floor, wafting one of Maeve's studies up into her hand with a cool breeze. *Speaking of, I want this one for my cover.*

"Mmm. And how close are you to done?" Imogen chose a new piece of art every time she came into the studio, and every time Maeve teased her with the same question.

I've got sixteen.

"Last week you had nineteen!"

Well, you're not the only one my dear brother is shredding to pieces. Imogen adjusted her laurels with a huff, then grinned. *Someone ought to murder him.*

With the pick-me-up of the tea, Maeve finished her work for the day, and set to cleaning up. She washed her brushes out, tidied her desk, and left the studio, then headed out to the bedroom to divest of her painting clothes and dress for dinner. She took her hair out of its working bun and put her hourglass necklace back on, checking her face in the mirror for stray smudges of paint on the way out. Imogen had busied herself in the kitchen, pulling out the ingredients she had picked up at the market at Maeve's behest. Maeve had fielded a couple of questions earlier in the day—apparently Imogen's culinary expertise was severely limited to tea—but the lobster was clearly high-quality and the spices smelled strong. She pulled on an apron and set up a stock pot on the stove, watching amusedly as Imogen poked at the lobster with a paring knife.

"The meat's in the tail and the claws."

Imogen bristled. *I know that!* She tossed the knife onto the counter and grumbled. *Caught the damn things for a year and a half. I just never cooked one.*

The bell rang, and Maeve waved placatingly as she headed for the door. "You will now!"

A bottle of white wine was thrust at her nearly as soon as she opened the door, and with her hands freed up Shivani placed them on her hips.

"Has she been practicing? No, don't tell me, I'll quiz her!" She brushed past Maeve and sprinted up the stairs, shouting. "Drop everything, Madrigal! Fourth etude!"

The sound of slightly harried piano issued down the stairs as Maeve welcomed Thalia and Frances in a more leisurely manner. "She's in a good mood."

"Mother Superior put her in charge of the spring community outreach project," Thalia told her. "So, she's taking revenge on Imogen—she insists Mother Superior's giving her all the responsibilities since you left."

"You'll make her feel bad," Frances protested, nudging Thalia's arm. "Shivani's fine," she told Maeve dryly. "Community outreach so far consists of going out to teahouses and asking cute boys if they've ever seen a ghost."

They mounted the stairs to find Imogen carefully picking out the piece at the old upright with Shivani watching hawkishly over her shoulder. Maeve was still rather on edge whenever the two of them interacted, but, apparently, they had organ lessons together every Sunday that occurred without murder attempts. She took Frances' and Thalia's coats, then brought them into the kitchen and uncorked the wine.

"Lobster stew," Thalia said approvingly, picking up the paring knife and beginning to clean the lobster with a sure hand. "Classic."

To the accompaniment of Imogen's unwilling exam, the three of them began to cook, and once Shivani was satisfied they all worked together to make the stew and drink the wine. It was much easier to cook for five than twenty-five, and they had plenty of time while the stew simmered to catch up on events since the previous week's meal together. Maeve led a blushing tour of the studio, Shivani taking the opportunity to gleefully deride Orion's critiques, and Thalia started in on the most recent updates to the legal status of the Warwick estate.

A contract, signed extravagantly by Orion and Imogen and more demurely by Mother Superior, sat ready to hand the deed to the cemetery and half of each sibling's share of the inheritance to the convent the moment the red tape was peeled off the estate, but for months progress had stalled. Lady Marlene's outstanding disappearance and Orion's attempts to take the money without the title had added several layers of complication—as Thalia was now explaining in loving detail. Maeve and Frances escaped to the kitchen while Shivani snooped through the bookcase and Imogen listened, her confusion plain on her face.

"She's explained it to me twice now and I still can't understand a thing she says about it," Frances giggled, topping her wine back up. "But it makes her happy."

"Good thing it makes someone happy," Maeve said wryly. "You couldn't pay me to care about all that bureaucracy."

"Cheers," Frances agreed, and clinked her glass against Maeve's. She crossed to the stew, gave it a few stirs. "I'm glad you are, though. Happy, I mean."

Maeve paused, then swirled her wine around her glass and gazed into it. Her face looked back, her curls frizzy and exuberant, her lips curled up in a smile.

"I'm glad, too."

They brought the stew to the table with crusty bread and too-fancy cutlery, and everyone ate their fill. The sun wrapped around the corner of the house, and Thalia won the privilege of switching on the electric lights as Imogen brought out the rare treat of sherbet. The conversation lasted long after dessert was gone, and at last, Shivani and Thalia and Frances made their way to the door—the convent just a few minutes' walk away. Maeve waved them goodbye, feeling the usual twinge of sadness as she watched them turn the corner and fade from sight. It was getting smaller and smaller every time, but still she had a moment of melancholy, nostalgia for ways of life passed. It was the way of things—a tiny bit of grief for small deaths along the way.

But the apartment, once she finished the climb up the stairs, was cool and breezy and cast in that blue light she had so come to love, and Imogen was nearly finished washing up. Maeve helped her put the dishes away, earning a kiss on the nose for her troubles, and laughed as Imogen immediately pulled the kettle back out.

"This time of night?"

Chamomile, darling, Imogen assured her. *A salve for a weary body, a nepenthe for a troubled mind.*

"I'll need a nepenthe for that pretentiousness. Poets."

And yet you knew what it meant. Imogen kissed her again on the cheek. *Want some?*

"I suppose." The kettle whistled, and Imogen expertly made up a tray, taking it into the bedroom and setting it on her bedside table. Maeve followed, flopping onto the mattress with a sigh, then sat up against her pillows and took her mug. She tasted sugar and spice and listened to the sounds outside—motorcars out on the street, and the rustle of the trees, and the soughing of the waves at the edge of hearing and the edge of the sea.

Imogen reached across and took her free hand with her own, cool and narrow and graceful, and Maeve watched the last dregs of sun glint off her laurels and cut her face in half, one eye sparkling warm and purplish and the other blue in shadow. She saw, heard, tasted and felt all of this, and knew that to move to record it would be to destroy it. So, she set the tea on her bedside table, laid on her back on the soft gingham comforter in the growing dusk, and contented herself with painting the moment into her memories. And when Imogen stroked the back of her hand with her thumb and sighed with contentment, she knew she was writing the same.

A good life is made up of good moments. And this golden, blue evening—the end of the beginning, the start of something new, and the promise of sweet summer—was to be one of many for Imogen Madrigal, and for Maeve.

FINIS

A Note on the Type

The text of this book is set in Adobe Caslon Pro, a serif typeface designed by Carol Twombly for Adobe, and is based on a typeface first designed by William Caslon (1693–1766). Caslon was an English typefounder and was born in Cradley, Worcestershire in 1692 or 1693. He trained as an engraver in nearby Birmingham, and in 1716, he worked in London as an engraver of gun locks and barrels, and as a bookbinder's tool cutter. Having contact with printers, he was induced to fit up a type foundry, largely through the encouragement of William Bowyer. The distinction and legibility of his type secured him the patronage of the leading printers of the day in England and on the continent. His typefaces transformed English type design and first established an English national typographic style.

Caslon released his first typefaces in 1722. Caslon's types were based on seventeenth-century Dutch old style designs, which were then used extensively in England. Because of their remarkable practicality, Caslon's designs met with instant success. Caslon's types became popular throughout Europe and the American colonies; printer Benjamin Franklin hardly used any other typeface. The first printings of the American Declaration of Independence and the Constitution were set in Caslon. The Caslon types fell out of favour in the century after his death, but were revived in the 1840s. Several revivals of the Caslon types are widely used today.

For her own Caslon revival, designer Carol Twombly studied specimen pages printed by William Caslon between 1734 and 1770. The OpenType "Pro" version merges formerly separate fonts (expert, swash, small caps, etc.), and adds both central European language support and several additional ligatures.

The titles and chapter headings of this book are set in Franklin's Caslon, designed by Richard Kegler and Paul D. Hunt for the P22 Type Foundry. The font set was created in collaboration with the Philadelphia Museum of Art to coincide with the Benjamin Franklin Tercentenary. The font set includes faithfully reproduced letterforms digitized directly from images of impressions made by Benjamin Franklin and his printing office circa 1750.

Composed by Clever Crow Consulting and Design
Pittsburgh Pennsylvania

ACKNOWLEDGMENTS

This book, as well as everything that led up to it, would not have been possible without the support of my family, blood and water both.

Thank you to my beta readers—Kielan Donahue for tireless proofing and baby-agent skills, Brenna Peterson for those wonderfully inspiring rainy weekends in Gloucester, Jean Allen for randomly showing up at my apartment with chili and love, and of course Jane Plomp for being there from the very first plot twist to that panicky whiteboarding session of the ending. I wouldn't have kept writing without the love and encouragement you all have given me for these five years, from witches to whales, and I truly owe you one of the greatest joys of my life.

I also owe this book to my mother Jen, who has always supported my creativity, even when it frequently veers into weirdness. Thank you for calling me every single morning while I was living alone, and letting me lament this story's many difficulties along the way. I can't wait to put my book on the shelf next to yours and brag that you taught me everything I know about art. A shout out to Mike, Ethan, and Brian Daly as well, for the lessons in adulthood, the Zaftig's, and the group-chat hype respectively. You all got me through a tough year, and I hope this story is a worthy payoff.

A strange thank you across time to F.E. Anderson, whose mausoleum I passed every day on the way to work, and who I slowly built Imogen's crypt around during those cold January drives.

And last but not least, to Dave Neal and Christine Scott. Your insight and art have transformed my scrubby little draft into something so beautiful I sometimes forget I even wrote it. Thank you for giving me this incredible opportunity to tell Imogen and Maeve's story, and to fulfill a long-held dream.

ABOUT THE AUTHOR

Grayson Daly is a writer and lover of fantasy, mystery, and any genre with the word "gothic" appended to the front. She grew up in a New England village and moved to the slightly larger one of Boston, where she lives with her childhood best friend and thirteen houseplants. When not writing, Grayson can be found building robots, learning to play the banjo, and haunting the bubble tea shop down the street. *The Untimely Undeath of Imogen Madrigal* is her debut novel.

Find her on Instagram, or in your local cemetery.

NOSETOUCH PRESS™

Nosetouch Press is an independent book publisher
tandemly based in Chicago and Pittsburgh.
We are dedicated to bringing some of today's most
energizing fiction to readers around the world.

Our commitment to classic book design in a digital
environment brings an innovative and authentic
approach to the traditions of literary excellence.

***We're Out There*™**
NOSETOUCHPRESS.COM
Horror | Science Fiction | Fantasy | Mystery
Supernatural | Gothic | Weird